Sequel to Winds of Change

Beneath *the* Lemonwood Tree

Buried, But Not Forgotten

Diana K Robinson

Contact dianarobinsonauthor@yahoo.com

Diana K Publications – https://dianakrobinson.com

First paperback edition

Book design by Publishing Push

ISBNs

978-1-80541-424-7 (paperback)

978-1-80541-423-0 (eBook)

"Don't give your son money; as far as you can afford it, give him horses. No one ever came to grief through riding horses. No hour of life is lost that is spent in the saddle."
    ~ Sir Winston Churchill.

*And, special thanks, as always,
to my very precious husband.*

The *Winds of Change*, the first book in the trilogy, sees Melonie Whitaker, nee Johns, the target of a vicious vendetta, spawned during the bush war in 1976, in a landlocked country known then as Rhodesia.

Melonie, a seventeen-year-old teenager experienced the worst of what war can serve up and survived the first attack on the farm homestead. The terrorists returned a few months later, abducted her and took her deep into Mozambiquan territory to a terrorist camp. She escaped, but her escape bred a vicious vendetta dreamed up by Solomon Tlale, her captor and survivor from the burned-out terrorist camp.

Melonie's passion for horses began as a child and continued with rapid growth when the family settled at Chanting Clover Stud in the heart of the picturesque Natal midlands in South Africa. Melonie not only achieved success, but the horses helped heal the wounds of the past.

But fame exposed her whereabout to her nemesis when she and her grandmother won the famous Durban July Handicap feature race with a homebred racehorse, Wind Power. Tragically, Iris, her grandmother, collapsed and died directly after the race. Under Hector Willis's tutelage, Melonie became the de facto successor.

Melonie falls in love with Gary Whitaker, Hector Willis's assistant trainer. They marry and have two sons, Garth, and Bradley, but Solomon has dedicated his life to retribution.

Melonie escaped two more attempts made on her life. In a hotel room in Harare, he promises she will not escape him again. Like an octopus hiding in a dark cave, his tentacles kept reaching out and affect not only Melonie's life, but the lives of everyone at Chanting Clover. His next failed attempt had been when she murdered Funani who'd come to hang her in her own garage, but she faced a murder charge. After many long months and delayed court hearings, she was acquitted. This burned a fire in Solomon's soul.

Chapter One

MELONIE WOKE SUDDENLY AND GASPED. Her heart raced. Sweat poured off her brow. Her nightie and the sheets were drenched. A terrifying nightmare. She'd not had one so vivid, and so terrifying, for months.

She wiped her brow, rubbed her eyes, and sat up. "Urgh" She moaned, unable to shed the images of the rope hanging from the rafters in this garage, not more than sixty paces from where she lay. She swung her legs over the side of the king size bed. Gary's side seemed hardly ruffled. He must've slithered out, so he didn't wake her. Cold from being damp, she shivered. Her heart still pounded, knocking against her ribcage. She'd never forget how hard she fought to prevent Funani from hanging her from that noose. The rope, the rafters the makeshift gallows seemed glued to her subconscious. It had been almost two years since that terrifying afternoon.

Gradually her heartbeat regulated, and she glanced at her watch, a beautiful gold watch that Gary had given her for her thirty-fifth birthday with a diamond at the number twelve. Ten minutes past seven. Gary would be at the training track. She would've normally been there too by now, watching her beloved horses in action, but for the horrific nightmare, she wondered why he hadn't woken her.

Her hands trembled. One of the symptoms of PTSD. They were hot and clammy too, in contrast to the damp, cold nighty clinging to her chilled skin. Mid-winter in the Natal midlands is renowned for its brisk weather and she noticed Gary had switched on the heaters for her.

She stood, stretched, and walked to her closet, eager to get the nighty off. She pulled out a fleecy tracksuit and dressed in front of the heater trying to work out what had triggered the nightmare. It may have been a documentary she watched last night on Nelson Mandela's release from jail and the elections. Her thoughts drifted back to that day when they'd taken their farm staff to the polling stations. How excited everyone had been. Most of their staff had never voted before. The excitement had been infectious. Funani, the man who'd tried to kill her had been on one of those tractor and trailer trips.

Despite the comfort of Prime Security guarding the three-thousand-hectare Thoroughbred stud farm, making sure the Whitakers and their horses were kept safe, Mel lived on a diet of fear and anxiety. Maybe it would be a good idea to visit Tony Brink, her psychologist from years ago.

She slid her feet into her warm sheepskin slippers and wandered to the kitchen. She needed a dose of caffeine. Mandela filled her mind. How lucky South Africans were to have a statesman like him, not a madman like Mugabe. Maybe they'd still be there had the populace voted in a man like Madiba, as he was affectionately known.

Her fears were inextricably linked to Zimbabwe, and now there were stronger connections between the two countries.

Being the last two countries to cast off colonialism, it gave them a kinship, thus making it easier for her nemesis Solomon Tlale to threaten her livelihood and life on a more menacing level.

Angelina's happy smiling face greeted her. She'd been serving the family for years. She started work with Iris. A very dear Zulu lady Mel couldn't imagine life without. "Morning Ma'am."

"Morning Angelina, how are you today?" Mel held her arm gently. "You look so fresh and beautiful in that lovely ethnic print overcoat and apron."

"Yes, I like the colour blue, and I'm very good, ma'am. Can I make you breakfast?"

"That's sweet, but I'll wait for Gary. Right now, I need coffee. A strong one." Mel switched on the kettle which had recently boiled. She spooned in the coffee, poured in milk, filled the cup with boiling water, gave it a stir and realised Angelina stood watching her.

"Oh, Ma'am, that's too strong." Angelina had a worried expression.

Mel simply smiled. Strong coffee would wake her, and hopefully give her mind clarity. There'd been brief footage of violent eruptions on that documentary. Clips of white radical groups causing disruption, culminating in the assassination of Chris Hani, a senior ANC leader. It must've been the violent footage that had triggered her nightmare. 'No more watching violence. Silly girly flicks and animal movies from now on. Except,' She paused in thought, 'animal movies make me bawl my eyes out. Silly girly flicks didn't really appeal.

The list of horses entered for the Durban July still lay on the dining table where she'd left it last night. She slid a chair out and sat down at granny Iris's beautiful old walnut table she loved so much. Sometimes, when alone, she'd study the grain of the wood and wonder which forest in England the tree had grown, and what history it'd seen before being felled for furniture, or had it just fallen, in a hectic storm perhaps. From forests to horses.

Four home-bred horses were running on this day. Two in the feature race. Still sipping coffee, Gary arrived for breakfast, rubbing his hands together. The jeans he wore, stiff from the cold, clung to his long legs.

"Brr, it's freezing out there. Morning honey." He kissed her. "Are you feeling, okay?"

"Just a bit rattled. I had a dreadful nightmare. I woke as if I'd just fought off another attack." Her shoulders slumped.

"Oh no. You haven't had one for months. What brought that on?" Gary's handsome face wrinkled with concern. He always felt so helpless in times like this.

"Either a psychic warning or the documentary we were watching on Madiba. I can't think of anything else." The fleecy emerald-green tracksuit she wore matched her eye colour, but today those beautiful eyes weren't shimmering with her normal enthusiasm for life.

Gary grimaced. He knew all about Mel's connection with the universe.

"I don't like the sound of that, my angel. Your admirable sixth sense is rarely wrong."

"I'm probably over-reacting. Left over from the nightmare. Have you seen Brad this morning?" Brad had been home from school recovering from a bout of flu.

"No, I haven't. He's around terrorising someone." A warm, loving smile rose on Gary's face, likely proud of his little rascal.

The vision made Mel laugh. Few could keep up with the eight-year-old Brad and his delightful, curious ways. Ways that often got him into trouble, Mel thought.

"The nightmare's still eating you, isn't it?"

"Yes. It's either a visit to Doctor Brink, or getting back in the saddle, or both." She stopped fiddling with her butter knife and looked at her adoring husband, thinking how lucky she is to have him in her life. So kind, So dependable. So thoughtful.

Gary rested his knife and fork on the side of his plate. "Do both but have a full medical check-up first. Remember Tony warned a blackout at full gallop might take your life." Yes, that thought frightened her.

"You're right, but this morning I'm just going out on a gentle hack, I won't be doing any galloping."

Brad came bounding into the dining room, huffing, and puffing, his auburn hair sticking up like it'd been gelled, and one side of his jacket had fallen off his shoulder. "Hey, Mum, can we go for a ride this morning?" He pulled out his chair and sat down.

"Hey, big boy, where are your manners?" Gary frowned at him.

"Oops." He scrambled off his heavy wooden chair, rushed around the antique rectangle walnut table, shook his dad's hand, and hurried round to Mel and hugged her.

Mel always loved a tight little morning hug from her youngest son. "Good morning, you rascal. You're supposed to be sick. But to answer your question, yes, we can go ride. And the good news, I've decided I am going to ride every day."

"Oh cool. Can I have some Rice Crispies?" Brad steepled his little, cold hands.

"Only if you have some scrambled egg after your cereal." Mel warned.

"Aaaw, Muuum." His little face puckered, and his pink cheeks got rosier.

"Come on Brad, do what your mother says. No scrambled egg, no ride." Gary cautioned his son.

Brad exaggerated a pout and folded his arms across his chest. But hunger likely got the better of him because he gobbled his breakfast. Then excused himself and he ran out. Mel shouted after him. "Ask Thomas to saddle up Peanut for you, and Tropical Sun for me."

"Hey, get back here young man." Gary shouted to him.

Brad made a u turn with the sound of screeching tyres and slid to a halt on the parquet flooring next to his mother. Mel couldn't help herself and burst out laughing.

Gary barely held his mirth.

"Wrap up warmly, don't forget to brush your teeth, then you can go." Mel advised him.

Brad screwed up his face and tilted his head to one side with a crooked smile, "I love you, Mum."

Mel pinched his flushed cheeks. "Off you go."

The two horses were ready when Mel got to the stables.

Brad sat, straight and tall on Peanut.

Mel and Brad hadn't had a hack together for a few weeks, so Mel was thrilled to have this chance. They moved off, and a smile as wide as the ocean and with as much energy, stretched across Brad's face. He kicked Peanut's sides, then turned in the saddle and waved to the groom. "Bye Thomas."

"Sssta." Thomas clicked his tongue against the roof of his mouth and grinned.

They'd not walked but for a few minutes, when Brad begged. "Mum, can we canter."

"Not yet, Brad. The horses need to warm up first. You can't take a horse out of the stable and expect to canter straight away. It's not fair on the horse. We'll canter when we get to the long uphill road that leads to the top of the farm. That'll give you lots of practice."

"But I want to canter properly now before I go back to school." He whinged.

"There's plenty of time to learn. Besides, there'll be lots of children your age still struggling with canter." Mel advised wisely.

Riding beneath the canopy of ancient Oak trees which led past the top end of the training track shaded them from the sun. "Well can we at least trot, it's so cold under these trees." Brad pleaded. When they reached the end of the long avenue the winter sun quickly warmed them, and they went on trotting until they reached the edge of the post and railed weanling paddocks. Mel slowed to a walk. She knew the clip-clopping sounds of trotting horses would alert the young horses and they'd bolt off around the paddock, tails high, and likely spook Peanut, though she felt sure it wouldn't un-nerve her courageous little Brad.

The situation unfolded exactly as Mel thought. Peanut bounced forward, jogged, and pranced next to Tropical Sun. Brad got the giggles and lost his foot from the stirrup. "Ooh, that's fun." Without a fuss, put his foot back in the stirrup.

Mel leant forward to attach the lead rein.

Brad stopped her. "I can control Peanut, Mum."

"Okay, but we're going to canter. Do you remember what I taught you?" Mel asked.

Brad nodded.

"Are you ready?"

"Yes, go Mum." He said impatiently.

Riding side by side, Mel squeezed her legs against Tropical Sun's sides. He broke into canter. Peanut did the same. Mel knew Peanut had an enviably comfortable canter. It wasn't long and Brad was sitting into the rocking chair movement in perfect rhythm with the movement. When they reached the summit, Brad's face was flushed the colour of a pink moon, and his eyes shone bright.

"Well done," Mel praised her fearless child. They'd cantered two and a half kilometres non-stop. Mel knew he cantered in the school's arena, and occasionally on a ride at home, but never more than a kilometre.

Bubbles of perspiration covered Brad's nose. He whipped off his riding helmet and rubbed his itchy scalp. "That was so fun, Mum. Did you see how well I sat?"

"I did, and I'm going to tell Miss Cheryl. Maybe then you can do bigger jumps and more cantering." Mel kept her tone enthusiastic.

They walked toward the ancient Lemonwood tree. Sheltering from the sun beneath the shade of the White Stinkwood trees nearby. Her grandmother, Iris Paige had planted the stand of trees which, along with the ancient Lemonwood tree, marked the northern tip of the farm. Crevices and uncovered granite boulders from erosion over the years filled the valley below. The old, gnarled Lemonwood was one of Mel's favourite trees. Large strips of bark hung off the trunk, as if the tree was undressing itself to reveal the wisdom of its years and radiated its understanding of the world around it. Mel loved hugging its trunk and feeling its vibration, but today. It stood as the keeper of the farm.

Two hours later, and a few shorter canters, they arrived back at the stables. Thomas stood at the gate and Brad waved. "Hey, Thomas, I cantered a lot. It's so easy."

"You're too clever, Brad." Thomas praised him.

Brad slid off Peanuts back, flipped the reins over her head and led her to her stable.

Back inside the house, thirsty and hot, Brad downed a glass of fruit juice. Minutes later, he was sound asleep on the veranda sofa. The sofa, covered in duck egg blue striped material was long enough for Brad to stretch out on, and the big comfy cushions enveloped him.

Mel left him sleeping. She marvelled at how quickly children fell asleep. She wandered back to the kitchen, downed a glass of cold water and quizzed Angelina on what she'd prepared for lunch. It smelt so good.

"Chicken casserole," she bent and opened the wide Aga oven door. Steam whooshed out. She screwed up her eyes and stood to one side. "Oooh, that smells awesome." And looked away. "Is that pudding I spy?" Mel grinned at her faithful cook.

"It is, Ma'am. Bradley's favourite apple crumble and I've made hot custard. He'll be hungry when he wakes."

Warmed by Angelina's thoughtfulness, Mel thanked her and left the kitchen to check on Brad. He lay motionless, still sound asleep. She sat beside him, opened her book, put her feet up on the ottoman. And read until Gary returned for lunch. He crept up to the couch and whispered, "How was your ride, Brad?"

His eyes flew open. "Hey Dad!" He sat up. The evidence of sleep gone in a heartbeat. "Gee, Dad. Ask Mum how well I did. I can really canter properly now."

"I knew you could do it. Well done. I'll bet you're hungry after that?" Gary looked down at his youngest son with pride.

"Yes! I'm starving." Brad pushed himself off the sofa.

"Go and wash your hands and tell me all about it at the table." Gary said.

Brad dashed off to the bathroom, then joined his parents in the dining room wiping excess water from his hands on his jodhpurs. He pulled out his chair and shifted himself onto the seat. Angelina brought the meal through on a tray and laid it on the beautiful antique walnut sideboard. Heat resistant mats were spread along the top. It was a prize piece of furniture Mel had inherited from Granny Iris.

Mel dished out the meal and put Brad's plate in front of him first. She reminded him to place his serviette on his lap, then she served Gary and herself.

"Brad will be showing his friends how to canter now. I'm going to ask Cheryl if she'll let them practice the canter more often and do bigger jumps." Mel picked up her knife and fork, then Brad and Gary followed.

"Dad. Why does Mum always have to start first?" Brad's head was cocked to one side. The angelic look on his face melted Mel's heart.

"Because ladies always go first." Gary said, "and it is good manners."

Brad thought for a moment, then loudly said, Yesss," and stabbed the air with his fist after the first mouthful.

"I presume you're talking about Mum's suggestion to Miss Cheryl, not that Mum comes first?" Gary said with a smile. Brad nodded vigorously. "And... and... Peanut got all frisky and pranced sideways when we passed the yearlings. I lost my stirrup and didn't fall. I'm going to show Garth what I can do this weekend."

Warmed by Brad's enthusiasm for riding, Mel realised she'd better have the medical check sooner rather than later so she could ride out with both her sons more often. And, with doctor's approval, start riding racehorses in training again.

"Angelina's done it again. This casserole is delicious." Gary glanced at Brad shovelling his food into his mouth so fast he barely chewed it. "Slow down, Brad, you'll give yourself indigestion."

His mouth was so full he couldn't answer but he sat more upright and did as he was told. Mel laughed, marvelling at his zealous appetite.

After the brutal attack, and the blow to her head, Mel experienced frequent black outs and hadn't been allowed to drive or ride for six months. When cleared to drive, she'd been advised not to train racehorses. It was too dangerous, but she missed the adrenaline punch it gave her, but it would be fun to hack with her sons and Gary, and maybe ride work once more.

Chapter Two

A YEAR HAD PASSED since Mel and Brad took that wonderful hack together and Brad mastered the canter. Mel had also past her medical examination and got back to training racehorses.

It was late June. The winter holidays in the Southern hemisphere for Garth and Brad who were helping staff as they geared up for the annual Durban July race meeting, the family's favourite race day.

Being winter, Mel, Gary and Garth wrapped up warmly in thick, all-weather coats to be at the track by the time the sun rose. Brad stayed snuggled up in bed. He wasn't as keen to go out in the cold and watch horses galloping down the track, but Garth had been bitten by the horse racing bug.

Standing beside his parents at the rails, squinting against the sun's early morning rays. "I want to train racehorses as a career, like you two."

"Well, you can take over from Dad and I once you've finished uni." Mel advised him and got the reaction she expected. Garth didn't see the point in going to uni.

"It's still a long way to go. You'll change your mind." Gary nudged him. "A tertiary education is a good idea."

Mel remembered the first day she'd ever stood where they were standing now. Emotional, seventeen, badly traumatised and the only thing that gave her hope were the racehorses. She'd stood beside Hector in awe, watching the Thoroughbreds walking around the large oval warm-up area, their coats glistening in the early morning sun. It was full summer then and nice and warm.

"Look around, treasure what your grandmother established, and you'll soon realise what you two boys have and you won't want to lose it because you know nothing about business." Mel said. The mention of university always got him sulking, but Mel's words made sense. Garth turned to her.

"But you two can do the sums." Gary and Mel laughed, likely his twelve-year-old logic made sense to him, but he quickly changed the subject. "Do you think Vision Quest will win this year?"

"We can only hope so, my boy." Gary noted Garth's foot tapping on the ground excitedly when the horses left the warmup oval.

"It's a tough race, but Vision Quest could win it. He's already broken the track record at Clairwood, but it's not just speed that wins a Group One feature race like the Durban July. It must be ridden with strategy."

Garth lifted his binoculars to his eyes and studied what the jockeys were doing.

"Dad's so right. It takes years to perfect. So, though you may not like what we both say from time to time, it's said because we've made mistakes, we don't want you to make."

"Yeah, thanks Mum," Garth still had his binoculars trained on Vision Quest as he slowly galloped down the side road to the start of the training track. The horse turned into the start and took off. "Gee Mum, he's flying. I reckon he'll win. I've heard all the commentary about the July on the radio."

Garth lowered the binoculars and turned to his mum. "James did nothing wrong in the gallop, but I heard you say to Dad you didn't approve of him riding Vision Quest. Why?"

Mel glanced at Gary, then gave Garth her full attention. "You are quite right. James rode the horse very well. You've heard Dad and I use the term, over-horsed, haven't you?"

Garth nodded.

"Well, I was worried that James might not handle the power and wilfulness of the colt, plus he's enormously strong. James hasn't had any experience riding in a Group one race before." Garth's body language indicated tactics and strategy fascinated him, and he was no longer filled with thoughts about university. Mel went on, "I thought Dad had over-horsed him, and that would not have done James's confidence any good, but we've seen now that Dad was quite right."

Gary's eyebrows had raised, pushed upward by his beaming smile. He put a hand on Garth's shoulder, "I didn't have the heart to say no when he begged me for the ride, and I'm glad I didn't." He ruffled Garth's hair. "Sometimes we must listen to instinct. You'll make a great trainer one day. You are very observant and that is what breeds wisdom."

They rushed toward the end of the track and stood fifty metres from the end of the grass track. They waited for James and Vision to pull up and walk back to where they stood in the sun. Garth kicked at the frost covered grass and it crunched noisily underfoot.

Gary shouted, "Superbly ridden, James. He's your mount for the feature race. Even Garth is impressed."

Garth blew steamy condensation in rings from his mouth,

imitating a smoker and chuckled, "So, Mum, does this mean Dad's not in trouble anymore?" He teased.

"You wicked child." Mel tried to tickle him, but he jumped away. He hated being tickled; he was so ticklish.

Moving off the frost covered, wheaten yellow brittle grass, they wandered down the gravel road on the side of the track in the sun, chatting.

"James told me about how he got into the Jockey Academy. Do you know his sad story?"

Mel felt a pang of affection. Heart warmed by Garth's youthful empathy for young James.

"Yes, we do know and aren't you and Brad lucky."

"We are, and we both know it. I can't imagine being raised in a tiny flay in town by just you, Ma. That would be terrible."

"You're right but they overcame their difficulties and look what a super chap James is. His mum must be a very strong person for she raised him very well."

Mel opened the Landcruiser door and Garth jumped into the backseat. "James told me he won a bursary from the State Lottery and started at the Academy when he was fourteen." Garth spoke.

Gary turned the ignition key, and the heater came on which almost instantly warmed the interior.

"Ooh, that's so nice, my hands are frozen." Garth put them around Mel's face.

She shrieked. "You little devil." She pulled Garth's freezing hands from her face and rubbed her cheeks.

Arriving at the house, they piled out and hurried to the door knowing the inside of the house would be toastie warm.

"Who do you think we should put Kgabu on?" Gary asked, opening the front door. "Ooh, it's so lovely and cosy in here. Let's have breakfast. The cold makes me hungry."

Mel hung their coats on the jacket stand and her teeth finally stopped chattering. Then she answered Gary's question about Kgabu. "He's been riding Green Mists."

"That mare can be a super-bitch from hell." Gary said, always concerned about her temperament.

"Hey Dad! No swearing." Brad had crept up behind his father.

"Okay Brad. I'll not swear again." Gary turned to face his youngest son and hugged him.

"You lie, doesn't he Mum?" Brad put his hands on his hips accusingly.

Mel laughed. "Not often. But Dad's right about Green Mists, she can be nasty yet, Kgabu rides her well."

During breakfast, an urgent call came through on the internal radio from the stables. Kgabu had been kicked.

Mel cocked her head to one side listening to Gary on the radio. "Oh no. What did I tell you about Green Mists. She can be truly nasty. You boys finish breakfast. Sounds like Dad and I might need to get Kgabu to hospital. Go down to grandpa when you've finished. If you're good, he'll take you fishing."

Mel grabbed their coats. She met Gary at the stables in the Landcruiser. As she approached the gate, she saw Kgabu lying on the stretch of lawn between the two stable blocks, writhing in agony, crying out, "my leg, my leg."

Mel knelt beside Kgabu. "How did this happen?" A horseshoe imprint marked his mid-shin. It must have been so hard it had virtually burned its mark into Kgabu's jodhpurs. She could only imagine how painful it must be.

"I...I was...tacking off, Ma'am. Mists suddenly swung on me. I think she's.... she's broken my leg." Kgabu grimaced.

"I think you might be right. It's swelling fast. Let's get you to hospital." Mel spoke calmly. Gay had called for two grooms, and they lifted Kgabu onto the back seat of the Landcruiser. Gary sped off, wasting no time to get the lad to hospital.

From the back seat came his shuddering voice. "The thought of not riding in the July pains me more than this broken leg." A brave attempt at humour, Mel thought and turned to smile at Kgabu, though she noticed his face contorted from the pain.

"I'm so sorry this has happened to you. Green Mists is a cunning little witch. I'm ashamed to say we bred her. I jumped on her the other day and her back come up immediately."

"She can be cunning, Ma'am, but she's a great ride." Kgabu's voice barely audible. "Maybe there's a problem the physiotherapist needs to look at. I loosened the girth, then she suddenly cow kicked. It happened so quickly I didn't have time to get out the way."

"Anything else you can think of that may have made her so uncomfortable. She looked fabulous on the gallop." Gary spoke, looking in his rear-view mirror. Kgabu grimaced.

"Oh man, Gary, she ran a brilliant training gallop. She's a good horse in many ways." Kgabu put his head back and closed his eyes.

FORTY-FIVE MINUTES LATER, they pulled up outside the emergency admissions at Gray's hospital in Pietermaritzburg.

Mel hurried inside, explained she needed a wheelchair and why. A nurse followed and between them they lifted Kgabu into the wheelchair and transferred him to the inspection bed when they got inside.

Kgabu gritted his teeth bravely as the nurse snipped through his jodhpurs with a pair of sharp scissors. They were stuck to his swollen leg like glued paper.

Mel and Gary walked to admissions at the front of the hospital where they Kgabu's father for the first time. A debonair looking man, of medium height but he carried an air of professionalism dressed in a navy-blue suit. A red handkerchief peeked out of the top pocket and matched his tie.

"Steven Dube, Hillcrest town Councillor," his hand was out to shake Gary's. He took Mel's hand next and shook it more gently. "Nice to meet you."

"And you. It's a pity about the circumstances." Mel said. She liked the look of the man and could see the resemblance to his son.

"It is, but it's not the first time. He got some nasty kicks and bites at the Academy, but none broke a bone."

"Would you like a coffee?" Gary asked.

"I'd love one, but where's my son?"

"Having the leg X rayed." Gary pulled Mel's chair out.

"I'll wait for Kgabu to get back from X rays. I'm sure you two need to get back to the farm. Thank you ever so much for getting Kgabu here so promptly. I'll get my wife to call this evening, Melonie."

"Thank you, Steve." Gary and Mel finished their coffee and left for the farm.

THE PHONE RANG AT EIGHT. Mel stretched across and reached for the handset sitting in her armchair in the sitting room. "Good evening, is that Mrs. Whitaker?"

"Yes, it is." Mel answered.

"It's Mrs. Dube here. I'd like to thank you and your husband for helping Kgabu at the hospital. He's doing fine. Horses are so dangerous, aren't they?" Her voice tapered off.

"They're not normally dangerous, but these unfortunate

accidents happen from time to time. I'm glad Kgabu's okay. How long does that wretched plaster cast stay on for?" Mel asked imagining how itchy Kgabu's leg would be a week from now.

"Eight weeks, poor Kgabu. Two breaks to the tibia and two plates. He's all plastered up and no longer in pain. He's watching racing on TV. Nothing will put him off." Mrs. Dube chuckled.

"I'm glad to hear he's doing well." Mel felt relief there was no finger pointing.

"Kgabu would like to know if we can meet you at Greyville? Is there any possibility you can get us complimentary tickets to the owners and trainers' lounge?" Mrs. Dube asked hesitantly.

"Yes, of course. We'd be delighted to have the three of you join us." Mel thought how nice it would be to spend the afternoon with Kgabu's parents and get to know them.

"Oh, wonderful. Kgabu will be so happy. Have a good evening and thank you." Mrs. Dube hung up.

Gary and Mel were in a quandary as to what to do with Green Mists or who could ride her. John MacIntosh would have been the best person, but he'd been chosen to ride Enchantrix in the fourth race at the Durban July, plus he was riding Ebony and Ivory in the feature race.

Their conundrum was answered when Kgabu called and suggested a lady apprentice at the academy could manage Green Mists. But there were only three days left before the big day.

Mel called the Academy. Gert, the head of the riders confirmed Julie Mokoena clicked with mares, and said she was a competent rider. He'd ask Julie. She agreed and would stay at the farm for the next three days.

The Academy bus brought Julie to the stud. Gert assured Mel Julie had ridden fractious, difficult mares before.

The two ladies shook hands. "Thank you for agreeing to ride our only difficult horse."

"It's a pleasure Ma'am," Julie said politely. Julie was the first black lady jockey at the Academy.

"If you don't click with her, please let me know immediately. I don't want another accident." Mel's brows creased with concern. Julie was tiny and very fine boned. She hoped she'd manage Green Mists.

"Yes Ma'am." Julie nodded.

That afternoon Mel sat on the white post and rail and watched Julie ride Green Mists in the oval warm-up area, then scrutinised the gallop. Julie pulled the mare up and walked to where Mel sat.

"Very nicely ridden. If Green Mists comes last tomorrow, it doesn't matter. It's her maiden race, but she seems to go well for you."

"Thank you, Ma'am. I'll still do my best." Julie ran a hand down Green Mists' neck, then walked her slowly back to the stables to cool her off.

THE FAMOUS DURBAN July is always run on the first Saturday of July. Gary and Mel met Kgabu, and his parents, in the Owner's and Trainer's lounge at twelve thirty.

Sitting in a comfy chair with his plastered leg resting on a foot stool, he grinned happily.

"Hi Kgabu, what a fancy outfit you're wearing." Mel thought how well the red shirt went with khaki shorts.

"I'm taking a couple of bets when the Tote opens," Kgabu announced full of cheer.

"On whom?" Gary asked.

"Aww, Mr. Whitaker," Kgabu laughed. "I think you know."

"You're dead right about Julie. She rides the mare well. Thank you for recommending her, at least the wicked witch of Chanting Clover can run her first race." Gary joked.

"I'm putting ten Rand for a win, and ten for a place, even though I'm sure Green Mists will win." Kgabu announced confidently. "Where are Garth and Brad?"

"On their way. They were fishing with their grandpa this morning." Gary replied. Kgabu screwed up his face, he didn't like fishing.

"I'm saving one hundred Rand for the feature race. Fifty for a win and fifty for a place on Vision Quest." Kgabu told Gary while Mel and Mrs. Dube went to the bar to order drinks. The waiter would deliver them to their table.

"Tell me all about this day famous race day, Mrs. Whitaker. This is my first time at the Durban July."

"Well, as you can see, from up here in the owners and trainers lounge you get a fabulous view of the course. As with Ascot in England, it's a day for the ladies to dress up. There's a different dress theme every year, which is quite fun, though I'm not a fashion fan." Mel pushed a wayward strand of hair from her face. "Fashion attracts many more visitors to the course, but for me it's about the magnificence of the Thoroughbred race-horse. Anyway, the theme this year is Rainbow Nation, which is rather nice."

"They certainly are colourful and a great addition to the day if one is not particularly horse orientated, like me. I love fashion and my favourite pastime is shopping. Steve hides his credit card every time I go." Mrs. Dube chuckled. Steve turned to look at her and raised his eyebrows, then he went on chatting to Gary.

"I suppose you're right." Mel took a sip of her gin and tonic the waiter had brought across. "It certainly adds a touch of colour and flamboyance to the day." Mel picked up her binoculars, "aah, the horses are being loaded for the first race."

Steve handed Kgabu a pair of binoculars.

"Green Mists loaded well. That's new." There was a yearning to his tone. "I wish it was me riding her."

"You may have lost her to Julie," Gary teased.

"Never. I'll be back on her when my leg has mended."

"Aaand... they're off." They heard the commentator say.

Mel watched Green Mists carefully. By the two hundred metre marker, Julie had placed Green Mists mid-field. The white cap with emerald diamonds, the stud farm's colours, bobbed along harmoniously as the field turned into the final straight and Julie turned on the magic. The filly burst from the group and won her maiden race as if she'd done it a hundred times.

Mel let her binoculars drop against her chest. She turned to Gary. "Can you believe it?"

"Wow," Kgabu shouted. "I'm rich."

Steve grabbed Kgabu's tote ticket and rushed down to the payout booths.

Mel's heart swelled with pride. Julie had ridden a textbook race, gotten her first win, and because of that, Kgabu had won a pocket full of cash.

Gary and Mel left their binoculars on their seats and moved to the elevator that took them downstairs and hurried across the paved walkways to meet Green Mists coming off the track.

Siyanda, the head work rider led the winning pair into the winner's enclosure. Julie couldn't stop smiling, but when the sash was placed around the filly's neck, Green Mists pinned her ears back and bared her teeth.

"Good God, she's never bared her teeth at anyone before." Mel whispered to Gary.

"Is this another champion in the making, Melonie Whitaker?" The commentator asked, a tall man who towered over Mel, he lowered the microphone close to Mel.

"Who? The horse or the jockey?" Mel smiled graciously hoping the sneer from Green Mists wasn't caught on camera.

Siyanda stepped forward and took the mare to the collecting ring for vet checking and Julie headed to the weigh-in rooms.

Gary and Mel took the elevator back to the lounge. Ivan, Garth and Brad had just arrived.

"Hi, Mum. Hi, Dad," Brad called out and Mel introduced them to Mr. and Mrs. Dube. When formalities were over Garth pulled a red marker from his backpack and made sure he was the first to sign Kgabu's plaster cast. He handed the pen to Brad who scribbled his name in bold down the side of the cast and drew a smiley face.

"Hey Garth, look how much I won on Green Mists." He held a bundle of notes in his hand.

"Gee, that's cool. How much?" Garth asked. Mel smiled. She knew how her eldest son loved money.

"Four hundred and twenty-seven rand and some cents." Kgabu tucked the cash in his shorts pocket.

"Wow, that's awesome. I'm jealous. Who's running in the next race?" Garth asked.

"Enchantrix, and John's riding her," Kgabu had his racing form open and showed Garth the listing. Mel tapped Garth on the shoulder and handed him two racing forms.

John got snagged mid-field in the second race. Mel felt the fist of disappointment clench at her chest.

"Did you see that, Mrs. Whitaker? Enchantrix should've won her race with ease." Kgabu commented, flabbergasted, and tore up his tote ticket. He'd lost on that race. But not much.

Gary excused himself. He stood at the gate leading off the track, waiting for John. Disheartened, he found it hard to believe Enchantrix didn't even place. He needed to know what had gone wrong.

John rode straight to him.

"What happened?" John pulled up and dismounted. "There are some trainers and jockeys who don't like your success, Gary. They'll go to any length to stop us."

"What do you mean, they'll stop us?" Through his binoculars he'd noticed some tussling on the track during the race.

John removed his helmet. "The two horses that galloped on either side of me are from the same stable. They made sure I stayed stuck mid-field. Report them, Gary. It's race-fixing. It had been well planned."

Gary swore under his breath and walked with John to the collecting ring. Before they parted company John told Gary, "Just watch, they'll target James and me in the main race. The Josi Manor stud have two good horses running — Chilly Willy and Dingo Boy. These two jockeys have a bad reputation. And the last thing I need is another fall."

"Don't worry. Let's go and plan some tactical riding with James."

After laying out plans with John and James, Gary went back to the Owner's and Trainer's lounge and joined the others. He leant in close to Mel and asked, "did you notice anything peculiar in the Enchantrix race?"

"I noticed John got himself snookered mid-pack, but that can happen." A questioning frown crossed her brow.

"I've just asked John about it. He was kept there on purpose by two other riders. Race fixing." Gary explained what John had told him. "John and James and I've worked out a strategy for the main race. If anything untoward happens, I'll report the riders and the stable."

Mel looked worried. She didn't want John to have another ghastly fall. "I pray the tactics work. I couldn't deal with an accident during the race."

Standing inside the parade ring at ten to four, other owners and trainers gathered to view the horses in the feature race. Gary watched Siyanda lead John's horse, a feisty Vision Quest ready to run his heart out. Ebony, James' mount who was striding out calmly was led by Thomas.

Siyanda hoisted John into the saddle who raised his hands to the heavens. The gesture had become his trademark since conquering paraplegia. Then the other jockeys were legged-up.

Twelve top-class Thoroughbreds, their shimmering coats glistening in the afternoon sun, moved gracefully around the collecting ring. Their powerful, toned muscles rippled with each step, a testament to their rigorous training and elite breeding.

The air buzzed with anticipation and a low hum of murmurs could be heard. Punters exchanged last-minute tips. Their voices a mix of hopeful speculation and confident assertion. Once a horse was chosen the crowd quickly dispersed to place their bets and excitement grew while Gary and Mel exchanged a few quick words and nods to John and James and returned to their seats.

Garth waved a tote ticket at them. "I took a ten Rand trifecta on both horses, spreading my chances and Brad equalled my amount. But he stupidly put it all on a win for Vision Quest."

"Aah, not," Brad shouted at his brother. "You're the stupid one."

"See Brad, did you hear that? Chilly Willy is now the favourite. At least I've got a chance to win something. You've got no chance." Garth goaded. "No need to clutch your ticket like your life depends on it. You may as well bin it."

"That's quite enough, you two." Ivan scolded before either Gary or Mel got the chance.

The boys sat quietly next to Kgabu and waited.

Brad's face grim. Garth wore a smug look.

Mel fidgeted with her binoculars. "I wonder why Vision Quest is no longer the race favourite. Perhaps the punters have been put off because a black, second-year apprentice is riding him."

Gary took her hand in his. "Maybe, but I doubt that's it."

The horses had galloped down to the start and milled around waiting to be loaded.

"I'm excited to see how James handles his ride," Kgabu said.

The sounds in the stadiums buzzed and the starter's flag went down. The gates burst open, and the horses galloped away seeking a good position.

Chilly Willy and Dingo Boy, the Josi Manor horses pushed through, flanking Vision Quest and Ebony and Ivory just as John had said they would. John and James were ready for them. John eased across to the left and James to the right which forced the Josi Manor horses into centre field.

Gary smiled as he watched through his binoculars. The carefully planned manipulation resembled a game of chess. John and James had ridden it perfectly. The Josi boys were snookered. Their own making, Gary thought.

Mel pulled her binoculars from her eyes and grinned at Gary.

Brad yelled, "Go faster, Vision Boy. Go. Go. GO! I need to double my pocket money and prove Garth wrong. GO."

Suddenly, Chilly Willy came up alongside Vision Quest.

"See, Brad, what did I tell you." Garth gloated.

Gary held his breath, hoping James could stay clear of Chilly Willy.

James urged his horse on, striking with his whip, and Vision Quest answered. Both horses crossed the line in photo finish.

A moment of stunned silence fell over the crowd while everyone waited.

Finally, the announcement came. "Vision Quest has won the Durban July."

The grandstands erupted.

"Yippee, I'm rich. See, I told you, Garth." Brad's face shone with excitement.

Gary hugged Mel and lifted her off the floor in a bear hug. "None of this would be possible without you, my darling."

Chapter Three

ENGORGED AND BLOATED, Colonel Solomon Tlale sat in his office at Army Headquarters in Harare, growing more and more agitated reading reports on large groups of teenagers and unionists rebelling against the Mugabe regime. These uprisings and street marches were happening in all the major cities around the country and the news didn't please him.

After reading through the tenth report, he fidgeted with his pen, slammed it down on the desk. Time to reign the rebels in and do it with force.

A quick swig of Johnny Walker Blue Label from his hip flask helped alleviate his tension before he had to join his fellow officers and the President in the boardroom of Army Head-quarters.

Hopes and aspirations of wealth and peace in Zimbabwe had all but evaporated for most people under the authoritarian leadership of President Robert Mugabe. But Solomon didn't see it that way. The rebels marching in the streets would be dealt with. He'd see to that. He glanced at his watch. Thirty minutes until the meeting. He scribed some notes to present.

Half an hour later, Solomon joined members of the military who'd gathered for the closed session. The President entered the room, followed by his personal guard.

The men at the table rose.

"Greetings," Mugabe said. "Today's meeting concerns only the military men seated at this table. There will be no discussion on this matter outside of this room. Thank you for your attendance." His voice was stern and uncompromising, then he seated himself comfortably at the head of the table, Solomon to his right and the guard left the room.

The meeting went on for an hour.

Solomon looked up from his notes and spoke. "It's time to engage the military more ruthlessly and with more force against these young rebel upstarts, then no-one will dare question your leadership, Sir."

Mugabe stared down his nose through thick lensed spectacles. He shook his head. "No-one questions my leadership, Colonel."

"I'm aware of that, Sir. But there is always opposition and by actioning my plan, the masses will be too afraid of the consequences if they rebel again, Sir." Solomon smiled to hide his cruel intentions.

Mugabe remained silent.

Solomon continued. "Fear, Sir." Solomon pushed the heavy wooden chair back to give more space for his theatrics and his stomach. "Fear ...... is an excellent... control mechanism, as we both know so well." The exertion of waving his arms around to make his point made him breathless.

At first, Mugabe made eye contact with Solomon, then he

looked down, no doubt admiring the highly polished black Armani shoes he wore, then he focussed on Solomon again.

Mugabe's ageing, watery eyes glistened beneath the lenses of his glasses. Very slowly he moved his head and shoulders in acknowledgement and pursed his lips, accentuating his square lower jaw. Sweat had risen on his brow, and he wiped it away with a handkerchief. In that moment, Solomon wished he could read the president's mind.

The President then spoke. "You know what to do, Colonel. I have another meeting to attend." He stood, and left the room, entrusting Solomon to work out the next phase of dealing with the rebels.

After the president left, Solomon sat, and with the other seven men they compared the Zimbabwean rebellion with what was happening across the Limpopo River, in South Africa. They all agreed that in South Africa, the unrest was more evident, though handled differently.

Solomon sensed this even among his connections and family living in Soweto.

His mind refocussed on the national task. Plans were quickly put in place to deal with the teenage rebellions across Zimbabwe. The military, supported by elements of the police would be in action in the next twenty-four hours.

The meeting ended and Solomon watched his officers file out. He remained, alone and brooding. Not about the country's unrest, but the unrest in his personal life. Family and associates were beginning to tire of feeding him information on the Whitaker family likely because there was no remuneration, and they were taking huge risks.

He demanded loyalty, of his informants, related or not, but still, information on the Whitakers had become sporadic, and often unreliable. He'd work ways to remedy this.

Knowing he had support from the top tiers of the Zimbabwean government eased his discomfort. This support also created the desired fear among his family and associates. They understood it wasn't wise to go against him.

Solomon stood, smoothed his military uniform, picked up his notepad and pen and walked slowly back to his office. He collapsed into his chair, which groaned, then he pulled out the top drawer of his desk.

At least his good friend, Johnny Walker Blue Label, ten-year-old whiskey, remained by his side, and dependable. He opened the silver hip flask, took a large swig and felt its comforting burn down his throat, and into the pit of his stomach.

Delicious.

He took another swig, then put the flask back in the drawer. The only glitch to this friendship was that the opulence of the liquor didn't endear him to his comrades, and especially not to his family working tirelessly in South Africa to gather information for his revenge mission. For fifteen years, and still he had no revenge.

He leaned back in his chair and burped with appreciation for the alcohol. Solomon smiled. He'd syphoned significant funds to his Swiss bank account, despite the economic plunge in the country, and now the unrest. One day he'd take over the Mugabe government and rule his people like the mighty King Lobengula had once done.

He opened and read a sitrep that had been put on his desk when he was in the meeting.

The sitrep informed him of another scheduled meeting with the President. An urgent meeting with the Department of Agriculture.

He flung the paper down. The fact his brethren in

Zimbabwe faced poverty on an unprecedented scale, didn't matter to him. This was President Mugabe's problem. Solomon had known hunger. He'd survived.

Solomon's problem was the murderer, Melonie Whitaker. He bunched his fists. How he would love to wrap his huge strong hands around her skinny little neck and squeeze the life out of her.

His hands tingled and his groin stirred. But he knew he'd grown too fat and sluggish to kill her himself. Soon his hired assassins would end her life, and he'd rest easy knowing he'd served all those comrades who'd died in the fire she'd ignited.

His thoughts shifted to his granddaughter, Tanya Khumalo. She'd proven to be a reliable ally. The only family member he paid in pursuit of his vendetta. He covered the rental on her upmarket flat in Durban, and, on the rare occasion when he visited South Africa, Tanya fed and accommodated him.

Through his connections he'd found Tanya the job working for local Government in Durban and a year later she'd reported she'd developed a reliable network of friends who'd become her sources of information on the Whitakers. She'd woven exaggerated stories about why she needed their help to get rid of Melonie Whitaker, the person who'd murdered her uncle, Funani Khumalo.

A slow, comforting warmth filled Solomon's body. The whiskey, and his thoughts, fuelled the flames of darker, more fearsome revengeful thoughts.

It was time to contact Tanya again. He'd not heard from her for a few months. He hoped she'd not fail him like her uncle had done years ago. Funani had failed and lost his life — that memory pained Solomon. The pain was not the fact that he'd lost his son, but because Melonie Whitaker had not only escaped death, again, but she'd escaped a murder conviction too. What further enraged him, he'd learned the judge was a Black woman.

He slid open the desk drawer and took another swig of Johnny Walker, then coughed up the bittersweet taste of revenge.

Chapter Four

ON THE BACK of her horse, riding over rolling hills and grasslands with three-sixty-degree views around her, Mel always felt her most relaxed. She stopped Tropical Sun for a moment and gazed at the dramatic Drakensburg range of mountains in the far distance. She could just make out Giants Castle from where they stood.

She reflected.

Riding every day had been what she'd needed. No more blackouts, no more nightmares, and physically, she felt strong and vibrant again. The stud's recent successes had lifted her spirits too.

Kgabu, Julie and James had proudly carried the rainbow nation flag for the stud and like her, Kgabu had also worked on his fitness since the plaster cast had come off.

Mel and Mrs. Dube had developed a comfortable friendship since the Durban July. Later that morning they were shopping together in Durban for the first time. She looked forward to that and tapped Tropical Sun's sides gently and asked for a canter. From stand still to canter always took Mel's breath away.

When she got home, Mel quickly jumped into the shower and was ready when Mrs. Dube pulled up in front of the house.

"Hi, Mrs. Dube," Mel opened the door of the Mercedes sports. "It's absurd that I'm still calling you Mrs. Dube," Mel laughed and wriggled into the bucket seat, pulled the seat belt over her shoulder and clipped it in. "What's your first name?"

"My given name is an unpronounceable Zulu name, so I'm known to my friends as Synthia — spelt with an S, not a C."

"Fantastic. Calling you by your surname was far too formal. Like a barrier, preventing a more relaxed, meaningful friendship."

"I worried that our cross-cultural friendship wouldn't get a chance to develop." Synthia said rather shyly as she put the car in gear. "These friendships are still observed as weird, and with some white people, totally unacceptable, but it's good change is happening, slow as it may be."

Mel glanced around the inside of the sports car, appreciating its excellence. "Well, I don't give a damn what other people think of my choice of friends. We enjoy each other's company which is none of anyone else's business." Mel smiled at Synthia.

"Great! What a refreshing attitude." Synthia let the clutch out a bit fast and the car spun out of the driveway, kicking up gravel as they left.

Over coffee, Synthia leant closer to Mel and said, "I'm not quite sure how to ask a question that's been on my mind since the day at the races. If I come across clumsy with my words, or I sound rude, please forgive me." Synthia sat back and sliced off a chunk of lemon drizzle cake with her fork.

Synthia went on. "Steve and I happened across some information on your past. If what we have read is true, how do you cope with the threats?" Synthia's smile had a sympathetic warmth. She sliced off another chunk of cake and crossed her long, coffee-coloured legs.

Mel leant back in her chair. "Let me begin by saying I don't know your sources. For me to say that what you've read is true or not, is presumptuous. You know how the media twist things."

"Oh yes, I do. And such a dangerous practice it is. That's why I thought it best to hear it from the horse's mouth, so to speak." Synthia chuckled. "Steve is very selective about what he reads nowadays. We did however, read about the court case, which seemed to be detailed, and often quoted your attorney. There's a part about what happened to you as a teenage girl in Rhodesia during the bush war. The attack on your homestead, the abduction, and then the attack in a hotel room in Harare. What a horrific tale. I guess the worst attack had to be the one in your home at Chanting Clover?"

"Probably, but they were all horrific. All traumatic on different levels. I guess what you've read is close to the truth." Mel took the first bite of her lemon drizzle cake.

"Ooh, good choice. This is delicious." Mel finished her mouthful. "Moreish." Mel licked her lips. "The attack at home came as a huge shock. I still get rattled by the memories. In fact, when I think of the killer's hand around my neck I get cold shivers, like now." She rubbed the goosebumps away from her arms. "I can still feel the knife going into my side, then the rough rope around my neck. It took months of psychological help to overcome that. I haven't had nightmares for a long time, thank goodness. Before I go to bed, I pray nothing like that ever happens again. I don't have the physical strength to fight off a man intent on killing me. The worst part is the attacker always has the element of surprise."

Synthia put her hand on Mel's arm. "My dear, special friend, I simply cannot imagine living with the trauma and fear you've known. And worse still, knowing he's still after you. I hope you don't mind, but we shared what we'd read with Kgabu."

"No, I don't mind at all. Kgabu is a gem and a special part of Chanting Clover." Mel said and swallowed quickly. The cake had made her mouth water.

"Steve thought he should know. He's so fond of you both, and now he feels very protective. Perhaps, in his way, he can keep an eye out for you, if you know what I mean? Poor Kgabu, he said he felt ashamed that a Black person had treated you like that. Steve and I feel the same way. And, after all you've endured, you're so loving and kind toward us and our son. As we've said before, we have huge respect for that." Synthia recognised the pain that lingered in Mel's eyes now. She'd seen that pain reflected in her mother's eyes when her father was murdered in front of her as a by-stander during riots in Soweto in the 70s. She'd never forgotten the look. "You're amazing. A very brave woman, and I hope we stay friends forever."

Mel changed the subject. "I love your autumnal ethnic wrap-around skirt, and that blouse is lovely too. Where did you get them?"

"There's a quaint little ethnic shop not far from here. The lady who makes them, Amanda is her name. A delightful designer who really has a flair for what African women like and all the fabrics she uses are pure cotton. I'll take you there, it's only a ten-minute walk from here. Spoil yourself." Mel thought about it as she stared out the window at the Indian Ocean.

"Yes, why not," Mel said, and they quickly finished their

cake and off they went. Mel fell in love with the shop. Amanda had called it, Dreamz.

Both ladies spent a fortune.

Mel bought a wraparound skirt like the one Synthia was wearing today, then she indulged herself and bought four lovely cotton blouses. "This is so unlike me," Mel laughed and shook Synthia's shoulder affectionately, "you're such a bad influence."

Synthia thoroughly enjoyed the shopping spree. She didn't stop at five items though.

"No wonder Steve hides his credit card," Mel chuckled. By the time they got back to the farm, Mel admitted that retail therapy with Synthia was a much-needed tonic.

Synthia switched off the engine and placed a hand on Mel's arm. "Before I go, I just want to say that if you ever need to call on Steve or me, just pick up the phone. Steve will be more than happy to help if he can, especially on that tiresome political side. He has contacts in Zimbabwe, he can call on. And, if you need a shoulder to cry on, you have mine." She leant over and gave Mel a peck on the cheek and a quick hug.

"Thank you, Synthia. I've enjoyed every moment. You might turn me into a shopper yet." Mel laughed, grateful for the friendship.

Mel had many friends, but most were still living in Zimbabwe. Befriending Synthia was comforting, having someone close that had become a trustworthy ally.

Before Mel left the car she shared her suspicions about Julie. "Since Julie's win on Green Mists, the filly has become more fractious. She's displaying the most unusual equine behaviour. Has Kgabu said anything?"

"No, he hasn't. Should I ask him?" Synthia seemed worried.

"She's always been a bit difficult, as Kgabu knows, but since the July everyone refuses to go near her. Only Julie can work with her. I explained to Gary what I suspect. Prime Security conducted an in-depth investigation and found nothing. But my gut instinct still burns with caution."

"Call her into your office. Question her at length and read her body language. If I'd gone through what you have, I'd also be suspicious."

Mel kissed Synthia on the cheek. "I'll let you know what happens."

MEL TOOK Synthia's advice and called for Julie to meet her in her office at the admin block.

She heard the knock on the door. "Hi Julie, come in. Have a seat."

Julie nervously sat on the edge of the chair.

"Tell me about your secret with Green Mists." Mel let her pen drop and kept her penetrating green eyes focussed on the young jockey. "You seem to have a magic touch with that witch of a mare."

Julie shifted in the chair. She'd obviously enjoyed the compliment, but Mel could see she was edgy about being questioned. Julie didn't offer an answer.

Mel continued. "The connection between you and the mare has posed a problem. None of our grooms or work riders will, or can, handle her. William tells me everyone in the stable complex refuses to do anything with her." Mel took a moment to let her words penetrate. "She's even tried to bite me on occasions."

Julie's hands fidgeted in her lap. She crossed her feet at the ankles and slid them back. A nervous smile tickled the sides of her mouth. Mel wasn't sure if she was about to burst into tears or out laughing.

"It's just.... one of those clicks, Mrs. Whitaker. Like you said you have with Tropical Sun. I love her, Ma'am." Julie spoke to the floor.

"Well, whatever it is that makes her love you, thank you for doing so much with her." Julie's head flicked up. She looked confused.

"Who's William?" She asked. Her feet shuffled nervously.

"He's our Union official. I'm not sure you realise what all this means."

Julie withered in her seat at the mention of the union.

"Gary said you're riding her at Clairwood on Saturday?" Mel asked, to confirm this.

"Yes, Ma'am." Julie sat a little straighter.

"Let me explain our concerns. Only you can feed her, groom her, tack her up, clean her stable, walk her to the paddock, load her, and so on. Is that correct?"

"Yes Ma'am. I'm happy to do it all, Ma'am."

"We have a problem with that. Not because you've offered to go the extra mile but working that number of hours is against the law." Mel emphasised the word, 'law.' She watched Julie's facial expressions and body language change. The mention of the law made her nervous, Mel noticed. Her snappy answer confirmed it.

"She prefers women anyway."

"That may be so, Julie, but it's not the point. Even our special Maria won't go near her, and Maria was with her at birth. It's against the law to work those hours. I've spoken to Gert at the Academy to get his advice. He agrees that what you're doing is a problem with the unions and applies at the Academy too. And Chanting Clover does nothing against the law."

A truly rattled Julie now fiddled with the hem of her T-shirt. Mel thought she might cry. Instead, she sat in obstinate silence.

"I'll chat to William, but I'd like you to give this situation some thought. We need a solution rather urgently."

"Yes, Ma'am." She stood up and hurried out of Mel's office. Mel smiled, if she'd been a judge, the gavel would have fallen.

Guilty.

That evening, relaxing in the sitting room, Labradors asleep at Gary's feet, he asked Mel how the meeting with Julie had gone.

"My questioning made her snappy and nervous. Exactly what I thought it'd do. She's guilty of something, but heaven knows what. She unnerves me, even though security can't connect her to Solomon. I don't believe it for a moment. I've asked her to come up with a solution. She's to let either one of us know in the morning."

"It certainly is weird" Gary's mood changed the minute he felt there may be a threat to Mel's life. "Horses don't change from fractious to demonic unless something is very wrong. And why is it that only Julie can handle her now? It's fishy. Since the July, the mare's gone bonkers. I don't like it at all." Gary's broad handsome brow creased with fresh lines.

"Mists bared her teeth and ran at me when I popped my head over her stable door. She's never done that before. Some- times I've felt like putting the bloody horse to sleep." Mel sighed. "I feel defeated for the first time, and when William reported that the Unions would act against us if one of our staff gets injured, I started to think more seriously. Somehow, some- where, Julie is tied up with Solomon."

"Sweetheart, let's see how the mare performs at Clairwood, then we can decide what to do."

"I'm not happy with that decision, Gary. We can't take the

risk."

"What do you think we do then?"

"Scratch her from the race. I want Vic to take blood samples and check what's going on."

Gary raised his eyebrows. He hadn't thought of getting their trusted vet involved, but Mel had a point. "Yes, okay. Good idea."

AFTER A RESTLESS NIGHT, Gary decided to tackle Julie once she'd finished her training gallop. Standing near the end of the track, he motioned for her to join him.

She rode across and greeted Gary politely. To anyone making a casual observation, there appeared to be nothing wrong with the mare, but as they trotted toward him, he noticed one of the mare's ears had lopped to one side quite dramatically and stayed in that position. He'd never seen that before.

"Morning, Julie. Mists went well. Have you come up with any brilliant ideas on solving the mystery of her aggressive behaviour? I believe my wife said you'd let either of us know this morning."

Julie looked shocked. "No, Sir. I'm sorry, I haven't."

"Well, as Mel explained, we can't turn a blind eye to your working beyond the legal limits, and we need......" Julie never gave Gary a chance to finish. She turned Green Mists and trotted away defiantly.

"Arrogant little wench," Gary uttered under his breath, slammed the Landcruiser into gear, returned to the house and irritably flung his coat and hat on the hall table, then stormed into the dining room.

"She's guilty, and I'm not sure I want her around." He pulled out his chair and sat.

"What happened?" Mel asked. She could hear in his tone he was angry.

Gary described the incident. Whenever Gary spoke fast, Mel knew he'd been seriously annoyed. "Based on the filly's performance this morning, let's not scratch her, but Julie needs to learn some manners. She can ride the race because I don't want Green Mists to be held hostage to the situation." Gary poured himself a cup of coffee. "Just this once let's play the watch-and-wait game. Time often solves riddles. I know Mists' behaviour is an enigma, but I'd like to see her run at Clairwood, then Vic can take blood tests and do what he thinks is best."

Mel picked up her cup of coffee, wrapped her hands around the mug and agreed, knowing it was the best thing to do when Gary was in this mood, which was rare. She'd stay at home.

On Saturday morning Mel and the boys went for a hack. She needed to clear her head of Julie and Green Mists.

To add, Phil Levy's resignation had come as a shock. He'd been with them for a few years, and though he was a shy, introverted man, he knew horses and he'd been a wonderful asset. He and his wife were emigrating to New Zealand. Mel had some CVs to study before the races would be screened live on television.

After lunch Garth and Brad went off with their grandfather on quad bikes. She read through the CVs, then she called Vic.

Vic answered after a few rings. "Hi Mel, everything okay?"

"Well, not really. Do you have a moment?"

"Yes, of course, fire away."

"You know that difficult, fractious mare of ours, Green Mists?"

"Err... um.... Yes. Yes, yes, I do. What's the problem?"

"Apart from breaking Kgabu's leg, she's now caused a bit of a Union revolt."

"Union revolt? What on earth do you mean?" He laughed. "Sorry Mel, I'm not following."

"All our grooms, in fact everyone here, including me, refuse to go near Mists. Julie, a testy young trainee jockey from the Academy is the only one the mare allows near her. She's been doing everything with her, including riding her, for the past eight or nine weeks. We agreed to let her stay here after the July, but now we're regretting it. They're racing at Clairwood today. In fact, she'll be running in a few hours. Gary's there." Mel looked at her watch to check the time. "I know this sounds off the charts, but I think Julie's feeding her something. When she's with Julie, she's like a lamb on dope. If she's doping the horse, why? And if she is drugging her, surely there're no drugs that would exempt the person administering them from the horse's aggression."

"Mel...." Vic paused, about to laugh again. "In all my years in practice I've never heard of anything more absurd, especially coming from you."

"I know. I know," Mel attempted to laugh, but it sounded more like acute frustration caught in her gullet. "It's ridiculous, and not funny. I've never seen such dramatic changes to a horse's character, and I'm pretty sure Julie's working with Solomon Tlale, that fucking colonel in Zimbabwe hell bent on revenge. Excuse me swearing. I couldn't cope with another attack, Vic. Especially not on our horses, and it's the kind of evil thing he'd get someone to do."

"I understand your fears. And if I'd heard this from anyone else, I would've suggested they seek psychiatric help." Vic did laugh this time. "It may be possible she's doping the mare, but in all my years in practice, there's no drug that fits the description. Let's take the Zimbabwean bastard out of the equation. If the filly is cleared to race, it's unlikely she's being doped. If she wins her race, blood tests are done anyway. I can take blood if she loses, but why would any jockey want to lose a race on a proven horse?"

"I know, nothing makes logical sense. Nonetheless. I'm concerned."

"Hmmm, does Julie have access to any of your drug cupboards and fridges?"

"No. Only Gary and I have keys, and we don't keep illegal substances anyway."

"From a clinical perspective, I'm at a loss, so let's take Julie out of the equation too. Send her back to the Academy, then gauge the mare's behaviour."

"I can't do that, Vic. The bitch has got us over a barrel. Everyone refuses to handle Mists, and our Union official has warned that if anyone gets hurt, there's going to be trouble."

"Well, then I suggest we keep Mists mildly sedated. Would you try and handle her sedated?"

"Yes! Sedation will work. What do I tell Julie without arousing suspicion?"

"Mel, my dear, you're not obliged to tell her anything. But if you want to justify sending her back to the Academy, tell her I want to do a series of hormone tests, and I don't want her ridden. That should give adequate time to get to the bottom of what's going on."

"Thanks Vic. I knew you'd come up with something."

"Keep on smiling, Mel, we'll work it out."

"What time will you be here tomorrow?"

"About ten. Julie can hold the horse while I take blood and sedate her."

"Thanks, Vic." Mel ended the call and sat staring into space, then she called William.

"Good afternoon, William. Green Mists, the difficult horse, will not be ridden again for some time. The vet is doing some tests on her tomorrow and Julie is going back to the academy."

"That's good news. Thank you for letting me know."

Mel didn't need trouble with the Union. They'd become rather touchy in the new South Africa. Mel thought they over-react, and many of the new rules stifled progress for they were so inflexible, especially in instances with animals. But she'd keep the peace and stay on side.

She glanced at her watch, and just then the boys came rushing in covered in mud and smiles. "Where did Grandpa take you?"

"To the river. Man, that was fun. Isn't the race on just now?" Garth asked.

"Yes, it is. I was just about to switch on the telly. Go and get yourselves cleaned up."

Ten minutes later, Mel, Garth and Brad watched Green Mists gallop down the track into a well-ridden win. The thought of putting the mare to sleep was no longer an option for Mel.

Garth and Brad bounced around the sitting room, whooping with excitement and watched Gary lead Green Mists into the winner's enclosure.

The lop ear still hung.

Despite Mel's anxieties, the easy win made her more determined to find a solution.

She called Gary. "Hi, honey. What an awesome win. Hold on, the boys want a word." Mel passed the phone to Brad.

"Hi Dad, I've just seen you on television. You're famous." He shrieked happily. "Here's Garth." Garth congratulated his dad and asked what time he'd be home.

"About six." Gary said and Garth handed the phone back to Mel. "I chatted to Vic earlier. He's coming here at ten tomorrow. He's going to take blood for hormone tests. He made another suggestion that I'll discuss with you when you get home."

Exhausted from the long day, Julie walked Green Mists to her stable, watered and fed her, closed the stable door with a bang, irritated by having to report to Mel.

It was almost dark when Julie stepped onto the veranda. "Sorry I'm late."

Mel accepted her apology with a nod. "A very nice win, well done. You look tired." Julie never answered Mel.

"How's Green Mists? Fed? Watered?" Gary asked.

"Yes, Sir. She's tired, but fine." Julie said and remained standing.

"Julie, I'll be taking you back to the academy tomorrow. The vet wants to do blood tests on Green Mists, and he's keeping her sedated for a week." Gary informed the young jockey.

Julie burst into tears and stormed off the veranda without saying a word.

"That's what she did at the track. We'll see how she behaves with Vic here in the morning." Gary said.

Julie had fed and groomed Green Mists and was mucking out her stable when Vic arrived.

"Morning, morning, morning," Vic greeted, placed his drug box outside Green Mists stable and peered over the stable door. Green Mists lunged at him. He narrowly escaped a vicious bite.

"Whoa! You cow." Vic reeled backwards out of harm's way.

He opened the medicine box and pulled up the tranquilizer. Julie said nothing but grabbed the side of Green Mists head-collar and clipped on the lead.

Vic entered the stable. "Pull her head away, please, and keep tension on the lead." Vic instructed. Though Green Mists could still swing her head around and take a chunk out of Vic's side, Julie was prepared.

Vic ran his finger down the vein in her neck, then inserted the needle. Green Mists flinched, but Julie held her head. Rich dark blood bubbled into the ampules. Once four ampules were full, Vic injected the tranquiliser into the vein.

Gary and Mel arrived just as Green Mists head drooped, her bottom lip dropped open, and her eyelids fluttered sleepily.

The lop ear was still in the same position, even after sedation, Mel noted.

Before Vic left, Julie asked him, "What are you testing for?"

Gary shot Mel a surreptitious glance.

"Hormones," Vic said casually. That information didn't settle the anxious Julie.

Vic turned to Gary. "I'll let you know the minute the results are back. Any trouble, give me a shout."

Julie put an arm over the drowsy mare's neck and whispered, "I'll see you in two weeks." She glanced at Mel, then ran to the cottage to gather her belongings.

"I'll collect you at the cottage," Gary called after her.

The journey passed in silence. As they pulled up to the Academy, Julie said, "Sir, I think I've been treated unfairly. There are plenty of other horses I could ride for you."

"We've got enough work riders, Julie." Gary said sharply.

Julie grabbed her things, slammed the car door, and walked off without uttering thanks, or goodbye. Gary didn't care, he was happy to see her go.

Later that evening Mel, Gary and the boys wandered down to the stables. Mel carried the syringe with the tranquiliser and cautiously stood at the stable door. Green Mists took no notice and tugged at her hay, still mildly sedated. Mel entered the stable and stood. Green Mists turned her head to look at Mel then went on eating. Mel cooed to her and took a step forward, clipped the lead onto the halter and stroked Green Mists neck.

"Nice work," Gary said and held the lead while Mel injected the prescribed amount into the vein.

Garth and Brad watched with worried expressions, concerned for the safety of their mother.

When Mel pulled the needle from the vein, she said to Gary, "I'm sure this is too much. She's still quite sleepy. Probably why she let me handle her without being nasty."

"Vic said we could reduce the dose. If she's still dopey by morning, halve it. What do you think?" Gary suggested.

Mel smoothed her hand down the mare's neck again. "Good girlie," she said, unclipped the lead and left the stable.

"Phew. I thought she might hurt you. Why do you and Dad comment on the lop ear all the time?" Garth asked curiously.

"Because, in the past, when a racehorse has had an overdose of steroids, or there's a certain drug in their system, the muscles of the ear are affected and they have no control over it, so it drops to one side." Mel explained and pinched Garth's cheek affectionately. "You two boys, straight to bed now, you've got school tomorrow."

Garth and Brad raced each other back to the house while Gary and Mel followed at a slower pace.

"I can't tell you how relived I am that Julie is no longer on the property." Gary said and took Mel's hand.

"I am too, and by the way, Thomas has agreed to see to Green Mists."

Gary squeezed Mel's hand comfortingly. "I've instructed the night watchman to pass her stable every hour."

"Shall we set our alarm for midnight and come down ourselves and check?" Mel asked.

"No, I'm sure security will inform us if anything goes wrong. I've got to be up early to get the boys to school. I'll check on her then."

TWO DAYS after Green Mists had been off all medication, Thomas legged Kgabu into the saddle.

Gary insisted on going with Kgabu and rode Mr Miracle. A big, calm horse who walked sensibly alongside Mists. During the ride Gary asked Kgabu what he knew about Julie.

"Are you suspicious of her? I feel bad that I suggested her, but she did ride Mists well." Kgabu stroked her neck.

"Please don't feel bad about anything. We'll solve the mystery soon enough." Gary assured Kgabu.

"I hope so. I'm suspicious of Julie too. Do you think she's connected to that nasty man in Zimbabwe?"

"I hope not, but it's not impossible."

"Well, thank goodness Mel never put Greenie to sleep. Look how beautifully she's going. She even gave me a little nicker at the stable this morning." Kgabu dropped forward and gave Mists neck a hug. "Sometimes we don't need science to confirm what's glaring at us, hey?"

Gary nodded. "Quite right. I'm going to call Vic. He'll be interested that the lop ear has returned to its normal position. I don't think I've ever seen her this calm. And Julie's never coming back here." He said categorically.

Chapter Five

TANYA KHUMALO FELT confident that she was Solomon's favourite granddaughter. She left her flat at 6:30 every morning and walked briskly along the esplanade to her office in the Council building. A time of the morning when fresh sea breezes douse the city with tiny droplets of moisture before the sun gets hot and burns it off. This was the time when Tanya felt the most invigorated with the sea breezes whipping at her face. By the time she reached the office her heartrate was up and her mind clear and ready for the demands of the day ahead.

Today she'd arranged to meet her friend Julie Mokoena for lunch to discuss the recent call Julie had received from Solomon that had stressed her.

Just before twelve, Tanya hurried down a side street that led to the beachfront. She found a table at the window in her favourite Ocean View restaurant.

Tanya selected a table for two at the window and sat gazing at the ocean, waiting for Julie to arrive. A cheerful waiter appeared, and she ordered her favourite coffee. A delicious double expresso latte, then she continued admiring the rise and swell of the sea. Lost in thought about her grandfather and his vendetta against Melonie Whitaker, Tanya became aware of a familiar voice behind her.

"Finally, I'm here."

Tanya jumped up, spilling a little of her coffee. "Oops," she hugged Julie. "It's so nice to see you. And that orange sweater really suits you." Tanya wiped the coffee spill off the table with a napkin.

Julie pulled out her chair and sat. "Thanks. You look great too. Very sassy in your dark green slack suit. Sorry I'm a bit late. As expected, the transport let me down."

The waiter popped back, and Julie ordered lemonade.

She stretched her arms above her head then dropped them by her sides. "I can't get that call from your grandfather off my mind. Every part of my body is tense."

"What did you discuss?" Tanya enquired, knowing how difficult and frightening her grandfather could be.

"That I'm back at the Academy. Nothing went to plan and I'm sure the Whitaker's won't take me back." Julie was shaking and fiddled with her napkin.

"Why?" Tanya couldn't imagine what could have happened to cause this riff with the Whitakers.

"They got the vet to take blood tests after Green Mists last win at Clairwood, then they sedated the horse." Julie's eyes were wide.

"I know nothing about horses. Then what happens?"

"They'll get the results back in a week, but I'll not ever know because I was fired. I tried to explain it to your grandfather, then I heard his breathing change. I knew he'd start yelling at me, so I cut the call. I'm scared, Tanya, really scared."

Tanya didn't answer immediately. She glanced out the

window. None of what Julie was saying made much sense. The skies were moody. Dark clouds were building. "I love watching the ocean when a storm is brewing. When lightning strikes across the sky, the atmosphere changes, doesn't it?" Tanya looked back at Julie.

"I hope I don't get wet when I walk back to the station. I never brought a raincoat or an umbrella. It was brilliant sunshine when I left the academy. And I must meet the transport back at 3 p.m." Julie fidgeted nervously.

"I'll walk with you. Gives us more time together to work out another plan." Tanya laid a comforting hand on Julie's arm.

"Ready to order?" The waiter asked, returning with Julie's lemonade.

"A Hawaiian burger and chips, for me." Tanya was hungry.

"Make that two," Julie said. I don't usually eat hamburgers and chips. Jockey's dietary requirements are so strict. But today I need a treat."

When the waiter was out of earshot, Tanya said, "Explain to me what happened with that mare."

"A fucking disaster. Though the Whitakers have no proof I fed the horse the herbal potion you got, but Mrs. Whitaker is sharp. When that stupid mare went nuts, I thought it was better to stop giving it to her."

"Wise move."

"I don't think the Whitaker's have connected me to you grandfather. But I'm spooked by all this." Julie spread her napkin across her lap.

"Relax. Grandfather says we must be patient."

"He did say that tome." Julie looked at Tanya with wide, frightened eyes.

"Tell me, how's the Academy going? Are you getting more

rides?" Tanya asked with interest, not wanting to lose the friendship because of her grandfather.

"Yeah, I am. Since winning on Green Mists, rides are easier to get, but it's still a man's world. It's tough, especially when I have a period and I'm bedridden for two days. No ride, no income. The physical demand is a killer."

The women finished lunch and walked from the Plaza to the Durban bus station where the minibus taxis waited.

The clouds overhead had swelled and were ready to burst.

"I'll give you a shout when grandfather calls me again." Tanya's parting words to Julie as she stepped into the waiting taxi.

The wind howled and blew Tanya about as she left the station. Then the first raindrops landed on her arms, and she picked up her pace. In minutes, the rain got heavier. When she stepped into the office foyer, she was drenched. She took the stairs to get warm, dashed to the bathrooms, grabbed the only hand towel, dried off, and then hurried to her office.

Shirley, her PA looked up from her desk. "I wondered if you'd taken your umbrella. I've got a spare jersey. Do you want to borrow it?"

"Thanks. I'm freezing." Tanya's teeth chattered and she gratefully pulled on the jersey. "Ah, that's better, thank you."

Outside the wind picked up, battering the palm trees and shrubs in the garden below. "At least I'm not outside in that," Tanya said with relief. The palm trees bent to their full extension, left and right, threatening to snap.

"Amazing how quickly this storm came up," Shirley said carrying a mug of tea. "Hopefully this will help warm you." Shirley put the mug on Tanya's desk. "Just listen to those waves."

The waves crashed against the beach, then tree branches

gave way, and the wind flung them across the pavement. Even the building felt the force of mother nature's power.

The windows shook. "Did you feel that?" Tanya asked. "I hope my friend Julie gets back to Shongweni okay."

The following morning at the office, Tanya's phone buzzed. She glanced at her watch. 7:45 a.m. Early for a business call. She answered.

"Hi Tanya, did you get caught in the storm?" Julie asked.

"Yes. I got drenched, but I got into the office before the wind got up. Did you get wet?"

"No, but the wind nearly blew the taxi off the road. I forgot to ask for the contact details of that Sangoma, traditional healer friend of yours. The one who gave you the herbal potion. Can you give me her number, please?"

"Yes, sure," Tanya read out the telephone number.

"Good luck."

During Julie's lunch break, she sat on a bench under the trees and dialled the Sangoma's number. Julie waited anxiously for the call to be answered.

"Hello." A soft, feminine voice finally answered.

"Hello, is that Lerato Msizi, the best Sangoma in Natal?" Julie asked politely. According to Tanya, Lerato fulfilled a vital role, not only in the KwaZulu-Natal community, but in all the provinces and was a highly respected and sought after healer.

"Yes, my dear, that's me. How can I be of service?" Her tone was serene and compassionate.

"I'd like to see you next week, if possible. Do you have a practice in the Shongweni valley?"

"Yes, I can see you in the valley, my friend. Do you require special healing for yourself?"

"No, Ma'am, it's not for me. I'll explain while we're in consultation, if that's alright?" Julie knew Lerato had special healing gifts and a thorough understanding of herbal treatments. She also offered divination and protection spells and was highly sought, even by African politicians helping guide them in making vital decisions based on spiritual guidance from their ancestors. Excited to get an appointment Julie answered, "yes, that's fine, thank you.

"Give me your name and number. I'll call you when I'm in the valley."

Julie gave Lerato the details and rang off.

Chapter Six

ANNE, Chanting Clover's valued equine physiotherapist arrived to work on Green Mists once again. A slight woman, with long blonde hair. Dressed in a purple track suit her fine complexion glowed.

"Hi, Kgabu. Do you mind holding her while I work?"

"No problem, but I'm sure she won't be aggressive with you."

Anne began her work, probing with her fingers and the heel of her palm over areas that had once caused the mare to bite or kick. "Gee, what a different horse!" Anne exclaimed while she massaged the pectorals. "This was where she got reactive, but all seems good now. Amazing how tight the thoracic sling becomes when a horse is in emotional tension." Anne gently massaged while Green Mists mouthed and yawned, enjoying the treatment.

"She's been so good on the walk rides, textbook perfect in her training gallops, well behaved in her stable, she even lets me wrap my arms around her neck and cuddle her." Kgabu smiled happily.

"If I didn't know better, I'd say I was working with a different horse." Anne stood beside the mare's shoulder. "The transformation is hard to believe."

Anne finished after an hour, picked up her bag, washed her hands outside the stable and thanked Kgabu for his assistance. "Hey, good luck at Scottsville on Saturday. It's your first race on her since that awful day she broke your leg, isn't it?"

"Yes, and I'm so excited. Thanks, Anne. I hope we win."

In the jockey's rooms at Scottsville racecourse in Pietermaritzburg, Kgabu waited as usual. He'd weighed, sat on a bench, rested his head in his hands and contemplated the race ahead. When he looked up, he caught a glimpse of Julie walking out.

Kgabu panicked. Why was she in the weigh-in rooms? She wasn't riding today. Then he looked at the wall clock and nerves took a hold. It was time to go out and mount.

Siyanda led Green Mists around the parade ring. Both her ears were pricked forward. She even nickered when she saw Kgabu approach. That made his day and melted his nerves. Siyanda legged him up. Green Mists shook her head, sneezed and pranced happily, eager to get on with her job.

Standing in the centre of the parade ring Synthia held Mel's arm. "I'm so proud of my boy."

"I know you are, and so are we. Let's get back to our seats and watch them win this race." Mel said happily.

In fine style, Green Mists romped home, winning by four lengths.

"What a magical race," Synthia uttered tearfully as she watched Kgabu stand in the saddle and punch the air triumphantly.

"Textbook. Thank God, I didn't put her to sleep." Mel cheered her decision.

Kgabu had three other races to ride and at the end of the day, he reported to Mel that Julie had been sneaking around in the jockeys' rooms.

"She's up to no good, Mel. Guaranteed."

IT WAS the first day home for Garth and Brad. Their mid-term break. Garth raced into the house shouting, "Mum. Mum. Come quickly. It's, it's... Warriors Robe." Garth jumped up and down, his arms flapped wildly. "He's thrashing about in his stable. I, I.... think he's going to die. Dad wants you to call Vic." Garth tore out the house again. Mel followed, her phone to her ear. Vic assured her he would get to the stables shortly.

Even though Gary had injected Warriors Robe with a painkiller, he still rolled around, trying to alleviate the pain in his gut.

"Vic's on his way." Mel said breathlessly and stepped into the stable.

"He's in dire straits, poor boy. A nasty colic, but this is a weird one." Gary said, sweat dripped off his brow. Though it was humid inside the stable Gary had been trying to pacify the horse.

Mel watched the beautiful jet-black colt for a few minutes. As the painkiller began to filter through the horse's veins, the thrashing slowed. Finally, he lay still. Mel stroked his neck and massaged his forehead. "Look at the colour of his eyes. The membranes are scarlet, Gary."

"I noticed that too. It looks more like biliary." A tick-borne disease.

Gary squatted beside Mel. She gently pulled the lower eyelid down for a closer inspection of the membranes. "Vic wasn't far away when I called. He'd just pulled a calf next door, so he should be here in a few minutes."

Garth stood by and watched. "I hate seeing a horse in so much pain." He was almost in tears as if he was feeling the horse's pain too. Although he'd panicked, Mel knew the younger children at school always asked Garth questions about their horses. It was important to Garth to have answers, so he stayed, despite his angst, listening to Warrior moaning and swishing his tail, flicking the straw bedding around. Every now and then he'd lift his head, then drop it back into the straw.

Ten minutes later, Vic arrived, accompanied by his new assistant, Dr. Richard Stevens.

Gary shook his hand. "Hi Vic, thanks for getting here so promptly." Vic nodded and introduced Richard.

Both men wore green overalls cut off at the sleeves and smudged with blood, obviously from pulling a big calf.

"Richard has many years of acquired knowledge on these beasts." Vic pointed to Warrior.

"Yeah, and they're full of surprises. Nice to meet you." He turned, "you must be Garth." And shook Garth's hand.

Warrior still lay with his head stretched back while Thomas gently stroked his neck and fiddled with his mane. Perspiration shone through the horse's coat.

Vic checked the heart rate and listened to gut sounds with his stethoscope. "Are you sure this isn't a snake bite?" He asked, examining the eye membrane.

"Hadn't given that a thought. Except he's not been in the field for the last twenty-four hours. It's unlikely." Gary looked at Thomas. "Have you seen any puff adders around the stables lately?"

"No, Sir. Not for many months."

Richard checked the limbs for any minor puncture wounds, just in case. There'd be small droplets of blood coming from each fang puncture. The tell-tale sign of a snake bite. There were none, and no swelling. Snakebite ruled out, but a small heap of dark, hard droppings caught Richard's attention. "When was this passed?"

"About two hours ago," Thomas answered. Vic had a look too.

"Internal bleeding. The faeces are blotched black." Vic put his stethoscope on the stomach near the flank and listened to the gut noises, then checked the noise coming from the horse's lungs.

Richard pulled on a rubber glove and rubbed on soapy liquid, then carefully inserted two fingers into Warrior's anus.

"Oh yuk, that stinks," Garth commented and held his nose while Richard removed more hard, black faeces and inspected the boluses. Some were coated with mucous, others had strands of dark red blood on the surface.

"I hope I don't ever have to shove my hand up a horse's bum." Garth broke the silent inspection, and everyone laughed.

"If you're going to be involved with horses, my boy, you'll have to do it one day," Gary advised him with the truth.

"I don't like the look of those, or the smell." Mel said, frowning as she inspected.

"I'm taking blood tests. We've already had one weird plant poisoning. Let's not take chances given the recent history here." Vic said.

Richard placed a handful of dark faeces in a plastic bag, then pulled the rubber glove off his hand.

"Thomas, who is Warrior's groom?" Mel asked.

"Jackson."

"Jackson, the union spokesman?" Thomas nodded.

Mel didn't voice her thoughts then, but an hour later, when Warrior seemed more comfortable and showed an interest in his hay, she shared her thoughts with Gary outside the stable.

She popped her head around the stable door, "We'll pop back in half an hour," Thomas acknowledged with a nod.

Mel called Synthia when they got back to the house.

"Hi, is everything okay?" It had become an automatic question nowadays.

"Well, I hope so. I need to have a chat with Kgabu, if he's there." Mel asked.

"Yes, sure, let me call him. He's watching a race on TV." Mel heard Synthia call.

Kgabu picked up the phone. "Hello, ma'am."

"Hi, Kgabu. Sorry to interrupt your race. Do you know which groom was allocated to Warriors Robe for his first race?"

"Um. A guy called Jackson. I think. Why, ma'am?"

"Before I answer that, is Julie listed to ride on that day? I can't remember."

"Yes, she is. Is everything alright with Warrior?"

"Yes, everything's fine now. We got him through an unusual, almost life-threatening colic. You can go on with your game, and don't forget to show Garth and Brad. They'd enjoy having TV horse racing games. Sadly, Warrior won't be racing for a few weeks, but you know how many other horses you've got to ride."

"Yes, I do, and I love them all. Please let me know about Warrior."

"Of course." Mel rang off. "Damn." She murmured, convinced more than ever that Julie was somehow connected to the colonel, and now Jackson may be the link. An uncomfortable vulnerability prickled, like a hairy caterpillar had just crawled along the back of her neck. She shuddered.

She needed to get away. The whole family needed a break from the drama they'd been through recently. Gary had said their next holiday should be in Botswana, and right now the Okavango called.

Mel's game-viewing holiday thoughts were soon interrupted though. Brad raced into her office carrying a rainbow trout he'd caught — on a fly line for the first time. He almost shoved the fish under her nose. "It weighs 700grams, Mum." Brad shrieked happily, "and Grandpa showed me how to gut it. Look," he bared open the fish's stomach to show her the empty cavern.

"Wow, what a clever boy you are." Pushing his hand away.

"Can we cook it for dinner?" His little nose wrinkled with his enquiry.

"Of course, darling. Angelina will show you how to fillet it."

"Oh, yay." He raced to the kitchen and Angelina happily showed him what to do, then patiently watched. "You're so clever, Bradley," she said affectionately. Angelina had known both the boys since their birth. She adored them.

After each person had a morsel of trout fillet, served as an entrée and dinner was over the family wandered down to the stables to check on Warrior. Mel was the first to peer over his stable door.

One hand shot to cover her mouth and the other held the door as she wailed, "Oh God, Gary, he's dead." She cried.

Mortified, Gary shepherded the family back to the house, then called Vic.

Mel sat in their room and sobbed with them. She left when

Vic arrived to do the post-mortem. Heart failure and appalling liver damage. The liver was three times the size of a healthy one.

Gary and Mel fell into bed after midnight, emotionally and physically exhausted. Staring at the roof Mel whispered, "he hasn't been able to kill me, now he's targeting what we love. There's somebody here working for Solomon. I think it might be Jackson." She rolled into Gary's arms and wept.

Chapter Seven

"Good evening, Julie. Did the potion work?"

"Yes! Thank you, it did." Lerato clicked off the call. Julie looked at the phone, puzzled.

She called Tanya. "Hi, the potion worked this time, but I'm puzzled." Julie said.

"Why? What's puzzled you?" Tanya asked.

"Lerato called me and asked if the potion had worked, then clicked off the call. She had no idea what I was using the plant poison for."

Tanya explained. "She never questions what her potions are used for or on. She would've only called to ensure you were happy with the results. The concoctions she prescribes are made for multiple uses, both for human and animal."

"Yeah, I know. I expected her to say something else instead of cut the call."

"Well now you know how potent the potion is. It must have been a different one you used on Green Mists. The one you've just used is also prescribed for humans who want quick relief from terminal illness. It causes death within an hour after consumption. It begins with a gradual onset of stomach cramps, the pain reaches a peak, then subsides quickly, and the human patient goes to sleep forever. But I'm told, with large animals, like cows and horses, it takes longer — a painful death by any accounts. That's not so nice to think about, but well done anyway. Grandfather will be pleased. You'll hop back onto his good-girl list."

"I hope so. But the Whitakers are mega suspicious. They're questioning all their staff which scares me."

"Stop worrying, my friend, they can't pin it to you. You're not even part of them any longer. I'm surprised grandfather hasn't asked someone to use the tincture on Mrs. Whitaker. Just 2mls ends the life of a human. What did she prescribe for that horse?"

"Twenty-five millilitres." Julie heaved a deep breath. "Tanya, I don't feel good about this. I know I didn't feed it to the horse myself, but I arranged it. He was a magnificent horse, and I love horses. I don't want to carry on."

A suffocated silence followed. "Does this mean you're no longer going to help my poor grandfather?"

"I'm worried. What if......I.... get caught." Julie stammered.

"I understand. I'm going to ask grandfather to pay you for the next instruction."

Julie whispered, "Okay, but that will be the last."

Tanya and Julie went to visit Lerato. Julie was curious to meet her in person. They took a taxi to the given address. It was more than an hour's drive from Durban, deep into the hills beyond Marrion Hill, almost opposite to where the Academy was situated, but ten to fifteen kilometres away as the crow flies.

The taxi filled with people booked to see Lerato for divination and healing. A long row of Taxi's waited for their return journey. Tanya and Julie disembarked and followed the others along a pathway that led to a cave.

Lerato lived and practiced from inside the cave. It was huge. On their left, built against the rock was a line of small huts. "Do people stay over?" Julie whispered to Tanya.

"Yes. I'm told those huts are for ladies struggling with fertility. They spend a week here with Lerato and apparently when they return to their husbands, they fall pregnant quickly. It's called, fertility blessing."

The cave opened wide as they walked deeper in. The floor covered with a mixture of sand and a white dusty powder with occasional scrubby plants and thirsty grass clumps trying to survive. In the centre stood Lerato's dwelling. A stone hut built on a raised platform. Three clay covered steps led onto the platform. Lerato held council on this platform.

"I'm told no one has ever been inside her room," Tanya whispered to Julie as they approached. They were the first in line and stood together at the base of the steps.

Julie's eyes were wide with a mix of fear and awe. The Sangoma sat in a handmade wicker chair in front of her bedroom door dressed in a red and white cloak. Around her head she wore a white veil, held in place by bands of red and white beads. Beads of the same colour hung in chains around her neck, wrists, and ankles and jingled eerily as she beckoned to them. Despite the unsettling sound, the old woman's wrinkled face held a kind smile.

Tanya led the way up the steps, and they knelt before Lerato. The Sangoma placed a wrinkled hand on each of their shoulders and began to chant quietly. A sound so peaceful and soulful it seemed to embody kindness and wisdom. When she finished, she blessed the two girls.

"That was amazing. I feel so cleansed," Tanya whispered as she looked up at the elderly woman. "Thank you Lerato."

Lerato nodded and took Tanya's hand. "What are you here for today?" The wise old sage asked.

"Julie wanted to meet you and thank you for the previous prescriptions. We don't need anything more right now." Tanya said. Julie bowed her head submissively.

"I'll schedule a divination session when you are in Durban again." Tanya added, taking the old woman's hand, kissing it, and then bowing before paying her.

As they left the cave, Julie hesitated. "Since you didn't ask for more potions, does that mean I'm free to stop poisoning the Whitaker horses?"

"Yes, but there's one more task my grandfather has for you," Tanya replied. "But he says you're to do nothing for a few months. I'll notify you after Christmas."

That wasn't news Julie had hoped to hear, but for now, she could focus on with her racing career.

THE HOLIDAY in the wilds of Botswana was booked. Mel surprised the boys the day they came home from school for the winter holidays late into June. "We've booked a ten-day safari in the Okavango Delta, and we leave the day after tomorrow," she announced that evening at dinner.

"Where's the Vanga Delta?" Brad asked.

"In Botswana. A luxury safari. How does that sound?" Her eyes glittered with excitement at the thought.

"Yippee." Brad shouted. "Are we flying there?"

"Yes, we certainly are." Gary answered Brad's question, and they chatted merrily throughout dinner going over the brochures.

"Ah, Mum, Dad, this is so cool." Garth yawned and stretched. "So, when exactly do we leave?"

"Monday morning," Mel said enthusiastically.

"Oh, wow. Well, I'm going to bed. Night Mum. Night Dad." Garth kissed them goodnight and Brad followed.

After they'd gone to bed Mel and Gary glanced through the brochures once more and laid out the map of Botswana.

"I can't wait to get there. Looks idyllic. Just what we need after what the past year has dished out." Gary stretched. "Do you want anything to drink before we go to bed?"

"No thanks, my love. How do you think our new trainer, Tinus Terblanche will cope while we're away?" Mel was interested to know Gary's thoughts.

"Working with him for the past month has been a pleasure. He's a super guy, great with the horses and it seems the staff like him too. He'd be perfectly capable of running everything in our absence. He knows the ropes and is a very experienced horseman. We chose the right man. No doubt about it."

"Well, if he runs into any snags, Dad's here to help." Mel extended her weary legs out in front of her, braced the muscle, then stood up. "Let's get to bed, I can't stay awake a moment longer."

Gary followed her to their bedroom after switching off all the lights, and in minutes they were both sound asleep.

After saying a sad farewell to Grandpa Ivan, the family were eager to get to the airport. It was Garth and Brad's first time flying to a new country.

They arrived in Gaborone, cleared customs, collected their luggage, and met the pilot for their onward journey. He was waiting for them in the arrivals hall holding a banner – Whitaker in front of him.

Ivan Geldenhuys, the pilot, led the family onto the runway.

A light aircraft waited near the main hangers. They boarded and in twenty minutes they were in the air on their way to their first destination.

After an hour flying time, Garth shouted to his brother above the hum of the engines, "Hey, Brad, check this out."

Ivan, the pilot tilted the plane slightly. He'd also seen the herd of elephant below. "It's a huge herd. Probably about a hundred elephant in that herd." Ivan announced.

Brad whistled. "Gee, Ma, can you see them all, and baby jumbo's too," Brad squealed with delight.

"What a great way to begin our safari." Mel leant over Gary to get a better look.

The Big Africa Safaris plane landed at Maun airport. The family were met by Craig Willoughby, their appointed guide who also had a banner with the Whitaker's name on it.

Craig led the family on foot across the apron to the airport terminal. The heat was stifling creating mirages above the hot tarmac.

Airport staff loaded the Whitaker family luggage onto a twin-engine Cessna Caravan they were flying to the Leroo le Tau airstrip in.

"God it's sweltering, isn't it?" Mel commented. Inside the building Brad and Garth took off their hats and wiped the sweat off their forehead. Hot, sweaty and irritable, patience was a big ask. Their parents finished the paperwork formalities as quickly as possible, and they clambered aboard the plane. A bigger plane, but the air-conditioning wasn't working efficiently and made the flight a prickly, uncomfortable journey. Drinking copious amounts of water kept them hydrated.

The cabin temperature registered 44 °C on the aircraft dashboard.

"We'll be touching down at Leroo le Tau in approximately

twenty minutes" The outside temperature is hovering around 40°C, the pilot announced. "The airstrip is on the western bank of the Boteti River. I hope there's no game on the airstrip."

"What if there is game on the airstrip?" Concerned, Brad's eyebrows met in the middle of his forehead as he asked.

Craig answered. "That's why we fly at the hottest time of the day. The game rests beneath the trees or wallows in a waterhole or in the river when the sun is at its zenith. We often see warthog on the runway, but they run, in their comic way, with their tails held up like ariel's and get off the runway."

"Like Timon and Pumba," Brad shrieked with joy, momentarily forgetting his discomfort. "This will be like a real-life Lion King movie holiday, hey Mum?" Mel smiled. Brad's enthusiasm was infectious, despite the heat.

No game lurked on the runway and the aircraft came to a dusty halt. A safari vehicle waited to take them to the lodge.

The welcome cool inside the lodge raised their spirits. Hippo Lodge, nestled right on Boteti River could not have been more idyllic surrounded by indigenous trees and snaking waterways creating little islands, but soon joined the main body of the Boteti River.

After unpacking and washing their faces with cold water, Gary slung his camera bag over his shoulder and walked out onto their private deck.

"Two idyllic days game-viewing here." He pulled a brand-new lens from its bag and attached it to his camera. "I'm getting ready for the game drive in the morning." He explained to Brad who'd sat beside him.

That evening, sitting on the main lodge deck, Gary got some magnificent shots of game coming down to the river's edge to draw up their water needs for the night. The sun, molten gold and silver cast provocative colours over the landscape and bounced off the backs of wet elephant, turning their thick grey hides to a glossy black.

The family were woken at dawn for the early morning game drive. They'd not been out long when a massive herd of elephant crossed the road in front of them. Gary clicked away on his camera, while Mel and the boys watched through binoculars. The herd was heading down to the river to drink. Water the focus of their attention.

By 8 a.m. Garth and Brad had ticked off elephant, buffalo, hippo, crocodile, lion, giraffe, zebra, wildebeest, impala, and kudu on their viewing list. Not far from the lodge, tall Acacia trees shaded the road ahead, and a pack of colourful African Wild Dog played in the cool of the shade. A rare sighting indeed. One young dog curiously played with a giant tortoise, trying to tip it onto its back so it could rip out the soft flesh of the underbelly.

Craig stopped the vehicle and switched off the engine. Two more dogs came to help and between them they flipped the tortoise over and devoured its innards. In less than a few minutes only a shell remained on the road. A macabre sight. Licking their lips the pack wandered off to seek something bigger to satisfy their hunger.

"Poor tortoise." Brad muttered sadly, staring at the empty shell.

"It's the way of nature, my boy. They must eat too."

After a late breakfast the family enjoyed a peaceful day wallowing in the pool, reading and sleeping. That evening they packed in preparation for the onward journey to Green Heron Camp in the Moremi Game Reserve, where they were spending five nights.

. . .

Back on the same runway where they'd seen the warthog, the pilot took off. When he'd levelled the plane, Gary broke the silence. "Thank goodness the aircon is working properly today. Garth, Brad let's see what game we can spot."

Mel had her head pressed against the aircraft window as she gazed at the expanse of Africa beneath her, she soaked up the peace and the quality time with her family. They'd been flying for half an hour when Gary's words burst from his mouth. "Good God, it's vast." The Okavango Delta myriad fingers of water spread like a fan for miles and miles and miles.

Craig shared some interesting wildlife tales about the Moremi Game Reserve and a little of its history. The plane landed and taxied across the red earth runway and parked beside two waiting Landcruiser safari vehicles.

"You two boys, jump out and get straight onto the waiting vehicle. Lion often lie in the grass nearby. They're so well camouflaged, so don't waste time."

The distance between the plane and the vehicle was no more than ten metres, but the thought of lion close made Garth and Brad's legs fly across the space. Gary and Mel laughed as they followed. The two boys sailed into the safety of their seats like two swallows diving into the nest.

"Hurry, Mum," Brad urged as their luggage was hoisted onto the second vehicle. Once Gary was seated Craig introduced the family to their driver and new guide. Craig was going back to Gaborone.

"Hi, I'm Simon, your driver and guide for the duration of your stay. Welcome to Botswana and the famous Moremi Wildlife reserve. We think it's the best in Africa, and I'm sure you'll agree." Simon drove slowly to the lodge. "We might see lion. They like to lurk close to the camp and rest in the shade when it's hot like this."

They weren't lucky.

Simon parked, then showed the Whitaker's to their luxury tent and carried their cases.

"Whoa, I've never seen a tent this posh, or this big," Garth looked around, astonished.

Brad tested his bed by bouncing on it.

"Hey, Brad, it's not a trampoline." Garth scolded, sounding just like Gary which made Mel laugh. She took Gary's arm and looked up at him. "Like father, like son." She smiled affectionately.

The tent had two separate bedrooms. Each bedroom had its own bathroom and both rooms had stunning, uninterrupted river views. A long wooden deck ran the length of the tent and on one end, a large, jute shaded jacuzzi welcomed hot, sweaty bodies as it bubbled like champagne.

"Hey, Mum, can we jump in there to cool down?" Garth asked.

"Not yet, Garth. Let's get unpacked, then you two can jump in." Gary said.

After obediently packing away their clothes, Garth and Brad sampled the jacuzzi. "Mum, Dad, are you going to jump in with us? It's so cool." Garth asked.

"We'll get in later. We're going to reception to book a Mokoro boat trip for this evening. It leaves at four, so you'd better get out and dressed soon. We'll leave in thirty to forty-five minutes."

Gary and Garth travelled in one canoe. Mel and Brad in the other. Each Mokoro had a guide. They'd not been on the river long when suddenly, not far from them, a hippo surfaced and opened its massive mouth in warning.

"WOW!" Garth shouted in fright as he stared into the mouth of the beast with foot long teeth razor sharp. The sound of Garth's voice startled the hippo, and it ducked beneath the water.

"Can a hippo bite this boat in half?" Brad asked Sampson, their guide as he considered the size of hippo teeth.

"Yes, but don't worry, we understand them. We never take our visitors that close." He assured Brad.

"But what if one suddenly comes out right beside us?" Brad's eyes were wide. He didn't trust what was going on beneath the murky green waters.

"We know each pod here, Brad. They are used to the mokoro's and just warn us to stay clear. I always take a wide berth around females with young."

The answer hadn't completely satisfied Brad, but when a few more hippo rose above the surface of the water fifteen metres from the mokoro and grunted, he settled. Gary had his camera close to his face the whole time and captured the Green-backed Heron preening in the reeds. The camp was named after this rare heron.

They returned to camp just before sunset when the buzzing, irritating mosquitoes came out to bite.

After a dinner served under the stars, they clambered into a safari vehicle and headed off into the night. Their night guide, Johaan spoke about what they might see in the bush at night and the nocturnal animals they could expect to see and asked if they'd covered themselves with insect repellent.

The highlight of the evening's drive, and with the help of Johaan's spotlight, they came upon a leopard hauling the lifeless body of an impala antelope up into a tree.

"Whoa, now that's power," Garth commented.

"Sssh," Mel put her index finger to her lips. The leopard quickly hauled its kill onto a sturdy branch a few metres above the ground, then stopped and considered what to do next. Startled by voices and the blinding light, its large yellow eyes dazzled red. She watched cautiously for a few seconds. Cameras clicked quickly. Then she turned her head away and hauled the carcass further into the tree.

"Let's leave her to devour her dinner in peace." Johann suggested and drove on. The only other nightlife they saw were a group of bushbabies darting across metres of open space between the trees. With the light on their little bodies, they looked like shooting stars.

Brad had fallen asleep. Gary woke him when Johann cut the engine back at camp. In the quiet they heard the deep grunting of lion on the move close to the camp. They stayed in the vehicle listening to the eerie sounds of the wilds of Africa at night. Brad was wide awake now.

"Will the lions come into the camp?" Brad whispered.

"Not this early in the night, but in the early hours of the morning they often pass through." Johaan answered. Brad's shoulders slumped from relief, he'd be tucked up in bed and sound asleep by then.

"The sound of lion on the prowl sends shivers down my back," Mel sat in bed leaning against Gary's shoulder, "but this is just what we all needed," she yawned. "We've been so lucky with sightings."

She snuggled down under the sheets with Gary, who whispered back. "We'll do this again, just the two of us next time." They melted into each other's arms, kissed passionately and slipped into a world only they knew.

Refreshed from a good night's sleep, the family boarded the safari vehicle at 5:30 a.m. and set off on another early morning game drive. Time passed slowly, stopping to photograph and admire the beauty of African wildlife in abundance. Mel had worried that constant game viewing might bore the two boys.

On the contrary, they were absorbed by it and kept asking Johaan impressive questions.

Topping a morning filled with excitement and spectacular viewing, they thought they'd seen it all until they passed a cheetah lying not more than three metres off the edge of the gravel road lying in the grass feeding five, fluffy, spotted cubs.

"Aah, those are so cute, aren't they, Mum?" Brad looked at the cubs then back to his mother. "I just want to cuddle them." Brad had always been the real animal lover of the two boys, and the more sensitive of the two.

Back in camp for a late breakfast Brad and Garth entertained everyone with their take on what they'd seen, and everyone else shared their sightings too, which were noted on a map of the area at the entrance to the lodge.

"What are we doing now?" Brad asked.

"We're doing what all the animals do in the heat of the day. Sleep," Gary answered.

"I'm not sleeping, I'm going to swim." Brad followed Garth to the communal pool and joined their newfound friends. Gary and Mel lay on sun loungers in the shade, reading. A welcome cool breeze wafted over them. Mel's book dropped on her chest as she dozed off.

After her revitalising catnap she asked Garth and Brad if they'd be happy with another early morning drive. They enthusiastically agreed. The kitchen had packed brunch and refreshments for everyone. Johaan would stop at a convenient spot when they all got hungry.

They passed through Third Bridge campsite where monkeys and baboons were busy ripping into dustbins and litter blemished the landscape. A large troop of grey vervet monkeys raced up trees as the vehicle approached and sat chattering as they watched the retreating vehicle. A hefty male baboon arrogantly sauntered away, looking over his shoulders, likely irritated by the intrusion, and sat metres away watching as the Landcruiser passed. The rest of his troop had scattered.

Garth chuckled. "I wonder what they're thinking. They're so like humans."

Once they'd passed, the baboon hurried back to the dustbins.

"Why don't the Parks Board put secure lids on the bins?" Mel asked Johaan.

"They used to, but the baboons still managed to break them open."

Third Bridge camp site facilities were not to be confused with the luxury tented camps that they were in. The camping areas within the reserve are not fenced and offered a truly wild experience.

"So, you just put up your tent and hope a lion doesn't eat you?" Garth stated, shocked by what Johaan had said.

"That's about it, Garth. Lion and Hyena come into the camp if they're drawn in by the scent of campers' leftovers, especially cooked meat, but animals respect the area is human inhabited, and seldom attack unless they're threatened, or some idiot takes cooked meat into the tent and leaves the tent flap open. Even elephant wander through."

"Leave their tent open?" Garth couldn't believe what he was hearing.

"Yes, believe it or not there are people who do that, but it doesn't happen often."

"Don't elephant get caught up in the guy ropes and pull the tents over?" Brad asked.

"As big as they are, they know where not to tread." Johaan answered.

"Can we come and camp and rough it here?" The thought suddenly appealed to Brad.

"It would've appealed to me ten years ago, but now I prefer the catered luxury we're in." Mel said categorically.

"Aaw. When we get home, can we go camping again?" Brad pleaded.

"YES! Then Grandpa can come with us." Garth said joyously.

"What do you think?" Gary asked Mel, but before she could answer, a massive buffalo bull exploded from the bush, charging across the road just feet in front of the vehicle. Its eyes were wide with terror, muscle straining with the desperate need to survive. He was followed by three hungry lionesses in hot pursuit. Their bodies rippling with raw power as they pursued their prey with ruthless precision. Johaan slammed on brakes, the Landcruiser skidding to a jolting stop. Then in a blur of movement, two more lionesses darted past the front of the vehicle, their eyes locked on the bull. The earth shook under the relentless charge. A fifth lioness nearly collided with the back of the Landcruiser.

Motionless, everyone watched the sheer ferocity of nature on full display.

Though the chase happened quickly and dramatically, Gary had his camera on his lap and managed to capture the kill.

The lionesses had planned their attack with deadly efficiency. Two launched themselves at the bull's throat, jaws clamping down with savage strength, while two others clung with claws spread, tearing into the thick hide of the bull's back. The bull bucked and twisted in a desperate attempt to shake them off. The fifth lioness circled from the side, her timing perfect until the bull's hoof connected with a sickening thud, sending her sprawling into the grass. She lay there, dazed, the breath knocked from her lungs, but her eyes remained fixed on the struggle.

The bull fought with every ounce of strength he had left, his bellows of rage and pain echoing through the air. He flung the lioness form his throat and her body tumbled through the air like a rag doll. She quickly rejoined the fight, but she miscalculated, and the bull met her with a brutal blow from his massive boss, sending her flying. She hit the ground hard, the impact reverberating through the earth with an almighty thud.

The bull's cries grew weaker as he felt his hindquarters begin to give way, the strength of the lionesses finally overcoming his will to fight. The end approached. Too exhausted to continue, he let out one last, defiant roar before he succumbed, collapsing under the weight of his attacker. The lioness who'd connected with the bull's boss still lay in the grass, panting heavily.

The mighty bull's dying cries upset Brad. He turned away and rested his forehead on the back of Mel's seat trying to block out the sounds of death.

"It's not often you witness such a spectacle at such close range," Johaan murmured, his voice low with awe. "Thank God the bull didn't crash into us." He turned to Gary, "did you get it all on camera?"

"I certainly did." There was a strange mixture of satisfaction and sorrow in his eyes. Gary put a hand on Brad's head. "You okay, son?"

"Yes. I just feel sorry for the buffalo. He didn't stand a chance."

Johaan resumed driving. The atmosphere still heavy with the aftermath of the kill.

Fifty metres down the road they spotted two thickly maned

male lions trotting along to join the lionesses, knowing their meal awaited.

"Lazy buggers," Garth muttered, his attempt at humour cut through the tension and brought a reluctant laugh from Brad.

They hadn't gone far when they came across a herd of elephant crossing the road ahead.

"Aah, the Lone Ranger herd," Johann stopped, leaving the vehicle idling.

"See the calf with half his trunk missing. I saw his mother fight off the crocodile who'd caught him at a water hole when he was small. One of the hardest things I've ever watched. I felt so helpless. Eventually the croc let go, taking half the calf's trunk. I thought the calf might die, but he learned to drink water by going down on his knees. The matriarch and the mother guarded him while he drank. It's a herd that's very special to me."

"Shame, poor thing. Mother nature is so cruel," Brad said sadly.

"It is, but it's the way of life in the wild." Johaan said matter-of-factly.

Brad shook his head. He was counting. "Fifty-one, fifty-two, fifty-three, fifty-four elephants."

Garth had also counted. He'd counted fifty-nine.

As the last elephant crossed the road, Johaan edged the vehicle forward, but he hadn't noticed a cow with a very young calf browsing on the left. He knew that cow and noticed her presence a bit late. He slammed the vehicle into reverse, but she shot out the bush and came after the reversing vehicle trumpeting a warning, then she charged. Her ears flapped angrily as she gathered speed.

The engine whined at the speed of the reverse. Johaan managed to stay on the road, watching his rearview mirrors.

Garth's smile had frozen in place. Brad couldn't look and gripped Mel's arm and closed his eyes. Gary kept a running commentary as the elephant cow gained on the revving vehicle, then unexpectedly she slowed, as if she'd suddenly remembered her calf, who by now stood alone in the middle of the road more than five hundred metres away. The cow stopped, bellowed loudly and flicked her trunk at the vehicle, then turned back to attend to her calf.

"Phew! Feel," Brad took Mel's hand and placed it over his heart. "Bet you've never felt my heart race like this before."

"Mel took Brad's hand and placed it over her heart. "I'm sure mine's beating faster. What an exciting morning."

Johaan laughed. "Probably not as fast as mine. For a moment I thought she might catch us and then we'd have been in trouble."

"Would she have trampled us?" Garth asked breathlessly.

"You're damn right she would've. She's one cow I stay well clear of. She's chased me a few times before. She's very bad tempered when she has a newborn calf. She's tipped over a few vehicles before and injured many. Thankfully she's never killed anyone."

"That was seriously scary." Garth stood up and held onto the back of Gary's seat.

"That's why I always leave the vehicle running when elephant or rhino are near."

"Aren't you scared?" Brad asked Johaan.

"Sometimes, like now." He admitted. "Up ahead is a look out point overlooking a big dam. We'll stop there and have some brunch."

Two adrenaline high's, one after the other, left Brad and Garth exhausted. They fell asleep on the return journey.

Near the camp gate, Gary woke them. Two particularly tall

male giraffe browsed lazily. They weren't in the least worried by the proximity of the Landcruiser.

Garth rubbed his eyes and whispered. "I could reach out and touch his neck."

"But don't," Johaan warned.

"So, boys, here's a question. What do you call a large collection of giraffe?" Gary put his camera on the seat.

"A herd," Garth volunteered first.

Gary shook his head. "Giraffe is both plural and singular."

"Aaw, Dad. Well, it's not a flock," Garth's voice was mocking. "So, if it's not a herd, what is it then?"

"It's a tower of giraffe," Gary informed them. Brad thought he was joking and burst out laughing. "That's stupid. A tower? Come on, Dad, tell us the truth."

Gary chuckled. "I promise, that's what a group of giraffe are called. Ask Johaan."

"Is that true Johaan?" Brad needed confirmation from his safari idol.

"Yes, your dad is right. It's a tower of giraffe." He confirmed while Gary packed the lens and camera into its holder.

THAT AFTERNOON the air was filled with the sound of laughter as Brad and Garth played an intense game of table tennis. Their spirits high, they plunged into the cool, blue pool splashing their parents and shouting, "come and join us!" Tired after a vigorous game with the boys Gary and Mel wandered back to their tent and lay on the hammocks and chatted while the sun began its decent. Garth and Brad were still in the pool, but when the suns golden hues rippled over the water, they decided it was time to get out and joked as they ran to the tent, comparing whose fingers were the most wrinkled.

Gary and Mel lay side by side, the gentle sway lulling them into quiet conversation, the world outside the tent forgotten. It was a serene intimate moment until the sharp ring of the internal phone shattered their tranquillity.

Mel, closest to the phone, reluctantly untangled herself from the hammock, her body heavy with contentment, she reached for the receiver. "Hello."

A pause, then the voice on the other end, their trainer, Tinus spoke with sombre weight that immediately pulled Mel into the present. "Mrs. Whitaker. I'm so sorry to disturb you. It's Tinus here. I have some very sad news. Your father.... He passed away this morning. He had a heart attack."

The world stopped. Mel's breath caught in her throat as the words pierced through her, each syllable a blow to her heart. Her mind struggled to grasp the meaning, to connect the words to the reality they represented. Her father, gone? How could that be? The phone trembled in her hand as the truth settled in a heavy, suffocating reality. She handed the phone to Gary, and ran to bathroom, where grief overwhelmed her.

Gary's voice, steady but thick with emotion, filled the space left by Mel's silence. He spoke to Tinus, gathering, gathering the necessary details but his heart was with Mel, breaking for the woman he loved and the pain she was enduring. When he hung up, he found her emerging from the bathroom, her eyes red, a crumpled handful of tissues clutched in her fist. She tumbled into his arms.

"Oh God sweetheart," Mel's voice cracked as she spoke. "I can't believe he's gone. How will we live without him? And how will we tell the boys. They loved him so much...."

Gary's own tears flowed freely, unrestrained. "We'll all miss him, my angel," he whispered, pulling her closer as if he could shield her from the unbearable reality. Mel's body shook as she inhaled sharply, trying to regain some semblance of control, but the grief was too raw, too immediate.

"I feel like I'm drowning," she choked out the words."

Gary whispered into her hair. "I know, sweetheart. I've asked Tinus to arrange a flight. We'll leave tomorrow if we can. We'll stay in Gaborone for the night and get the direct flight to Durban the next day."

Mel nodded, her voice small and broken, "Home... it won't be the same without him."

Her sobs grew louder. Garth stirred. In a sleepy voice he called out, "What's wrong Mum?"

Gary's voice, thick with the effort of holding it together, called back. "Garth, wake your brother. We need you both here."

Moments later both boys stood in the doorway, their faces pale with confusion. Mel gathered them in her arms, her voice breaking as she delivered the news that would shatter their world. "Grandpa died this morning."

Their reactions immediate and heartbreaking. Brad let out a wail of anguish, his young mind unable to comprehend the loss. Garth buried his face in his mother's chest, his body racked with sobs. Gary wrapped his arms around them all, a protective cocoon of love and grief as they mourned together.

Chapter Eight

A YEAR HAD PASSED since the family holiday in Botswana and Ivan's passing, and now they were preparing horses for the first race in the legendary Durban July.

The year had been an endless emotional struggle for Mel and even now she couldn't amass the normal level of excitement for her favourite Raceday.

Gary tried his best to lift her out of the void. "This July will be fun, my angel. And what an honour to have Nelson Mandela as the special guest in the owners and trainers VIP lounge. I know how hard the year's been since Dad passed but Garth would love your attention." Gary prodded gently, trying to snap her out of her numbed emotional state.

"Oh, I know. I'm sorry, my love. You're right. I'm incredibly proud of him. I'll make a concerted effort."

"Wonderful. He'll feel so bucked if you pay attention to his efforts in training Provocation. He's a schoolboy after all. The more praise and encouragement the better."

Mel rubbed her forehead, pushed strands of hair from her face and hugged Gary. "Where's Garth now?"

"He's at the stables. They both are. We have half an hour before the first race. Let's go down there together."

They found Garth outside Provocations stable, laughing and joking with Siyanda. When he saw Gary and Mel approach, he threw the brush he was holding in the air. "Yay, you've joined us."

Mel put her arms around him. "I can't tell you how proud I am of your achievements. Well done, sweetheart. Prov looks incredible."

"Gee, thanks, Mum. It's been real fun. We've missed you at the track."

Those words hit home. Mel realised how secluded she'd been, and it hadn't been fair on any of them.

Just then Brad came scooting round the side of the stable block.

"And where have you been?" Mel asked, grabbing his arm playfully.

"I needed a pee really badly," he chuckled, "no-one saw." He yanked the last half of the zipper up on his shorts with a naughty grin.

Mel envied their resilience though she knew they missed their grandfather, but they'd moved on and stopped mourning long ago. It was time she did too.

Garth, adamant Provocation would win, took a bet with Gary. "Double my pocket money." He tested his dad as he sat at the table they'd reserved in the VIP lounge.

"What if he doesn't win?" Gary asked, curious to hear Garth's answer.

"Well, Dad, can we discuss that after his race?" He cocked his head to one side, having not considered that outcome.

"Nice try, my boy. A bet is a bet. If he loses, no pocket money for August. Deal?"

"Aaw, Dad." The thought of losing his pocket money for a month didn't appeal.

Suddenly, loud cheering erupted below the grandstand. People were chanting as the President's cavalcade stopped adjacent to the VIP lounge entrance.

"Okay, Dad, deal," then a thought struck him. "The President will be dining with us when Prov is running. Will it be rude to come back in late?" Garth asked, feeling torn between the two. Did he wait and see the President, or was the horse he'd trained more important?

"My boy, the President loves ambitious children, "besides he's not sitting at our table." Garth sighed with relief.

The President, heavily guarded by his entourage, stepped out the Mercedes and waved to the crowds. The bodyguards escorted him and the First Lady to the lift. They stepped into the VIP lounge to loud applause, and everyone stood. Though Chanting Clover's table was one away from the President's, he was close enough for he and Steve to have a jolly reunion before taking his seat.

Mel noticed Garth fidgeting. "When it's time, quietly excuse yourself."

Moments after everyone was seated, Garth slipped away and ran down to the collecting ring. Siyanda led Provocation around and gave James the sign they'd devised for luck. Their fists balled and the signal resembled a game they played at junior school. One potato, two potato..... Tinus stood on the edge of the paddock.

"He's looking good." Tinus patted Garth on the back. "You'll make a great trainer one day."

"Ah, thanks, Tinus. We'd better get upstairs. They're

serving lunch while this race is on."

They dashed upstairs and took their seats. The waitresses had just begun to serve the hors d'oeuvre. Garth moved to the edge of the room and stood by the large expanse of windows and focused his binoculars on the starting stalls.

"Yesss," he shouted a little louder than he meant to as the horses jumped free. Mel joined him. The waitresses hadn't reached their table yet.

"James is holding him well, Ma. Better than I can." Garth said honestly. "Look, he's gathering speed nicely." Garth gripped his binoculars so tight his knuckles turned white. Provocation moved into third place. "Gooo boy. GO."

As if the horse heard Garth's screams in the last heart-stopping moment, Provocation surged ahead and reached into first place by a nose. Garth jumped up and down, his entire world exploded into pure, unfiltered joy, oblivious to everything and everyone around him, including the President. He lowered his binoculars and hugged his mother, then they walked back to the table.

"See, what did I tell you, Dad." Garth gloated as he sat.

"Well done. An awesome feeling, isn't it?"

Garth nodded vigorously. Mel noticed Madiba watching him. A smile had spread across the President's face in the same way a father would look proudly at his son.

Once lunch was over, the President asked to meet Garth. Garth couldn't believe his ears. Garth and Brad went to meet him. Madiba shook hands with Garth first, then Brad. He asked them questions about their love of horses and racing with such interest he put them at ease almost immediately.

When they got back to their table, Garth said excitedly, "he spoke to us like he knew us. Like he wasn't even a president. How awesome is that?"

Mel smiled. It would certainly be something to tell their friends at school. Shortly after lunch a fashion parade began in the VIP lounge, showcasing young African designers work from all over the country, and other parts of Africa. The fashion theme of the day — Ethnic.

Mel noticed the President, his wife and two of his daughters were suitable impressed by the international standard and he said so when he gave his speech.

At the end of the speech, Synthia whispered to Mel, "it's going to be interesting to see Kgabu ride Green Mists in the feature race today. Two thousand metres is a tough call for a mare." Mel agreed. It was rare for a mare to win the feature race here at Greyville on this day.

"And Ebony and Ivory is going to be a challenge for her. The colt has excelled in the last eight months."

"Well," Synthia smiled knowingly. "My money is still on my boy."

"I'm sure it is. I've been so out of touch since Dad died. I'm just happy to have our horses running today. Gary, Tinus and Garth have done all the work."

"Only four running this year, darling. Green Mists, Ebony and Ivory, Provocation, and Silver Flame." Gary reminded Mel, who then turned to Synthia.

"One year we had horses in every race! Madness." She shook her head.

"I'm sure." Synthia put her hand over Mel's, "last year was hard on you, my friend. Just enjoy the day and the gracious presence of our President. Isn't he wonderful."

"Yes, he is, and he was so good chatting to Garth and Brad. Do you know the President well?"

"Oh no, I wish I did, but Steve does, as you saw."

"Mum, we're popping out." Garth interrupted. Mel knew

they were bored with adult conversation. Fifteen minutes later they ran back, breathless and flustered.

"What's up?" Gary asked a panicked Garth.

"I've, I've... just seen Julie." Garth whispered, trying to get his breath back. "Standing.... at Green Mists stable and when she saw us, she quickly disappeared." Garth took a deep breath. "I hate that girl. I wish she'd never come into our lives. I don't trust her."

Gary, Steve, Tinus and the boys hurried down to the stables, but Julie had gone.

"That bitch has it in for us, Dad." Garth said, his cheeks flushed with anger.

"Relax Garth. Everything will be fine, Siyanda will be bringing her up to the parade ring now," Gary assured him, and they wandered back to the lawned centre of the parade ring to watch the line-up of horses for the feature race.

Green Mists entered and pranced around, showing off, ready to take on the geldings and colts. When Ebony entered the collecting ring he looked every bit the champion.

"Owning a magnificent Thoroughbred, especially one ready for a Group One race, is an honour I shall treasured for the rest of my life." Emotion sounded in her voice as she watched the jet-black colt stride out, showing off four stark white stockings and a white diamond-shaped blaze. She'd named him after the famous song and in that moment, she wished his half-brother, Warriors Robe had never died. He'd be racing today had he not been poisoned.

Kgabu walked confidently into the paddock with the other jockeys. Siyanda legged him into the saddle. Synthia held Mel's arm. "They look so good together, don't they?"

"They certainly do. I see Ebony and Ivory and Mighty Skies have moved into joint favourite."

"I'm not worried. My eyes are on Kgabu, of course. I'd still be proud of them even if they came last."

The stadiums buzzed, voices on the big screen grew louder, and the course hummed with anticipation. Last-minute bets were hurriedly placed, and the cameramen regularly zoomed in on the President, which simultaneously flashed onto the big screen.

The horses had gone down to the start. Most of them had gone in, but there were two the handlers were having difficulty loading.

"Come on, come on," Mel urged under her breath.

The horses were in and jumped away. James positioned Ebony perfectly from the start, lying fourth. Mel knew without doubt now, Ebony would win the Durban July, but suddenly from nowhere Green Mists was catching him.

Still leading at the three hundred metre marker James began to use his whip. Mel was biting down on her bottom lip. James didn't know how close Green Mists was. Only a length behind at the two hundred metre marker now. A space in time where everything seemed to stand still for Mel.

The crowds were going ballistic, jumping up and down, waving their racing forms, hats, and hands, screaming for their favourite. The screams reached a fever pitch when Ebony and Ivory crossed the line. Mel's legs felt like jelly. For a moment she thought the feisty Green Mists would take it, but she wasn't unhappy with a first and a second for Chanting Clover.

She could hear people moaning, those who wanted Green Mists to win, while other's chanted and danced to the melody of the money they'd won.

Melonie let out a little sob. Gary squeezed her hand. "Is that a sob of happy, or a sob of sad?" He grinned and she gave Gary an affectionate punch on the arm.

"Both. Happy that Ebony won, happy that Green Mists beat the favourite, Mighty Skies, but sad Dad couldn't be with us to share this incredible day. And now, Ebony stands a good chance of winning the J&B Met in Cape Town in January. Wouldn't that be something?" Mel wiped her eyes before the hurried down to the walk their winner in.

In the jockey's room, Kgabu was dealing with different emotion. He was seething. Not because Green Mists hadn't won, but because he'd walked straight into Julie.

"What the fuck?" He groaned angrily at her. "You didn't ride today, yet you are everywhere around horses and people connected to Chanting Clover. What stupid games are you playing at?" He'd gripped her shoulders with both hands and glared into her eyes.

"What do you mean, what am I playing at?" She spat and shrugged herself free of Kgabu's grip.

"Why are you in here when you haven't ridden today? And why were you down at Green Mists stable today? Huh?" He grabbed her arm as she was about to leave.

"Let...go...of me," she wrenched herself away, but Kgabu wasn't going to let her go easily.

"Not until you promise not to harass any of us again. I never want to see you in the jockeys' room, unless you're riding, or I swear, I'll report you. Touch any of the Chanting Clover Stud horses anywhere, and I'll come after you with an army of brutes who'll break your arms, legs and neck, and do it slowly, so you feel the same painful death that Warriors Robe felt. Do you hear me?"

A sly grin smeared across her face.

Tempted to slap it off, he managed to contain his anger. In that moment Kgabu had never hated anyone so much. He loosened his grip on her arm, and she ran from the jockey's room.

Chapter Nine

THE MUSICAL TONES of randy stallions calling, the singsong nickers from mares in season, answering sounded across the stud. Mel sat in her office daydreaming for a moment. She loved those sounds, even though they indicated madness over the next two months, and she happened to be studying pedigrees.

She jumped when the phone rang.

"Melonie Whitaker." She answered.

"Good afternoon, Mrs. Whitaker. My name is Jeremy Katz. Is this a good time to talk?"

"Er, yes, yes. Good afternoon, Jeremy. What can I do for you?"

"Firstly, I would like to congratulate you on your win on Saturday. A stunning horse you have there, and you bagged the second place too. That mare is also exquisite."

"Thank you. We're very proud of our two horses."

"Ebony is a magnificent beast, but they all are. The reason for my call, ma'am, is related to the Durban July, but not the horses. Let me explain if I may?"

"Go ahead." Mel answered with a curious smile on her face.

"I own the largest modelling agency in Durban, and though young ladies are relatively easy to find, good looking young boys, like your sons, are not. Would they be interested in earning some well-paid hours in front of the camera?"

Melonie threw her head back and guffawed. "Are you serious? I cannot for one moment imagine my two boys being remotely interested. They're farm kids, Jeremy, and both attend boarding school. They'd be ragged to death if they started modelling."

Jeremy remained silent for a moment. "We're serious, Mrs. Whitaker. You have two very good-looking boys."

"Jeremy, I'm sorry to disappoint you. I honestly don't think either of them would be interested." Mel sighed. "Apologies for being candid, it saddens me the Durban July is no longer about the brilliance and nobility of the magnificent Thoroughbred." Mel had never approved of the fashion side show, and now it was almost taking precedence.

"Yes, well... I'm sure most of the spectators are there primarily for the horses, but the colourful display of clothing adds a little spice and variety to an already spectacular day."

"Clothing. What clothing? Most of the models are hardly wearing more than a few sequins and ostrich feathers. It's hardly a 'design'." She hadn't meant to sound rude.

It was Jeremy's turn to laugh. "Being a lady of class, as you are, I understand."

"Perhaps if the designs were tasteful and elegant, I wouldn't mind so much."

"I noted that your eldest son was admiring the ladies who were modelling some of Durban's latest ethnic designs."

"I'd say that would be perfectly normal for a young lad, wouldn't you? I'm quite sure he wasn't there to admire what they weren't wearing." Mel took in a deep breath. "Well, Mr. Katz, thank you for calling and considering my boys." His tone made Mel feel a little uncomfortable.

"Before you put the phone down, Mrs. Whitaker, please ask your boys."

"I'll ask them. I think they'll be quite amused. If you don't hear from me, you'll know they're not keen. Tell me, before I go, what sort of modelling would they be doing?"

"Mainly branded clothing ranges for stores like Edgars and Woolworths. I have, however, just recently received a request for young models to wear and show off some of the latest imported equestrian wear from Germany." The hook, Mel thought. "They're looking for models from the ages of seven to eighteen. Your boys instantly came to mind. Being in the equine industry, they would be perfect for such an assignment. Should they agree to model, perhaps we could use your venue for the photoshoot?"

"That's very interesting. I'll let you know next week. Thank you for calling and have a wonderful day." Though the offer sounded straightforward, she'd heard some gory stories of modelling agency men. There was no way her boys were going to be Mr. Katz's pray. But, she thought, perhaps that was unfair judgement, and if they did the photoshoot at the stud, she'd feel happier.

That evening she discussed the call with Gary. He wasn't opposed to it. "It might be a good opportunity for them to experience earning their own money, teach them about investing it, especially as I paid Garth a double whammy of pocket money after I lost the bet." Gary chuckled while he stroked Bessie lying at his feet. "I'm not entirely sure Brad would be keen, but I think Garth might be. Money excites Garth."

When they got home for the weekend, Mel told them about Mr. Katz's telephone call.

"Eeeew, no Ma. Never! Modelling is for pansies." Brad reacted just the way she thought.

Garth piped up. "Hey, Ma. Did you ask how much he pays?" Gary knew he'd be attracted to the money.

"No. I didn't think either of you would be interested. Besides, you know how I feel about modelling."

Garth half grunted. "Mum, you're so old-fashioned. I like mod clothes, and maybe we'll get given some designer riding gear."

"So, does this mean you're interested?" Gary asked.

"If the money's good, yes, why not? I mean, it's just sticking on clothes and smiling at a camera. What can be so bad about that? And, the best thing is, we get paid, and it's done right here." Suddenly Brad's interest perked now his brother mentioned money. He didn't think modelling was for sissies anymore.

Mel raised her eyebrows. "Okay, I'll call Mr. Katz and ask how much he pays before I commit you to the assignment?"

"It's got to be good." Garth said smugly.

Mel smiled. "I'll call him after breakfast, so hang around." Her son's had surprised her.

"Katz Modelling Agency," a lady answered the switchboard.

"Good morning. Mr. Katz, please."

"Whom may I say is calling?" A friendly voice asked.

"Mrs. Whitaker."

"Hold on, please, Mrs. Whitaker, I'll put you through." The phone crackled as she transferred the call.

"Hello, and good morning, Mrs. Whitaker. I can only

assume your sons have agreed?" Jeremy said. Mel could imagine the type of smile on his face.

"Tentatively. They want to know what the payment is. Per assignment? Per hour?"

"Aaaah. Smart boys. We pay well, Mrs. Whitaker." Jeremy briefly explained. Mel asked him to break it down and fax it through.

"Of course. I'll get my secretary to send it through within the hour. It'll be done by midday. We close our offices at one on a Saturday."

"Thank you. They're both keen on the equestrian clothing, more than the other clothing, and we're happy for you to do the shoot here at the stud. The stallions are safe with the children."

"Oh goodness, that sounds faaabulus, Mrs. Whitaker. Oooooh, all that shiim...mmering horsepower, makes me go quite goose pimply." His voice raised with excitement and confirmed Melonie's suspicions.

An hour later, the fax arrived. The family sat on the veranda perusing the different assignments. The money was good. Garth and Brad approved.

Two weeks later, the Katz Modelling agency arrived at the stud.

Two Combi minibuses parked near the stallion barn. Four young ladies between the ages of twelve and sixteen got out of one minibus. Garth's eyes lit up. They were followed by two younger girls and two boys about Brad's age. The lighting engineer parked away from the front of the barn.

The second vehicle carried the cameras and stands, lighting and equipment, plus the suitcases of clothing, and driven by the photographer, with Jeremy in the passenger seat.

Mel and Gary walked over to the vehicles. Garth and Brad followed and introduced themselves. Chris, the photographer unpacked the one minibus, while Greg, the lighting engineer unloaded the equipment. All the models and Garth and Brad helped unload while Jeremy clucked around outside the stallion barn like a broody hen.

Brad whispered to his mum he thought Jeremy was the funniest looking man he'd ever seen. "Whenever he glances my way, I get the giggles." Mel put her index finger to her mouth.

Chris busied himself hanging up the clothing on a mobile wardrobe, with Greg set up the lighting and the screens.

Once everything was in place near the entrance to the elegant stallion barn, the models were asked to change. Jeremey allocated the clothing, and Mel showed the ladies to laboratory inside the barn. Garth and Brad showed the boys to an empty stable that had been cleaned out for the occasion.

Jeremy called. "Ladies first with Garth, then the younger models all together, please." His arms waved theatrically.

Brad, standing close by, collapsed in mirth, soiling the beautiful designer riding jacket. Jeremy was quick to reprimand. Brad stood up, dusted himself off and stood quietly, his cheeks pink with embarrassment.

The stallions were led out one at a time. Chris, Jeremy and the models gasped when Kagiso led Bold Warrior out into the sunlight. His coat gleamed.

Garth stepped forward and helped the young ladies, shifting them around the stallion. The very nervous girls stood on the outside and the girls used to horses stood closer to the stallion. Mel watch Chris capture magnificent shots of the group as Warrior sniffed and snuggled his nose into the crook of Garth's arm and touched noses with one of the girls, then Garth led the stallion to a nearby tree. Greg followed and set up the lighting. Bold Warrior was thoroughly enjoying being in the limelight and behaved like a perfect gentleman.

Jeremy was so impressed with the stallions' impeccable manners. He suggested that the eldest young lady join Garth. She stood on one side and Garth on the other and they peeked at each other beneath the stallion's neck. Bold Warrior arched his neck, his ears pricked rigid. Chris clicked the camera on rapid succession and adjusted the shutter speed, all the while checking lighting and exposure. Bold Warrior stood fascinated, flicking his ears back and forth and turning to examine Garth and Lucinda. The pictures were prize winners. Garth led Bold Warrior back into the barn and put him in his stables while Kagiso brought out Master Vision.

Master Vision loved the younger children. They were a bit nervous of the huge, powerful horse and they tucked in close to Brad, in awe.

"Wow," Jeremy uttered, then whistled when Brad kissed Master Vision's nose. "Your boys are so photogenic." He smiled at Mel and between Chris and Greg, these shots are going to be all over the fashion world.

Jeremy, a small man who could have been mistaken for a character from Hans Christian Anderson's fairy tales had a withered look, a wizard-like profile, a round bald head, and a long, 'salt and pepper' coloured beard, but despite his strange looks, Mel had warmed to him.

To add to his unfortunate looks he had two rather large pointed, pixie-like appendages for ears, that moved when he spoke. Mel knew it must be them that fascinated and amused Brad. When the stallion session was over, Brad tried to imitate Jeremy's ear movement, and everyone burst into fits of giggles. Thankfully, Jeremy seemed oblivious he was target of such mirth and confirmed this by saying to Mel what a cheerful, delightful child Brad was. She wasn't sure Chris and Greg agreed.

When the photoshoot was over and the minibuses packed, Gary took Jeremy, Chris Greg and the models around the other stables.

It had been a long day where extreme patience had been exercised, not just because of the naughty Brad, but taking pictures of horses always required patience.

Garth and Brad were left with the designer clothing they'd modelled. Garth was thrilled, but Brad seemed unmoved by Jeremy's generosity. "Never again, Mum. Well, not if that weirdo Mr. Katz is around."

Chapter Ten

"Hɪ Jᴜʟɪᴇ," Tanya greeted when Julie answered her phone. "Grandfather tells me you're leaving us for a while and heading upcountry to Johannesburg."

"Yes, that's true. I have an offer to ride at a stable in Randjesfontein. Too good to refuse, plus I'll be closer to family in Soweto."

"Which side of Joburg is that place?" Tanya asked curiously, having seldom been in Johannesburg.

"It's north where all the well-known trainers have their horses. It's a training centre like Summerveld. Not so pretty, but who cares about that."

"So, when will I see you again?"

"I'll be up and down the country, riding in Durban and Pietermaritzburg often, so when I'm there, I'll call and stay over, if I may. I leave the Academy tomorrow. I'm so excited."

"Oh! Great for you, but I'll miss you."

"I'll miss you too." Julie remained silent for a few moments.

"Hello.... Hello, are you there, Julie?" Tanya thought the call had been cut.

"Yes, I am. I...I...um...I want you to know.... I'll not be involved with anything to do with Chanting Clover for a while. I'm sorry Tanya. I accidently ran into one of their jockeys in the jockey's rooms. He was with me at the Academy and rides for the Whitakers. He grabbed my shoulders and swore at me, telling me neither he, nor the Whitakers, ever want to see me again. They're suspicious. He also warned me if anything happens to the Whitaker horses or any of them, he and his father will come after me with men who will beat me to an inch of my life. His father is a high up Town Councillor in Hillcrest. I want to get on with my career and let things settle."

"I understand. I'll let grandfather know. We'll speak again soon." Tanya said.

Tanya sounded disappointed, but Julie didn't care. She was scared now, plus she didn't get a dime for her efforts.

IN A FIT OF RAGE, Solomon banged his mobile phone down on the desk and cracked the screen. Anger churned his insides. His body began to shake violently, and he felt his heart thump in his chest.

Weakened by such extremes of wrath, his legs grew too weak to move his massive frame from his chair. Finally, he bellowed for his secretary, who came running. She took one look at the Colonel, whose face and neck were lined with rivulets of sweat. She felt panicky, unsure of what to do.

"Are you ill, Sir?"

"NO!" He yelled. "I'm fucking angry. Get Nkizwi on the line this instant."

"Yes, Sir," Anette leant down, picked up his mobile phone

and noticed the damaged screen. She quickly dialled Nkizwi's South African number.

Though Nkizwi was a distant relative, he'd willingly agreed to help the Colonel. Anette imagined he'd also been fed the same sad lies about the demise of Funani Khumalo.

She handed the Colonel the ringing phone and quickly exited the office.

"Nkizwi... hello.... hello. Nkizwi are you there?" Solomon shouted, scarcely able to hold the phone between shaking, sweaty hands. The signal was poor and crackly. He disconnected and slammed the phone on the table, shattering the phone's glass face completely and yelled for Anette, who hurried back.

"Get hold of Nkizwi from the switchboard and order me a new phone." Anette crept out of the office, terrified he may throw something at her as she left. He'd just missed hitting her with the stapler, earlier. Even if the next missile were not aimed at her, she was likely to get hurt if she didn't leave quickly. She hurriedly closed the office door and dialled Nkizwi's number.

"Hello, Colonel," Nkizwi answered.

"It's Anette. Hold on, and I'll put you through."

Before leaving his office, Anette carefully placed the landline telephone instrument next to him. He grabbed the receiver.

"Hello Nkizwi, how are you?"

"I'm well, thank you, Uncle." He used the term 'uncle' out of respect, for the relationship was not that close.

"I've just spoken to Tanya. She tells me that Julie refused to take on the next assignment. Why?" He yelled, spittle flying. "It's time to act again. The lull of years will be to our advantage, but no more excuses. I'm tired of them. Julie has changed her number, I believe. I want it. I don't even know where she's based anymore. Is she such a hotshot jockey now that she has lost her manners?" He asked sarcastically. "So high and mighty. Has she forgotten her fucking loyalties? Nkizwi, the plan must continue, and it must go ahead NOW." Solomon yelled. His stomach so distended, taking a deep breath had become difficult nowadays.

"She's scared, uncle. She......"

"Fucking bullshit. She turned one horse mental with a potion, and another lost its life in 1998. She wasn't scared then. What's wrong with her now? It's December 2001. Everyone has forgotten those details." Solomon yelled.

"Yes, uncle, I understand. The Whitakers became suspicious of her and employed a highly effective undercover security company to protect them. She was nearly caught and now has a successful career she doesn't want to jeopardise for something that does not concern her." Nkizwi advised him.

So incensed, the Colonel couldn't speak. He grumbled something Nkizwi failed to interpret. It sounded gibberish as the colonel's anger and hatred grew to frenzied heights.

"Uncle, uncle. Stop. Please listen." Nkizwi pleaded with the mad man. None of the people who assisted the colonel truly understood the levels his malevolence. Surely it could not just be the murder of Funani that made him hell-bent on crippling the Whitaker's, Nkizwi thought.

"I'll ask her. Maybe she'll apply her mind to your plan if you were to offer her a reward of some sort. She knows you pay Tanya's flat rental, and you reneged on a payment you once promised her. She told me that angered her, for she was the one who would suffer if she were caught."

The Colonel's breathing had turned to deep wheezing. The sound subsided, then there was silence. Nkizwi thought he might have expired.

"Uncle, are you there?"

Solomon didn't like to pay for favours — ever.

"Tell……," he took a breath, "tell her… I will …. pay her fifty thousand Rand, ……and she's not to fail. She understands the consequences if she does."

"I'll tell her, uncle. I'll report to you after I've spoken to her. When must your plan be implemented?"

"January. After that, we'll see. Do you understand? Colonel Solomon Tlale will not fail again. I will not...rest until that Whitaker bitch is...dead. Do you hear me? In the meantime, creating fear again is what we must do. Then we strike."

"I hear you, Colonel." Nkizwi addressed him by his rank this time.

The phone went dead.

From her office next door, Anette had heard Solomon screaming at Nkizwi. His words laced with venom. She'd heard more than she could comprehend. The words, 'until she is dead. Do you hear me?' echoed in her mind, hanging in the air like a noxious cloud, suffocating her with their sheer malice. Her stomach twisted violently. No man had ever made her so frightened. It was more than just fear, this was terror, cold and paralyzing.

Colonel Tlale was not just cruel, but the evillest person she'd ever encountered.

For two long years she'd suffered and served. She had children to raise, but listening to him now confirmed her thoughts — she had to seek alternative employment as quickly as possible, if only for her own safety. Secretaries are easily implicated, and she was not going to be dragged into a plan to murder some woman called Melonie Whitaker, who resided in South Africa.

Chapter Eleven

"OH MY GOD," Mel cried out as she sank to the kitchen floor. Angelina, her precious and beloved housekeeper, companion of many years, lay spread on the terracotta tiled floor. Mel shook her body. No response. She turned the old over ready to render first aid, but it was too late.

Mel stared at Angelina's face. A peaceful, happy expression covered Angelina's wrinkled, kind face. Through her tears Mel wondered how long she'd been dead. It couldn't have been more than half an hour. Her heart must have stopped mid-stride. 'A desirable way to come to the end of one's life,' Mel thought, pushing her hair away from her face and drying her tears. The expression on Angelina's face had left an impression on Mel. Was the crossing that beautiful, she wondered.

The kettle was still hot, the breakfast had just been placed in the warmer, and suddenly the old dear was gone.

Mel stood up, thinking how fragile life is. She'd miss Angelina, so would the rest of the family. She'd been a special part of the farm and the family since Iris's days. No-one knew

Angelina's age. Even Angelina never knew, but Mel one calculated she must've been in her early to mid-eighties.

Gary found Mel resting up against the centre consol in the kitchen, weeping quietly.

"Good Lord, what on earth happened?" He asked, shocked to see the old lady lying dead on the floor.

"No idea. She must've had a massive heart attack." Mel said sadly. "But I can't believe how at peace she looks."

"She does, doesn't she? But what a loss. Where's Salina?"

"She's gone to the clinic. She asked yesterday for time off. We need to organise an ambulance, my love. I'll contact her family. Can you arrange the rest?" Mel went to collect a blanket to cover the old lady's body.

Breakfast had long since gone cold. A quiet day proceeded. All the staff were in mourning.

ANGELINA WAS LAID to rest in the staff quarters' gardens. A request made by her family, many of whom still lived and worked at Chanting Clover.

Salina, Angelina's youngest daughter took over as head of the kitchen.

"You can't cope with this big house on your own. Do you have anyone in mind to help you?" Mel asked the day of the funeral.

"May I train my daughter, Edwina?"

"Yes, of course. That would be wonderful. How old is Edwina?"

"She's just turned eighteen and cannot find a job."

"Well, now she has one," Mel smiled, and Salina hugged her.

There was no need for security to research Edwina's past. She'd been born at Chanting Clover.

GARY AND MEL had celebrated in style at the Kenilworth racecourse after their beloved horse, Ebony and Ivory won the J&B Met and made history by breaking the 2000m track record.

"The best way to start the year, I'd say." Gary raised his glass and tapped it against Mel's.

They'd gone to bed at the normal time despite their win. They were transporting the three horses back home the following day and Gary didn't want to be tired and hung over with that responsibility.

Gary's mobile phone vibrated on the bedside table and woke him. He reached out and grabbed it, noticing the time on the face of the phone. 5:10a.m.

"What the hell," he moaned and answered.

"Whitaker."

"Mr. Gary, Ebony is dead." Siyanda sobbed. His words hit with shocking clarity.

"What?" He uttered with disbelief. Siyanda's words were like a shot to the head. Those words, 'Ebony is dead,' would be seared into his memory for life. A cruel reminder of the vendetta, and what may happen next.

Siyanda muttered something Gary couldn't make out. "Siyanda, I can't hear you nicely. What happened?" After a long, jerky exhalation, Siyanda explained.

"Baas, his throat is cut. My Ebony boy... he...he die a terrible, painful death." Through his angst and sadness came his broken English. His grief as raw and overwhelming as Gary's.

Mel, sat upright beside him, her lips and hands trembling. She knew another tragedy had befallen them.

"Where are you now, Siyanda?" Gary asked, feeling nauseous, he glanced at Mel. Tears had begun to roll down his cheeks. Their prize horse killed the morning after winning the prestigious J&B Met feature race. A race by invitation only.

Master minded by the bastard Colonel. Gary felt sure, but who could do such a thing? Who could kill a horse by slitting its throat? Thoughts ran riot in his head as he listened to Siyanda.

"I'm outside Ebony's stable. I came to check the horses before the grooms feed and prepare for the journey home. This is bad. There is blood everywhere."

"Siyanda, listen to me carefully. Don't touch the stable door, the horse, the walls, the halter, rope — nothing. Do not clean up, do you hear me?"

"Yes, Mr. Gary, I hear you."

"Good. Stay there and do not let anyone near Ebony's stable. Was the door locked last night?"

"Yes, but the lock is broken off. It's still hanging on the door."

"Leave it there, do not touch it." Gary reiterated. "All you must do is wait. Instruct the grooms to feed the other two horses and prepare them for travel. We will be there soon, but first, I must call the police."

"Okay, Mr Gary."

"Good man, and...." Gary paused. "I'm sad you had to find Ebony. I'll see you in half an hour. We'll load ......" Mel interrupted. "Tell me what's happened. You can sort out with Siyanda when we get to the stables," she shook Gary's arm.

He ended the call. Ebony was murdered last night. Someone slit his throat."

Mel gasped and put her head in her hands. "NO! No, no, no," she uttered trying to shake the sordid visions from her mind. She got out of bed. "Poor Siyanda, to have found him like that. We need to get there as fast as possible."

Mel whipped open the wardrobe door, flung on her jeans and a shirt and bundled the rest of her clothes into her suitcase, rushed to the bathroom, cleaned her teeth and chucked her wash bag into the case and zipped it up. Gary did the same and within fifteen minutes they were on their way to the racecourse stables.

"A revenge killing. That bastard is sick." Mel pulled a tissue from her jeans pocket. "Because he hasn't been able to kill me yet, he's terrorising us by killing our horses."

"I'm sure you're right. Poor Siyanda, he's beside himself."

"How the hell did this happen without roving security hearing something?"

"God knows, we'll find out in a few minutes," Gary said, concentrating on the early morning commuter traffic.

Siyanda had alerted racecourse security. The police, who Gary had called before leaving the hotel, had got to the stables just before Gary and Mel arrived.

Gary parked and strode across to the police van and introduced himself.

"A massive manhunt has been launched to find the sick-minded person who killed your horse. Yesterday's champion. I won money on him. I'm so sorry Mr. Whitaker, but we'll find that person." The policeman said.

Mel had raced to Ebony's stable but stopped mid-stride when she saw the pools of dark red blood that had flowed from beneath the stable door and had run down the concrete paving outside the stable and merged with the grass.

A security guard rushed to her side.

Mel snapped. "Did you have roving guards on duty all night?"

"Yes, ma'am, we did."

"And you're telling me that no one heard that padlock being cut?" The guard wasn't sure what to say and fidgeted. Mel shook her head and walked away. Her anger, white-hot. How could anyone do this?

Realising it wasn't the guard's fault, she turned to face him again. "How many guards were on duty last night?

"Four," he answered nervously.

"Do you rove around, or do you sleep?" So filled with bitter hatred for the person who'd done this, she found it impossible to be polite, but the guard looked guilty. She knew in an instant, he'd been sleeping.

Mel did a wide berth around the pool of blood and moved to check on Provocation and Dashing Clover. They'd eaten but were clearly stressed. The powerful, metallic smell of blood had been drifting up their noses all night triggering the fright/flight instinct. She opened Provocation stable, and he nickered, comforted by Mel's presence. She sat on the edge of the concrete manger feeling sure Julie had something to do with this unspeakable savagery, but she must've had help.

The police cordoned off the entire stable block. Photographs were taken. The stable door, the cut padlock, the manger, and the walls on either side of the door were dusted for fingerprints.

Mel stayed out of sight in Provocations stable.

Once the police were finished, the carcass removal company removed the dead horse. Gary was thankful Mel had hidden herself away. He was rooted to the spot, paralysed by the weight of his sorrow. When Ebony's head fell back, exposing the windpipe, muscles and sinew, Gary bolted round the side of the stable and vomited. Gary could stomach most things, but seeing a horse he deeply loved, with his throat gaping open, the once noble head held on only by skin, made his gut churn.

Composed once more, wiping his nose and mouth with a handkerchief, he called Tinus, then joined Mel.

Loaded and on the open road, Gary kept a close eye on his rear-view mirrors, just in case they were being followed by someone other than their security van. He could see the horse's heads move about while they pulled hay from the nets hanging in the horse carrier. The two horses seemed to have settled, knowing they were going home.

It was a very long journey from Cape Town to home, especially towing horses. They stayed overnight with friends in Colesburg and set off early the following morning. After a few hours travelling Gary pulled into a service station to re-fuel, check the horses and grab a coffee. On the newsstand outside the kiosk the story of the slain racehorse featured on the front page of many daily newspapers. Mel wanted to sob. She swallowed hard, bought a newspaper and refreshments and read it in the car.

It said the news of the slain champion had shocked the racing world in South Africa, and abroad. The journalist compared the death of Ebony and Ivory to the 1966 shooting of the famous South African horse, Sea Cottage. There were no answers at this point, but reporters had vowed to keep their readers informed.

"At least Sea Cottage wasn't killed," Mel sobbed in the privacy of the cab. "If Julie did kill Ebony, she had help. She's too small to slit a horses' throat."

"Thank God the cut didn't separate his head from his body.

I couldn't have dealt with seeing that. Seeing what I did was bad enough." Gary kept glancing behind them instinctively.

"How are we going to protect our horses from now on?" Mel asked, not expecting an immediate answer, it was just a thought that had crossed her mind.

Gary shook his head but vowed he'd find a solution.

Five hours later he pulled into the off-load bay at home and parked. Tinus was there waiting.

"I'm so happy you're home safely," he said and opened Mel's door. "I'm so sorry for your loss, Mel."

"So are we. It's too ghastly, isn't it? Seems almost impossible. Gary and I are still trying to deal with it."

Tinus greeted Gary then unbolted the back ramp of the trailer and reversed Provocation out, while Siyanda backed Dashing Clover out. Both horses whinnied, the sounds and smells of home drifted up their noses.

"How are you doing, Siyanda?" Mel asked, concerned the poor man had sat in the horse box with the two horses all the way.

"I'm fine thank you, Ma'am. I could not have left these two alone." He said protectively and led Dashing Clover down to the stable block.

Tinus glanced at his employers. They were grey from exhaustion. "You go home. I'll deal with everything."

"Thanks. That would be great, we're both so tired."

Desperate times required desperate measures, Tinus thought. He thanked Siyanda for the information on what had taken place in Cape Town and then he wandered up to the main house, knocked on the door, opened it and followed the sound of Gary and Mel's voices and found them in the sitting room.

"All done. Provocation and Dashing Clover are fine.

Siyanda is a master. He's brushed them down and settled them in. I think you need to look at installing a sophisticated monitoring at the stables now," Tinus said and sat down. "Siyanda has just told me he overheard some small talk that Julie is connected to a well-respected Sangoma, and a lady called Tanya, who lives in Durban. I think you need to ask the security company to engage a PI. Maybe Steve has some contacts too."

"Thanks, Tinus. I'll get onto that tomorrow. Good of Siyanda to tell you. He probably didn't want to give us more bad news."

"How's Kgabu?" Tinus asked.

"He's taken this badly. He's still trying to deal with the guilt of introducing Julie to us, even though I keep telling him it is not his fault." Mel felt her head and shoulders droop. "I'm just about asleep, will you excuse me?" She left the room.

THE PHONE RANG in the Chanting Clover Reception office. "Good morning. May I speak to Mr Whitaker, please."

"Yes certainly, who may I ask who is calling?" Iris, the receptionist asked.

"It's the CID from Kenilworth."

"Hold on please, I'll put you through."

"Gary, it's the CID from Kenilworth for you." She connected the caller but kept listening.

"Gary Whitaker."

"Good day, Mr. Whitaker. We've traced the fingerprints. There are three sets, two of which match those that belong to your grooms. The third set belongs to a woman." Gary went cold. "Her name is Julie Mokena. Do you know this woman?"

"Unfortunately, yes, we do." Gary felt his anger burn.

That was all Iris needed to hear.

"We have her address in Johannesburg. May we fax all the details through to you now?"

"Yes, please, and as soon as possible."

"We will do that immediately, Mr. Whitaker. There is a warrant out for her arrest."

"Great. The sooner you arrest her, the better. I want justice. Let me know when you have her in cuffs and behind bars."

"We shall do that, Mr. Whitaker. Can I confirm your mobile phone number, please?"

"Yes, certainly." Gary gave his and Mel's numbers.

"Thank you. I shall call again as soon as we have more news."

"Wonderful. I look forward to receiving the fax."

Gary placed the receiver and joined Mel in her office. Her head jerked up when he walked through the door. "Look at these terrific photos of our last crop of gorgeous babies?"

"They certainly are beauties. I've just had a call from Kenilworth."

"And?" She asked expectantly.

"It was Julie who killed our beautiful Ebony. Her fingerprints were found on the stable door. CID is faxing through the details in a few minutes. A warrant is out for her arrest. Let's hope she'll be behind bars before the end of the day. As soon as they have her, they'll let us know."

"The bitch." Mel snapped vehemently. "I wonder how she's connected to that woman named Tanya, the Sangoma and Solomon?"

"Willem must find out as a matter of urgency. I'm glad he's in charge now and not that useless Pieter, but this just confirms our suspicions, doesn't it? It still sickens me to think that she killed an innocent creature to exact vengeance. Had the little devil been here a week longer, Mists would be dead too." Gary felt his jaw clench and his fists ball. The frustration, anger and anxiety taking its toll. He'd make sure Julie was locked up. But what of the others.

Mel stretched her arms above her head and took a deep breath. "There was never any doubt in my mind that Solomon was behind the slaying of our precious boy. I hope the police interrogate her in the most uncomfortable way possible. To kill an innocent, defenceless animal in the most grotesque way is so cowardly. Just the sort of thing Solomon would instruct his accomplices to do. And I bet he's cooking up something else as we speak."

"I certainly hope not, sweetheart, but I fear you're right. Worrying times again, even though we have better security. I think Tinus is right about added security in the main block of stables and the stallion barn."

"I've always dreaded it would come to this. That bastard won't rest till I'm dead." Gary looked away. He couldn't bear to see her expression. The thought of losing her was incomprehensible.

Chapter Twelve

GARTH'S senior years had passed so quickly. Even he found it difficult to comprehend that he was in his last term, with final exams straight after the ten-day short study break.

He was proud of his academic achievements, and he knew he'd pass the final exams. He was hesitant to bring up the subject of university with his dad again for it always seemed to end in an argument. Garth saw no reason why his dad was so eager for him to study a course he had no interest in. He enjoyed earning money, but that didn't give rise to a desire to take a business degree.

Just prior to the start of this study break Jeremy had offered him a modelling contract in Durban. He happily agreed to do it. He'd discuss doing an MBA at college when he returned from the assignment.

"Garth, my darling, I've booked you into the Maharani Hotel. Jeremy will reimburse me."

"Oh cool. Thanks, Mum. Wow, the Maharani. Five-star luxury. Did Jeremy agree?"

"Yes, he did."

Just then Brad butted in. "Why the hell do you get such red-carpet treatment when most of the other models don't. I hope I get that kind of treatment when I get my next offer from Jeremy."

"Jeremy will look after you when you've finished school, even before then, boet." Garth said, itching to get on the road.

"Well, I must be off. Bye Mum." He gave her a hug. "Bye Boet. Please tell Dad I say cheers."

Garth picked up his case, hopped down the front steps, jumped in his Audi sports car and drove off. Once he'd left the farm road, he put his foot down, accelerating through the twists and turns of the scenic motorway to Durban. Security personnel had difficulty keeping up, but they rarely lost sight of Garth's Audi.

Wind swept from the journey with the car roof open, he arrived at the hotel and checked in. After dumping his bags in his room, he set off for the beach.

Though the beach wasn't far from the hotel, he drove his flashy Audi sports car to the beachfront and parked. A young, good-looking man in a silver sports car drew a lot of attention from the fairer sex, and today the beach was full of teenagers enjoying the ten break away from school, which should be a time to study but when the sun is hot, who wants to study.

Surfers were already out, and lifeguards kept an eye on bathers. Garth noticed a handful of pretty girls ogling their bronzed, toned bodies in the mirrors at the beach showers.

He pulled his beach bag off the back seat, zipped up the hood, locked the doors and headed down the steps and onto the beach.

Then two blonde girls appeared at the showers.

He found a spot, keeping the shower cubicles in sight,

pulled a towel from his bag, laid it on the sand and slipped off his tracksuit, revealing a colourful speedo costume, shapely thighs, and calves. Then pulled his T-shirt over his head.

The blonde girls were now in the shower playing like otters under the jet of water. Mesmerised, he watched them play. Their play aroused him. Their giggles lasted a few more minutes and they stepped out, their bodies washed free of sand.

Garth beckoned to them.

The girls glanced at each other. One girl grabbed her towel and wrapped it around her waist while the other shrugged her shoulders and sauntered toward Garth, dragging her towel provocatively.

"Hello, lovely ladies." Garth towered over them.

"Hi," the taller of the two replied.

Garth had spent time bodybuilding in preparation for this beachwear assignment. He knew his body was as toned and chiselled as the lifeguards' bodies. The way the girls looked him over, they approved too.

"I'm Cindy, and this is Theresa." Cindy introduced them both.

"Great to meet you. I'm Garth Whitaker. Do you two live in Durban?"

"Yes, we do, and you?"

"Near Nottingham Road. My folks own the Chanting Clover racehorse stud. I've come down for a modelling assignment."

"Oh wow, that's nice. What kind of modelling?" Cindy asked.

"Hey, spread out your towels and sit," Garth suggested before answering Cindy, who laid her towel as close to Garth's as she could get it.

They chatted about racehorses for a while, but Garth was

getting thirsty. "How about I get you two something to drink? I'm thirsty."

"Sounds like a cool idea. Thanks." Cindy answered for them both. In the short time they'd chatted Garth had summed Cindy up. He found her shallow, and noticed she constantly dominated Theresa. He felt sorry for Theresa.

He slipped his tracksuit pants back on, stuffed his towel and shirt into his beach bag and they wandered along the beach to the Blue Lagoon restaurant. Garth selected a table on the balcony with a view of the sea. It was a nice hot day, but a cool sea breeze kept them comfortable. A waiter rushed over to serve them.

"What would you like, Madam?" The waiter addressed Theresa who had the menu in her hand.

"I'd like a coke float, please."

"Theresa!" Cindy immediately scolded her, startling Garth with the ferocity of her tone. "That's so fattening."

Theresa blushed and scowled at her friend.

"One won't make the slightest difference. I've already been swimming for an hour." Theresa snapped at Cindy. Garth came to Theresa's aid.

"You're so slim. I cannot imagine a coke float will make the slightest difference."

Cindy glared at him while the waiter stood patiently by. "And for you, Madam?" He turned to Cindy.

"I'll have a lime cordial with soda water and ice. Thank you." Cindy's tone falsely polite. Garth decided he didn't like Cindy.

"And for you, sir?" The waiter asked.

"I'll have a coke. Thanks, mate." Garth answered casually. "My Mum calls a coke float, a brown cow. Same thing, I think. Is it your favourite?" He asked Theresa.

"Not really, I just felt like one now. Brown cow, that's a cool name. I seldom drink them because if we put on more than 1.5kg, Jeremy has a heart attack.

"Jeremy! Jeremy who?" Garth's interest peeked.

"A weird looking fag who owns our modelling agency," Cindy piped up.

"Are you two on the modelling assignment tomorrow? Beachwear stuff."

"Yes, we are."

"How uncanny. So am I. I've been with the agency for the last four years. Amazing that I've never bumped into you two before. Seems my luck has changed." Garth's smile was the kind that lit up a room, as if the sun had chosen that very moment to break through the clouds. His lips curved with effortless charm and left the two girls staring at him. "The first time my boet and I modelled for Jeremy, the shoot was done at our Stud. We were modelling rider clothing from Germany and a range from Woolworths and Edgars. My boet found Jeremy so bizarre, he couldn't stop giggling. When we finished, my dad took Jeremy, the crew and the other models on a tour of the stud."

"So, we'll be together for the next three days. How cool is that?" Cindy cooed.

"Very cool. So where are you staying?" Theresa asked.

"In the Maharani."

The girls whistled. The Maharani hotel was one of the most impressive hotels along the Durban beachfront.

"I'm not paying. Jeremy is." Garth smiled, a dimple appeared, deepening the impact and he directed it at Theresa. Cindy noticed and pouted. Garth went on sucking on the straw standing up in his glass.

Theresa enjoyed Garth's attention. It rarely happened that a man paid more attention to her when Cindy was around.

Theresa picked up her long-handled teaspoon and scooped vanilla ice cream off the top of the coke, seductively sucked it into her mouth then licked the remains off the spoon before taking a sip of coke with half an eye on Garth.

"Where are you two having lunch today?" Garth asked.

Cindy quickly answered, "with you?" But Garth's eyes were still focussed on Theresa.

"And what about you?" He asked Theresa.

"Excuse me! Did you hear me?" Cindy's snarky tone irritated him.

"Yes, I did, but I asked you both."

"Well," she said, "seems you're only interested in what Theresa wants to do." She pushed her chair back, stood up, glared at Theresa accusingly and let her towel drop. "You don't know what you're missing, you jerk." She said to Garth and swaggered out the restaurant, dragging the towel behind her. The other patrons turned to watch, amused.

Garth held a mischievous smile, then turned his attention back to Theresa whose cheeks glowed ruby red.

"Well, well, well. One little lady who must be the centre of attention. So, what are you doing this afternoon?"

"I had no plans, but Cindy's going to make me pay for this. Sometimes I wonder why I'm friends with her. She believes she's the most beautiful model in our group and flaunts herself. I must admit, she's good in front of the camera, and she's more beautiful than me, but she's a bitch."

"Sweetheart, there's nothing wrong with your looks," Garth assured her truthfully. "So, back to what you're doing this afternoon?"

"I guess I should go for a swim and work off the ice cream and coke. We're not allowed to get sunburned. Jeremy will throttle me, but a little more colour over this," she pulled her bikini top down and revealed the paler skin at the top of her breasts, "will blend nicely."

"It certainly will." Garth said, appreciating the view. "Shall we go for a swim now?"

"Great idea." Theresa answered enthusiastically.

"After a swim I'll treat you to a buffet luncheon at the hotel. Then we can catch a little bit of sun. How does that sound?"

"Wow, cool. Gee. Thanks." Theresa pulled Garths arm and looked up at him, "So tell me, why did you choose me over the gorgeous Cindy?"

"Because you're not false like her."

They left the restaurant, wandered down to the beach and found a spot to dump their towels and belongings, then raced each other into the sea.

Theresa splashed water at Garth playfully. He responded and waded closer to her. While they frolicked in the shallows they joked about Jeremy, and Cindy's tantrum at the restaurant. As they pulled themselves deeper into the sea a wave caught Theresa and dumped her. Garth wondered where she'd surface, imagining her tumbling beneath the water. She rose in the shallows, coughing, spluttering and spitting sand from her mouth. Garth swam toward her until he found his footing on the seabed, then paddled to her.

"Errrrr, I hate it when that happens," she coughed, kneeling in a foot of water when another wave caught her. Garth grabbed her arm, pulled her up against him and moved to deeper water feeling her nipples brush against his chest. His loins tingled.

Still able to stand, Theresa rubbed her eyes with her other hand, then pushed wet blonde hair from her face. "Ugh, I must look terrible." The last bit of wet hair caught in her mouth as she spoke. Standing in front of Garth she gazed into his mesmerising blue eyes. Their faces now inches apart. He put his lips to hers and kissed her hungrily just before another wave separated them.

Her head popped up above the water a few feet from him. Theresa twisted her head, flicking her wet hair away from her face.

"Oooh. You kiss so well." She giggled happily. Garth moved to her and gripped her bare waist. He had lady friends, but none kept his attention for longer than a short kiss. The opportunity for anything more had often come his way, but he'd declined, but Theresa captivated him. Dizzy with desire she pushed her body against his, skin against skin, "have you ever done it in the sea?"

It was Garth's turn to blush. "I've never done it before."

"Serious? How can such a good-looking lad like you still be a virgin?"

He shrugged. "So, let's change the situation." Theresa began rubbing her body against his as the waves lifted them buoyantly about and they drifted into deeper water. They kissed again and held each other, still feeling the ocean floor with their toes. Suddenly Theresa pulled away, ducked beneath the water, and surfaced holding her bikini pants in her hand, chuckling wickedly.

"Theresa!" Garth pretended to be shocked, but he felt eager to find out what the guys at school raved about. "I thought you were a good girl."

"I am. Very good at it." She ducked under the water again and took a handful of Garth. He almost choked as Theresa held his testicles, the skin, tight from the cold. His body tingled. She rose out of the water, "let's have some fun, feels like you're ready.

"Theresa, there're...... people around." He stammered shyly, having imagined his first sexual encounter to be on a comfortable bed without spectators.

"So? They can't see what we're doing below the water. Take your cossie off." Garth obeyed, and she groped for him again.

Garth moaned. He'd never felt so aroused in his life. Theresa wrapped her legs around his waist and guided him in until they were neatly coupled together, dipping rhythmically with the rise and swell of the waves. To avoid screaming as they orgasmed, they kissed hungrily. Slowly the thrill of lovemaking in the sea subsided. They pulled apart, Garth's virginity swept away across the ocean. Still gripping their costume bottoms, their legs too weak and wobbly to stand on the sandy base of the ocean, they fell about chuckling while trying to refit their costumes.

Garth's legs could hardly carry him up the beach to where they'd left their belongings. He hoped Theresa would stay with him at the hotel after lunch, instead of tanning on the beach.

They reached his car. "Wow, is this your dad's car?" Theresa asked as he unzipped the hood and pushed it down.

"No, it's mine. I bought it with money I earned in Milan at the beginning of this year."

"Wow. I wish Jeremy paid us this well." She said with awe and envy. "The bastard doesn't get us assignments overseas. Actually, that's unfair of me to say. He looks after me."

"It was a month of bloody hard work. Then I had to catch up missed schoolwork in my most important year. Training racehorses is easier and considerably more fun. Geez, I hated all the make-up, hair dos and fussing, flashing lights and Jeremy, but I wanted the money. I won't do another overseas assignment, and this one will be my last."

"A month? That's a long time away from school," Theresa said with admiration.

"Yeah, but I caught up. It's just my final exams left now. Dad wants me to go to Varsity and I am dead against it." Garth tossed his bag on the back seat. "Well, come on, get in, I'm famished," he smiled, trying to shake away the weakening sensations of his first sexual encounter.

He drove to the hotel and parked in the residents parking and grabbed his bag. They took the elevator to the reception, then another lift to his room on the fifth floor.

Theresa walked in ahead of Garth. Her mouth ajar. "I've never been inside this fancy hotel before, even though I've lived in Durbs all my life. It's really posh, isn't it? And what a view," she said as she walked across the room to the balcony then turned back to face Garth, "this is a real treat. Do we really need lunch," she joked and rolled onto the king size bed.

Garth needed food. And she admitted she did too.

They walked hand in hand into the dining room. The cold buffet, professionally spread down three long tables in the cool dining room, had Theresa staring in wonder.

"Oh my God, I've never seen so much food in my life. And what stunning decorations. Those vases of strelitzia are magnificent. If Cindy were here, she'd yell at me and tell me all of this is fattening. She'd suggest I stick to lettuce and cucumber." Theresa kissed him on the cheek like they were lovers. "I can't wait to eat those prawns," she pointed to a beautifully decorated platter of king prawns. "My folks could never afford prawns. I've only tasted them once at a buffet with Jeremy, but the buffet was nothing like this."

"Pig out then." Garth picked up two plates, handed one to her and they joined the queue. Garth stood behind her and rested his chin on her shoulder, "don't worry about what Cindy would eat. You're prettier and nicer than she'll ever be." Theresa turned and blew him a kiss, "I'll need some help, stand beside me. I don't know what half of this food is," she whispered so the fancy, rich ladies in the queue couldn't hear.

As they made their way down the length of the buffet tables Garth helped Theresa choose and explained what various dishes were when she asked.

It didn't take long to fill their plates, and they found a table for two in the corner of the dining room. Garth opened his napkin, shook it out and laid it across his lap. Theresa noticed and quickly did the same. She sat for a moment starring at her plate of food.

"What are you thinking?" He'd noticed a sadness in her eyes suddenly.

"I'm an only child. My parents are dirt poor. My father is an alcoholic, and I grew up in a frightening household. My poor mother found it hard to cope, but she's always been a wonderful mother. When I reached twelve, she took me to Jeremy who agreed to take me on as a paid child model, and he took me under his wing. Like I said, he's been so good to me ever since. I was his first full-time child model for a whole year, then Cindy came along and stole the prime spot. Theresa closed her eyes. Garth thought she might cry, and he wasn't very good at handling crying women.

"What's troubling you now?" He asked, puzzled that she wasn't tucking into the food.

"I don't know what all these knives and forks and spoons are for." She uttered. He felt the pain of her embarrassment. Appalled by his thoughtlessness. He took it for granted she'd know what to use.

"You know, my Mum always said that one day I would realise how fortunate I am. You've shown me that today." He leaned in close to her and whispered, "Thank you, beautiful Theresa. I'm so blessed to have met such a sweet, humble, kind, fun-loving beautiful young lady. Please don't cry. It doesn't matter to me what knife and fork you use. Use what's comfortable."

His tenderness made her want to weep. She remembered Jeremy telling her once to start from the outside and work in.

Relieved by what Garth said, she picked up a knife and fork, cut a prawn in half and put it in her mouth. "Yum, this is so good." She pushed the other half onto her fork, then devoured the rest. "What are those funny little black balls you have on your plate?"

"Caviar. Fish roe."

"What's roe?"

"Fish eggs. They're quite salty. An acquired taste. I'm not sure you'd like them, but here," he put a small amount of his fork. She opened her mouth like a fledgling in the nest being fed by its mother.

"Hmm, that's good. And what's that?" Theresa pointed to another food she'd never seen.

"Carpaccio." Garth picked up a few slices and placed them on her plate.

"Car...what...si...o." Theresa laughed.

"Very finely sliced raw beef. It is delicious. Try it."

Theresa put a slice in her mouth and chewed. Oooh, that's awesome. I'm a carnivore. Always have loved my meat."

"Get a little when we go back for a second helping. We can go back as often as we like."

"Really?" She said, flabbergasted.

Garth enjoyed her company and found her ignorance delightfully refreshing.

They dined on the buffet for two hours. A taste tester for Theresa, plus a culinary education she thoroughly enjoyed.

Garth revelled in watching her expressions with each new dish, especially as she no longer felt intimidated by them.

"I've never eaten so much in my life," she scrunched up her linen napkin and placed it on the side plate.

"Shall we go and work it off?" Garth asked playfully. "The sea or my room?"

Theresa looked at Garth for a few moments. "You've just taught me about fine dining, it's my turn to teach you about fine lovemaking." She taunted.

They left the dining room, hurried to the elevator and dashed to the room. Theresa started stripping off as the door closed and bounced onto the king size bed pulling off her shorts. Feeling self-conscious he undressed sitting on the edge of the bed, but Theresa pulled him onto his back and playfully said, "come on, hurry up," and yanked off his underpants, and as soon as he bounced free, she squealed with delight at the sight of him and was soon on top of him. Their lovemaking was urgent. There'd be time later to explore. Satiated, they lay naked together on the bed chatting.

"Would you be able to spend the next three days with me?" Garth asked.

"I'd love to." She sat up. Garth couldn't resist. He cupped her beautiful breasts in his hands. Theresa smiled and gestured with her arms waving above her head. "I've never known this kind of luxurious space. Even on the modelling assignments, we always shared rooms and a mid-level budget."

Garth let his hands drop from her breasts. "Will your parents want to know where you are?"

She burst out laughing, completely unphased by her nudity.

"I moved away from my parents two years ago. I left school at sixteen and earned enough from modelling to support myself. Besides, my father doesn't care whether I live or die, he's drunk all the time. He's been drunk as long as I've known him." Theresa lay back, her mouth pursed, wondering how much she should share. "I've not told anyone about my life, other than Jeremy, but I feel comfortable telling you, if you want to know."

"I'd love to know." Garth lay naked, his arms folded behind his head and watched her. She now sat cross-legged beside him. Distracted by her beautiful body, he focussed on the ceiling while she spoke.

"My poor mother had three miscarriages. My drunken father caused them all he beat her so often. I guess I was lucky to survive, though sometimes I wonder." A tear escaped and rolled down her cheek, settling on her breast. Garth wiped it off and caressed them again.

"My mum spends her days painting. Her art provides her with a reasonable living, and if she needs help, I give her a couple of hundred Rand. She's an excellent artist and does stunning mosaics too. Her favourite medium is oils. She has a little art studio-cum-bedroom in the garden where she locks herself away from my father. She cooks for them, then retreats to her studio." She leant forward and kissed Garth tenderly. "Am I boring you?"

"Not at all. Keep on talking."

"Mum's studio is wooden, stands on quite high stilts and has a lovely spacious veranda with steps that lead up to it. She loves working there in the early mornings, listening to the birds in the garden. Her easel is set up so she can do the oil painting work outside. The strong odour of turpentine is too much to paint inside. And, if dad staggers down the garden, she can quickly lock herself inside, though most of the time he's too drunk to get up the steps.

"Who supports his drinking habit?" Garth asked, placing a hand on her knee affectionately.

She took in a deep breath. "He steals, he's basically a tramp. Years ago, if he didn't come home, she knew he'd be sleeping in a gutter somewhere. She pays a cleaner twice a week. That lady does all the ironing too. Now he's older he manages to stagger home most days, and since she's moved into her studio, he doesn't get to beat her up any longer. If he does become loud and aggressive, she calls the cops and doesn't get a meal. He's figured it's easier to leave her alone." Theresa shook her head and rubbed her eyes, but tears still streamed. "He's probably the most well-known drunk in Durban." She snuggled into Garth's side. "That's.... that's been my....my childhood. Maybe one day I'll look back and feel sorry for him, but now it just makes me sad, angry, and bitter — all horrid, negative emotions."

Garth stroked her hair. "Does your mum rent the house?"

"No, it's hers. She inherited it from her mother, thank goodness. Dad never held a job for long. If it wasn't for gran, I can't imagine what I would've lived in growing up."

Garth had never met anyone who'd lived such a dreadful life. He'd always been surrounded by children from affluent parents. He lifted her head and kissed her fully on the mouth. When he stopped kissing her, he held her face in his hands. "I'm sorry you've had such a terrible childhood." He wrapped her in his arms and held her while she cried. "You truly are beautiful and thank God for it. Is your mother beautiful?"

"I guess she is. Dad was a nice-looking man when they got married. She didn't know then he was an alcoholic."

"Well, your looks are your fortune, as they say. You'll rise to be an international model if you stay with Jeremy."

Garth rolled onto his side and propped himself up on one arm ogling her shapely breasts, significant for her petite frame and slender waist. "You certainly know how to use your sensual hips and beautifully toned, shapely legs. I enjoyed them around me. You could easily model for Playboy. The guys at school bring naughty magazines into the dorms after holidays. Chicks with long blonde hair, high cheek bones, dark blue eyes, kissable lips, and lovely creamy complexions, just like you, are on the pages and they are no more beautiful than you."

Her big blue eyes looked up at him now.

"In fact, you're even more desirable." He took one of her nipples between his teeth and gently nuzzled till she squirmed.

"Ouch," she slapped his arm and playfully pushed him away, but he'd aroused her by playing with her nipples and she expertly guided him back inside her, rotating her hips, riding him. He grew harder as she moved, drawing him in and pressing him out. Garth felt like bursting. This time the sensation went far beyond anything he'd experienced in the sea or after lunch.

In the late afternoon, after a shower, they walked along the beach hand in hand.

"I can't remember a time when I've felt happier." Theresa moved closer to him. The wind had picked up and tossed her long, curly blonde hair around her face.

"Nor me." Garth kissed her and got a mouthful of hair. The rest of her golden curls wrapped around the side of his face. "May I ask you something personal?"

"Yes, of course."

"How did you learn to be such an expert in matters of the bedroom, or is it just me being the novice?"

Theresa brushed hair from her face, pulled away and walked off. "Hey," he caught her arm and pulled her back.

"If I tell, you'll think I'm a whore." She looked down and kicked at the sand with her bare feet. Garth waited. Eventually she spoke.

"Jeremy has loads of porno films, and we all watch them. He's sex mad, but obviously not with girls."

"Whaaat?"

"Don't look so shocked. You know he's gay."

"Yes, I do. So, when did you start watching porno movies?"

"About two years ago. Just after I left school."

Garth couldn't hide his surprise.

"Ja, I thought you'd be shocked. I was fifteen when I had my first orgasm with one of the male models. I don't remember much of it. I was goofed on cocaine while making a porno movie."

Could her life story get gorier, Garth wondered.

"Do you still take cocaine and act in porn movies?" He didn't like that thought.

She giggled. "You really have lived a protected life, haven't you?"

"I guess so," he reflected with a smile. Once again quietly thanking his parents for bringing him up the way they had. "Well, do you still make porn movies and take drugs?"

"Nah, I don't want to end up like my dad. I only did two porno movies. They paid brilliantly, but they made me feel dirty and cheap. Most of the other models, especially those who are still involved in making porno films take cocaine to enhance the experience. I personally think it weakens it. Being in the moment is way better. I decided to stay clean for the last eighteen months. I've had some great sex with some of the models. But it's purely for the orgasm and the rush of endorphins. No strings, if you get my meaning and it has been ages since I've had good sex."

They kept walking, and Theresa kept talking. It seemed to relieve the burden of her past, and Garth enjoyed listening now he'd got over the shock.

"Jeremy's a serious perve. He loves watching us orgasm. He gets his rocks off then too. You know what that means, hey?"

"Yeah, the guys at school use that expression when they have a wet dream."

"Jeremy masturbates while he watches, and" she covered her mouth, "the only thing big about Jeremy is his dick. I've never seen such a huge one."

Garth cringed. He didn't want that thought on his mind.

"I'm sorry. Is this too much for your good upbringing?"

"Hey," he pulled her to him again. They stood facing each other. "I'm saddened and shocked at the same time. I've never been exposed to stuff like this. You're teaching me so much, but please believe me, I'm not judging you." He hugged her.

Theresa pushed her head against his chest. "You rich boys will never understand, but if you really want to know, I'll tell you everything." Garth ran his fingers through her hair, starting at the base of her neck which made her shudder and melt into him.

"That's not entirely true. Not all of us are rich and selfish. In fact, I'd say most of my friends come from average homes. Like all blokes in their last year at school, we fantasise about what we'd like to do to pretty girls like you, and now you've taught me how beautiful it is to be with someone like you." Garth had his chin on her head, his eyes gazing straight into the setting sun across the ocean.

"It's been hard." She began to weep.

"I'm sure it has. I can't begin to imagine how hard, but think of it as an advantage, for you are wise from it." He reassured her, thinking how naïve he is.

"Sometimes, after a photo session, the models have a bit of an orgy. I don't get involved nowadays." She looked at him. "What I've told you has upset you, hasn't it?"

"In a way. I'm upset you've had to experience so much, so young. I must tell you, I'll never engage in a gang bang. Not ever. I just couldn't do that. If you want to stay with me over the next few days, I'd love it, but it's just you and me. I'll pay for everything. Let's enjoy each other."

"Absolutely. I had no intention of doing anything else. I want you all to myself." Theresa seemed happier now.

Though she shocked him, he admired her honesty and loved her frivolous ways.

They got back to the hotel after dark and ordered dinner at reception.

Theresa was hooked on prawns, so he ordered a seafood platter which arrived with a bottle of sparkling wine and two crystal flutes.

They ate supper on the balcony. The clear sky glistened with sparkling stars and shone as brightly as Theresa's beautiful eyes. They sat silently listening to the sounds of the waves crashing onto the beach at high tide while they dined and sipped on the wine.

"Cheers. Here's to the next two days." Theresa took a sip. "Now tell me about your life." She picked up a ring of calamari in her fingers and nibbled on it.

"I'm not sure where to start, but I've had my fair share of trauma."

"Really? How so?" Theresa imagined his life to have been eighteen idyllic years.

"As we speak, there's a security detail outside the hotel, guarding us."

Her big blue eyes got bigger. "Why?" Theresa instinctively looked over the balcony nervously.

"It's a very long story. My beautiful, kind, caring mother is the target of a nasty vendetta. She's come close to losing her life a few times. The last time, I was old enough to remember. It was traumatic. The bastard is targeting our best racehorses now.

Someone killed two of mum and dad's best horses. It's terrible, and we live knowing mum is the desired target."

"Oh my God." Theresa had stopped eating. "I'm sorry, Garth. That's more difficult than what I've been through." There was no mistaking the sympathy in her voice which touched Garth. "Why is your mum the target of this demonic killer?"

"It's a long story. I'll tell you one day."

Theresa understood, though she wanted to know more. Suddenly she felt differently about Garth. Perhaps he wasn't the spoilt brat she assumed.

They finished eating and took their drinks inside. Garth left the balcony door open; the air cooled them as it washed over them sitting on the bed with their backs resting against the headboard, sipping the last of the wine.

Garth broke the silence. "What's on your mind?"

"You must think I'm so self-centred." Theresa dropped her head, seemingly ashamed. Garth put his drink down and took her hand. "You've been through far more trauma than me and no, I don't think you are self-centred. In fact, you're remarkably balanced considering."

"Yeah, perhaps. I was frequently taken away to live in the safety of foster care and returned home when father sobered." Theresa put her glass down and snuggled up to Garth. "No-one has ever spoilt me like this. I'm so grateful to you."

"I couldn't think of someone I'd like to spoil more." And Garth genuinely meant it.

"Despite what I've told you, I blessed the day when Jeremy came into my life. He's been my lifeline. I forgive him for his unusual habits. He's always treated me well. Unlike my father, who raped me several times until I eventually moved into mum's bedroom."

"WHAT?" Now Garth really was horrified. "He should've been locked up, or castrated." Intensely angry suddenly.

"Mum wanted to have him jailed on numerous occasions. I never asked why she didn't report it to Child Welfare, but I think she feared losing me. Soon after Jeremy became my protector, I hardly ever saw my father. Now he's dead, thank goodness."

"When did he die?"

"A few months ago. Cirrhosis of the liver."

Despite the way he felt about Theresa, he knew she wasn't the sort of girl he could take home to meet his parents as a prospective wife, but he wanted to stay friends with her. Friends with benefits, he thought ruefully. He had a lot to thank her for.

The following day after a healthy breakfast they headed down to Jeremy's offices. Four men and four women were modelling the beachwear.

Cindy gave them a curt glance as they walked into the office. Burning jealousy showed in her eyes as she glared at Theresa.

Theresa whispered to Garth, "you're by far the hottest man here."

Jeremy's voice boomed through the offices. "Morning, morning, sweet things. Exciting day ahead." He glanced at his watch. "Let's get our little selves down to the beach, shall we? The photographers are meeting us at nine-thirty. Deary me, a little windy poo today, isn't it, Garthy?" Jeremy swept past him wearing a black and white kaftan. Garth smiled but he didn't dare look at Theresa.

The models wandered down to the beach and on the way down Cindy sauntered across to Garth. "Why did you choose this slut over me?" The words left her mouth with a sting.

Garth wisely squeezed Theresa's hand. He sensed she was

about to slap Cindy for calling her a slut. Garth ignored Cindy and kept walking.

"If you hadn't held my hand I would have climbed into the bitch," Theresa scoffed. Garth nodded. "I thought as much but by not answering defused a fight."

By the end of the day, the group were exhausted, sunburned and in vile, anti-social moods. They all quickly dispersed. Jeremy walked across to Garth and Theresa and asked what was up with Cindy. Theresa explained. Jeremy walked off shaking his head.

The following day the photo shoot was held a few miles north in the dunes, and where black rocks protruded into the sky and the waves crashed over them.

Jeremy took six models in his SUV. Garth and Theresa went together in Garth's Audi.

He and Theresa enjoyed this shoot with a swim in the sea at mid-day. Jeremy asked them all to rest in the afternoon, it would be along night with the evening shoot at the Suncoast Casino.

Theresa and Garth arrived at seven and walked through the entrance to the casino and into the lobby. Suddenly someone yanked her head back with a handful of her hair. Theresa screamed and as she turned Cindy launched a punch that sent Theresa to the floor.

Garth yelled at Cindy, but it was too late. While he helped Theresa up, blood poured down her front, Jeremy raced to her side, grabbed Cindy's arm and dragged her away with alarming force. Fuming, he reprimanded her in front of the other models while she fought to free her arm. Theresa's scream alerted security who'd called the casino emergency nurse. She arrived on the scene and took Theresa to the medical rooms. Garth ran after

Jeremy. "Tell that bitch not to come near me for the rest of the assignment."

The following day Theresa stayed in the hotel watching soapies, while Garth joined the other models at Jeremy's studio. He got back to the hotel at four o'clock in a bad mood, but when he saw Theresa, he calmed.

"Wow, the swelling has gone down fast," he kissed her. "How did you manage that?"

"The hotel staff have been fantastic. They kept bringing me ice. I've had a day of luxury, thanks to you. I've been watching TV and ordered lunch on your tab, which they brought to the room. I can't thank you enough."

"Well, I'm delighted you were so well looked after. How's the head?"

"Just a bit tender. How much hair is missing?"

Garth inspected the back of her head. "Yeah, a bit has gone, but it's not noticeable. God what a cow. I'd be surprised if Jeremy keeps her on. On my way in I ordered a cocktail. It should be here in a minute or two."

"You're amazing." She kissed him hungrily. "How was your day?"

"Boring. I would've preferred to stay here with you," he grinned. "Tomorrow, I'll drop you at home. I'm sure you won't be modelling for a few days. Where do you live?"

"In a very small furnished one bedroomed flat on the Berea. It's not great, but it's all I can afford. I'll never speak to that cow again. She's cost me a lot of money." Theresa's lips curled and her eyes became slits as she thought.

"Don't worry. Jeremy assured me he'd take care of you. He's making Cindy pay for the time you lost. She was spitting like a viper. He took no notice. He was furious." Garth pulled his wallet from his pocket. "Here, have this," he handed over two hundred Rand.

"No! I can't take that. I've paid my rent for the month, and I have money left."

"I insist." Garth shoved the money into her handbag.

They moved onto the balcony and quietly gazed at the ocean. Eventually Garth asked, "What would you like for supper?"

"Pizza would be nice."

After they'd eaten and showered, they fell into bed.

"Can we see each other again?" Theresa's voice was almost a whisper. She didn't want to let him go.

"Of course, but I must warn you I'm going to college and working for my dad too. I don't want a steady relationship with anyone right now, it wouldn't be fair." Garth thought she was about to cry, but she smiled bravely.

Garth dropped Theresa at her flat, then set off for home. The drive home passed quickly as he thought about what Theresa had taught him. He parked, grabbed his bags and strode up the front steps.

Mel waited in the hall. "Hello, my child," she hugged him. "You look happy." She was relieved he'd got home safely.

"It's good to be home, Ma." He kissed her hello.

"Tell me all about the assignment."

"Let me dump my bags." Tell Ma all about it. Not likely, he smiled at his reflection in the mirror and ran a comb through his hair. It looked like a birds nest after the journey home with the hood down.

"Hey, howzit boet. How did it go?" Brad wandered into his brother's room.

"It was okay — you know what it's like. All the bloody

pampering and photographers screaming and Jeremy flapping around. I'm not modelling anymore."

"Any hot chicks?" Brad asked casually.

"Plenty bru, plenty. Some seriously hot chicks on the beach. Hey, Mum's waiting for me on the veranda."

The brothers joined her and flopped into easy chairs. "No more modelling for me, Ma."

"Oh, why?" Mel asked with a half-cocked grin.

"I hate it. This one is definitely the last and I've told Jeremy." He put in a good word about Theresa and told them about Cindy attacking her. "It's all so bitchy and uncomfortable. Training racehorses is far more fun, and I'm way better suited to it."

Chapter Thirteen

GARY GOT HIS WAY. Garth agreed to do an MBA online
with college attendance twice a week. Now all he wanted was
his final A level exams and school to be behind him. Eight weeks
later, there he was, sitting in his mother's office chatting about
training racehorses when the phone on her desk rang.

"Hi, Mrs. Whitaker," Theresa greeted Mel.

"Hello Theresa, how are you?" Garth waved his hand, indi-
cating he didn't want to speak to her. Mel nodded as he left.
"This is a very early morning call. Garth is down at the track,
training racehorses." She fibbed.

"Yes, I know. He told me his early mornings are busy, but I
wanted to tell you that I'm pregnant, and Garth is the father."

"Gosh! Are you sure, Theresa?" Mel hadn't expected that
kind of news.

"Yes, I'm very sure, Mrs. Whitaker."

"Have you told Garth?"

"No, I haven't. I wanted to tell you first. He'll probably
deny it's his."

"Now, why would he do that?"

"Because it would interrupt his studies and his career. He's told me he only wants to be friends. I'm not of his class or breeding you see." Mel didn't like Theresa's snarky tone.

"Theresa, my dear, there are many ways of sorting this out without getting nasty. May I ask, do you want the child?"

"Yes, of course I want the child. I'm not having an abortion if that's what you're inferring."

"Theresa, if you want to keep the child, that's your choice. I'm not suggesting an abortion at all. What I'm suggesting is that you think about giving it up for adoption." Mel heard Theresa gasp. "Let me explain my reasoning before you argue with me. It's a huge responsibility raising a child and being a single parent, and it would hugely hinder your career, being the sought-after model that you are."

"You.... you don't..." Theresa was about to start shouting as Mel had anticipated.

"Let's chat about this in a calm and sensible manner," Mel said sympathetically, with genuine warmth in her voice.

"Don't patronise me. You're speaking to me like I'm a child, incapable of making decisions."

Mel kept her tone relaxed and friendly. "I understand you're upset. I also understand you and Garth are not in a relationship, you're just friends. He speaks very highly of you, and he doesn't think you're below him. We never raised Garth or Brad to be like that, which I believe you know. What would you like me to do? I gather that's why you called me first?"

"I...I...love Garth." Theresa began to cry. Mel felt sorry for her but happy she'd defused her anger. She liked Theresa, though their meeting had been brief. "Please convince your son to marry me." She sniffed.

"Theresa, no one can force marriage on anyone. Besides,

situations like that never last, they simply end in pain. Suppose you decide to keep the child, keeping in mind that it's your choice and yours alone, we'll insist on a paternity test to ascertain that it is, in fact, Garth's child." Theresa's sobbing grew louder. "If those results are positive, there will be adequate financial support, but Garth's not ready for marriage, and not under these circumstances. You're a street wise young lady, why didn't you ensure you had some form of protection before sleeping with my son?"

Theresa slammed the phone down.

Mel hadn't intended to upset Theresa but hoped Theresa would give her suggestion some thought.

Garth returned to the office half an hour later. "So, what did Theresa want?"

"To tell me she's pregnant and carrying your child." Garth's tanned face turned a deep shade of red, his mouth dropped open, and he collapsed into the chair opposite his mother.

"I doubt she'd know whose child it is, but it's not impossible." He said with blatant honesty. He patted his face. "Shit, talk about awkward."

"Go on," Mel said.

"I like her, as you know. But as a friend."

"I like her too, but now we need to chat about what we're going to do about the situation. Theresa said she loves you and wants to marry you which I know you won't entertain. When I challenged her about not protecting herself from unwanted pregnancy, she slammed the phone down. I hope she thinks about what I said."

"I'll never marry her. She was fun for three days, we chat on the phone quite regularly, and I've seen her a few times, one of those times was with you. But marry her? No way. Besides, how can she be sure it's my child?"

"I asked her that. I said a DNA test would have to be done to confirm whether the child is yours, if she keeps it, of course. I didn't suggest an abortion, but I did tell her the cons of keeping the child and recommended adoption."

"Thanks Ma. I intend staying single for at least another ten years." Gary had heard snippets of the conversation from his office. He crossed the passage and joined them.

"This is going to be difficult, Garth. You're a good catch — a very eligible bachelor. I think we must convince Theresa that keeping the child would ruin her career. Let's put the emphasis more on her life. She doesn't need the burden of raising a child. She must focus on her modelling career. I agree with Mum. Encourage her to give the child up for adoption. We'd pay for the costs of the birth and give her financial support for three months while she gets her figure back." Gary stayed standing in the doorway. Mel smiled at his straightforward male logic.

"I made it clear that if she wants to keep the child, it's her choice, and the consequences are hers, and hers alone." Mel added.

"That's all very well, sweetheart, but I think she'll need financial assistance. You know the plight of her mother. You two are good friends, aren't you?" He pointed the question at Garth who nodded. "Well then, let's do the honourable thing and pay. But marriage is out of the question."

"I agree, Dad. There's no way I'll marry her, besides I'm far too young. I'll call her and see if I can talk some sense into her. If she keeps the child and it's not mine, we shouldn't pay a dime. She may just be trying to scare me into marrying her. Maybe she thinks an illegit child will tarnish our reputation." Garth wondered if she'd think like that. He hoped not.

"Dad and I will wait to hear from you. We're behind you, whatever you choose to do." Mel said comfortingly. "And, apart from financial support, be sensitive Garth, this is a huge emotional upheaval for her."

Gary looked at his wonderful caring wife, then to his handsome eldest son. "I hope Theresa can be swayed without a fight."

Garth called Theresa. "Hi, I'm curious to know why you called my mum first?" A manipulative move he'd felt uncomfortable about.

"I was scared you'd laugh and tell me to go and jump."

"I wouldn't do that. I'll never dump you. You should know that. I'm disappointed you slammed the phone down on her. That's rude. She's trying to help."

"I love you, Garth Whitaker." Theresa burst into tears. She meant it, and Garth knew that.

"That may be so, but I'm too young to marry and take on the responsibility of a family. I've only been out of school two months. I've always been honest with you, and I've told you I don't want a serious relationship with anyone. We had a short fling, and it was great. You're great, but we agreed to be friends. What about all those other male models you told me about? How sure can you be sure it's my baby?"

"Because I've not slept with anyone for three or four months before you. Remember I told you."

"Theresa, I promise I'll do the right thing financially, but nothing else. I know it's hard, but I think you should put the child up for adoption." Garth now felt the pressure of being caught so innocently. "There are options, sensible options. Let's look at them without anger. I'll do what I can to help emotionally, but if you decide to keep the child, then we need the paternity test mum spoke to you about. If it's not mine, there'll be no financial support."

"You bastard. You're just like the rest of them." Theresa began to cry again.

"The rest of who, Theresa?" Garth raised his voice a little. "I'm not paying for someone else's child. There's no need to call me a bastard."

"Men," she stammered. "You are all the bloody same."

"No, we're not. I've been honest with you from the beginning. I told you I didn't want a relationship, and I told you why. It's up to you to protect yourself from an unwanted pregnancy. Especially if you want multiple sexual partners. When we met that afternoon, you could've told me you were not on the pill, but you didn't. That's dishonest. And now you're begging me to trust you and you're calling me a bastard."

"You can fucking trust me. I am not lying." She yelled. "I'll have this child."

"That's defiant, and quite frankly, stupid. Give it some thought. You might think more clearly when you're not so emotional. Keep in mind that a child now might ruin your life. It won't ruin mine."

"You're so fucking dishonourable." She yelled.

"Theresa, when you can talk nicely, let's discuss the options." Garth ended the call.

The following day Theresa called back.

"Morning, Theresa, how are you doing?"

"I'm okay. I want to apologise for the way I spoke to you yesterday."

"I understand, and your apology is accepted. It's a massive shock for everyone, and I'm sure an emotional one for you. What have you decided to do?" Garth closed his eyes, hoping for the best outcome.

"I've decided not to keep the child. I had a great conversation with my mother after our fight. She said she'd love to be a grandmother, but not this way. It was the best chat we've had in years. Will you honour the expenses until I hand it over to new parents?" Garth heard the quiver of emotion in her voice and felt for her.

"Absolutely, even if it's not mine. A hard decision for you to make and you have all my sympathy, but for all our sakes, it's the most sensible one. No one needs to know, and I'm told post-birth recovery is quick being as fit and strong as you are. You can get on with your modelling soon afterwards. I must admit, I'm relieved."

"I appreciate your help, and I hope we can always remain friends."

"Of course. Mum has also said she'll be happy to give any emotional help you may need, just pick up the phone. The same applies with me."

"That's very kind. Please pass on my thanks to your mum. Can I ask you one more question?"

"Yes, fire away."

"You know my mother is an artist. Would your parents be interested in seeing some of my mother's work and, if they like it, commissioning something? She's good at landscapes and very good at painting animal portraits."

"Ask my Mum, T. She'll be happy to hear from you too."

"I love it when you call me T. Will you see me off and on during the pregnancy? I'd like that."

"Yes, of course. I don't want to sound rude, but I must go, Dad's waiting for me. Chat later. Don't forget to call my Mum."

Garth looked at her profile picture on his mobile screen. He couldn't deny relief outweighed all other sensations.

Chapter Fourteen

"Good morning. May I speak with Mr. Whitaker, please? It is CID Johannesburg."

"Hold on, please, I'll put you through."

The phone buzzed on Gary's desk. He grabbed the receiver, "Whitaker."

"Good morning, Mr. Whitaker. Sergeant Nkoni from the CID in Soweto, speaking."

"Yes, good morning, sergeant. Have you finally got good news for us?"

"Unfortunately, not. I've got bad news. We arrested Julie Mokena yesterday, but she escaped police custody. The search is on again to find her."

Gary sat in silent disbelief. The dwindling efficiencies within the police force over the past five years had become an infuriating part of life in South Africa. More and more of the force fell prey to festering greed bred by corruption and bribery. Gary had a feeling this was one such case. Someone had paid a bribe to free her.

"Escaped police custody?" Gary repeated. "What now? This is inexcusable." Gary seethed, thinking chaos creates opportunity, but he didn't voice it.

"Yes, I understand. I'll keep you informed of any future progress. I'm sorry I've had to pass on bad news."

"This is extremely serious. I hope it won't take more bloody wasted years to find her again?" Gary swore in frustration.

"I'm sorry. I'll get back to you when we know more."

"Thank you." Gary slammed the phone down, left his hand resting on the instrument and shook his head. He picked it up again and called the CEO of their security company.

"Willem, Gary here."

"Morning Gary, what's up?"

"CID in Johannesburg called — they arrested Julie yesterday, but she escaped police custody. Can you fucking believe it?" Gary stared out his office window wondering if they'd ever escape the consequences of the vendetta against Mel.

"Oh yes, I can believe it. I can't tell you how often it happens nowadays. It drives me nuts. I bet it's a bribery debacle. Your man in Zimbabwe is playing games again."

"My thoughts precisely. He must've got someone here to pay the right cop." Gary took a deep breath. "By the way, I've not told Mel. I don't think she needs to know."

"Got ya." Willem rang off.

Gary continued staring out the window wondering if they'd ever find Julie Mokena.

IN HIS ROOM studying after breakfast, Garth answered his ringing phone abruptly without taking notice of the number or name on the mobile screen.

"Garth Whitaker." All he heard was Theresa sobbing.

"What's wrong, T?"

"I've lost the baby. I had a miscarriage last night. I'm.... in hospital...." She stammered, "but I'll be home.... tomorrow."

"I'm so sorry. Are you okay?"

"Yeah. Sort of. Physically, a bit painful and tender. Emotionally, numb. In a weird way, I feel relieved I'm not carrying full term."

"That's very brave. I'm proud of you for taking such an emotional situation so well. I'll come and see you. You can't go home and be alone."

"I'm going to mum's sister for a week. I'll text you the address."

"Great. I'm busy studying. Exams next week, but I'll see you tomorrow.

Garth rushed to the house to tell Mel.

"Ma! I've just had a call from Theresa. She had a miscarriage last night. She's in hospital. Coping very courageously."

"Oh, Garth, I'm so sorry. But it's a relief." She took off her reading glasses and pushed them onto her head. "Let this be a lesson, my boy." She raised an eyebrow.

"I promised Theresa, I'd visit her, but I don't know what to take her. Give me some ideas, please."

"That's good of you. Get her some expensive perfume, a vase of lovely flowers, a card, some chocolates and...."

"Whoa, Mum. That'll cost me a fortune."

With a wry smile, she said, "mistakes often do, my son, but my suggestion will be considerably cheaper than paying for four more months of her pregnancy needs, a paternity test and everything afterwards."

"True." Her words made him feel selfish.

His mother's words hit home. Garth left for Durban. He'd decided to surprise Theresa before she left hospital and walked into the ward carrying a bowl of mixed flowers and a box of chocolates.

Theresa's face lit up when she saw him. "How sweet of you to come."

He leant down and gave her a kiss. "I said I'd not let you down. I'll pop through tomorrow too." He put the flowers and chocolates on the locker beside her.

"Thank you. The flowers are gorgeous. I love all the different colours. I'm going to gorge on those chocolates when you've gone, simply because I can," she smiled sheepishly. "Imagine what Cindy would say," she laughed.

"Bugger Cindy, just enjoy every one of them. I can't stay long. I just wanted to ensure you're okay."

"I'm fine. Lying here thinking about it, it's the best thing that could've happened. "She reached up and hugged him. "You've been so good to me it makes it harder for me not to love you more. Gentlemen like you are hard to find."

Sometimes Garth had thought a relationship with Theresa would've been fun, but common sense prevailed. The friendship was good. They chatted for a short while.

"I'll see you tomorrow."

GARTH SHOPPED ACCORDING to his mother's list and swallowed hard when he tallied it all up, then he drove to the address Theresa had given him and knocked on the door.

A dirty, bedraggled looking woman flung the door open. Her stare was bristly, and the smell of stale cigarette smoke stuck in Garth's nostrils.

"Wait here," she closed the door.

He waited, annoyed by the woman's rudeness and wondered if she was the auntie. The stench from within would ensure he didn't stay long. He held the bad of his pièce de resistance gifts and a large vase of white roses. Inside the floral-patterned carrier bag that hung over his arm were more chocolates, Dior perfume, a silk nighty, an assortment of body lotions, bath oils, soaps, and bath bombs and a little pink envelope.

The front door burst open again. The unkept woman glared at Garth with a murderous, accusing look in her eyes.

"Go down the passage, second door on the left." She stood to one side and let Garth in. He

stepped inside, almost wishing he hadn't. The house stank. He found Theresa lying on a single bed covered by a threadbare bedspread as old and ugly as the aunt. He couldn't help wondering why Theresa wasn't staying with her mother.

Garth put the vase of roses next to the bowl he'd brought her the day before. He handed her the bag of goodies. "Hi, how are you today?"

"Feeling a bit weak, and depressed. More flowers, and this bag?" She looked up at him questioningly.

"It's the least I can do. I haven't had to go through what you've just been through."

"Aaw, you are so thoughtful." She opened the bag of goodies and opened the envelope first. She read the card with tears in her eyes then unfolded the cheque he'd slipped into the envelope. She gasped and reached for a tissue. "Thank you, but I can't take the money. You've already been so good to me."

"I insist. Were the nursing staff nice to you?" Purposefully changing the subject.

"They were amazing. Mum is relieved too. I spoke to your Mum. She very generously gave my Mum two great commissions. A pastel portrait of that special horse you lost — Ebony and Ivory, I think she said. The other is a project she's really excited about. Six mosaic mirrors in your stud colours and six matching lampshades. The income from that commission is more than she made the whole of last year and changes everything for her. Having your family name on her portfolio means a lot."

"Why aren't you staying with her, instead of this ghastly place?" He looked about disapprovingly.

"Won't you sit." She patted the bed. "Mum is busy with the commissions and doesn't have time to look after me." She started opening the bag of goodies.

"I wish you loved me, like I love you." Theresa sprayed some perfume on her wrist. "This is the first time I've smelt Channel No 5. It's gorgeous." Garth held her hand. He did love her, just not the same way she loved him.

"You'll find the right man, but for now, keep the focus on your career, and save as much money as you can. There has been a huge lesson in this for me too."

Tears rolled down her cheeks. "A horrid lesson, but I'm so grateful for all these goodies, the cheque and our friendship."

Garth said goodbye, relieved to get out of the smelly flat. On the way home he thought a lot about Theresa, but even the lure of the bedroom didn't change his mind.

She's a good lass, just not for me.

Chapter Fifteen

"You won't believe who called this morning." Mel said happily as she walked into the boardroom at the admin offices after doing her rounds of the broodmare barn.

"It wasn't Theresa again, was it?" She'd called frequently over the past few weeks, suffering from a form of postpartum depression.

Garth's textbooks were spread out on the boardroom table. Gary had been testing him.

"No. A refreshing change. The wonderful James Khumalo is back."

"Goodness. How nice to hear from him. Where is he?" Gary asked.

"With his mother in Pinetown. He's back from the UK for good and asked if he can visit us."

"Brilliant, when?" Garth asked. He'd always liked James.

"He should be here in about an hour. He said it's been an amazing experience, five years racing in England. Hard to believe he's been away that long, isn't it?"

"I bet he's missed the sunshine and the smell of the African earth after the rains. He always said he loved that smell when we hacked around the farm together." The memory brought a smile. to Garth's serious study face.

Gary poured himself a glass of water. "We'd better get finished then Garth."

"Yeah, for sure, Dad."

Mel closed the boardroom door and went back to her office.

James arrived driving a snow-white Toyota double cab he'd just driven off the showroom floor and parked at the admin block.

Mel saw him arrive, dashed down the steps and flung her arms around him. "It's so exciting to have you back. Time has flown." She stepped back. "Gosh you're looking well."

"I can hardly believe I've been away nearly six years. You're looking well too, Mel. How's everyone else?"

"Excited to see you. Gary and Garth are in the boardroom. Garth has an exam coming up. Come in."

Gary shook James's hand. "Welcome back, young man. It's good to see you."

Garth gave James a hug and a handshake.

"I can't tell you how special it is to be back here. I got the foundations to do well in the UK here on this farm and I'll never forget that. I hope there's an opportunity for me to ride for you again."

"Absolutely. You and Kgabu can work with the junior jockeys. Knock'em into shape," Gary joked.

"Fantastic. Chuffed to hear Kgabu's still here."

"Very much so. He rides all our top horses, plus some of the horses we train for other owners.

"You and I will have a blast." Garth bounced up the veranda steps. The normal Whitaker gathering place with a stunning view of the garden and the brood mare paddocks beyond, with the faint outline of the Drakensburg in the far distance.

"Will you have lunch with us, James?" Mel asked.

"That would be lovely, thank you." His face shone with good health and excitement.

"How long will lunch be, Mum?" Garth asked.

"About an hour."

"Cool. Can I show James the horses he'll be riding?"

"Of course."

They rushed down to the main stable block. James was in awe.

"Jesus, your horses look fantastic. Better than most of the yards I worked for in the UK. The Irish horses were big solid Thoroughbreds for the most part, but some of the yards in England should be inspected. The horses look like greyhounds, not horses."

"Really? I thought England produced some of the best racehorses in the world."

"Of course, and they do in the top studs, and there are loads of very professional yards but there's loads of sleezy ones too, sadly. Seen in both flat and jump racing yards." As they walked down the line of stables, peering in at the horses, many of the staff remembered James fondly and rushed to greet him.

"Your horses are so much more relaxed too. They might be racehorses, but at least they get hacked out and live out for a couple of hours a day and are not confined to a bloody stable for most of the day."

It was nearly lunch time. They wandered back to the house and at the sitting room doorway, James suddenly stopped. "Wow. What a stunning painting of Ebony. He almost looks alive."

"It's beautiful, isn't it? The mother of a friend of Garth's painted it. Poor darling horse, never deserved to die."

"That's for sure. I couldn't believe it when I heard." James shook his head.

They moved through to the dining room. It had always been James's favourite room. Not because he had an alarming appetite, but the walls were adorned with racing photographs from as early as the late 1960s. He'd also always admired the twelve-seater walnut dining room suite Mel had inherited from her grandmother. It had a smell that reminded James of old-fashioned values and exceptional taste, for which this family were renowned.

At lunch, tale and tale gushed forth from James. There was so much to tell and he had an uncanny knack of embroidering them with a hysterical mix of African, British and slapstick South African humour — making his tales all the funnier coming from a young Zulu.

"It's your turn, Garth. Get over there and learn from some of the greats. They are still around, and they know how to bring on racehorses, not that we don't, but it's very different. An industry worth billions of pounds. It stinks of bucks, my boy. You can smell it, even in their poop." He joked. "'Strue, bru, genuine." Garth loved the tales, descriptions and slang. A refreshing change from the recent trauma with Theresa.

"The equine industry in the UK contributes something like eight billion pounds a year to the GDP. It's mind-blowing. You don't smell money like that here. The quid has a special smell." A crooked grin ran up one side of James's face. "Back here, one pound is worth a fortune. I bought my Toyota, and a flat for my mum, cash. It felt so good to bargain for their best cash price." He took a mouthful of water and went on talking. "There's racing of some sort or another almost every day in the UK. The competition is scary. Prize money is big bucks, bru," he looked at Garth. "For the big races', the bag is bigger than you and I can comprehend. There's no room for passengers. It's a 'shape up or ship out' attitude and in most of the best yards, the race-horses are cared for like royalty, my man, until......" James's expression changed from cocky cheer to melancholy as he suddenly thought of his friend Charles.

"This will be my last story." He grinned at Mel. "Charles and I rode a stunning horse called News Reel. Charles adored him. One day he started pulling and then went lame. Two days later we were told he'd gone to spelling, but in fact he'd been thrown out and a rescue centre got hold of him. When Charles found out he gave the trainer a piece of his mind and told him all the horse needed was a chiropractor. The trainer laughed at Charles, 'What the fuck do you know about chiropractors? Twerp.' Charles resigned and went in search of the rescue centre. He finally found News Reel." James took mouthful of lunch.

"One weekend we visited News Reel. It was appalling. We left the stable devastated and made it our mission to find a better yard for him. During our search we found out what happens to too many racehorses when their racing lives end. We went undercover, as it were. In our time off we visited countless sanctuaries. Many of them are amazing. Sadly, some of the best small ones are very poorly supported. From our research, some of the rescue centres are just a political lark. Titled, monied — don't question them and some of the worst cases came out of those centres owned by the mega rich. Even the RSPCA couldn't close them, but there were some heartwarming stories too. We wanted to report the worst cases, but we knew we'd lose our jobs if we got involved. We eventually adopted News Reel and moved him to another yard. He'd just got over serious laminitis and was as thin as a rake. Between us, we collected two thousand pounds for News Reel's welfare, and just before I left, I gave Charles another thousand pounds."

"What a heartwarming story. Well done, James." Mel's eyes were glistening.

"Five weeks after we moved News Reel to the new yard, Charles received some photos of how well he was doing. Just before I got here, the yard owner called. A young teenage girl had fallen in love with him. She wanted to know if Charles would part with him. He agreed but insisted on paying for one more chiropractic treatment. The young girl events him now."

The Whitakers, though saddened to hear of the racehorse abuse, knew it happened all over the world — the UK was no different. And, as with sad tales, there are many happy endings too. The Whitakers were not strangers to this vexing time in the cycle. They understood how important it was to be responsible and humane.

"I'm thrilled to hear you remembered how important the chiropractor is to the horses physical comfort." Mel said.

"I will always remember your strict rules. During the ten-day rest period every racehorse has one or two chiropractic treatments before they go back into training. It works and mitigates countless unsoundness issues."

Chanting Clover never sold on problems. Owning race-horses requires knowledge. In Mel's opinion, the only humane way to 'let down' a racehorse is under supervision. She only sold horses to persons with experience in caring for Thoroughbreds. Churning out racehorses like used pieces of sports equipment wasn't her style.

"When I die, I want to come back as a racehorse here." He laughed. "I learned so much here. I loved it in the UK, and I did well because of the grounding you gave me. UK was a massive education and a huge culture shock. The first few months I could hardly understand what half of the people were talking about — all the different English accents — oh my word. Then, to add, their health and safety rules are mostly anal, but I realise some are essential."

"I agree, James. We find lots of the health and safety regulations to be counterproductive." Gary offered his opinion.

"Before I go, I must give you another shocking tale, just for fun." James took the last mouthful of cottage pie.

"The jump races," James whistled. "Jeez, bru, now that's a tough ride." This time he addressed Garth.

"Sorry to interrupt you, James. Dessert?" Mel asked.

"Yes please."

"I had the good fortune of riding the Cheltenham Gold Cup a couple of times. Little beats that for an adrenaline rush. Those fences, oh my word. I went flying on a few occasions and made an arse of myself." James chuckled. "The fences are built with the horse's welfare in mind, but it's still tough. When I fell at my first jump race, I was winded so badly I thought I would never breathe again. All I saw were hooves flying past me as I sat, ego dented as badly as I'd dented the turf." Laughing, he took the bowl of dessert from Mel.

"Yum, this looks good. Apple pie, it's a popular pudding in England."

"When you fall at a fence, do you duck and stay put until all the horses are clear?" Mel asked as she passed the bowls around.

"You cover your head and pray you don't get stepped on. I guess it's a bit like eventing, when you interfere with their stride, it's a total cock-up." Garth said.

"Exactly. When I started, I was covered in grass burns." James picked up his spoon and cut into the apple pie, and savoured the taste sensations of toffee, apple and cream. "This is delicious.

"Hurdles can't be higher than 3.5ft. Those are cool. But most of the time I was riding flat races, which I preferred. I have big respect for jockeys who ride in the Grand National at Aintree. Right in front of the grandstand, the highest jump is 5ft:3" high. That's 1.6metres, Bru. And, if that's not enough, they put a bloody great ditch in front of it measuring 6ft wide. I was lucky to go as a spectator. Mega-thrilling day for sure but I can see why the bunny huggers come out in their hordes." James swallowed another mouthful of apple so quickly he almost choked. "It gets quite rough out there, horses go down, jockeys take nasty tumbles, some even lose their lives. It's a mammoth test. I got choked up watching those horses give their all."

"Oh, I do that too. Sometimes I can't talk when I watch the races. There's a lump the size of a rugby ball in my throat." Mel said.

"It's all so different, Hey?" James was looking at Mel, then he went on chatting to everyone. "And the mega-rich Arabs." James shook his head. "They glare down their eagle-like noses at you as if they're looking at a waif from the Oliver tale. You're a nothing, like lower than shark shit, low. It's flippin' intimidating."

"Sorry, I've forgotten my manners. I shouldn't be swearing." James's sheepish expression made Gary laugh.

"Would you go back?" Mel asked.

"Oh, you bet I would, ma'am. The plusses far outweigh the negatives, but for the racism there. Gee. I can't speak for our pre-independence politics, and I don't wish to draw attention to it with you, my friends, but I can tell you, mark my words, it's there. Even with my post-independence rose-tinted glasses on, I'm more comfortable here as an emerging Zulu male than I was there. It's a world of many contrasts and contradictions. Governed by class and all that crap. I had it pretty tough in some places."

"What's the pay for jockeys like?" Garth asked. Money never far from his thoughts.

"It's not too bad. Converted into our weak Rand, it's bloody excellent." A smile stretched across James's face. "Here, I'm considered rich."

They finished lunch and Garth took James to see the stallions.

"This is a manicured haven for horses, that's for sure. In the UK, you get quite a mix of yards. I never worked in any of the very grand places that are hundreds of years old. Newmarket, even the built-up part of the town, at a guess, there are at least fifty training stables. It's unreal. You can walk down a street and within three hundred meters of the High Street there will be one, two or even three stables hidden on either side of the narrow lane. The town is wall-to-wall horses."

"Really? I must go over one day, but I've got this MBA to finish first." Garth shrugged his shoulders. He wasn't enjoying the course.

"Every day, at the crack of dawn, we rode to the Gallops from our stables. There's a strictly enforced law in Newmarket that cars are to give way to riders. If a driver disregards this rule, there's shit to pay. On horseback, we trek. Bugger the cars. The worst thing about negotiating the streets was the flipping weather. If it wasn't snowing, or dark, or raining, we weren't in our reality. Belting up the Gallops on the great Heath on the outskirts of town was an exercise in sheer willpower. Fuck bru, it's cold. But come rain or shine, we were there. And blow me down, there are about twelve different tracks in Newmarket for horses to exercise on. Guess your Mum and Dad know that."

"Yes, they do. Mum said they fell in love with the place after seeing the flat dear old Hector had left mum."

"Jeez, but some of those people did my head in. This little Zulu boy didn't get the culture, growing up the way I did," James pointed to himself.

They got back to Jame's new pick-up after viewing the stallions. "Eish, my man, it's good to be home." James gave Garth a hug.

"It's good to have you back. What are you up to tomorrow?" Garth asked.

"Nothing planned. Helping Mum, probably."

"Come out on the gallops with me in the morning. Could you get here by five-thirty?"

"Of course." James answered with the type of enthusiasm Garth remembered. "Who are you going to put me on?"

"Would you like a spin on Prov?"

"Bloody A. I'd love to ride your boy."

"Deal," Garth said. They shook hands, "till tomorrow. Cheers mate you better get back to your Ma before she frets."

THE FOLLOWING morning Siyanda and Thomas chatted to James while they waited for Garth.

"Hey man, it's so good to speak Zulu again." James tittered. "It must sound fucking ridiculous with a bit of a Pommie accent." The grooms agreed it did sound strange, but they were loving it.

"It does, bru, but hey, starting the morning with laughter is what everyone needs." Garth said as he joined them.

* * *

GARTH RODE a youngster from the mare, Melonie's Rival, by Bold Warrior. The young horse was a whopper, standing at 17hands and only two and a half years old.

"That's one powerful horse. What's his name?" James asked.

"Warriors Rival. I think mum is hoping he'll make the grade to race overseas. He's got a lovely steady temperament, like his parents. A cruise to back, only bucked a few times and off we went. With you on Prov, carrying less weight, I'm curious to see how he performs."

Garth felt sure the strapping Warriors Rival might give Provocation a challenge, but being so young, he wasn't going to push the horse too hard, for he was handicapped by carrying Garth's weight.

"Provocation's a lovely horse. He's as comfy as a rocking chair with a lovely soft mouth. Kudos to you. Can I ride him in his next race?"

"Yeah, 'course. Mum reckons, with me on his back he'd make a great ponsie dressage horse. Show mum what he's made of. He can be bloody lazy though. My hopes are he'll qualify for the July handicap next year. Put some spark into him, James."

James touched Provocation with his magic touch, and he flew down the 1600m track.

Tinus, who was standing at the end of the track, shouted, "now that's the Provocation we need to see more of."

"Can James ride him in his next race?" Garth shouted back as he trotted over to join them.

"You'll have to fight Kgabu. If he's happy, it's fine by me. Next Saturday, in Johannesburg. An important group two race. I'm mighty impressed with Warriors Rival, Garth. He ran well next to Prov. He's got the potential your mother speaks of."

Tinus ruminated as he spoke, "and especially as you weren't asking anything of him."

"He sure has, Tinus. I'm excited about this horse." Garth patted Rivals neck then gave James a slap on the back. "I can't get that kind of enthusiasm out of Prov. Well done."

Unreserved excitement filled their chatter all the way back to the house. Garth called Kgabu. Kgabu obliged, happy to let James ride Provocation. He wasn't Kgabu's favourite.

James's warm, easy-going nature endeared him to everyone. The work riders considered him a British racing idol, and when Gary offered him a full-time position at the stud, it was met with great jubilation. Once his mother was settled in her new flat he'd move to Chanting Clover.

Siyanda, elated by the news, took James by the arm and said, "me, Siyanda, getting old now."

"Oh, come on Siyanda. You're as fit as when I last saw you." But James could see the years of wear and tear showed.

"Eish," he laughed. "On outside, not inside." He shook his head. "Next year, Siyanda be fifty. Too old for this now. Mr. James, you take my place."

"Hardly. You've got another ten years in you, Siyanda. You're part of the furniture here." It was true. Siyanda had been with the stud for many years. He couldn't imagine living anywhere else. "My son John, he take over from me then. You teach him all you learnt across the seas." He said in his broken English and toothless grin. Arthritis had started to weaken Siyanda.

The following day James rode Warriors Rival down the two thousand metres. Tinus and Garth waited at the end with their mouths open.

"Jesus, this horse can fly. A 17hand fighter jet. I think he's the fastest horse I've ever ridden." James shouted joyfully." James walked him over to where Garth and Tinus stood.

"Mel knows this horse's potential and when she says he's a champion, you know she's right. But with the so-called, big ears around, please don't talk about his potential." The statement made James shudder. Suddenly he realised how serious the threat was.

JAMES RODE Provocation into second place in his race at Gosforth Park, near Johannesburg and then went on to win on Warriors Rival.

"This horse, my man — he's a world champion." James's lips stuck together. His mouth dry from the speed Warriors had taken him down the track. Garth grabbed the rein and led them into the winner's enclosure.

Rival whinnied loudly when they arrived back at the stud the following day. Siyanda led him out of the horse carrier. Security guards stood close, armed this time. They'd been posted outside the stables at the Gosforth racecourse too.

Garth stroked Rival's neck and whispered, "And tomorrow, my boy, you'll be spoilt by the Chiropractor and the physio."

"Horses here are different," James walked next to Warriors Rival listening to the welcoming response from the other horses in training. "They are such happy horses. No sirens, no buzz of endless traffic. The calm of this place chills them out. This is how every racehorse should live." James slapped Kgabu on the back. "Hey?"

"For sure, Bru. I'm chuffed you brought your skills and wisdom back here. What a team we have now."

"I'm pleased to be back. And this boy, shit, he's a dream to race. He fucking gives everything he has, right past the post. You ride him next."

"For sure. No question." Before Kgabu left to head home, Garth suggested they all have a bit of a celebration in Durban on Friday night.

Due to strict security measures, Mel and Gary wouldn't permit Garth and James to drive home after a night on the town, so she booked them into the Parade Hotel. Kgabu insisted he'd drive home, not being a drinker. Mel made sure Synthia was happy with his decision. She agreed.

"Drive safely and have a good time." Mel waved them goodbye on Friday afternoon.

Garth spun his sportscar out the driveway. Mel stood on the top step shaking her head.

'Boys,' she uttered under her breath.

GARTH HAD NOTICED her shake her head. "Mum's so protective over us. Watch when Brad gets home tomorrow. It gets worse. Most days she's fine, then something triggers a horrid memory and she's a nervous wreck for a few days."

"Can't say I blame her, Garth. She's been through so much trauma." James said thoughtfully.

"Yeah, she has. I worry about her. We all do. The threat on her life, or one of us, or even more horses being killed or poisoned, is constant and extremely hard to live with. Most of the time I don't think about it, but some days it gets to me too."

James was quiet for a while. The fresh air on his face and the freedom compared to life in the UK he'd forgotten about, but now he relished the lack of restriction. Security followed though.

"Hey bru, two nights ago, I got a prank call?" Garth spun his head, alarmed.

"What kind of prank call?"

"My phone rang twice, then it stopped before I could answer. Five minutes later it rang again. I answered after the fourth ring, worried it might be mum. When I said, 'Hello,' a voice said, 'we are watching you.' I shat myself. I never got back to sleep, plus I didn't sleep well last night either, so if you don't mind, I'm the party-pooper tonight — not a late night for me."

"Heck, James. We need to let Dad know, now. Dial his number from my phone."

"What's the hurry?"

"Just dial my dad." James dialled Gary's number. When he answered, James, handed the phone to Garth. "Dad, I need to pull off the road. Hold on." Garth slowed the car and pulled onto the shoulder. "James had a threatening call on Wednesday night." Garth held the phone away and asked James, "what time was it?"

"Around 2 a.m."

"Did you hear that, Dad?"

"Yes, I did. What was said?"

"The voice said, 'someone is watching you.' This means he's being watched at home." Garth suddenly felt scared.

"Yeah, you're right. I'll get onto Willem now. Keep vigilant, my boy. The security van is following you, right?"

"Yeah, they are behind us." Garth peered in the rearview mirror to make sure.

"Whatever you do, don't get drunk. Drive safely and have fun."

"Thanks, Dad, we will." Garth pulled back onto the motor-way. The security van followed. Garth turned to James. "It's pretty shitty having security following our every move but you can see how vital it is. Sorry you've got caught up in the shit now."

"I had no idea how bad it is." James was worried.

"The impact on our lives is horrendous. I can't get my head around the level of vengeance, aimed directly or indirectly at mum. Dad will arrange extra security. And they'll check your cottage. It's a shit situation and we'll have to watch our backs tonight. I'm surprised Dad didn't ask us to go home."

"This scares me," James said.

"You get used to it. Remember they're after mum, not you. Let's have a good time tonight, but anything peculiar in future, let us know immediately."

They arrived at the Parade hotel, checked in, dumped their bags, and headed to Beach Boys, Garth's favourite pub. Garth called Theresa to join them, but she couldn't make it.

Kgabu called to find out where they were. He them twenty minutes later, but he wasn't in the mood for a party either. The evening turned into a quiet celebration. They outside chatting and listening to the city noises and the waves crashing onto the beach discussing the Chanting Clover security situation.

Every now and again when an attractive girl walked past, Garth let out a loud wolf whistle. Kgabu and James teased him, but soon the conversation reverted to the vendetta against Mel. If James was a target now, they decided to get back to the hotel by ten.

Kgabu stood up. "Sorry guys, I'm going to be a party-pooper. I can't stay awake any longer." James stretched and yawned. "I'm ready."

"Yup, let's head back." Garth downed the last of his beer.

Not even the drinks had relaxed them. They walked Kgabu to his car then Garth and James crossed the road to the hotel. They heard running feet close behind them. Before James had time to turn, he felt the powerful grip of a hand at his throat. Then, almost simultaneously, he felt the thrust of the attacker's knife penetrate deep into his side. Kgabu had seen the attack but too far away to prevent it. He parked and raced across the road to help. James lay on the pavement moaning in pain. Garth took off after the assailant and Kgabu knelt beside James.

The assailant was too fast for Garth and ducked down a side street. Too dark, despite the streetlamps, Garth couldn't get a description of the man's face, except he wore a blue jacket with denim trousers and a balaclava. Garth hurried back to where James lay. Kgabu had already dialled 911. Garth unbuttoned James' shirt and peeled it back.

"Hold my phone, please." Garth handed it to Kgabu while Garth pulled off his shirt, folded it a few times and plugged it into the wound to slow the bleeding.

Kgabu called Steve. The stab wound had gone in deep. It bled profusely. Garth kept James talking as he applied pressure to help ease the flow of blood. People gathered to see if they could help.

"The bastard ran up behind us and rammed a knife into James's side." Kgabu told Steve. Garth could hear the stammer in Kgabu's voice, then he called Gary.

"Did the mugger say anything to James?" Gary asked. Kgabu lent down, "James did the attacker say anything to you?"

"Um... yes.... he said, 'you're a dead man.'"

"It happened so fast, Gary. James said the voice sounded the same as the threatening call he got two nights ago."

"Are you and Garth, okay?"

"Yes, we're fine. The ambulance should be here soon. Garth's trying to stop the bleeding. He sprinted after the attacker, but he was too fast."

"Kgabu, have you seen our security detail?"

"No, we haven't."

Gary was furious. "Where are you exactly?"

"Right opposite the Marine Parade hotel. The ambulance has just arrived, Gary."

"Okay, I'll call back in ten minutes." Gary ended the call. Garth surrendered James to the medics who quickly assessed the wound and lifted James onto the stretcher. The chief medic said, "We're taking him to Addington hospital."

Garth nodded. "We'll follow."

Kgabu called Steve again. "Dad, Garth and I are following the ambulance, meet us at Addington hospital."

As the elevator doors opened on the second floor of the hospital, two policemen stood by. Garth introduced himself and Kgabu.

The taller of the two policemen spoke first. "We've seen the crime scene. Did you see the attacker?"

"Not his face, he was so fast I couldn't catch him. He wore a balaclava, denim jeans and a blue Jacket. That's all I can give you."

The cop made a note. "Pity, he's probably changed from those clothes already."

It wasn't long before Steve and Synthia stepped out the elevator. Synthia wrapped her arms around Kgabu. "Have you called James's mother?" She addressed the question to Garth.

"No, not yet. The Doctor said he'd meet us here once he's out of theatre, then I'll call."

"Good man." Steve squeezed Garth's arm.

"This is the work of that bastard Colonel." Steve said. "And where the hell are the security who're supposed to look out for you."

Garth's mouth was set. He never answered as he contemplated the earlier events. Twenty minutes later two nurses pushed a sleeping James from the lift and the doctor followed.

"Will he live?" Garth asked the doctor.

"Yes, son, he's not badly injured. Fortunately, the stab wound isn't as deep as we first suspected. He's all stitched up. You can call his mother."

"PHEW! Thank you, Doctor." Garth sighed loudly. A few minutes later Gary and Mel arrived.

The doctor greeted them and hurried back to theatre. A car crash victim had been wheeled in.

MEL AND SYNTHIA stayed with Kgabu and Garth at James' bedside for half an hour. Every now again he'd sleepily open his eyes, smile and go back to sleep while Steve and Gary went to the Durban Central Police station. Once the statement was verified, they went back to the hospital and noticed the Prime Security vehicles in the car park.

They were alert and jumpy when Gary approached. They'd not done their job. They'd already been severely reprimanded and given a warning.

"One van to me back to the stud. The other to follow Garth back to the hotel and home in the morning. Is that clear?" Gary stated angrily.

"Yes Sir." One of the guards answered.

Garth visited James the following morning who was sitting up in bed drinking tea when Garth walked into the ward.

"Hi. You look better." Garth could hardly believe how good James looked.

"I'm fine. Bit tender, but I can go home tomorrow. Doc saw me at seven."

"Brilliant news."

"I've let my mum know. She's taken the day off work tomorrow. I'll stay with her for a week, then I'll be back at the farm. Seven days the stitches come out. No riding for another two weeks, doc says." He grimaced, not from the tenderness in his side, but the thought of not riding for almost a month.

"Yeah, that's pretty shitty, but my worry this proves someone knows our every move. Dad needs to question our security company. Anyway, I must head home. I just wanted to make sure you're okay. Let me know when you're with your mum."

"Thanks mate. I'll be fine."

Garth's thoughts were racing as he drove home but smiled when he heard Gary giving someone at Prime Security a piece of his mind. "No fucking excuses, put me through to Willem."

Garth didn't wait to hear the rest, besides Brad was home.

"Hi boet." He gave Brad a brotherly hug. "Is Mum, okay?" Garth asked Brad.

"Not really. She's worried the knife was destined for you, not James."

"It was James who got the threatening call, but someone here has a link to that bastard in Zimbabwe. Our safety is dependent upon the security firm finding the leak as fast as possible."

"Eery, isn't it? That pig Colonel to be assassinated. Everyone knows where he lives. Can't be that hard to take him out, surely?" Garth questioned, using his arms to express his astonishment.

"Well at least James will be with his mum for a week and wasn't badly hurt. Should give Prime Security time to up their game here."

Chapter Sixteen

Solomon reached for his telephone. "You failed, again," he bellowed into the mouthpiece. "What's wrong with you useless idiots. You'd have lost the war for us if we'd relied on types like you."

Nkizwi remained silent. He wanted to say, 'You didn't win the war because of your military prowess, it was all political, arsehole.' He kept his tongue and wondered how much more abuse he could tolerate.

Joseph, the assassin, had been the man recommended by Tanya to kill James. She'd assured Nkizwi and her grandfather he could do the job quickly and efficiently. He was known in Durban as a reliable hitman.

"Nkizwi, Nkizwi, are you there?" Solomon bellowed like a wounded bull.

"Yes, Colonel, I'm here."

"Listen carefully. I've explained this to Tanya, too." He briefed Nkizwi on the next plan. "And this one cannot fail. Do you hear me?"

"Yes, Sir."

Nkizwi put the phone down. He sat for a moment contemplating calling Tanya. He wondered whether he should continue helping with this bizarre revenge mission. The colonel had lost his mind, but he knew if he told Solomon to go to hell, find someone else,

his life would be at risk. He'd got himself caught in the colonel's web.

IN 2006 CHANTING Clover's plans for their two champions to race in America and Dubai had been thwarted by trade union strikes that year.

Thankfully with that behind them and security beefed up to an all-time high they felt safe to delve into the possibilities of pursuing their dream. To follow Horse Chestnut's footsteps. A horse owned by Harry Oppenheimer who was sent to compete in America in 2000. This South African Thoroughbred racehorse, hailed to be the most successful in South African history might be matched by two homebred horses from Chanting Clover. The thought caused a welcome surge of excitement.

The colt, Warriors Rival had wowed crowds across South Africa, breaking many track time records. 17.1hands of power, class and nobility. A dark bay Thoroughbred with spectacular cadence. He seemed to float over the racetracks and like the going, but he'd also proved himself when the going was soft, but he didn't like it wet.

The filly, Tsotsi, Chanting Clover's other rising star, born at the end of August 2005 and named after the famous, award-winning film. A bright red bay with black points. 16 hands and so striking it was hard to take your eyes off her when she pranced daintily around the parade rings at courses across the country. I a relatively short time she'd become the tote darling and

Mel had a massive soft spot for her.

In May 2007, she won the Pietermaritzburg Fillies Sprint in spectacular style. Not unlike the famous Oscar-winning film, Chanting Clover's Tsotsi was destined for great things. When she won the Ipi Tombie Challenge for fillies and mares in a jaw-dropping performance Mel knew in her gut, she could take on any filly, worldwide. But her brilliance exposed her as target for Solomon's grudge against Mel. The sooner the two horses left South Africa, the better.

In early 2008, Gary, Mel and Tinus sat browsing through the rules and guidelines for taking South African horses across the seas.

Mel's concern was whether the horses had enough time to acclimatise in Mauritius before March 2009, when the first races begin in the Dubai season. They took their guidelines from those who'd done it before. A compulsory quarantine period in the Western Cape lasted six-weeks then they could be flown to Mauritius for a minimum of three months training before going on to Dubai.

"It's going to be a bit of a squeeze," Mel said, glancing at Gary and Tinus. "The thought of having Warriors Rival and Tsotsi run in two of the richest horse races in the world makes me tingle with anticipation. Look at my arms, they're already covered in goosebumps." She rubbed them away.

"If the horses perform well in Dubai, they'll race in France in October in the famous Prix de L'Arc de Triomphe. What an honour that would be." Gary said. Tinus clapped enthusiastically.

"Six weeks in quarantine and three months in Mauritius before the horses are permitted to compete in Dubai is tough on our horses. Once Mel and I get back, Tinus, you will join them."

"I'd like that. I think young Garth will pressurise you for a week or two there too." Tinus grinned. He'd never travelled out of South Africa before.

"Not just Garth, Brad too. At some point they'll be after a chance to see how it all operates on the island. Brad is so busy with extra-curricular events at school, but you can bet he'd jump at the chance to get to Mauritius and Dubai. He's said he wants to travel when he finishes school at the end of this year."

"Shall I book the horses into quarantine for the first week in August?"

Gary glanced at Mel. Their eyes spoke.

"Yes. Thanks, Tinus." They answered simultaneously.

Gary stretched his arms above his head. "I never thought it would be such a process getting our horses overseas, but it'll be worth it."

"For sure, Gary. These two are spectacular." Tinus admitted both horses were the best he'd ever worked with, but before they headed to the Western Cape, they had the feature race at the Durban July to run.

Provocation and Warriors Rival were the two Chanting Clover horses running in the feature race and Tsotsi in the third race. Dashing Clover and Silver Flame were running in the fourth race and Leap of Faith and Red Clover in their maiden race. An outstanding line-up of Chanting Clover's homebred talent.

This 2008 Durban July was an unexpected mix, like a bag of Liquorice All Sorts.

Jeremy offered Brad a modelling assignment that fell on the day. Mel didn't hide her disappointment.

Garth collapsed laughing when he saw what Brad was to

model. "Fuck, boet, don't let Mum see those clothes before the day. She'll forbid you from modelling them."

"They're ridiculous, aren't they, but I don't care. It's only an hour of making a fool of myself, and the money is good." Brad pointed out.

And Warriors Rival and Tsotsi competed for favourite in the odds.

Because of the modelling contract Brad left home the day before the big race day. Jeremy required all the models to practice on the ramp at the course. Before he left home he begged Mel to wear a glamorous designer dress he'd chosen for her. She was hesitant, but she eventually agreed and when he met up with the family in the Owners and Trainers Lounge, he saw his mother had the outfit on. He wanted to cry, she looked so beautiful.

Without trying, she takes centre stage, Brad thought proudly. Brad had chosen an eye-catching, elegant, mid-calf, figure-hugging white dress with black trim, worn with an elegant wide brimmed black hat trimmed with white braid, elbow length black gloves and elegant black court shoes.

"Mum, you look drop-dead gorgeous." He gazed at his beautiful mother. "You look like you've just stepped out of Vogue magazine, and I love the way you've done your hair," he whistled. Her long auburn locks tumbled over her shoulders in gentle waves to the middle of her back.

"Dad, I'm so touched you dressed to match Mum. This is a first, and we've been coming to the July since I was born. You two are the most handsome couple here today."

Gary wore a white suit with black trim, black shoes, and a black shirt. The suit jacket was a casual cut and highlighted his father's good looks and Garth agreed.

"Hmmm. Very sassy." He said, rubbing his chin.

"Oh, stop it you two." Mel suddenly felt self-conscious.

Later in the day they were voted the best-dressed owners and trainers. Mel loathed being thrust into the limelight. Essentially, a private person, but more importantly she felt frighteningly exposed for they would appear in newspapers across the country and on Television. She told Brad she'd never dress up again.

When Steve and Synthia arrived, they were also in matching outfits.

Synthia wore a beautiful bright amber, black and cream off the shoulder calf-length dress. A bold fusion of symmetrical patterns and around her slim waist, she wore a thick black leather belt with gold buckle detail. Against her dark skin she too looked every bit a super-model. Steve wore a pair of black slacks with a cheerful, Madiba-style shirt in the same colours as Synthia's dress.

Chanting Clover's fillies achieved second and fourth place in the first race. Leap of Faith galloped into first place in the second race. Steve and Synthia erupted in loud cheer and hurried down to lead Kgabu into the winner's enclosure.

Tsotsi, the racing darling won the third race, winning by three lengths. When Gary and Mel led her in, photographers surrounded them. The contrast of the white and black ensemble worn by them both, and Tsotsi's striking red bay body and black points made a perfect picture of the type of class one expects to see on a day like this, comparable to Ascot.

"Oh ma'am, they're celebrating at the stables too." Siyanda beamed.

"She's a gem, isn't she?" Siyanda handed the rein to Gary.

John McIntosh won the fifth race on Silver Flame. A flashy, silver dapple grey. John's first official race since his return from

Australia. He punched the air with his fist as he pulled the horse up and turned him back toward the grandstand.

The afternoon had gone so well and soon Gary and Mel, Brad and Garth, Synthia and Steve stood beneath the canopy of ancient trees in the centre of the parade ring watching the beautiful Warriors Rival strut around.

"I feel the same excitement today as I did all those years ago when Wind Power won the feature race." Mel steepled her hands and sent up a little prayer and gave Kgabu a thumbs up when Siyanda lifted him into the saddle.

"I'm not sure how to translate what I'm feeling right now." Synthia said. Her mouth quivered slightly, and she swallowed hard.

"Oh gosh, Synthia, I fully understand. My stomach's in a tight knot."

Once the horses left the arena the team hurried back to the Owners and Trainer's lounge.

The luminous green and white diamonds, Chanting Clover's racing colours, showed nicely through binoculars. Mel felt sure her pulse raced at the same speed as her horses. Provocation was running well mid-field. Warriors Rival gained ground skimming over the turf like a fighter jet and soon led the field to generous applause.

Excitement filled the stadiums. Even the grandstands vibrated with the encouraging chant which Warriors Rival seemed to respond to and crossed the line in winning style. The crowds were on their feet shouting and screaming waving their winning tickets about and throwing their racing forms in the air.

He'd just broken the track record that had stood unbroken for eleven years.

"It will be an even greater horse to beat today's record." Mel shouted as she made her way down the stairs holding onto Gary's arm.

"He's going to show them all in Dubai. Mark my words." Garth shouted as he took the stairs two at a time.

Siyanda and Johnny waited at the rails, ready to grab the rein of the champion and hand him over to his breeders and trainers. Gary and Mel were joined by Garth, Brad, Synthia, Steve and Tinus. It was a momentous occasion for them all and Kgabu was speechless from emotion.

A few tears escaped, which he wiped away then patted Warrior's neck. "The best ride I've ever had, Gary. He knew exactly what to do. I was just the passenger. There's nothing to compare the thrill of riding a Thoroughbred at top speed into first place in a race like this."

"That's for sure. Did you hear you broke the speed of sound," Gary laughed. Kgabu wasn't sure what he meant to begin with.

"Did we break the time record?" Kgabu asked, shocked.

"You didn't just beat it you smashed it. Best time in eleven years." Gary told him. He dropped both arms down the sides of Warriors neck and kissed his mane. "What a boyki," he shouted.

The happy group left the course that evening and slowly travelled home, exhausted, blissfully happy and a little intoxicated.

Security tailed them.

THE FRIDAY FOLLOWING the July race, the two champions were trucked to Touws River in the Western Cape where they'd spend six weeks in quarantine before flying to Mauritius.

"The dream has officially commenced," Tinus patted Mel

on the back and jumped into the driver's seat after loading the horses.

"Drive safely. Security will meet you at the crossroads and follow you there and back. Let me know when you get there," Mel told Tinus and checked he had everything. "You've got all their travel permits and logbooks?"

"Yes, Thomas popped it all in the cubbyhole." Tinus opened the passenger door and jumped in.

Seventeen hours later Tinus parked in the offloading zone at the Lettas Kraal Equine Quarantine station and called Mel.

"We've arrived. Horses travelled well."

"Thanks for letting me know, Tinus. Let me know when you are on your way back."

"Will do."

The quarantine station, situated in the only Africa Horse sickness free area in South Africa and chosen purposefully as the quarantine area for horses travelling abroad or coming into South Africa.

African Horse sickness, a truly horrible killer disease carried by the Culicoides midge. Tinus and Thomas led the horses to their stables, handed in their logbooks and travel permits, and drove into town. They grabbed a bit to eat and found a cheap B&B for the night and after a hot cup of coffee the next morning they set of home. The return journey was considerably faster when not towing millions of Rands worth of precious cargo.

That evening Mel sipped on her favourite Nederburg Cabinet Sauvignon in front of a roaring fire that glowed in the sitting room fireplace. The temperature outside had dropped to zero and Tinus and Thomas were home safely.

"This is really a nod to Mike de Kock." She raised her wine glass. "He's the person who turned racing around for us South

Africans in Dubai." She took another sip. "He achieved well deserved recognition across the world. I think our security situation, because of me, holds you back, my darling." She whispered sadly.

"It's not your fault, my angel. But I agree, here's to Mike," Gary raised his beer glass. Though Gary had often felt hindered by the vendetta, he'd never say so. Besides the setbacks, they'd done well having won Breeder of the Year status twice. Once when Iris Paige was alive, then eight years later under Mel's management. Gary had been in the running for Trainer of the Year twice, and their horses had broken many records. What more could they ask for?

"Here's to you, my love. The entrepreneur of the family. The next step, Mauritius." Gary too another sip which underlined his nose with white froth. "There must be millions of Rands' worth of South African horses in Mauritius being trained on the beaches and over the sand tracks that run through the forests. I'm certainly looking forward to seeing it all and learning the process first-hand."

"Yes, me too. Very exciting. I still pinch myself and remind myself that it's real. That it's happening. I don't mean to put a damper on our celebrations, but has extra security been put in place for the two horses at Lettas Kraal?"

"All taken care of, my love. Rest assured, there will never be another one of our horses slain or poisoned, anywhere on this planet and God help anyone who tries." Gary meant it. His jaw jutted and he held his mouth tight feeling the tension in his chin.

Chapter Seventeen

MAURITIUS WAS everything Gary and Mel had expected. An exquisite tropical island with crystal clear, ice-blue seas and golden beaches, fringed with an assortment of palm trees and tropical flora. The change they needed.

"I was reading that the racetrack in Port Louis is the oldest in the southern hemisphere. Did you know that?" Mel asked Gary as the taxi took them to their hotel.

"No, I didn't. How interesting. I can't wait to see the facilities, and our horses, of course." A relaxed, serene expression covered Mel's face. A look Gary remembered from bygone years. Secure and deeply happy far from the threat of Solomon.

Gary opened the car door and collected the luggage from the taxi boot and paid the driver.

As they walked into the cool reception area of the Summer Breeze hotel Mel chatted about her recent Mauritius racing research. Her cheerful banter reminded him of their honeymoon in Rome. Mel unpacked while Gary spoke to Chase, their Mauritian trainer.

By the sound of Gary's brief conversation, their horses had arrived safely. Chase D'Aboville, the trainer, French by birth, had come highly recommended. He'd grown up on a vineyard in the south of France. The horse bug bit him as a teenager, and shortly after leaving school his grandfather passed away, leaving the Mauritian estate and small private racehorse training centre, to Chase.

He'd flown out for the funeral. He'd fallen in love with the island when he'd visited as a child. He'd desperately wanted to live on the island, until he met his aristocratic wife, Adrienne. Together they flew to Mauritius for Adrienne to view the property, but she refused to live in Mauritius. Chase had to pursue his dream so after many years they compromised. Adrienne would visit, but she insisted on staying in France to run their vineyard and winery. Adrienne, a lovely French aristocrat, happened to be in residence when Gary called to speak to Chase.

Mel was curious. "So, what did Chase have to say?"

"He congratulated us on our horses' beautiful manners and said he looked forward to working with our team. All expressed in a broad French accent." Gary smiled. "When I said we'd get a taxi to his property, he said, 'Non, non, on vous trouve un taxi. We'll send our driver to fetch you. No taxi. Stay with us tomorrow night, s'il te plaît.'" Mel listened, amazed. She never knew Gary could speak a little French.

"Wow! Where did you learn French?" She chuckled.

"Aaah, oui, oui, merci beaucoup." I replied in my best schoolboy French. He winked at Mel. "Then Chase asked if I speak French. I disappointed him by saying that I only remember a few phrases, short sentences and the odd random word."

Chase politely responded. "Ah ha, I see. Ok, c'est pas grave

— that's alright." Gary repeated Chase's words and Mel laughed at Gary who'd put on his best French accent.

"We've got the afternoon to ourselves, sweetheart. Let's explore the shops and meander along the beach."

"Excellent idea. Synthia has taught me how to shop and I quite enjoy it now." A wicked grin rose on her face.

Mel rarely spent money on herself, so Gary tapped his shorts pocket. "Wallet's here and you deserve to spend what you like, my love." He picked her up and kissed her lovingly. They were feeling relaxed. Enjoying a long-forgotten freedom.

Their immersive shopping experience combined traditional markets, modern malls and vibrant street scenes, but they'd started at the Central Market, a bustling hub filled with locals and tourists, then they went on to explore Le Caudan Waterfront at the harbour. In this stylish shopping complex Mel found some lovely boutiques and spent a fortune, but when they sat munching on a local dholl puri – the islands flat bread filled with a taste of Creole-Indian delicacies, Mel looked at Gary, "I feel guilty for spending such a lot of money." Gary took now notice. He held his flatbread to his mouth and looked at her. She burst out laughing, half of the innards were spilling out the side.

They dropped the bags in their hotel room and ended the day with a long walk along the beach watching the sun set over the ocean.

They arrived at Chase's magnificent training centre after breakfast.

Chase, short in stature with finely chiselled features, salt and pepper grey hair, and deeply tanned skin rushed over to greet Gary and Mel and paid the taxi he'd arranged.

A maid had followed and gathered up their suitcases.

Adrienne stood at the grand entrance to the gabled, colonial style homestead and graciously descended the sweeping stairway to the bottom step and greeted the Whitakers in French. Despite the haughty welcome, Chase was quick to explain she spoke little English.

Adrienne's dark hair, swept neatly back in a French plait, wore a bright yellow kaftan and round her neck was a sting of large white beads. Mel had seen the same type of Kaftan's in the shops. She'd been tempted to buy one. Seeing Adrienne look so cool and carefree in hers, Mel decided to buy one when they ventured back into the city.

Mel stole a surreptitious look around as they wandered through the grand hall, tiled in a traditional black and white checkerboard pattern. Mel turned to Adrienne. "What a beautiful home you have." She acknowledged the compliment in French as they stepped onto the veranda.

"What a stunning view."

Adrienne motioned for Mel to take a seat. Gary and Chase followed. They were in deep conversation about training schedules.

A kidney-shaped swimming pool hugged the edged of the veranda. Shimmering crystal-clear water twinkled invitingly, beckoning hot, sweaty bodies to take a refreshing plunge. An expertly crafted bamboo deck on one edge of the pool where Adrienne had her favourite potted palms, exotic strelitzia and other tropical plants Mel had never seen before. Vast expanses of manicured lawns stretched beneath ancient Royal Cuban and Queen palms, extending all the way to the edge of the beach.

The lady who'd swiftly whisked away their cases appeared on the veranda like a ghost. She wore a crisp, perfectly starched white uniform that highlighted her lovely coffee-coloured complexion. She carried a silver tray with four tall crystal glasses filled with island punch, decorated with fresh mint and colourful paper umbrellas. A thin slice of pineapple embraced the rim. She placed the tray on the table next to Adrienne and vanished.

Adrienne offered Mel a glass before taking one for herself. "Thank you for making us feel so at home, and for taking care of our staff. Siyanda will be joined by our special jockey, Kgabu, tomorrow."

Adrienne smiled demurely and crossed her legs at the ankles. "Avec plaisir." She replied, sipping her cocktail. Adrienne's lack of conversation made Mel feel uncomfortable, but in every other way, the perfect, gracious host.

AFTER THEIR WELCOMING cocktail they walked along the pathway at the back of the house that led to the stables. The D'Aboville Training Centre. Twenty-two horses were housed there. Two of them belonged to the Whitakers. Mel couldn't wait to see them.

Because the yard was smaller than most, Chase was able to spend valuable time with each horse and was the main reason they chose Chase as their trainer.

The stables were not more than a five-minute ride from a quiet stretch of beach where they took the horses every morning.

As if on cue, Tsotsi and Warriors Rival were looking out over their stable doors, alert and interested, they'd recognised familiar voices. When they saw Gary and Meel approach, they whinnied. Mel kissed each one on the soft velvety part of their nose. Chase found it amusing. Gary explained it was Mel's tradition.

"In Mel's research, she tells me that Le Champ de Mars racecourse is the oldest in the Southern Hemisphere. Is that so?"

"Oui, oui. Tous sais. Because the French and English have spent many generations at loggerheads with each other." Chase wore a crooked smile. "In 1812, a British colonel, Edward Alured Draper, designed the racecourse and introduced horseracing to an effort to unite the French population with the English, through leisure for nothing else worked. This did. Ca a marché grâce à l'anglais, thanks to the Englishman they formed the Mauritius Turf Club. The first race was held at the small Le Champ de Mars track, which, over the years, has been upgraded, but it's still a very narrow track which limits the number of entrants for any race." Chase explained.

While Chase and Gary chatted, Mel wandered through the stables, enjoying the peace and tranquillity of the D'Aboville estate, draped by towering palms and other exotic trees.

Siyanda joined Mel on her walkabout.

"This is like heaven." They wandered around looking at the other horses. Siyanda couldn't stop talking about the island, more especially, riding on the beach. Siyanda would remain on the D'Aboville property for the next three months, then he'd accompany the horses on the flight to Dubai and stay there with them.

The following morning the quiet, ghostly lady in white knocked on Gary and Mel's bedroom door at 5 a.m., crept in carrying a tray with hibiscus tea and homemade biscuits and like ghosts do, disappeared again. Mel found her silence eery.

At six they followed seven horses to the beach.

Despite his previous daily walks to the beach, Warriors Rival still found the sounds of the ocean, and the rushing and residing of the frothy water, frightening. Not even a lead from the bold and brave Tsotsi, who loved being in the sea encouraged him in, but after a lot of snorting and pawing at the sand Warrior finally conceded. Only because Mel led him into the shallow waves and reassured him that nothing was going to leap out of the sea and gobble him up.

"Parfait!" Chase stated as he observed Mel.

"He adores Mel, as you can see," Gary said proudly.

"Beaux chevaux. Beaux chevaux," Chase shook his head. "Magnifique." He bunched the fingers of his right hand and kissed the tips, then sent the kiss into the air. "Such quality, and your wife is brilliant with the horse."

"She's that with way with all of them."

Chase smiled at Gary. He understood.

The next ten days seemed to pass in a blur. Chase introduced them to trainers, farriers, vets, and other owners. He took them to the Guy Desmarais Training Centre situated on a high plateau with stunning views of the ocean and the island. It was considerably cooler on the plateau than down at sea level. Chase often boxed the horses to the forest tracks, especially when they arrived after long stressful flights. They acclimatised quicker up there.

When they got back, Kgabu, Steve and Synthia had arrived. Kgabu was introduced to Chase and Adrienne. Like Siyanda, Kgabu would be living at the D'Aboville training centre in the workers rooms, built in a row the wooden building was on stilts. There was also a circular bar, dining and lounge area with a pool table, darts and other board games and bookcases filled with racing books to keep them occupied in the evening. All meals were prepared for them in a kitchen not far from the circular building. Like everything else at the D'Aboville training centre, it was stylish and comfortable. Now wonder Siyanda said it was heaven, Mel smiled to herself.

Neither the Whitakers nor the Dube's wanted to leave the island after ten days. They envied Kgabu and Siyanda.

Synthia cried when she hugged Kgabu and said goodbye. "It's going to be a lonely three months without you, my boy." Kgabu held his mother tight, then shook hands with Steve. "Cheers dad."

"Dr Richard Stevens will join you two days before you fly to Dubai." Gary said holding Kgabu's hand after the handshake then he shook Siyanda's hand. "Keep our horses in tip top shape."" He patted Siyanda on the back knowing Siyanda would die for the two for them.

Mel turned to Chase. "Thank you for everything." Chase bowed his head and opened the taxi door for her.

"Au revoir." He kissed the top of her hand.

Chapter Eighteen

IT WAS Brad's final day at school. The parents gathered in the hall for the farewell assembly. Gary, Mel and Garth took their seats.

"I wonder if Brad will miss school." Garth leant in close to Mel.

"I doubt it. He'll be like you. Eager to get on with his life." She nudged him gently in the side.

As deputy head boy, a competitive sportsman who represented his school in tennis, swimming, gymnastics, and cricket and excelled in his academics, he'd get a mention from the headmaster, just as Garth had.

"I love this school and all its rich history and tradition. I'm going to miss coming here." Mel commented. "I think this school has the most beautiful grounds in the country."

"Well, it's one of the finest schools in South Africa." Garth whispered, a proud ex-student. "And it gave Brad and I an incredible education and the old boy network is fabulous. Traditions and standards are vital in this modern world."

Sounding more like his dad than Mel had heard before. She wanted to say something but didn't for the final year students filed into the hall.

Proud parents turned to look as they walked in and stood at the back of the hall, then the headmaster, Mr Sharp, entered from the side of the stage and stood at the lectern while the teachers filed in from both sides of the stage and stood behind him.

The gathered parents stood as the headmaster welcomed everyone, then invited them to take their seats after the singing of the national anthem and the reciting of the Lord's prayer.

The 2008 final year students remained standing. Mr. Sharp announced the 2009 prefects to loud applause and called the current head boy and deputy to the stage.

Eric Sinclair and Brad stood on the stage while Mr. Sharp praised their achievements, saying he hoped the new Head boy and Deputy head would uphold the same standards that Eric and Brad had. The parents and students clapped. Eric and Brad left the stage and took their positions at the back of the hall.

Mr Sharp then gave a brief history of the final year students' achievements. "I know you all want to get out of here, so I won't go on talking, but let me end in wishing you all a very successful future."

Everyone clapped and a hum of conversation followed the parents and students as they filed out of the hall.

Gary, Mel and Garth wandered back to the car and collected Brad from Founders. The boarding house Brad had resided in for the last five years.

"It's good to see the old hostel again," Garth said as they parked.

Brad was waiting, sitting on his suitcase, with his extra

luggage at his feet. He'd already said 'cheers' to his mates after assembly.

Brad whipped open the car boot and flung his bags and case inside and slammed it shut.

"Whoopee," he shouted, handed his laptop to Garth and jumped into the back seat. "I'm actually going to miss this school, even though I'm chuffed my school years are over." He took a long deep breath. "I feel so lucky to have attended this school, don't you boet?"

"For sure. We're all going to miss it. It's thanks to you two special parents for providing us the chance to be educated here." Garth squeezed his mum's shoulders. "It must feel quite surreal to think this is the last time you'll ever do a school run?"

"I'm sad at the thought," Mel admitted.

"It certainly has been a wonderful place for you Brad, and you've excelled here. We're enormously proud of both of you." Gary turned the key in the ignition. "The friends you've made here will be with you forever."

Gary drove slowly out of the school grounds and took the scenic route home from Balgowan, where Michaelhouse school was situated. So much of the drive reminded Gary and Mel of parts of rural England. Early British settlers had planted English oaks, London Plane, Maple, Ash and Sycamore and other imported tree varieties in bygone years. At the end of November, the countryside was a feast of lush greens, and the sides of the roads littered with an assortment of indigenous flowers and shrubs.

When they arrived home, James was there to meet them.

"Hey, bud, feels good to be an adult, hey?" James shook Brad's hand.

"Yeah. Feels weird. Howzit, James." Then John appeared.

"Good'ay, mate." He shot Brad with his broad Australian

accent.

"Howzit, John. Jeez, that bloody accent blows my mind." Brad laughed.

"Aah, easy to pick up, mate. I've bloody well been there for three years. But hey, it's good to see ya. Finished ya school days and all? Good on ya, mate."

It was times like these, with the house full of young people, Mel felt alive and re-energised.

Their time in Mauritius made her realise she had to hand more of the admin over and get back into the saddle. Even start work riding again with her sons. Boring routine had never been good for her.

"One big happy team all gathered to welcome you home." Gary remarked and patted Brad on the back. "Has it sunk in yet? School is over, forever?"

"No, it hasn't. Guess it will take a while."

"It takes a few days, Boet." Garth remembered those first few days home.

Jovial conversation continued as the group of young men who'd grown up together, were re-united.

Mel sighed, irritated by the interruption of the phone ringing in the hall. Brad ran to answer it. "The Whitaker residence."

"My, my, my! Now isn't that the luck?" Jeremy's effeminate voice blurted in Brad's ear.

"Hello Jeremy. What can I do for you?" Brad asked.

"I have a few assignments for you and Garth, but before I explain, congratulations on finishing school."

"Thanks, Jeremy. So, tell me, what are the assignments?"

"They're in Italy. Can I tickle your interest?" He chuckled hopefully.

"Italy? Yeah, I'm keen. Not sure about Garth. It's best you

speak to him yourself. When and what's the deal?"

"I'll fax it through. Please call me on Monday and let me know."

"Will do. Thanks for considering me." Brad hurried back to join the others.

"So, what did Jeremy want?" Garth asked as Brad sat.

"He's got two contracts for us in Italy. Five days on a yacht near Naples, then in Rome, Pisa, and Florence. Gucci, Versace, the whole shooting match. Top Brands. Rome, your favourite city, Mum. All flights paid. Three thousand US for the time on the yacht, and twelve thousand for the other days. All flights, hotels and meals paid for. Bloody amazing deal. Fifteen thousand US$ for twelve days. Fucking awesome, I'd say. Jeremy will fax it through just now and you can have a look."

"When?" Garth asked, tempted by the money. Mel frowned.

"I've just told you. He's faxing it through just now."

"No, Brad. When does the assignment start?"

"Oh! 3rd of January. Ma, can I go?" Brad looked at her with pleading eyes. Brad fancied earning that amount of money at the beginning of the year. Converted in Rand, it could not be easier money. He'd never get that amount of money in South Africa unless he did something illegal for twelve days.

Mel always loved the expression he'd just shown. "You're a free man, Brad. You can officially start working with us on 1st of February. How does that sound?"

"Great, Ma. Thanks. I'll let Jeremy know. And you, Garth?"

"Not a shit, Boet. I'm done with modelling. The money is tempting, but I'm not working for that twat again, besides I have college to complete." Mel was relieved.

Gary arrived back from the stallion barn while everyone was reading through the fax. "Sounds like I've missed something."

Chapter Nineteen

MALPENSA AIRPORT, from the air, looked enormous. Way bigger than our Johannesburg airport, Brad thought, staring out the aircraft window. In his imagination he'd expected bright blue skies, forgetting January is winter in Europe.

The Alps were covered in snow — a spectacular sight from the air, with the early morning sun peeping through the clouds on the horizon. The brilliant rays of light turned the mountain tops dazzling white. A dramatic and awe-inspiring sight. Though he'd seen snow on the Drakensburg mountains and played in it as a small boy, he'd not seen it like this, or from the air.

"Amazing," he turned to Barbara, one of the Katz models who sat beside him. "Now I know where the phrase, 'snow white' comes from."

"Do you think Jeremy will let us ski?"

"Ski?" Brad asked, amazed. "Do you know how to ski?"

"Yes, I do. The last time Jeremy brought us here, we did a lot of skiing. We were here for a month."

"Gee, lucky you," Brad whistled. The intercom pinged, the captain announced the flight was on time and would be landing in five minutes. He wished everyone an enjoyable stay in Italy. Then the chief stewardess announced the normal blurb about seatbelts and cellular phones in Italian and English.

When the plane parked, Brad, Barbara, Joanna, and Eric unclipped their seatbelts, gathered their bags from the overhead compartments, and waited for Jeremy. A few minutes later he opened the toilet door, the light above pinged green, much the same colour as Jeremy's face. Jeremy wasn't good at flying, and the landing made him nauseous and panicky.

"Follow me to passport control," Jeremy said to the group once he composed himself. "Stick together, my lovelies. It's a big airport."

They passed through immigration and took the Malpensa Express into Milan. The train took them to the city centre, twenty-five miles north of the airport. Jeremy had booked the models into the Station Hotel for the first night and they weren't impressed. Jeremy was meeting an old friend from his early modelling days in Milan.

"We have no say, let's just go with the flow, he's paying," Brad said to the three whinging girls.

"Yeah, I guess, except he could've put us on a direct flight to Naples." Then, as if they could see the thought passing through her mind, she laughed, "how the hell Jeremy ever became a model, only the Lord knows."

Jeremy left them in the hotel, and he went off to visit his friend. It was the perfect opportunity for a group gossip guessing what kind of person Jeremy's friend was like which made for an amusing evening of Jeremy related charades.

"Gee, you girls are cruel." Brad was glad he wasn't the topic of attack.

The Station Hotel offered quick access for the trip south to Naples the following day. The first assignment was being shot on board a fancy yacht moored at R.Y.C.C Savoia and owned by another friend of Jeremy's. He certainly had friends in all the right places, Brad thought. This first shoot, a nautical flavoured Versace and Gucci brands. The South African models were always sought after, and Jeremy knew how to choose the right ones for particular brands.

Another group of Italian models, doing a different assignment, were using the same yacht.

"Fok, those Italians are baai mooi," Joanna said, using a mix of Afrikaans, her mother tongue, and English, but even her garish sense of humour that always came out of her mouth in a mix of the two languages didn't manage to keep them entertained while they waited their turn on the yacht."

"I hate sitting around. I'm going to ask Jeremy if we can explore. Who's with me?" Brad asked.

Everyone put their hands up. As much a Jeremy didn't want to relent, Brad finally got his way. "We must stick together, guys. We could easily get lost, and I don't want to get into trouble."

"Let's check out the streets and alleyways. Ja, we S'efricans could get helluva lost, you know." Joanna said in her strong Afrikaans accent.

They took a taxi into the city centre, clambered out and stood gaping.

Once again Joanna had them all in hysterics. "Fok, check out that statue," Joanna pointed. "Just somma a leaf to cover the mooi bits."

Brad unfolded the map.

"Jeremy said the city centre is filled with majestic old architecture, monuments and fountains, and loads of little trinket shops." Barbara reminded the group but after studying the map for a few minutes they agreed to pay for a guide, otherwise they would get lost. They followed the map to the big 'I' and secured a guide. They all contributed to the cost.

Joanna, the group clown kept every body's spirits up while they absorbed the glorious, chaotic history of the 4000-year-old city. Even the guide's spirits were lifted by her. He liked Joanna, her rough accent and her exotic beauty he stood close to her while he spoke. Joanna lapped up the attention.

"Mount Vesuvius is dormant, not extinct. It looks down on the bay and reminds us of its potential for destruction." The guide spoke briefly about the destruction of the famous Roman town of Pompeii.

"Sjoe, imagine being buried under molten lava," Joanna commented and rested her head on the guide's shoulder who gazed at her longingly.

Brad laughed, "You wouldn't have known, Joanna."

"Ja, true, Brad." She chuckled, realising what a stupid state-ment she'd made.

They said goodbye to the tour guide who quickly kissed Joanna and gave her his phone number.

The four lugged their bags of souvenirs back to the marina and got back at six.

Jeremy hovered, like a broody mother-hen.

The two days of modelling on board the yacht Brad found thoroughly boring and thankfully they were now on their way to Rome.

IN ROME they modelled a new summer range for men and women by Valentino. Brad modelled the men's casual wear, showing off his perfect build, tanned shapely arms and a well-defined six-pack.

The hairdresser fell in love with Brad the instant he saw his emerald-green eyes twinkling like gems under the glaring studio lights. The photographer couldn't get enough of young Brad and the dimples on either side of his mouth when he smiled. Brad was brilliant in front of the camera. His natural, authentic ways shone through, nothing ever appeared put on or false, and the ladies in Rome begged for this sun-idol's attention when they crowded around during the first assignment at the Colosseum.

From Rome, they travelled by coach to Florence, and finally finished on the lawns below Pisa, then took the guided tour up the Tower. Because of Jeremy's friend, they had to trek all the way back to Milan and catch their flight home and by this time the travel weary ladies were snarky, sarcastic and hormonal. Brad felt sorry for Jeremy for he was their target.

Brad was the only happy one. He'd met Indigo, a stunning American ramp model, raised on a Thoroughbred stud farm in Kentucky. She spoke Brad's language, in more ways than one.

Indigo Hughes swept Bradley Whitaker off his feet. Her parent's had a large farm, home to ninety Thoroughbreds, situated twenty miles south of Lexington, Kentucky. They'd instantly clicked. The zingy chemistry was tantalising, but they only had three days together before the South African group flew home. They promised to stay in touch.

On the flight home, Brads thoughts were filled with Indigo, but he also began to think like Garth. He loathed the fuss of make-up artists, hairdressers, irritated photographers, snobby directors, glaring lights, Jeremy in a flap most of the time, bitchy girls, train trips, hotels, and endless flights. It certainly wasn't a romantic profession. Bloody hard work and exhausting.

. . .

Brad's phone pinged constantly as Indigo sent endless pictures of barns and horses and foals and her parents. Brad responded by doing the same.

"I love the name Chanting Clover." She typed back. "The name of our farm is Brook's End. It belonged to my paternal grandfather and his father before that. It's been owned by six generations of the same family since 1849."

And a whole lot more photos came through.

Garth stood behind his brother. "Shit Brad, she's fucking gorgeous," he commented and playfully grabbed the phone away from his brother to get a closer look and zoom in on the tall, blonde American lass.

"She is, isn't she. She's fun, has an awesome sense of humour, and is a down-to-earth farm girl. She made the last three days in Europe, wonderful. She models to earn extra money, much like us. She wants her own horses one day. Her Dad told her if she wants horses, she must buy them. Apparently, her brother will be taking over the farm. Family tradition. She says her father is a male chauvinist and wouldn't hear of her running it."

"Oh boy, one of those types, is he?" Garth commented. "Tits to die for though, Boet," he teased, and Brad seized the phone back.

"Hey, no need to be rude." Brad said sternly.

"So, my boet, did you do it with her. Like lose your virginity, my man?"

"No, sadly not." Brad demeanour instantly changed.

"Pity. Long-distance relationships never last, so maybe it's just as well." In that moment Garth remembered Theresa explaining the orgies they'd had with Jeremy masturbating on the side. "No orgies while you were away. Jeremy enjoys them."

"Hey, Boet. What kind of bloke do you think I am? Joanna told me that once Cindy left the agency, the orgies calmed down. Theresa still gets top positions. Not sex positions, Garth, modelling positions. She's been overseas plenty of times and is making good money now. You should have hung in there, boet." Brad joked.

"Not a shit. A sweet girl, but not for me. I see her all over Facebook and we chat regularly. We're still good friends."

"I guess she's still nurturing a broken heart."

Garth didn't comment.

"Hey, Indigo is a good contact to have in the US. Especially if Mum and Dad start sending horses over there."

"Yeah, that's for sure. She's asked if she can come over here and stay with us for a few weeks, which is cool."

"Hey, does she have a sister?" Garth asked.

"As a matter of fact, she does, but she's five years your junior." Garth looked disappointed. "What are you going to spend all those dollars on?"

"Property for sure."

"Property? What kind of property would you get for that? Some shitty little bedsit in Berea?" Garth laughed.

"You'd be surprised. I've seen what I want. An up-market, one-bedroom apartment. I have more than two thirds deposit and I'll rent it out. Someone else can pay the rest of the mortgage."

"Good idea. So, when's the beautiful Indigo going to grace us with her presence?" Garth wanted to meet the blonde bombshell.

"In a few weeks. She has to help her father with horses going to the sales first. Maybe Easter?"

Chapter Twenty

VALENTINE'S DAY with two good looking sons in the house caused non-stop ringing of telephones. Eventually Mel couldn't take any more and by lunch her mood was prickly and unlike her. When the house phone rang after lunch, she grabbed the receiver, almost dropping it and raised her voice. "Hellooo," she answered, her jaw held tight made her voice low and raspy.

"Hello, am I speaking to Mrs. Melonie Whitaker?" A softly spoken woman's voice asked.

"You certainly are." Mel took a breath, releasing the tension in her jaw, "please accept my apologies for sounding angry. I thought it was another Valentines call for either of my sons and the incessant interruption is enough to drive a lady mad. Who, may I ask, is calling?"

"I cannot give you my name over the phone. I'm sorry. The information I have for you is extremely sensitive."

A familiar shiver ran down Mel's back, but this voice didn't sound threatening.

"Can we meet at the Nottingham Road Hotel at two o'clock?" The lady asked.

"Yes, but... what...what is this all about?" Mel asked with caution.

"I have information that may save your life."

Mel wondered if this could be a set-up. She shuddered, but she'd take a team of strong, armed men with her, Gary and the boys would follow. "What will you be wearing so I can identify you?" She liked the sound of the lady's voice, and something deep within said she should meet this lady.

"I have on a red blouse and a black skirt. I'm a black woman."

Mel felt a prickle of tension run down her back and raise the hair at the back of her neck. "I'll be there at two o'clock." Mel said goodbye and instantly called Gary. Had she done the right thing? She felt she had, but she'd need a full security detail with her.

"I'll get onto Willem, sweetheart, but are you sure about this?"

"Yes." Mel said emphatically.

"Okay. Garth, Brad and I will arrive a few minutes after the big boys. This could be a set up, you know."

"I realise that sweetheart, but the way the woman spoke it just didn't feel like it or sound like it."

"Well, be super cautious. There'll be plenty of us protecting you."

"I will be, but something tells me this is important. Please bring Tinus too."

Despite her nerves, she had no fear of this meeting.

Mel parked in the parking area at the Nottingham Road

Hotel at two o'clock and hurried inside. Two large Zulu me in civilian clothing, armed with 9mm pistols tucked into their trousers, followed her.

Seated in the foyer was the lady she'd come to meet. She stood and greeted Mel, holding her hand. She kept Mel's hand in her warm one and placed the other over Mel's hand. "I'm pleased to meet you, Mrs. Whitaker. I'm Anette Ndada."

"Good afternoon, Anette, where would you like to sit."

"My dear, I'm not sure I want to sit inside the hotel. Would you mind if we walk around the gardens? I'll pass on to you what I need to, and then we go our separate ways."

"Yes, that suits me," Mel surreptitiously nodded to the two enormous guards who sauntered past as if they had nothing to do with Mel and wandered outside. Mel led Anette out into the garden.

"I know you must be wondering what this is all about. "Anette said as she pulled out a chair and sat. "You're a very brave lady to have met with me alone." They sat together in the shade. "I was Colonel Tlale's secretary." Anette watched Mel wither.

Mel felt her body recoil and edged away from Anette instinctively. Anette quickly placed her hand on Mel's arm and Mel froze.

"Please, Mrs. Whitaker, I'm not here to hurt you. I'm here to protect you. Can I get us some water?"

Mel's mouth had suddenly gone dry. "Yes, please, that would be nice." She watched Anette walk toward the door. A waiter was near the entrance. She spoke to him. Mel presumed she'd asked for the water. When she returned, she smiled warmly at Mel. "I'm going to get straight to the point of our meeting, if you don't mind," she asked Mel who shook her head.

"I heard conversations and plans on how the Colonel intended to get rid of you. I knew about the plan to terrorise you by killing some of your horses. I know there are plans in place to murder certain staff members, jockeys, and other heinous tactics to cause mayhem and pain in your life. I couldn't go on listening or take the abuse. He screamed at me endlessly."

The water arrived and she drank half the glass. Mel sipped on hers, swirling it around her dry mouth, but she wasn't feeling as anxious anymore.

"He threw things about the office and at me. I couldn't take it anymore and resigned. He's a very dangerous man, and what he has already done to you is inexcusable. There are many others he's had killed or maimed, and families destroyed. You are the only white person he has such a ferocious hatred for. He's determined he'll win, and my conscience wouldn't allow me to keep the information to myself any longer."

Mel's eyes widened by what Anette was saying. Her breathing had returned to normal, and she liked Anette. There was an angelic warmth about the little lady.

"I spent a couple of months looking for another job in Harare, but there's nothing for me in Zimbabwe. And......" She went quiet and took a swig of water. A gentle smile rose in her eyes, "we're kith and kin. We're Rhodesians. I was born under Smith rule, and when I look at my country now, the devastation and starvation of my people makes me want to weep. You were part of the mass exodus late 70s and early 80s. Well, now my dear, there's a mass exodus of us black people."

"Goodness, Anette, when I hear that Colonel's name, my body goes freezes. My survival instincts kick in — fight or flight. It's the most terrible sensation. Fortunately, I did neither.

Though I don't want to hear, I have to know. What are his evil plans?"

"The day I resigned was the same day Nkizwi informed me he wanted nothing more to do with Solomon and suggested I move to South Africa."

"Who is Nkizwi?" Mel focussed on Anette and sipped her water.

"He's a distant relative, I think. He works as a go-between in Soweto and communicates with Solomon's granddaughter, Tanya, who lives in Durban. I...." Mel interrupted.

"Anette, stop, stop. I have a security team in the car park, and my husband is there too. Would you mind explaining every-thing to them too? It would be better if we got this down in writing and not have such important information passed on second-hand from me. I might miss out something vital to my safety. My mind gets in a bit of a tangle nowadays when it comes to information on Colonel Solomon Tlale.

"Yes, of course, I understand." They walked to the car park together. Mel waved to Gary. Tinus, Garth and Brad jumped out of the car with Gary, relieved to see her.

"Hello, my darlings," Mel sounded frail and a bit over-whelmed. "This is Anette Ndaba. She was Colonel Solomon Tlale's secretary. She has valuable information to share. Can we get the security team to join us at the table in the garden? They can take down the details. I explained to Anette it's too much for me to digest and must pass on accurately."

"Of course," Gary said and turned to Anette. "Nice to meet you and thank you." He shook her hand. "These are our sons, Garth and Brad, and this is Tinus, our race-horse trainer."

Gary waved to the security personnel sitting in a double cab close by.

Anette glanced at the two large men. A gimmer of recognition showed in her expression.

Of course, Mel would've had protection, they'd followed her into the hotel.

The men towered over Mel and Anette. Mel wondered if Anette felt as intimidated by them as she did. They were men who'd snap someone's arm or leg without effort and feel no remorse.

They all followed Mel back to the tea garden. The two guards moved two tables together and took their seats. The larger of the two Zulus sat close to Anette. He held a pad and pen.

"I'm ready," he said.

Anette began. She spoke for forty-five minutes, answering a barrage of searching questions from everyone. It was after four o'clock when the Zulus walked back to their van.

"I'm too weakened to stand," Mel whispered. "Let's have some tea." Mel straightened her skirt, glanced at Gary, then Anette. "Please join us for tea. Where are you staying?"

"I'm going to book in right here, but I'd love some tea. Thank you. My throat is parched from all the talking." Anette smiled. "I wouldn't like to get on the wrong side of those two men."

Tea was brought to the garden. This time they chatted casually about the situation in the current Zimbabwe, then Anette asked, "Mr. and Mrs. Whitaker, you wouldn't by any chance have a position for me in your administration offices, would you? I'm qualified in Human Resources, a very good administrator and secretary. I've been in South Africa for a couple of weeks, but I've not found a suitable job yet and companies are hesitant taking on a Zimbabwean."

Before Anette got her answer from either of his parents,

Brad piped up. "Pity you didn't knock the colonel off, would've saved us all considerable stress."

Anette laughed. "I felt like it many times. I'm not someone who hates easily, but I can honestly say I hated the Colonel with a rabid hatred at the end. I knew I had to resign and leave before he ruined my life, my mother's and my two children."

'A position in admin?' Gary tried to read Mel's thoughts and when she raised her eyebrows, he knew what she was thinking.

"We've been looking for someone to help Mel with admin. The lovely lady we used to have retired a few months ago. I think it's a great idea, what do you think, my love?" Gary knew the paperwork overload had been depressing Mel.

"Absolutely. I'd be delighted to have an ally. Where will you live?"

"Well," Anette shifted in her chair, "I don't have anywhere to live, but I'm sure I could find a small cottage somewhere not too far from your farm."

"How about living temporarily in the guest cottage at Chanting Clover? It'll give you time to find something that suits you." Mel offered. "What do you think, Gary?"

"Sounds good to me."

"What a generous gesture. I'd love that, thank you." Anette was stunned and it showed which gave Mel more confidence she'd made the right decision.

"Drive out to Chanting Clover with your things in the morning," Mel suggested, and drew directions on a paper serviette which made Brad laugh.

"Mum!" Brad giggled, "you're so funny."

"I don't have any paper, and this will do, won't it Anette?"

"Of course it will, as long as I can read it." The fun banter was just what they needed.

"At least I have a reliable little Toyota Corolla, if nothing else." Anette joked. "My entire possessions fit in too."

Leaving Rhodesia back in 1979 with her parents, Mel remembered the day with such clarity and the emotion caught her now. She quietly prayed the same wouldn't happen in South Africa.

The following day Anette arrived and parked her Toyota at the admin office. Mel saw her arrive and watched Anette sit in her car for a few minutes. Mel wondered if she felt a little nervous, or perhaps it was the relief of having a job and a roof over her head.

Mel met her in reception. "Hi, and good morning."

"Good morning, Mrs. Whitaker. I still can't believe this is happening. I'll never know how to thank you."

"Not at all. And please, call me Mel." She ushered Anette into the boardroom.

"Coffee?"

"I'd love some, thank you. The hotel was a very pleasant stay."

"It's a great little place, isn't it? Garth and Brad love going there. They meet all their friends in the little pub there."

Mel brought the coffee and sat opposite Anette. "I guess the first thing you must be concerned about is what we're going to pay you?"

"It would be nice to know, but you've been so kind already. Free housing, trusting me, and offering me a job already leaves me speechless with gratitude. I brought the originals of my qualifications. I have no reference."

"I wouldn't want a reference written by that bastard. We can start you on four thousand rand a month with the free cottage for as long as you need to stay there."

Tears trickled down Anette's cheeks. She wiped them away

with the back of her hand. "I cannot tell you what this means to me. Now I can send money home. I've been so afraid my children and my mother might starve. They live in a shanty village on the outskirts of Harare. It's dreadful. Walls of mud and a roof of old corrugated iron, but what could I do? No job, and I depleted my savings moving to South Africa." Her hands trembled slightly, betraying the weight of her burden. She sniffed and reached into her handbag for a tissue.

"How many children do you have?" Mel asked.

"Two. Moses, the eldest, is seventeen. One year left at school. Shinzi is fifteen with two more years at school. Neither could have completed school, so this job is our lifeline."

"Four people?" Mel wondered if she'd missed something.

"Yes. Me, my elderly mother and my two children. Moses finds the odd job gardening on a Saturday and Sunday, but only now and again. His meagre earnings help keep the three of them alive. If Moses doesn't get work, he disappears into the farmlands and forages for edible roots and tubers, wild fruit, herbs and amaranth, but he tells me most days they go hungry."

Mel felt so heartsore listening to Anette's woes. Their home country used to be the breadbasket of Africa. "So, you'll send half your salary home, I guess?"

"Of course. More than half. They survive on one meal a day, and it's not a highly nutritious one." Anette sipped her coffee to stop her lower lip quivering. "I'm so grateful to you both. I cannot imagine why that awful man is so desperate to harm you when you are the kindest person I've ever met."

The door burst open, and Gary entered. "Aah, welcome to the Chanting Clover team," he said cheerfully. Gary had requested Willem to a check on Anette before she arrived at the farm. Anette posed no threat, instead what she'd told them was valuable to their intelligence network. "Have you shown Anette the cottage?"

"No, not yet, we've been having coffee and chatting, but we'll head down there now. Are you ready, Anette?"

Mel led the way and while they wandered down the pathway that led to the cottage they chatted like old friends.

"I love the gardens, it's like a carefully tended park." Anette said as Mel opened the front door of the cottage.

"Oh, err....... I...." Anette felt so overwhelmed she was at a loss for words. She looked so embarrassed; Mel hugged her. "I had all the windows opened this morning to let in some fresh air."

"In all my living years I've never lived in such luxury."

Mel understood. "I feel so happy I can share what we have with someone like you. It's fully furnished so you don't have to waste money on buying anything except food and personal things."

"Do you believe in gut feel?" Anette asked.

"Oh yes, and it's worked for me on so many occasions."

"Never in my wildest dreams did I expect this, Mel, but from the moment I made the decision to call you, I knew I was doing the right thing. Everything else I left to God to take care of and where ever I can help to protect you and your family, I will do so."

"Thank you, Anette. Get unpacked, settle in, and here is the internal phone." Mel showed her the telephone mounted on the wall in the passage. "My number is two, Gary's is one."

"I'll give you my certificates tomorrow, if that's okay?"

"Absolutely. I thought we'd go shopping this afternoon, stock you up with food for the rest of the month. It'll be a good opportunity to show you where things are in our little village.

There's always plenty of fruit and vegetables in our home garden, do help yourself."

Anette watched Mel hurry down the pathway back to the offices. She sent her thanks to her guardian angel, closed the door and called Moses.

When Mel got back to the office, she plonked herself in the chair in Gary's office. "I think we've employed a gem. I feel she's my saviour, somehow."

"Incredible, isn't it? Rather shattering information, she shared."

"Horrific. At least we can foil the bastard's next plan. After that, who knows. According to Anette, this Nkizwi fellow told Solomon to put his hatred to bed, but he wouldn't hear of it. That's a very scary thought. Let's hope nothing gets in the way of Dubai. We fly next month." Mel looked at her watch.

"I'm taking Anette grocery shopping. Poor dear has nothing to eat and only a few cents left."

ON THE JOURNEY to the grocery store, Mel learned more about Anette's life, her children, and the colonel.

Standing mid-isle in the store, Mel pushed the trolley. "Pile in what you need." Anette shopped sparingly.

"Is that all you want?" Mel asked when they got to the check-out. Anette insisted that she would live well on what they'd bought. On the way back to the farm, Anette shared the reasons why she still had contact with Nkizwi. It was one issue that had niggled at Mel.

"I'm not sure I trust him. He may still be supplying the colonel with more information than he lets on."

"Well, the connection will help our security company gather intel. We'll beat him at his nasty tactics. Karma has a way of doing that." Mel didn't let on that she often felt karma was paying her back for burning down the camp and killing the commander, Antonio, but as her parents, her psychologist and Gary had reiterated, she should be no guilt for that. Antonio had brutally raped her. He had to pay for that. The others were soldiers happy to die for the cause.

Chapter Twenty-One

"HAS THERE BEEN any feedback from Willem? They should've finished the investigation. We need to know where the leak might be, and who stabbed James." Irritated by the amount of time the police and Prime Security were taking to come up with something positive, Gary paced about Mel's office.

"Can you chivvy them along, sweetheart. I'm buried deep in other things today and scarcely know where to start." Mel asked, watching him move, his shoulders hunched from the strain and the worry. He nodded, went to his office and dialled Willem's number.

"Good morning, Willem. Any news?"

"Yes. I was about to call you. I'm just waiting for a report to be faxed through. When's a good time to call you back?"

Gary sighed. "At last! Give me a ring after two." He put the phone down and let Mel know. There was a notable release of tension on both her body and her face.

Gary gave Brad a call. "Where are you, son?"

"Helping Maria at the broodmare barn." Brad answered.

"How long will you be there?"

"I could be here all day. These babies are so lovely. I'm teaching them all to pick up their feet."

Gary felt a paternal warmth wash away the disquiet. "Wonderful. Mum and I are coming to join you."

From the brood mare barn, they ambled down the road to the ready-to-run barn. Mel wanted to check a filly who'd pulled up lame two days ago.

Thirteen youngsters were being prepared for starting-stall training. The lame filly wasn't among the group.

"Jackson, where's Mischief?" Mel called to him.

"In her stable," Jackson answered without taking his eyes off a new handler trying to calm a spirited young colt. Brad and Gary looked at Mel. "That's quite impressive handling."

"Certainly is. How long has he been here?" Gary asked, interested to know for the young groom was talented.

"No idea." Brad shouted, "Jackson, what's the new grooms name and how long has he been here?"

"Peter. He's been here a week. He's doing well." He raised his thumb with a smile.

Gary went on watching Peter communicate with the colt who was determined to avoid entry into the starting stalls while Mel and Brad went to check on the lame filly.

Mischief stood with her lame leg resting. "Clean out her foot Brad, let's see what going on." Mel suggested.

Brad picked up her front foot and scraped away the dirt caught in her hoof. With the handle end of the hood pick Brad prodded the sole and found a sensitive spot.

"Abscess."

He shouted to a nearby groom to bring him a hoof knife. While he waited, Gary leant over the door. "Found anything?"

"Yeah. I think I've located an abscess. I'm going to open it up with the hoof knife."

Brad made an incision, cut away some of the sole and pussy blood oozed out. Mischief sighed and mouthed, as if in thanks. The relief immense. Mel helped Brad with the dressings and left the filly standing on all four feet. She still favoured the sensitive foot, but she could put weight on it.

Satisfied the filly would be sound in a few days, they rushed back to the house, had lunch and waited for Willems call at two. One minute past the phone rang. Mel and Brad sat in on the call. Gary put it on speaker wishing Garth was there too. He'd gone out on a ride with James.

"Hi Willem. So, what does the report entail?"

"There are three staff members working in cahoots with a connection of the colonels."

"Three?" Gary repeated. And Willem rattled off the names.

"Jackson!" Brad said in shock. "We've just seen him." He looked at Mel. "Dad and I were chatting to him before lunch when we sorted out Mischief, the little lame filly." He said, flabbergasted.

Jackson is apparently the ringleader. Then there is a work rider called Fila, and a lady called Beauty." Willem read out. "They are all in cahoots with a lady called Tanya who is the Colonel's granddaughter."

Mel felt the blow to her chest. Her eyebrows shot up, knitting in disbelief, creating deep lines in her forehead. She gasped, "Beauty cleans James's and Anette's cottages, and their ironing. The cottages must be bugged."

"Willem, why was this not picked up months ago?" Gary's lips tightened into a fine line.

"No idea, Gary. But I'll have the three removed from the staff housing at one o'clock tonight. They'll be held in Prime

Security detention rooms until further notice, and they'll spend the rest of the night being interrogated. Some of my men's heads are going to roll, for sure." Willem assured them.

"Willem, if I recall correctly, Jackson's name was mentioned by Pieter, the last CEO of Prime. Surely that should've been on record?"

"I've not seen anything like that Mel," Willem answered, "but that would mean Jackson would've been involved with Green Mists debacle, and the other two."

The colour drained from Mel's face. "If only Pieter had done a better job those horses would still be with us."

"Willem, if the cottages are being bugged, I reckon we are too. Let's cut this call."

"Okay. Sending chaps to you now."

Gary held his index finger to his mouth and pointed to the glass doors that lead from his office into the gardens at the back of the admin block. Once they were outside, he spoke. "Beauty would be privy to the most inside information, and she must've been linked to the attack on James." Brad closed his eyes and rubbed his brow.

"I'm going to check my office drawers. My sixth sense is playing havoc with me." Mel went back inside, dashed to her office and ripped open the first drawer and there, stuck on the back of the drawer was a tiny device.

"Fuck." She swore. Something Mel rarely did. "Let's check all our drawers. Just don't let anyone know what's happening except Willem. Sweetheart, will you call him?" Mel addressed Gary, who left the office and went into the garden to call Willem.

Sure enough, Brad found the same tiny devices in his, Gary's and Garth desk drawers.

"Jesus. Smash them into bits." Willem instructed. "Do a

really good job, they are pretty tough. Hit them with a hammer and makes sure they're in bits. My guys are on their way."

"Christ, Willem. These fucking people are determined to ruin us, aren't they?"

"It appears that way, and all our previous conversations will have been recorded. They'll also know we'll be onto them at one o'clock in the morning. I'm going to change the time. At least this conversation won't be recorded."

Mel popped her head round the door. "Iris, we are heading home. Will you ask Anette to lock the building before she goes home. We won't be back later."

"Yes, sure. I'll let her know." Iris nodded.

Garth burst into the hall, flung his hat on the hall table and shouted, "Going to clean up."

When he joined them, he sensed the atmosphere. "What's up? It feels like bad news."

"We've found listening devices in our desk drawers. Willem is sending experts in to check your rooms, the tack rooms, the cottages and the rest of the offices after Anette locks up. Did you and James have a good ride?"

Garth stood still, momentarily paralysed by what Gary had said. Eventually he answered, "we had a great ride, but if I'm understanding all this correctly, that's how the bastards knew James, Kgabu and I were in Durban that night. It wasn't just the strange phone call during the night."

Gary was slowly nodding as the news registered with Garth. "How can I help?"

"Guide Willem's undercover guys around, as if you are showing visitors around. Behave as natural as possible, makes jokes with them but pre-warn them so they can play along too, for there may be other staff involved and watching."

"This means the stabbing was meant for James." Garth had always thought the assailant had the wrong guy.

"I heard my name," James faltered at the sitting room door, worried he'd interrupted something he wasn't supposed to hear.

"Yes, you did. Have a seat." Gary motioned.

James sat next to Garth with Brad on his right.

Gary went on. "Let's go into the garden." Garth and James followed Gary, and they stood together on the lawn while Gary explained what had happened and forewarned James that he should join Garth in showing the men around as if they were visitors wanting to invest in a racehorse.

"Holy cow," James said. Will Willem's guys search my cottage?"

"You bet they will. They are going to start here in the house, especially Mel's home office down the passage and the bedrooms. Then they will go to the tack room and look at the horses in the first block, as if they are interested in buying a horse, so chat to them like they are clients. By then Anette will have locked the admin office and Iris will have gone home. They will do the entire office block before moving down to the cottages."

WILLEM CALLED Gary the following morning. He and Mel were having coffee in their sitting room watching the morning news on television.

"The culprits were caught packing up their belongings and were forcefully removed at nine last night. They'd heard the plan to move them at one a.m. Just as well you located that device in Mel's desk drawer."

"Wonderful. Well done, Willem."

"Eight listening devices were found, and three hidden

cameras. Two devices in James' cottage, one in each of the three tack rooms, Garth and Brad had one their bedroom, and one strategically placed camera in the boardroom. Another camera in the reception, so visitors to the stud have been monitored too. Bastards. Interestingly, nothing was found in Anette's cottage. I'll call you in about an hour with details from the interrogation."

"Good. I look forward to hearing." Gary switched down the sound on the television and revealed what Willem had told him.

"Only Jackson could have put the tack room ones in place." A burning rage rose Mel's belly which glowed in her emerald eyes like a leopard caught in a spotlight.

An hour later Willem called back. "Hi Gary, too much has been revealed to talk on the phone. Can you and Mel meet me somewhere to discuss it. And to add, Anette is a completely trustworthy ally, it seems."

"That's great news. Hold on a mo." Gary asked Mel where she thought they could meet. "Rosie's tea garden in Nottie's village." He said to Willem.

"That's fine. What time?"

"Twelve, and we'll have a bite to eat there."

"Sounds good. See you at twelve." Willem ended the call.

Gary let Garth and Brad know of the meeting. They declined going. "We'll be back after three but we're on our phones if you need us."

Chapter Twenty-Two

QUESTIONS AND WHISPERED utterings sent ripples of unease among the staff after the disappearance of the three traitors. Gary, Mel, Garth, and Brad behaved as if it was a shock to them too.

James and Kgabu knew nothing either, so the staff soon stopped asking though James and Kgabu reported that speculation continued, especially from the work riders.

Kagiso, the stallion manager, put Sipho, one of his sons in Jackson's place which Gary and Mel approved of. Edwina, head of the household, suggested her niece, Bonny could fill Beauty's place, and James reckoned a replacement for Fila wasn't necessary.

"Great replacements, but don't drop your guard, Mel," Anette whispered into her ear. Mel had told her privately what had happened.

"The Colonel will be fuming he's been foiled again. I wish I was a fly on the wall in his office right now. I dare not ask

Nkizwi, but I suggest your security firm monitors Nkizwi and Tanya round the clock."

"Thanks, Anette. Nothing can get in the way of Dubai now." Mel worried they'd have to cancel their flight.

"Nothing will go wrong, not under my watch," Anette said confidently, and nothing did.

TRYING her best to quell the excitement bubbling inside her, Mel stood behind Gary as they checked-in at Durban International airport.

They were on their way to Dubai.

Even though it was cool inside the airconditioned building and Mel wiped droplets of perspiration from her brow. Anxiety is making me sweat, she thought as she handed her passport over.

"I have to keep pinching myself this is happening," she said to Gary. The check-in lady handed back their passports and the boarding passes. Next stop, the security checkpoint.

"Such a lot has gone on since we decided to get involved with racing on this level. It can't get better than this, my love. Let's celebrate." Gary put his arm around Mel's tiny waist and pulled her close to him. "And it's all your doing." He kissed the top of her head.

"Nonsense, sweetheart. It's our amazing team that has made this possible."

"I agree, but who heads the team?" He smiled affectionately and answered for her. "My wonderful, beautiful wife."

They'd worked hard to achieve this dream. "It's also marvellous having Steve and Synthia's investment in Tsotsi. Without that we would've struggled to afford to get the two horses across to Chase, and onward to Dubai. Did I tell you Steve has someone investigating Solomon?" Mel stopped so suddenly a lady behind her walked into her and apologised profusely, but Mel assured her it was all Mel's fault, then she faced him. "No, you didn't. Steve has a lot of clout on the political side, doesn't he?" Gary nodded. "What time do they land tomorrow?"

He kissed her nose. "I thought you and Synthia would have that detail firmly entrenched," he teased, as commuters pushed passed them.

MARCH 26TH, 2010, the day they'd dreamt about landing in Dubai and here they were waiting from the hotel shuttle to collect them. The Dube's were expected later in the afternoon.

On the 28th of March, they'd be shuttled to the racecourse by the hotel bus. There they'd meet Chase and Tinus in the grand owners and trainer's lounge and this year happened to be the final year races would be run at Nad Al Sheba racecourse. Set against the backdrop of the Dubai desert, surrounded by vast stretches of sand, the course held an old-world charm. The grandstand stood proudly, offering a comfortable viewing experience to watch horses galloping down the wide flat track with its long sweeping curves. Mel knew in an instant both horses would run well on its surface. The inner track was a marvel of creation in a desert. Stark against the golden sands, lush green turf was the inner circumference. It hosted the Dubai Sheema Classic.

The talk today was all about the new Meydan track, opening in twelve months. A model of what it was to look like stood on a massive stand in the VIP Owners and Trainers lounge, to which the Whitaker team were drawn.

However exciting the new, futuristic colossus appeared, with the new grandstand stretching over a mile, today was the final race day at Nad Al Sheba. Mel felt hugely privileged to be a part of its old-style grandeur. She'd treasure today forever and prayed she'd be here in twelve months to be a part of the opening of the grand Meydan, but now all she could focus on was what was around her in the moment.

Originally Chase said he wouldn't attend - pressing work to be done at the winery, but at the last minute he decided he couldn't miss this red-letter day. He patched it into his itinerary en route to France and met the Whitaker's and Dube's, who, he noted, were dressed as if they were South African aristocracy.

The Owners and Trainers lounge was packed with important breeders, trainers, their wives and associates, both locals and from afar. Royalty and sheiks were in specially allocated VIP boxes. Mel enjoyed a glimpse of the other world. Below them the course buzzed with people ducking in and out of queue's, rushing to place bets like busy ants in frenzied lines. The atmosphere was electric and after the introductions with Chase were done, Mel and Synthia discussed the fashions.

Though there were many interesting, dramatic, and creative outfits, the dress length had to be a modest length, falling on or below the knee, in stark contrast to the ladies at the Durban July. Most ladies today were dressed in expensive, designer outfits, those seen in high society magazines. Jeans are not permitted. Shorts and sportswear of any type is also not permitted.

"I love it that the standards are kept so high here. Seeing these fashions, I approve."

Synthia chuckled. Her precious friend could be so old-fashioned. She leant in close to Mel, "Milliner's must do well here." And without making it too obvious she pointed out some rather stylish hats worn by the ladies in the room.

"Sweetheart," Gary interrupted. "Chase is showing Steve

and I to the stables. I'll see you in a bit." Mel, though anxious to see her horses too, she knew, when in Dubai, it's a world dominated by men. She graciously stayed seated and glanced at Synthia, who also understood the silent messaging.

"What are Garth and Brad up to?" Synthia asked cheerfully. "I bet they wanted to be here with us on this historic day."

"Yeah, especially ogling these beautifully dressed ladies. They'll get their chance, but now it's up to them to keep an eye at home. It's our turn for fun." Mel's lips stretched, her brows raised slightly and Synthia, being the mother of Kgabu, agreed with Mel's sentiment.

"If all goes well here, France is the next destination, and then, of course, we can't discount America. Our sons have plenty to look forward to." Synthia's thoughts were on her son, who right now would be sitting in the jockeys' rooms, nervously waiting. "I still can't believe Steve and I are part owners of Tsotsi. It's so exciting, but my poor darling Kgabu must be a nervous wreck right now."

"I'm sure he's petrified. But knowing him, he's focussed on the race. That's what makes him such a good jockey, besides, his great love of horses, of course." Mel squeezed Synthia's hot clammy hands.

"Relax. Kgabu will be fine." Mel reassured her, though Mel knew she'd be a nervous, but happy wreck until the end of the day.

"So, the Golden Shaheen, Tsotsi's race. It's the shortest race on the card, isn't it?" Synthia asked, rubbing cream into her hands.

"Yes, that's right. It's a sprint over twelve hundred metres. Tsotsi stands an excellent chance of winning it because she's so fast, but we must remember, she's racing against world class fillies, so let's stay neutral, as hard as it is."

"What boggles my mind is the actual race. It lasts mere minutes and is worth a $1million."

Mel agreed. "Staggering isn't it. Even second and third places are worth a lot of money too."

"Pity it's not all mine. Just imagine the shopping spree I could have here with that amount in my pocket." Synthia smiled dreamily.

"I read your mind. I saw your thoughts with that grin on your face." Mel laughed, "but it wouldn't go far here. Everything's so expensive."

"Yeah, I know, but I'd have a house full of brand names most people only dream of owning and I'd sure have fun blowing it."

"Some brands do it for me, but you know in the clothing department, jeans and a cotton button up shirt, short or long sleeves, or jods are my go to." Mel liked the simple pleasures in life.

"What would you spend it on, Mel?"

"Another stallion."

"Really? How boring. The men are taking their time, aren't they. Let's get another drink." Synthia waved to a roving male waiter dressed in a black jacket with white trousers, a white shirt and red bow tie.

"Fancy outfits for waiters. Aren't they?" Synthia commented "I pray for Kgabu's sake he wins the big race this evening. It's the real important one for his career, isn't it?"

The waiter came back with their drinks and a small dish of assorted nuts for them to nibble on. "Now just imagine that bundle, Mel. Five fucking million dollars. Eish." Synthia wheezed when the waiter was out of earshot. "All that glitters is gold here."

. . .

IN THE JOCKEY'S ROOMS, Kgabu sat meditating through a strange mixture of sensations. One minute he felt numbed, the next he felt hyper-ware and could hear the rhythmic pulse of his heartbeat in his ears. His palms were sweaty inside his gloves. He slipped them off and wiped his hands down his silks.

In thirty minutes, the first race would begin. As with any big horse race meeting the buzz in the jockeys changing rooms is infectious nervous chatter, then as the time draws closer to mount, the room goes quiet. There's a surreal quality about the atmosphere and Kgabu was feeling it as he glanced around. Each jockey sat quietly with their own thoughts. As Synthia had worried about Kgabu, he sat thinking about his mother, imagining she would be more nervous than he was right now. But she had Mel to comfort her. He sat alone in disciplined silence, meditating. Like he was watching himself from outside his body. Is this really happening? Then he thought of the millions of people watching around the world. He felt both exhilarated and terrified at the same time. He began his breathing exercises. This was the most important day of his career. He needed to be razor sharp. The butterflies had already flown.

He glanced at his watch. Fifteen minutes left. He rested his head in his hands and prayed for a safe ride. Even if they didn't win this race, there was still the next, the richest race of all. Just being here, with mum and dad and the Whitakers on this final meet was an honour. He wondered how everyone else in the team felt. He knew Chase wouldn't be nervous or anxious, he'd been here too often. Then he wondered how Tsotsi would be feeling. He felt sure she'd be feeling the atmosphere, the vibrations of sound to ignite her. She loved racing, and she had the spirit of a champion.

Kgabu weighed and was cleared to ride. The horses would

be entering the grand paddock in five minutes. Were his team waiting?

Kgabu sat up straight and stared ahead of him, ignoring the whispering and conversations of the other jockeys. Most of whom spoke in their mother tongue, which Kgabu didn't understand. Not many of them spoke to him, and not all spoke English. None spoke Zulu, of course. He'd had a brief chat with an Australian jockey he'd met with Chase, but he wasn't riding in this race.

He call to mount sounded. Kgabu jumped to his feet, fitted his helmet, slipped his gloves back on and picked up his crop. He was fourth in line. His nerves had settled, he was ready for this ride.

Then he heard his mother shout, "There he comes." She held his dad's arm firmly, likely too weakened by nerves to hold herself up.

Siyanda legged him up onto the glowing Tsotsi. The grooms had turned her out to perfection. Her red-bay coat shone like a mirror, so shiny he felt sure he'd see his reflection there.

Lithe, fit muscle rippled beneath the royal blue saddle blanket. Number Two, in white, had been embroidered boldly on it.

That out-of-body feeling again. Was he really riding in Dubai? Siyanda led the prancing Tsotsi. Kgabu stretched his legs downward then lifted them and slid his feet into the tiny irons. Everything felt as if it was happening in slow motion, the weight of history and expectation pressed down on his shoulders. Then he left the paddock. Kgabu's focus switched to the task ahead and the roar from the grandstands became a distant hum as he and Tsotsi approached the starting gate. He could feel Tsotsi's nervous energy. It mirrored his own anticipation, but he felt connected by trust and mutual skill. They were poised on the edge of greatness.

Tsotsi was led in. Time stood still. The seconds stretched out. Kgabu took a deliberate deep breath, answered by a deeper one from Tsotsi. Every sound became amplified. Then suddenly the gates flew open and Kgabu's world exploded into action and all he heard were Tsotsi's thundering hooves pound against the golden sands beneath her feet and the wind whipping against his face as the other horses surged around him.

The track seemed purpose built for Tsotsi. The dirt track was fast, built for speed, and Kgabu felt the raw power beneath gather as she stretched ahead of the field and the wide track became the most exciting loneliness he'd ever felt. He rode her on and suddenly felt she'd already worked out her own strategy. He smiled to himself despite the kickback from the dirt stings on his face. That brought a reality back and he saw the final turn and the grandstand loom larger. Tsotsi's last few strides didn't need a flick of the whip, she crossed the line four lengths ahead to thunderous applause. Now he heard every sound with crystal clarity as the world rushes back.

Tsotsi had shown the world what she had in her limbs and her heart. Tsotsi was in a class of her own.

Kgabu stood in the saddle and punched the air triumphantly, then he ran his hand down her neck and whispered, "We got this babe." Like he was speaking to a lover. She'd done the dance of the angels. Her flight down the golden sands had broken a world record, he heard the announcement as he met Siyanda ready to lead her in and meet with the rest of the team,

Choked with emotion, Kgabu could hardly speak as faces peered up at him and microphones were shoved under his nose.

"What a win. That mare knows her job. How did the race

feel for you, Kgabu?" The interviewer asked as he jogged along beside Tsotsi who still had miles of petrol in her tank.

"She knows her job. She was born to win." Kgabu answered, ready to be overwhelmed by emotion. He felt he could blub his eyes out he as so ecstatic and wondered if the next race would feel the same. He'd just ridden a Thoroughbred Ferrari. Would Warriors Rival give him the same sort of ride.

Then he saw them. The Whitakers were walking hurriedly toward them.

Cheers had gathered momentum. The jockey on the horse in second, slapped Kgabu on the back and congratulated him, and soon the Whitakers took a rein on either side of Tsotsi and Siyanda walked beside Gary.

"Absolutely fabulously ridden," Mel's voice had an emotion timbre to it as she patted Kgabu's knee. "Your parents are waiting at the winners circle."

As they walked along the crowds congratulated them. The interviewer had moved on to talk to Mel, then he questioned Gary just before the grand moment.

Emotions ran high. Kgabu and Tsotsi had made history, breaking the track record on the last ever race on this track.

A glittering gold inlaid, navy blue winning lightweight blanket covered the magnificent Tsotsi and a sash was placed around her neck. Kgabu stood beside her, blinded by flash-lights. They'd won the Dubai Golden Shaheen one-million-dollar race. What was he supposed to say to the gentleman interviewing him?

Stuttering, he found his tongue and explained how well Tsotsi had paced herself. He laughed then. "I did nothing, she did it all." He patted Tsotsi vigorously and she snorted. The tears began to roll at last when he heard his mother's voice. "My.... precious son... has done it."

Then Kgabu saw him. Sheikh Hamdan bin Rashid Al Maktoum stood ready to praise the winning pair. He stood, tall and proud in all his finery. This race, the other races and the course was deeply rooted in Emirati culture and at this Nad Al Sheba course, the seeds of ambition had been planted from its inception in 1996.

And here, standing in front of a man who understood the Thoroughbred, was not only humbling but inspiring. Horse, rider, breeder, owner, trainer, all unknown South Africans would go down in the history books at And Al Sheba,

Kgabu had composed himself once more and shook the Shiekh's hand. He spoke perfect accented English as he congratulated Kgabu and said how much he liked Tsotsi. "A picture of Thoroughbred perfection."

Then it was time to leave the winners area.

A smiling Siyanda seemed to dance on light feet as he led Tsotsi to the veterinary area.

The stables, just beyond the track, housed some of the most prestigious racehorses in the world, and the Whitaker two formed part of that.

When the strict protocols of postrace checks were complete, Kgabu joined the team in the VIP area to loud applause once more, but all he needed was to rehydrate. He sat beside his mother and downed a litre of water. It didn't take long before the team were surrounded by well-wishers eager to meet the black South African jockey who'd just become an international star. They were generous and warm with their praise, but Kgabu couldn't stay. The Godolphin Mile would start in forty-five minutes. The feature race. The Dubai World Cup.

"Pray for us, please." Kgabu's departing words. In the elevator he closed his eyes and visualised crossing the line first, wearing the green and white stud colours. There were two green stars on Kgabu's white cap and the arms of his silks. He always thought of the stars on his cap as his guiding light.

"This is nerve wracking," Steve admitted to Gary.

Back in the jockey's room, he sat for ten minutes in the sauna, then had a cold shower. Refreshed, he slipped into boxer shorts and folded his clean silks in preparation. The Australian jockey, Bruce Robertson sat beside him. "You rode that last race brilliantly. Well done." He shook Kgabu's hand.

"Thanks mate, it wasn't me. I can't believe she beat the track record. The fastest sprint ever on this track. Fucking A man." Kgabu enjoyed chatting to Bruce and they chatted for another ten minutes, then they both sat in silence and contemplated the big race. In fifteen minutes, they'd be called from the dressing room for weighing and medical checks. Shortly thereafter he'd be thrown into the saddle on the back of Warriors Rival.

He couldn't wait. The colt was Kgabu's favourite horse. He heard the odds weren't good, but he expected nothing else. The pair were new to these sovereign grounds. Would he shine here like Tsotsi had just done, he wondered. There were world famous champion horses to beat in this most prestigious, richest race on the world calendar.

It'll be even more historic to win this race. The thoughts tickled the edges of his mind with an energy he'd never experienced before. Even the build up to Tsotsi's race. He didn't dare to hope.

Ten minutes to go. He knew the team would be gathered to watch the fourteen horses parading around the paddock. When this race was over, the doors would close for Nad Al Sheba and Kgabu wanted to make a memorable one for himself and for the global racing community who were watching.

It was a big field of top-class bloodstock. He felt the tension grip first, then the nerves took hold as he watched the other jockey's pace the room.

Then they were called. Siyanda was there, smart in white overalls with Chanting Clover Stud embroidered in emerald green thread across his back. His sparkling ivories beaming through a smile as wide as the track.

Kgabu felt he was floating. He felt himself being lifted into the saddle and suddenly he was out on the track going down to the start of the world's richest race. His mind was filled with bizarre out-of-body sensations more bizarre, more magical. Moments he'd never forget and though he wasn't religious, he felt the superpowers of the universe shining down on him now.

Warriors Rival loaded calmly and quietly, showing no hesitation. The strapping 17.1hand colt oozed self-confidence, so typical of the Whitaker's racehorses. Beautifully schooled animals that had been bred and raised with love, in the hands of one of the finest horse master's Kgabu had ever met. Melonie Whitaker.

The gates shot open. One thousand seven hundred and seventy-seven metres beckoned under the floodlights. Shadows danced about the galloping feet like playful fairies, teasing and cajoling. Horses galloping at full speed, powered by nerves and steered by men with nerves of steel rivalled Kgabu's ability to steer six hundred and forty kilograms of powerful horsepower down the track, but Warrior was loving every minute on the wide track with the surface he loved most.

He galloped effortlessly over the sand. They were soon heading toward the front of the pack. Kgabu delighted in how little encouragement Warrior needed. Like Tsotsi, he knew his job and he loved it.

'Come my boy, show them how to win a race like this,' Kgabu whispered as he felt the raw power of this huge Thoroughbred open his shoulders and engage his engine as his back legs lifted. Warriors ears flicked back and forth in answer to Kgabu's whispers and a cold thrill ran through his fingertips. The more he whispered, the faster Warrior ran.

Adrenaline pulsed as they took the lead, and he miraculously found more speed in his powerful legs. Kgabu encouraged him with the swipe of the whip, never touching Warrior's body. He didn't need to.

"We've got this boy. You're incredible. Thank you." Kgabu's voice faltered with emotion as Warrior stretched over the finish line two lengths ahead of the field.

They'd won the Dubai Duty Free, $5million race. The trophy belonged to Chanting Clover and their incredible team.

Kgabu stood in the saddle, shaking his head in wonder after he'd punched the air triumphantly. Warrior began to trot toward the exit gate and the thunderous crowds waving their arms in speechless wonder.

Warrior was a stayer. A distance horse and though he was fast, nothing like the flight of the angels with Tsotsi, but he was quite fast enough.

Kgabu stayed standing in the saddle patting Warriors neck and shouting his praises for his favourite horse.

Siyanda raced toward them, half crying, half cheering and grabbed the right rein to lead them toward the winner's enclosure. "Hey, Kgabu, you are a master. Well done."

Gary and Mel, Chase, Tinus and his parents were running toward him. Kgabu shouted at the top of his voice, "We've done it, by God's good grace, we've done it." Warriors Rival was breathing heavily, his nostrils flared, but he snorted and shook his head acknowledging Gary and Mel as they took the reins.

"Oh my God, two wins today. I can't believe it. On two great horses — thank you." He sobbed as he placed a hand on

Mel's shoulder. Mel couldn't answer, emotion had got her tongue.

Chase, Tinus, Synthia, and Steve jogged beside them on the right. Warrior seemed to have the energy to race another few hundred meters as they approached the flood-lit winner's paddock. The interviewers struggled to keep pace.

"I didn't know whether to laugh or cry as you crossed the line. A fabulous win. Huge congratulations."

Flood lights seemed to shine brighter as the pair were led into the circle. Kgabu bounced off Warriors back. The same navy and gold sheet covered him, and the sash was placed over his neck. What a moment that was for the Chanting Clover Team.

The purse was huge. A prize the Whitakers never imagined could possibly be theirs, but this evening, their world had changed, and so had Kgabu's. Too much to absorb the moment and within minutes Kgabu shook hands again with the deputy ruler of Dubai, Hamdan bin Rashid Al Maktoum. He warmly congratulated Kgabu on another sensational win and eyed the magnificent Warriors Rival with appreciation.

Suddenly the celebration and euphoria seemed to come to an abrupt halt. It was over. Siyanda led Warriors Rival back to the stables for vet checking and post-race care. The team answered more questions and spoke to royalty and high-end owners and adrenaline raced away as fast as it had risen. The team drifted away and re-united at the hotel.

MEANWHILE, back home, Garth and Brad had hired a projector and linked it to You Tube and watched the race with all the staff on the veranda. Before everyone was too inebriated to talk coherently, Garth called his parents.

"Hey Dad, now you and mum are mega famous. Well done. Kgabu must be over the moon." Garth shouted.

"I don't think Kgabu knows what's hit him, but yes, amazing wins. Mum and I are delighted and very proud of our horses. The whole day seemed surreal. You two can experience at the new Meydan racecourse next year. How does that sound?"

"Brilliant."

Then Brad grabbed the phone, "Hi Dad, Tsotsi and Warriors are two unbelievable horses. You and Mum must be so chuffed."

"We certainly are. It's still sinking in though." Gary laughed loudly. Even he couldn't believe what had taken place. The shock had been numbing and elating, then he handed the phone to Mel.

"Oh Mum, all your clever breeding skills have just paid off. You're amazing." Brad whooped proudly. "We hired a big screen and projector and invited the staff to celebrate and watch with us. It's been hysterical watching them. When Tsotsi won, I'm sure our staff's wails and shrieks were heard in Durban. Tell Kgabu we're all so proud of him."

"What a splendid idea. I'll tell Kgabu. He's floating on cloud nine right now."

"I bet he is. I would be too if I'd won that much fame and money. Hey, mum, did you enjoy meeting with the deputy ruler of Dubai?"

"I certainly did. A little intimidating, but he was full of gracious praises. We'll see you at home in forty-eight hours."

"You two deserve this radical win." Brad said with heartfelt sincerity.

"Thank you, sweetheart. It's been a team effort." '

The following morning, the cheer could still be felt despite most were nurturing horrific hangovers.

"Hey, boet, are you studying tonight?"

"Yeah, for sure. One last bloody exam I cannot fail. My plan is to come out with you in the early morning, then study the rest of the day. I'm giving myself one evening out with my mates at Notties."

"Sounds like you've got it all worked out. So, when the folks are back, it's Notties here we come."

"Something like that. Next year it's our turn, Mum said." Garth whistled and did a little gig, then stopped and held his head. "Fuck, I drank far too much last night."

"Yeah, me too. It's going to be a slow day today. Hey, who's fetching Mum and Dad, by the way?" Brad asked.

"No-one. Steve and Synthia are dropping them off. Have you spoken to Kgabu yet?"

"Yes, he's over the moon. He said it felt like an out-of-body experience. Swore blind he was dreaming. Said he worried he'd suddenly wake up and find it was all just a dream. Even though he'd won the earlier race, the sensation of winning the richest race in the world under lights must dreamlike. The Dubai Duty Free. Fuck, just imagine, boet. I'm still shaking my head in disbelief. Do you know what Kgabu gets paid for winning those two races? It almost makes me wish I was that small." Brad didn't really mean that, but the money would've been nice.

"Do you think those wins will go to his head?" Garth asked, holding his head.

"Never boet. He's way too humble. What worries me though, international stardom for him and the folks, puts Mum straight back into the spotlight, not matter the increased security we have around the place."

"Yeah, it's a serious concern. Did Dad tell you Steve is onto someone in Zim?"

"No, he didn't." Brad looked surprised at having not been told.

"Mark my words, his folks will protect us and Kgabu with their lives."

"You know, I still can't get my head around this fucking vendetta, can you?" Brad's jaw set grimly.

"No. Will anyone? Mum did nothing to that stupid fucker. He's just evil, like most terrorists. They have no feeling for other's lives." Garth replied angrily. "Let's hope Steve's man, or the security company, come up with something soon. I can't deal with the stress much longer."

"Yeah. Tuck yourself away and study, boet. No chatting to chicks on Facebook over the fame of our parents, now." Brad waved his index finger at Garth.

"Talking of chicks, your little beauty will be here soon." The thought of meeting her raised a grin on Garth's face.

"She sure will, and I can't wait. And boet, she's all mine. Hands off." Brad warned. "Fuck this hangover. I need paracetamol."

The following morning Gary finally answered Garth's endless missed calls.

"Fucking press, my boy. Sorry. We've been hounded since we stepped foot in arrivals. Mum's seething."

"We were just getting worried cos you said you'd be home by now."

"We'll be home and an hour and a half."

There were more celebrations when Gary, Mel, Steve and Synthia arrived.

Kgabu had stayed with the horses in Dubai.

Garth grabbed Gary's hand and shook it vigorously. "Geez Dad, that's one kak load of money you've just won."

Gary chuckled. "You and your money fixation, boy. How's the studies going?"

"Well. I'll pass this last exam. I'm confident."

"Good to hear."

Steve and Synthia stayed for mid-morning tea and cake celebration. Laughter and chatter went on for over an hour. Mel then mentioned racing in the States.

"If our horses go to the States, that's my call." Brad piped up.

Chapter Twenty-Three

As the sun rose in the salmon pink dawn sky, Garth and Brad stood shoulder to shoulder scrutinising Johnny and his team of work riders warming up frisky, alert, fractious, young racehorses who had the cool breeze under the tails.

Nine quality Thoroughbreds were testing their riders to see if they were awake or not.

"There's no better sight than this, don't you agree, boet?"

"Yeah, for sure. Some superb youngsters coming through. Watching them play around makes me feel so proud."

"The filly, Misty Vision. I think she could be another Tsotsi." Brad turned. They'd seen her run in the first group at six o'clock. "What do you think, Garth?'

"Yeah, you could be right. I don't know about you, but I'm starving. Let's get back for breakfast."

They wandered into the hall, hung up their hats, washed their hands and joined their parents who were already seated in the dining room.

"Morning Mum. Morning Dad. How did you sleep?" Garth pulled out his chair and sat.

"Like babes. Nothing like being back home." Mel answered.

"Great. Brad and I thought it'd be nice for all of us to go on a long hack to the top of the farm. Your favourite spot, Ma."

"What a wonderful idea. I'd love that. We're still in holiday mode, aren't we darling?" Mel glanced at Gary. Adoration smeared across her face.

"Excellent idea. I can't remember when the four of us last hacked to the top of the farm."

Garth had studied hard for the last four days. He felt he could forfeit time for the family ride.

Where the wild, ancient Lemonwood grew had to be Mel's favourite place on the farm. Today was a balmy, warm day as the family cantered abreast up the road toward the summit, chatting happily. The chief subject, the sensational wins in Dubai. At the top of the ridge where two folds of hillside meet, they pulled up to a walk. The horses were breathing heavily from the long canter.

Years ago, Mel's parents, Ivan and Margaret Johns had planted White Stinkwood saplings near the old, gnarled Lemonwood tree when they first arrived from Rhodesia. The trees were lovely and tall now and offered welcome shade.

"This was a brilliant idea, Garth." Mel said breathlessly.

"I agree, Mum. To think that in another eight days, I'm a qualified Marketing professional," he laughed and punched Brad's arm who wrestled his brother playfully in the saddle. Their mounts put their ears back irritably.

The Labradors and Jack Russel's finally made it to the top and collapsed in the shade nearby, panting loudly.

"Reckon you got this exam?" Gary asked.

"Bloody oath, Dad."

Mel spoke. "It was up here, years ago, when my mum said, 'this is as close to heaven as one can get.'" She turned to Gary, "do you remember her saying that, sweetheart?"

"Yes, I do, and the only thing that has changed is the Stinkwood trees have trebled in size." He moved closer and whispered, "I love you today, as much as I did back then, too." Mel felt a tingle in her gut and warmed by his words. She felt the same way. She gazed across the valley to the mountains in the distance. Their recent travels and extraordinary wins had done her good.

"I sometimes forget how much I love it up here. We must do this more often," Mel spoke in a quiet voice filled with maternal emotion.

Garth glanced at his mother. "I hope I find a woman like you one day. Ma." He too suddenly feeling unusually emotional. Something in his mother's tone must've prompted it.

"What a sweet thing to say, my precious." Mel felt the power of his words filter through every cell in her body. "I'll never tire of looking at this view, but I'll also not forget the three sixty-degree vistas that surrounded me as a child our farm, Blue Winds in the beautiful eastern highlands of Zimbabwe." Now she couldn't keep the sadness from her voice as she remembered. A view so dramatic in its enormity.

"I remember sitting on my beloved Firelight, much like we're doing now, looking into the Gairezi River valley, where icy cold waters ran. I'd not leave there until my eyes had scanned every inch of the view in front of me for two reasons. I'd sit on Firelight, side-arm strapped to my waist, and wonder where the terrorists were hiding until my eyes watered, and before leaving, I'd pray no harm would come to us as the war intensified." She shook her head. "It seems I'm still fighting it, and my prayers have not changed." A tear rolled down her cheek as her family listened. Even the horses stood motionless, then a painful, yet poignant memory filled her mind again.

"It wasn't just the view. The weather was ever-changing. So many times, I'd watch the full life of a tropical thunderstorm play out. From puffy white clouds blowing in from Mozambique to the horizon filled with dark grey bulbous clouds and lightning flashed in all directions. I'll never forget the rumble, crash and bang of thunder rolling in from as much as twenty miles away. Unbridled African storms are sights and deep-throated sounds to behold. I shall never forget them." Mel took a deep breath, "sadly, my battle rages on against us all. It's such a tiresome torment, and I'm so sorry."

The family remained silent. Her words wrenched at the souls. The horses also stood still, apart from the odd sneeze and the flick of the tail getting rid of annoying flies. The breeze picked up and the leaves of the trees rustled eerily.

"At the end of the storm, blue skies were restored. I guess that is what we hope for in life." Mel sighed. "The afternoon sun came out in all is warmth and glory and the strange stillness of the fresh air reclaimed the tranquillity of Nyanga. Sometimes I felt someone was watching me, but most times I'd wander home feeling blessed to have seen the powerful force of nature form in front of me. That exquisite, raw beauty was marred, though, for I was marched over that same terrain, barefooted and terrified, in the dark of night, tied to none other than my nemesis, the evil terrorist, Colonel, Solomon Tlale. Back then he was just a young cadre operative."

Melonie visibly shook.

Brad rubbed his arms. "Wow, Mum, you had us all absorbed, even the horses listened." Garth then spoke. "Thanks for sharing that truth, but it's provoked a deep primal fear within me, and a sadness that you keep thinking our traumas are all your fault. They're not, Ma. They belong to that bastard. We must bring him down. It's time we lived in peace."

"I'm sorry, my darling child. Sometimes I must shed those memories, it keeps me sane. Even though I love Chanting Clover, this view, and everything we have here, and my beautiful family sitting on our horses looking at the majestical Drakensburg, I still miss the views of the Eastern Highlands in Zimbabwe, but I won't say more. It's upsetting you, isn't it?"

Garth didn't answer. Instead, Gary put an arm across her shoulders. "One day we'll go there as a family. I'd like to see the Eastern Highlands and other parts of Zimbabwe too."

Mel didn't say it then, but she couldn't go back. She'd tried once before, and Solomon was waiting for her. She shuddered. Desert Rose felt the vibration in her back and fidgeted. It was visions of Solomon hanging over her in that hotel room in Harare that had made her shiver. She'd only go back when Solomon is dead.

Gary, Garth and Brad sat quietly and watched her. Her lips trembled slightly, "now Blue Winds stands abandoned and broken. My friend Julie said the farm is filled with squatter farmers eking out a living. Most of Dad's forests have been chopped out and they grow their maize and beans on that land. I'd never be welcome back in the country of my birth. I couldn't show you boys the dregs of what is left, it would break my heart."

"But the view they couldn't fuck up, Mum." Garth apologised for swearing, but he felt angered by what she'd just said.

Standing there, in peaceful and beautiful KwaZulu Natal, flanked by those she cherished most in the world. Chanting Clover was almost as precious to her as Blue Winds had been.

She wished her parents, and her grandmother could be with them.

Gary reached for her hand. Across the space between their two horses, he blew her a kiss. "We'd still love to see it all one day, wouldn't we boys?"

"Exactly Dad. Brad and I have often said we'd love to see it, even though the farm is nothing like it used to be."

Mel stretched her arms above her head. It felt like she'd been on a spiritual trip home. "This ride has been a treat. I'd forgotten how stunning it is to canter along with the wind in my hair for a few hours with my precious family beside me."

"It's magic, isn't it? I'm going to Notties tonight. Spur of the moment arrangement. I'm meeting a bunch of school and college mates. It's a farewell to two blokes going to work in the UK for a while driving tractors to earn some pounds."

"That's great. Don't drive home if you've drunk too much. Mr. Johnson will put you up in the hotel and send me the bill. Are you going too, Brad?" Gary asked.

"No, Dad, I'm staying home. Don't feel like being on the track in the early morning with a hangover. We both had a shocker after Dubai, and it's not fun." Brad grimaced at the thought.

"I've no intention of getting blotto either. I'll be at the track with you, boet."

Mel and Gary glanced at each other. "You've also got your final exam day after tomorrow." Gary reminded him.

"I suppose it's time to get these horses back home so they can graze and be horses." Mel peeked at her watch.

"And soon we'll have Indigo joining us on this ride," Brad said happily and, on the way home, cheerful banter replaced Mel's poignant tales.

Chapter Twenty-Four

IT WAS after seven when Garth finally crawled out of bed and staggered down to the stables to find his parents and apologise for not being at the track. He found them in the broodmare barn and greeted them sheepishly.

"You look like you should still be in bed," Mel said sharply.

"I feel like I should be too! There's one plus to a hangover, Mum. You get better as the day progresses."

He could see his joke didn't impress her. He thought he'd make light of an awkward situation, but it hadn't worked. He felt vile. "Who's this little cutie?" He pointed to a foal she was with. "He's stunning."

"His name is Storm in a Teacup. All the words join up as one." Gary replied curtly, annoyed with Garth for being irresponsible. He was a pitiful sight so hungover.

"Wha... a... fucking mouth....ful." He slurred. "Sorry, Mum."

"Oh Garth, go back to bed," she said irritably. "You reek of

250

stale alcohol and cigarette smoke. Go and sleep it off so tomorrow you can write your final exam."

"Believe it or not, I didn't drink much. I don't know what has made me feel so.... ill." Garth turned and staggered home.

He was still asleep at five that afternoon. Mel snuck into his room to wake him. Her senses were assaulted by the rancid smell of vomit as she opened the door. She held her breath and moved closer to the bed. Vomit had been spewed all over the floor, and the trail ended beneath the toilet in the bathroom. Though she tried not to look at the mess he'd made, she couldn't help noticing blood in the vomit, and tried waking him, but he was out cold. Panicked, she left his room, raced to her phone and called Gary, then their family doctor.

"Bring him in straight away," Doctor Sneddon said. "I'll meet you in emergency admissions."

Between Gary, Brad, and Mel, they heaved the semi-conscious Garth onto the back seat of the Mercedes and raced to Gray's hospital in Pietermaritzburg. Brad stayed at home.

Doctor Sneddon was waiting. Gary helped two nurses lift Garth into a wheelchair and pushed him into the curtained inspection room.

"Probably alcohol poisoning from what you described on the phone, but I'll do blood tests." He turned to one of the nurses. "Get him to ward two and put up a drip straight away."

"Yes Doctor," she answered and wheeled the delirious Garth to the lift.

"He'll respond quickly to the rehydration. I'll let you know the moment he's fully awake." Doctor Sneddon advised.

Gary and Mel sat beside the bed and watched the nurse insert the intravenous cannula in preparation for the drip. Garth had fallen asleep again.

"Oh, how I wish Garth wouldn't party so hard," Mel

moaned. "I thought it was going to be a few drinks to say cheers to his buds going overseas."

"He does tear the backside out of it sometimes, doesn't he? Though he did say he hadn't drunk much. Probably a little untruth cos I think he felt quite ashamed down at the broodmare barn. Thank goodness he did drive home and got back safely, or we wouldn't have known he was ill."

Brad and James waited anxiously for Gary and Mel to get home and to occupy their minds they sat watching movies with the sound turned up and never heard the car arrive.

Brad jumped up when he heard Gary's voice. "How's Garth?"

"Alcohol poisoning. He'll be in overnight on a drip. We'll collect him sometime tomorrow after Doctor Sneddon has seen him."

"Thank God it's only that," Brad heaved a sigh of relief. Let's hope he's better tomorrow. Doesn't he have his exam tomorrow?"

"Yes, he does, but it's only at two o'clock."

"That's good news, now I know he's fine, I'm off." James said good night. He was spending a few nights in Pinetown with his mother.

THE PHONE BUZZED BESIDE GARY. Woken from a deep sleep he reached out to answer it. "Hello," he said sleepily.

"Gary, Garth has slipped into a coma." Doctor Sneddon said.

"Oh my God, when?" Gary sat upright, wide awake now. So was Mel. She switched on the bedside light.

"The sister called me half an hour ago. I've given him an intravenous steroid and have taken more blood tests. This is more than alcohol poisoning. I think you should come through." Doctor Sneddon advised.

"We'll be there as soon as possible."

They jumped out of bed. Gary explained to Mel as they raced around getting dressed, then Mel hurried down the passage and woke Brad.

"Garths slipped into a coma. Please stay here, sweetheart. I'll call when we are at the hospital."

"Okay, Mum." Brad rubbed his eyes. "Drive safely. Everything will be fine. Whisper to Garth that I'm riding Prov in the morning. That'll wake him."

Mel leant down and kissed his forehead, then ran to the car.

AWAKE NOW, Brad lay in bed starring at the roof. A little light peeped through the curtain from the security lights outside and when a gentle breeze moved the curtains, the light danced across the ceiling distracting Brads disturbing thoughts. He soon found himself praying aloud. Garth had to come out of the coma.

Brad had no idea how long he'd been lying motionless in bed. Only the rise of his chest when he breathed reminded him, he was awake. Then suddenly a thought crossed his mind, and he flew out of bed, hauled on a tracksuit, and sprinted to Anette's cottage. Panting he glanced at his watch. It was four forty-five a.m. James would be on his way back to the farm to get to the gallops soon.

Brad knocked on the door. He waited. No answer. He knocked harder. Eventually Anette answered.

"Who is it?" she called out.

"It's Brad. Sorry to wake you." He heard her move around inside and switch on the lights. She opened the front door.

"Mum and Dad have raced off to the hospital. Garths in a coma. The Doctor believes it's more than alcohol poisoning."

Anette stood in the doorway, numbed into silence. Was this the work of Melonie's nemesis? The palm of her hand covered her heart. "Come in, Brad." She stammered. "I'll put the kettle on."

Brad followed her to the kitchen. "Anette, did Solomon discuss poisoning one of us, or was it just the horses?"

"Just the horses. When Julie refused to do any more work for Solomon, that conversation dried up. Do you think Garth's been poisoned?"

"I don't know. It's just a hunch. He went to a piss-up with friends at Notties. We all thought he had a dreadful hangover when he staggered down to the broodmare barn. Mum sent him back to the house to sleep it off. Thinking back, he said he'd not drunk much. When mum checked him at five, he was out cold. They rushed him to Gray's at six-thirty last night and the doc called Dad half an hour ago to say Garth had slipped into a coma."

Anette's hand froze on the kettle handle. She turned to Brad. "Oh my God. I'm sorry. This is something I've long feared." Anette was about to pour the water into the mugs when goosebumps rose along her arms. "Apart from you and your parents, who knew where Garth was?"

Brads eyes widened. Anette had a point. "The decision to meet with his buddies in Notties was a spur of the moment thing. He asked me to go too. His phone must be tapped." Brad broke into a sweat, the kind that rises when primal fear takes over. "It must be bugged. Garth made the arrangements while we were out riding."

"Have you called Willem?"

"No. I'm pretty sure either Mum or Dad would've, but not

for this." Anette offered Brad a rusk with his coffee.

"Don't assume, Brad. Their minds are focussed on Garth. Call Willem now. I gave the name of the Sangoma to the security team. Her name is Lerato Msizi. Perhaps Tanya got the poison from her, if it is poisoning. It would be strange, Lerato's the best there is. She's a healer and psychic, Brad, not a murderer."

"We were told that too. But Tanya operates under instructions from her grandfather. Lerato won't know what the poison is used for or on. Do you remember the name of the poison used on the horses. That would help the doctor give the right antidote to Garth to bring him out of the coma, if it's poisoning, of course."

"Just call Willem. Stop wasting time." Anette was close to tears with worry and frustration at not being able to remember.

"Willem, I's Brad Whitaker here. Sorry to wake you."

"No problem. How's Garth?"

"In a coma, but I want to tell you that his phone must have been bugged. He made the decision to go with his mates on the spur of the moment while we were all out on a family ride."

Willem didn't reply for a moment, so Brad blurted, "Anette and I think he's been poisoned. Do you have any documentation on the type of poison used to kill our horses. If you do, call the hospital immediately. There may be an antidote," Brad wailed in desperation. He couldn't lose his brother.

"I'll take and look and call your folks. Hang in there, Brad."

"Thanks Willem."

Anette went on speaking. "I heard many things, but I wasn't always in that murdering swine's office. Shall I make a call to Nkizwi, see if he's heard anything?"

"Do you trust that man?"

"No, but he may have heard something."

"If you're comfortable calling him." Brad began to fret.

Anette dialled. Nkizwi's number rang and rang, eventually he answered. "I'm sorry to wake you Nkizwi. It's Anette."

Brad couldn't hear what Nkizwi was saying, but when Anette fainted, he really panicked. He quickly jumped to Anette's aid. Her eyes fluttered open a few seconds later, but her coffee cup was shattered. The coffee strewn across the kitchen floor.

"Are you alright?" Brad asked, helping her up.

"Yes, I'm okay."

"What did he say, Anette?" Brad urged as she straightened her gown.

She didn't look at Brad, she couldn't. "Is he dead yet?"

"WHAT!" Brad screeched. The fear in his voice ricocheted off the walls, then his phone rang. His heart pounded as he answered.

"Hi, Dad."

"Garths gone. He died a few minutes ago." Gary sobbed. Brad collapsed onto the chair beside him holding the phone to his ear. A sob rose from the depths of his soul. It didn't sound like his.

"Brad, Brad." Gary shouted.

"Y....ye.... yes.... Dad. What happened? Oh God, Dad, why? Why Garth?" He bawled.

Anette knew, after what Nkizwi had said, that Garth had died. He'd been poisoned. She held Bradley's shoulders as he spoke to his dad.

"Bye, Dad. See you shortly." He sniffed and fell forward, his head on his knees and cried till there were no more tears. Anger now replaced them. He stood up and yelled.

"If nobody else kills that bastard, I'm going to."

"I'm so sorry, Brad. I wish I could have prevented it."

"You've done so much for us already. I'm going back to the house. I'll call Tinus and James later. Thank you, Anette. It seems Nkizwi is still working with Solomon." Anette couldn't bring herself to repeat Nkizwi's exact words, but Brad instinctively knew there was more. But he couldn't deal with more right now.

BRAD FELL onto his bed and wept his eyes out again, then he called Indigo. He knew he'd wake her, but he felt sure she'd understand. He needed to speak to her before his grieving parents arrived home. The phone rang and rang. Eventually she answered.

"Hi, Brad," she said sleepily and yawned. "What a surprise," but the moment of difficult silence told her something was wrong.

"My.... my brother's.... just," Brad sniffed, "died."

"Oh, my God, Brad. I'm so sorry. How? Car accident?" She asked and switched on her bedside lamp, fully awake now.

"He, um... he and....and...some mates," he paused and swallowed. Indigo waited. "Went out on a bender," he stopped talking and took a breath. "We thought Garth had got pissed. He got home okay, now we know his drink had been spiked with poison." Brad stopped speaking for a moment. "Oh God, this is so hard." He couldn't hold back the tears.

Indigo did her best to comfort him with sympathetic words. "I couldn't imagine anything worse. I'm so sad for you, my love. I'll be there in four days, or" an obvious pause of thought, "will this change now?"

"NO! I need you here, babe. I know that sounds selfish, but the road ahead is going to be stifling."

"Where are you now?" She asked.

"At home. I'm waiting for my parents to return from the hospital."

"Oh God, you poor thing. Even worse dealing with this all on your own. How come you never went with them to the hospital?"

"Mum asked me to stay to get things going in the morning. Never in a million years did anyone expect this. When the folks left here, Garth was still alive."

Was it really Garth he spoke about? Had he really died? In that moment the truth was impossible to comprehend. Garth? Dead. He'd never see his boet again. The thought tightened his chest. For a moment he didn't think he'd be able to talk, let alone breath. He wiped the tears from his face. "I.... I'll.... call.... in...... the afternoon.... my time."

"Be strong. That's what Garth would've wanted, babe."

Broken hearted and stuttering, Brad called Tinus with the tragic news.

"Oh, may fok." He said, using Afrikaans. "Yurrrrrr, Brad. Jesus, no. I'm so sorry. What the hell. How? Where are your parents? I wondered why no-one was at the track this morning." Distressed words tumbled from his mouth. Tinus was gutted.

"None of us can believe it either. Mum and Dad are at the hospital. They should be back in an hour. I don't know what to do with myself. I can't fucking believe I've lost my only boet." Brad held onto the phone and sobbed. Brad could hear Tinus quietly crying too.

"Listen, Brad. I'll come to the house after I've told Johnny. He can go on with everything. Have you let James know?"

"No. I'll do that now." Brad uttered.

"I'll do it. He's here with me."

"Thanks, Tinus." Brad cut the call. A knock on the door.

He didn't want to answer it, but it was Anette. She opened the door and called out. "Anything I can do to help?"

"Yes," he cried. "Bring my brother back."

Somehow, she managed to compose herself. "I wish I could, Brad. How I wish I could." She turned away, unable to face Brad's pain. She took it upon herself to advise the kitchen staff. Brad covered his ears. He couldn't listen to their mournful ululating. It only made Garth's passing more final.

The news spread like a runaway fire, leaving devastation in its wake. Work temporarily ground to a halt. Horses were let out for the day and even they seemed to sense the mourning as a crushing hush had befallen Chanting Clover.

Kagiso and James arrived at the house to support Brad. Tears streamed down their faces.

"Maria's mournful, chilling cries echoed through the broodmare barn. I couldn't stay. Bradley, we are deeply hurt by the loss of Garth," Kagiso hugged Brad with tears in his eyes.

James stepped forward. He took Brad's hand then pulled him into a comforting bear hug, even though he was almost a foot shorter than Brad, it felt good, then he heard the tyre sounds over the gravel on the driveway.

"My folks are here. I think we need to deal with this alone. Please leave via the kitchen." This was the moment Brad dreaded the most.

Mel walked into the hall first, pale and exhausted, her face puffy from crying and collapsed into Brads arms. They stood together and sobbed. Gary followed and wrapped the two of them in his arms. They wept rivers of tears together. Life would never be the same again.

Eventually Brad whispered. "Grandpa will be crying with us even though he's got Garth by his side. They'll be fishing together in heaven." Brad cried like a little boy then. His words choked his sobs, but the sentiment made Mel's worse. Tears ran down Gary's face as he shepherded them into the sitting room.

"Why did he have to die?" Brad sunk into an armchair. Tandy, the black Labrador rested her chin on his knees. Her soulful brown eyes conveyed a profound sense of empathy and understanding, as if she knew Garth was never returning. Tiger, the only surviving Jack Russel after an attack on a puff adder in the garden, jumped up on the arm of the chair to lick away Brad's tears, trying to comprehend the shift in energy and mood. Honey, the golden Labrador, sat between Mel and Gary and mirrored the emotions of the family she loved. She didn't move.

Brad stroked Tandy's head gently while he listened to Gary describe their last moments with his brother, then he rested his head on top of Tandy's.

"Dr Sneddon believes Garth was poisoned. Someone must've spiked his drinks. We don't know what poison yet."

"That's exactly what I thought. Murdering son-of-a-bitch must be stopped. Garth's phone is tapped. Where is it? No-one knew he was going to Notties. We discussed it at the top of the farm on our ride. I told Willem."

Mel's head snapped up. Gary eyes bore into Brads as he listened. "I ran to Anette when you called. I thought she may have heard the name of poisons that evil man prescribed. I also asked Willem if there was anything on file about the poison used to kill our horses. I thought if the doc got a name he'd find the antidote. Anette even called Nkizwi. He asked, 'is he dead yet.' Poor Anette fainted and hit the floor hard." Brad's mouth was quivering. "This confirmed he's still working with Solomon. Willem needs to know all this urgently. Is there going to be a murder enquiry?"

"Most definitely. Willem is already onto it. Now I need to

tell him about Nkizwi." Gary reached for the landline telephone and punched in Willem's number. Their conversation was brief, then he called for Anette.

Mel's eyes were closed. Honey's head rested protectively on her tummy.

"Sweetheart, are you okay with Anette coming over?" Without opening her eyes, she nodded.

"Solomon's hatred of me has ruined our lives. The burden of this is too much to bear now. It's all my fault we've lost Garth." Wracked with sobs, her shoulders shook. She stood and ran from the room.

Anger grasped the back of Gary's throat. It burned with bitter hatred. Would he or Brad be next, he wondered.

The meeting with Anette was emotional, heartbreaking and upsetting for Gary. Now that the realisation had fully penetrated, Brad sat like a statue, his mind grappling with not only a deep sense of loss, but an anger he never thought he'd ever experience as he listened to Anette relived the moment in her cottage, then Gary turned to Brad, "I'm going to check on Mum. Thank you, Anette."

Gary left Brad and Anette in the sitting room,

Mel lay face down on their bed.

"My body is so weakened by grief." She said into the bedclothes, but Gary deciphered her words. She sat up and swung her legs over the side of the bed. Gary sat beside her.

"I'll never get used to not seeing Garth, holding him, laughing with him, cuddling him. No wedding, no grandchildren, no happy times with him present. We'll never watch him ride, and...." Mel murmured something Gary couldn't decipher for she held a tissue firmly against her mouth.

Gary placed Mel in the protective circle of his arms and in the privacy of their room he shed tears of utter desolation.

Chapter Twenty-Five

THE NEWS of Garth Ivan Whitaker's death spread fast. The reception telephone rang constantly for days. Faxes, emails, cards and letters from all over the world arrived in bags. Flowers poured into the offices and Anette managed it all with panache and good grace despite her sadness.

Gary, Mel, and Brad remained numbed by their loss. The world around them blurred as their minds struggled to make sense of Garth's death, though warmed by the kindness and sympathy from friends and family who rallied together to help and support.

Iris manned the admin block, buffering the family from too many visitors, though she seemed unmoved. Anette monitored calls, and the rest of the staff took over while the family mourned.

It was Tinus who told Chase, Siyanda and Kgabu, both miles from home in Mauritius caring for Warrior and Tsotsi. Kgabu had broken down and cried unashamedly on the telephone. Chase vowed to look after him and Siyanda as best he could and offered heartfelt condolences.

Siyanda requested to fly home for the funeral. Garth had been like one of his own.

Gary had advised Steve and Synthia that morning. Apart from Willem, they were the first to know, and that same morning, Tinus had let the Mauritian team know.

Synthia checked on Mel regularly and called Kgabu every day, promising to let him know when the funeral was. They'd fly him home with Siyanda.

Today, a day that should have filled everyone with excitement and anticipation, was just another gloomy day, except for Brad. Indigo was arriving.

Brad woke early and scrambled out of bed, thinking how difficult the first few days at Chanting Clover would be for Indigo. He admired her bravery. Visiting a family she'd never met under such tragic circumstances, and she didn't even know Brad well.

As Indigo's plane landed in Durban.

Steven Dube's flight touched down in Harare at the same time.

BRAD STOOD and waited while passengers filtered into the arrival's hall. When Indigo came into view, his heart did a flutter. She'd seen him too. Pushing her luggage trolley, she rushed to him. They kissed passionately and finally she pulled out of Brad's embrace. "I'm so sorry about Garth, babe," she whispered.

"Thank you. I'm so happy you're here. I hope it's not going to be too awkward for you. I'll do my best to make it easier." He took the trolley and pushed it to the car.

Inside the Landcruiser cab hung a heavy sadness for a while. Brad did his best to lift his mood by pointing out landmarks as they travelled and never mentioned they were being closely followed by a security detail.

Brad took the most scenic route home, working his way through the hills and valleys of beautiful Durban suburbia. Then he weaved up back roads onto the plateau, leaving Kloof and Hillcrest behind them. As they travelled towards Camperdown, Indigo began to nod off. Jet lag was catching up with her after a twenty-six-hour flight. From Camperdown to Fields Hill on the other side of Pietermaritzburg, Indigo slept, but she woke as they passed through the breathtaking Midlands meander to the turn off to Chanting Clover.

Despite the void that Garth's death had left, Indigo's presence was a welcome disruption in the household, and everyone went out of their way to make her feel welcome, but by lunch, lack of sleep claimed her.

She went to lie down and only woke at lunchtime the following day. When she looked at her watch, she couldn't believe how long she'd slept. She jumped out of bed, dressed, and dashed to the dining room to join the family.

"Oh, my word, forgive me," she flashed a brilliant smile. "I'm so sorry, I can't believe how long I've been asleep." Brad jumped up and pulled out her chair. She gave him a quick kiss and sat.

"You needed it, my dear." Mel smiled graciously.

Indigo reminded Gary of a young Mel. They shared common interests, were both exquisitely beautiful and now they shared a mutual love of their surviving son.

Over the next few days Indigo helped lift Mel from a very dark place to one that had brief moments of light, but Mel was often lost in a whirlwind of unanswered questions.

When Indigo and Brad weren't busy with horses, she assisted with the painstaking task of organising Garth's funeral. She darted around like a ray of sunshine, shining her light in the admin offices too. She even managed to encourage Gary and Mel to join them at the track one early morning. They'd not been there for over a week.

Being with Indigo and Brad early in the morning, watching their young horses in training lifted their spirits and momentarily took their minds off their loss. Standing beside Indigo, leaning on the rails that lined the grass track, Mel placed a hand on Indigo's arm.

"Thank you for dragging us down here, it's done us good."

"Here, here," Brad chipped in.

"Aah, it's my pleasure," Indigo answered. Her broad American accent made Mel smile. They watched the training for a while, then visited the stallion barn. Gary wanted to check on a new stallion that had arrived a few weeks ago. A flea-bitten grey in colour with a bad attitude and no manners.

"Morning, madam," Kagiso greeted Mel first, then Gary, then Brad and Indigo.

"How are you coping with this bad-mannered horse?" Mel asked.

"Eish, ma'am, it's going to take time. He's very rude."

Gary could vouch for that. The horse had given Gary a nasty bite on the shoulder. But Gary was impressed. Looking at the horse now, he'd quietened down considerably. "Well done, Kagiso. What an improvement."

"What's his name?" Indigo asked.

"Gatherin'Storm, and he lives up to his name."

The angry clenching of his jaw when people arrived at his stable door had gone and his ears weren't pinned back. "You're doing a splendid job, Kagiso."

"He's got lovely conformation, but not a colour I've ever liked," Indigo commented.

"I agree, but his bloodlines are what we're after. We have a half share in him. Steve, who you haven't met yet, and Synthia bought the other share."

"So how many stallions do you have standing at stud here?" Indigo looked around the barn curiously, there were three stalls empty.

"Six, and that is quite enough." Gary smiled. They each have their own paddock with a stable in each. They all go out intervals, and often this barn is empty, and the stallions stay out all day."

Gary then spoke to Brad. "Mum and I are going to wander home. We'll see you for breakfast."

Brad and Indigo watched them go. "Your folks are holding up well."

"On the surface, but they'll never get over this. What parent does? I'm not sure I will either. We'll learn to manage life without Garth, but we'll never get over his death." Brad pulled Indigo into his arms. "You're amazing, considering how difficult this must be for you. I wish you'd known the folks before Garth was murdered."

"I wish I had too, babe. I don't want you worrying about me. I love being here with you and horses, horses, and more horses, it's awesome." Indigo ran her lips across Brad's lightly. "Healing takes ages. Don't be in a rush. I remember how long I mourned after losing my grandmother. Garth's tragic death will be far harder. First, it's the shock, then the emptiness, then the memories, then the confusion and the questions."

Brad held Indigo's hand as they strolled back to the house. When they entered the dining room Mel was on the phone to Steve in Zimbabwe.

"The line's shocking, Steve. Say that again."

"Okay. That's good news. We look forward to seeing Synthia tomorrow. Very sad you can't be with us."

THE DAY they all dreaded was upon them. Garth's funeral was being held in the church at Michael House school. When they arrived, the church was already overflowing.

The family took their seats on the front pew. Gary's jaw was clenched, feeling the bitterness of the loss of his eldest son now. Mel looked small and aged sitting next to him. She reached for his hand.

"The colonel will never win this war, no matter what." Brad said, leaning close to his dad.

A handful of senior staff had made sure their duties were complete, or they'd swopped with someone junior and were seated at the back of the church.

The Rector had been asked to keep the service short, with only two hymns. He opened the service by speaking about Garth's status as head boy. Brad squeezed Indigo's hand tight. The Rector then read a passage from the bible, which was followed by the Lord's Prayer. After the prayer the headmaster gave a touching eulogy.

"Garth Ivan Whitaker had what most of us envy. He was a tall, good looking, gregarious, young man with a tremendous sense of humour that I remember weakened one's limbs and hurt one's chest from laughing." He smiled, obviously remembering a joke Garth had told as he looked across the congregation. "Not only did he have this marvellous sense of humour, but he also had a deep sense of fairness too which made him an outstanding head boy. Garth's sporting prowess was legendary, and his sense of fun and loyalty was recognised by all. He had an amazing school career, and his last year here he led the scholars by example. His remarkable sporting legacy will live on forever, written on the boards of fame that hang in our school hall. Rest in Peace, Garth. You may not be with us in body, but your spirit shall be with us all forever. Taken too young but now you're in the safe hands of our dear Lord."

Two of the young men that were with Garth on that fateful night, spoke with intense emotion. There were no dry eyes in the church. Garth Whitaker had been loved and admired by all who knew him.

"I can't deal with anymore." Mel whimpered softly.

"It'll be over soon, honey."

She blew her nose and managed to sing part of the final hymn.

The Whitakers filed out of the church ahead of the congregation. They shook hands and thanked everyone for their support.

As they were about to get into the car, Theresa rushed over carrying an oil painting. A portrait of Garth, done by her mother. When Mel saw it, she gasped. All the emotion she'd held onto so bravely in the church, burst. She and Theresa held each other for a long time, silently sharing their tears and their terrible loss. "I wish I hadn't lost his child." Theresa whispered through her tears.

"So do I," Mel said with quivering lips.

They stood apart. "I'll never love another man like I loved Garth." Theresa confessed.

"Please thank your mother for this remarkable painting. It is a superb likeness of our beloved Garth." Mel turned to Gary, "We'll hang it in our bedroom." Gary nodded, too choked to answer with words.

Gary and Mel left the school grounds with the beautiful

painting of Garth on the back seat. While they drove home, Mel kept glancing at it.

When they emerged from the privacy of their bedroom, afternoon tea was ready. Brad and Indigo met them, but there was little conversation as they sat watching the sun going down. Finally, Mel spoke.

"I'm glad we flew Siyanda and home for the funeral. When's he flying back?"

"Day after tomorrow," Brad replied. "I believe Theresa's mum painted a portrait of Garth. May we see it?"

"Yes, darling, of course. Dad hung it in our room the moment we got home."

Brad and Indigo headed down the passage to the master bedroom.

"Wow, that's brilliant," Brad commented. Indigo was clearly taken by the painting as she stood staring at it. "God what a waste of a talented, good-looking guy."

When they got back to the veranda Mel mentioned she'd commission a painting of Garth and Brad together. That painting would hang above the fireplace in the formal drawing-room.

Chapter Twenty-Six

Soft autumn colours had taken over the vibrant summer colours in the garden and Mel spent a lot of time there. Being in the garden soothed Mel, though the cool evenings meant she spent less time on the veranda staring at the distant mountains, remembering the last ride the family had with Garth. Mel's detachment to everything concerned everyone close to her. A total severance to life and all she loved became a massive worry for Gary. Two weeks after Garth's funeral Gary called Tony Brink, the psychologist Mel visited after the Funani attack.

"Mel refuses to see anyone. She hardly speaks and even when her dear friend Synthia visits or calls, she sits with her in silence. I'm frantic with worry, Tony."

"Just leave her be. Let her mind disappear, it's part of the healing process. Continue being loving and kind and comforting, it's all she needs. Your wife is an emotionally strong person, but she's dealing with a kind of guilt none of us can comprehend. This can take months, sometimes years. I'll visit her, instead of you bringing her to my practice. She'll feel more comfortable being at home. How are you coping with your tragic and untimely loss?"

"It's a living hell losing a child, Tony. I'm managing the process because I simply have to. Brad helps me no-end, but the two of us are having more difficulty with anger issues right now."

"I fully relate to that. It's also an important part of the healing process. It may happen to Mel when she moves through the phases. She'll put the emotions into perspective, as you and Brad will too. I'll see Mel tomorrow. Would ten o'clock suit?"

"Yeah, dead right. Thanks, Tony."

The veranda, sheltered from the wind, offered the best view of the vast expanse of their beautiful, autumnal garden. Every now and again Mel caught glimpses of the broodmares in the pastures. She wondered if the Drakensburg mountains in the distance would be covered in snow this year, like the year it snowed heavily, and Garth and Brad built snowmen and got the grooms to make them toboggans and tow them around. A flicker of a smile creased the edges of her mouth. She sat gazing at the view, wishing she had artistic talents, or a novelist perhaps. How that would help her refocus. She needed something to fill the empty void her life had become.

"Mum," Brad broke her reverie. "Please join us on a ride tomorrow."

Mel turned slowly, the movement of an old woman, far older than her years. It was as if she'd heard only a noise.

"I wish I could. Tony Brink is coming to see me at ten." She looked up at her youngest son, "I wish was an artist or a brilliant writer, but as I'm neither, I must sit here and soak up the beauty that surrounds me. I'll ride with the two of you soon."

The following morning Tony arrived just as Mel was feebly

finishing off a slice of toast for breakfast. She found eating tiresome.

They sat together on the veranda with a cup of coffee and spoke for an hour and a half. Mel poured her heart out to Tony. She knew he'd understand and guide her. Gary joined them just before lunch.

"May I?" he asked Tony. He sat beside Mel and squeezed her hand. "How are you feeling, sweetheart?"

"Much better now that I've off loaded the horrors that lurk in my mind. Tony is wonderful."

"Thank you, Tony. Would you care for a bit of lunch?"

"That's awfully kind of you, but I must get back. I have another appointment at one-thirty."

Gary walked Tony to his car. "If you need me, give me a tinkle, but I think Mel will be fine. Let me know when she starts interacting again."

"Will do, and thanks again for making the effort to come here."

Three days later Mel agreed to ride to the top of the farm with Gary, Brad and Indigo.

Gary breathed a massive sigh of relief.

After breakfast they set off. Gary prayed the time spent on horseback would be the therapy she needed, but he also worried the memory of the last time they were all together in her favourite spot might send her back into her black hole.

They rode together in front, one hand on the reins, the other clasped together. The sight warmed Brad's heavy heart and he mouthed to Indigo, "thank you."

They stopped the horses in the normal spot, under the shade of the White Stinkwood trees and stood in silence. The only sounds that could be heard were horse's tails swishing away flies, their gentle sneezes and the odd bird call.

Mel broke the silence. "I'd like Garth's ashes to be buried over there, beneath the Lemonwood tree." A lone tear dribbled down Gary's cheek as he looked at the mountains, then to the base of the Lemonwood tree. For a moment he couldn't speak, then he said, "I couldn't think of a better place for Garth's ashes to be laid to rest."

It always irritated Gary when the phone rang before 6.30 a.m. He'd just got dressed. Mel was still asleep. He grabbed the phone. "Whitaker"

"Sorry to wake you," Steve said. "I've some more news. Can I talk?"

"I was awake, but Mel wasn't. What's up?"

"Some good news. My Zim associates have uncovered something I'm reluctant to discuss on the phone. Can we meet at the pub at lunchtime?"

"Sounds good to me. Hold on, let me ask Mel now she's compos mentis." Gary covered the mouthpiece with his hand and asked. She raised her thumb.

"Twelve-thirty's good for us."

"Wonderful. See you at Prime Italian?"

"Perfect." The thought of a bowl of their speciality Carbonara almost brought a rush of saliva to Gary's mouth. He could do with an Italian carbo-boost.

The Prime Italian restaurant in Durban was Steve and Synthia's favourite restaurant. Built on stilts over the rocks above the sea the upper deck had a spectacular view of the Indian ocean. A perfect place to meet and discuss sensitive cross border issues. As it happened, today there weren't many people sitting outside and though it was cool, the clear IBR roof and the gas.

"COME IN," Indigo answered the knock on her bedroom door. "Brad! Hi sweetheart, how are you this morning?"

"I finally had a restful night without nightmares, so I'm feeling great. Mum and Dad have gone to Durban, so, for the first time since you got here, the house is ours."

"Ooh, how amazing." She melted into Brad's arms, and they kissed passionately. The emotional tension of the past two and half weeks had not been easy for either of them.

"When I got back from the last modelling assignment, Garth asked if we'd slept together," Brad chuckled, thinking back.

"He was a naughty boy, that brother of yours, but we've waited long enough, haven't we?"

"I do believe so." He said affectionately. "Garth had lots of lady friends, but he rarely had them in bed. He didn't trust girls after the Theresa saga, which was sad for them both. Theresa is actually a very nice person and, if I am honest, they suited each other. I'm sure Mum wishes Theresa hadn't lost Garth's child, but enough about Garth for now."

"It's all so sad." Indigo whispered. She wasn't sure why she needed to whisper. It just felt right to talk quietly in that moment. "I must tell you, though, I'm missing not having you in my bed, Mr. Bradley Whitaker. If you'd been in my bed, wrapping your arms around me while falling asleep you may not have had nightmares."

"Out of respect to my folks and the fact that I'm a virgin, I didn't know how to approach it." Indigo knew from the modelling assignment Brad was still a virgin. They'd not had the opportunity to make love in the brief time they got to know each other.

"So, creep in here tonight, and stay here with me." She hadn't told Brad she was also a virgin. She'd surprise him later.

"I thought you'd never ask. But right now, it's time for a good long relaxing ride. What do you think?" Brad looked at her with a crooked grin. "Knowing I'll be in your bed tonight, has aroused me. Let's go."

Indigo teased him as they ran to the stables. It was the first time either of them had laughed in a week.

Thomas saddled Enchantrix for Indigo. She told him she felt like a queen having everything done for her. Thomas grinned. To him she could be a queen. He helped her mount while Brad brought Mr Miracle from his stable. Brad had done his own tacking-up.

It was well after mid-day by the time they reached the shade of the White Stinkwood trees, and they stared silently at the ancient Lemonwood tree knowing Garths ashes would soon be placed beneath it. Its branches spread to embrace the years and all the people it had seen pass its way. It emanated a soothing, healing energy and the horses sighed.

Brad and Indigo dismounted. Holding the reins, Mr Miracle nuzzled Brad's arm. Tears rolled down his face as they sat on the ground. The horses stood behind them.

Indigo cried too. "Oh, my word, I can't stop crying for so many reasons. I can see why your mum loves this place. I can feel mother earth's energy tapping into me right now, like a re-boot to my system. Sometimes I love the fast pace of modern life but being here makes me realise how that pace removes us from getting close to the earth's vibrations."

"Wow, that's profound. Believe it or not, it does the same for me too. I rarely discuss my feelings on that level. Mum and I have an unspoken understanding about intuition and our mutual connectedness to mother nature. She says I'm an old soul."

"I resonate with that sentiment. My happy place back home is on the range, along with my horse. I find horses more authentic and more comfortable company than being in a group of humans. I do the modelling because it's a good income. I can travel to parts of the globe that are fascinating. Not doing the modelling stuff, I'd not have those opportunities. I revel in my good fortune, store the memories in my heart, and in the photos I take. I love the cultures, the vibrance, the colours, the history, and the architecture. I'm blessed to be able to return home to my horses, saddle up and seek peace and solace after a hectic modelling assignment. Do you find the same?"

"Exactly the same. I find modern life invasive. It's too fast. Too techy. Especially when one is brought up to this." He spread his arms wide. "It's priceless."

"This place is like heaven, just as your mum says." Indigo sighed, picking off bits of grass around where she sat. "This is food for the soul. I'm not sure I've ever heard such quietness in my life — it alone, chokes me up." She rested her head on Brad's shoulder.

They sat in comfortable silence while insects buzzed about them. Butterflies of all shapes and colours floated past, flaunting their beauty in front of Indigo. Gentle breezes rustled the leaves through the canopy above. "I've never seen such beautiful butterflies in my life. They carry the spirit of Garth on their wings."

"The words, 'rest in peace,' could not be more apt. To lie up here, beneath the Lemonwood tree, is the perfect place for a perfect man, taken from us far too soon."

"He'll always be with you. You do know that don't you?" Indigo said with conviction.

The horses began to get restless. Flies and midges were pestering.

"Time to head home." Brad stood up and pulled Indigo to her feet.

"I could stay up here forever. Why don't you build a house here?"

"Now there's a plan. Perhaps one day I will. I'm dreading coming here with Mum and Dad to lay Garth's ashes, but I have enjoyed the peace it's offered us now."

"Yes, that's not going to be easy." On the way home Indigo spoke of her dreams. Brad couldn't speak of his, they'd been thwarted unexpectedly.

"If I'm left to live, maybe I'll dream again. If the colonel gets his way, he'll put me beneath the Lemonwood tree too."

"BRAD!" Indigo slapped his arm. "Don't even think such things."

"Well, it seems there's a good chance, given our history." The bitterness in his voice irritated Indigo, even though she tried to understand.

"Even if he doesn't get me, the politics in Africa are so volatile, anything may happen. I may not even inherit this farm. My family have been through the mill in Africa. It began with my great-grandparents who were chucked out of Kenya by the Mau Mau. Their successful cattle, sheep, and coffee farm was plundered and destroyed. Mum's parents were forced to abandon their farm in Zimbabwe. Mum said they died young. Their hearts were broken. I'd be blind not to see what is happening here. The post-independence ruling party, the ANC, is not what it used to be when Mandela was at the helm. The top boys are on the gravy train, raping the country of its wealth and pocketing it for themselves. One thing you must understand about these despots that rule in Africa, they do not give a continental about their own people, their welfare or the future of the youth and generations to come. It's all about living for now and what they can take. The EFF is another political party — the violent youth, pretenders to the throne. They're gathering youth and murdering white farmers at every opportunity — the very people who put food on their tables. Does that make any sense? So, with all this to consider, I wonder about the prospects for my future here."

Indigo didn't know what to say, but what he'd said was the truth even though she had no real grasp on the cultural divide in Africa. She scarcely understood it in America. What she wanted was for everyone to live in harmony, in peace with each other but that was an impossible dream.

"Surely the vendetta must end at some point."

"The only way it will end is when Solomon Tlale is dead. If I'd gone drinking with Garth, I wouldn't be here either. That's how terrifying it is. Steve says everyone in Zimbabwe lives in fear of the evil Mugabe and his henchmen, and of course, Solomon is right up there with him as one of his top men. They believe they're invincible. The man in the street has no future at all."

Indigo understood a little more now and she was afraid. African politics didn't make any sense to her, nor did the vendetta, but she feared for Brad's life.

Thomas was waiting when they got back to the stables. He took both horses and untacked. They wandered hand in hand back to the house. The mood had changed dramatically since leaving the Lemonwood tree.

The hall was filled with the scent of roses and other sweet-smelling flowers brought back from the church. Some had gone over, but a large crystal vase, full of St Joseph's lilies looked like they'd just been picked. They were one of Mel's favourites.

"Such a beautiful smell," Indigo's nostrils flared as she breathed in the delicate scents that filled the hall. "Pity some are going over."

Brad put his arms around her. "The ride was good, wasn't it?"

"Wonderful. I like Enchantrix, she's a lovely comfortable ride, and so safe." Indigo hung up her hat on the hat stand and went to wash her hands. Mel had heard them arrive and joined Brad in the hall holding a cup of coffee.

"Gosh, you two had a good long ride."

"Yeah, we did, it was great. Where's Dad?" Brad asked.

"He's in his office."

"Good, I need to ask him something. I'll pop down."

Indigo came out of the toilet rubbing hand cream into her hands and greeted Mel. "Hi, Mel, how was your lunch?"

"Wonderful, thank you. Did you enjoy your ride?"

"I certainly did." Brad held Indigo's arm. "Sweetheart, I'm just popping down to see Dad. I won't be long."

"That's fine. I think I'm going to have a rest and read my book." She bid Mel good afternoon and disappeared to her room.

Brad knocked on his dad's office door.

"Hi, my boy, how was your ride?"

"Fabulous, thanks, Dad. We rode two boundaries then up to our favourite spot and sat under the Stinkwood trees. I took Mr Miracle and Indigo rode Enchantrix. So, what did Steve find out?" Brad asked as he pulled out a chair and sat.

"Good news for a change. George, the contact, and friend engaged an ex-CID cop to help investigate the colonel's dubious dealings and uncovered most of the colonel's South African contacts. Prime Security are onto them now. It's a sensitive operation and may take a while before we have the evidence we need, but we'll get the bastard. He's done us enough damage."

"That's excellent news. I tried to explain it to Indigo, but it's way too hard for her to grasp. The thought it could be me next fucking scares the shit out of me."

"I'm sure it does. It scares us too. Rest assured; we're doing everything we can to prevent another tragedy." Gary's body shook involuntarily.

"What's the news on Tsotsi and Warriors Rival? Are they going to America?"

"We'll have to see how they feature in Paris. Only then can we decide. But, my boy, you will travel with them if it is to be."

"Great, that's all I wanted to hear. It looks like you want to say something more."

"Yes, I do. I just don't know where to start without bawling my eyes. Without our Garth, many things must change. You'll be the sole benefactor now, and in due course, we'll need to sit down, have a good heart to heart conversation and make the changes with our lawyer. Mum and I will have our wills changed too."

"I've been thinking about my future a lot, if I have one. I'm going to continue modelling for Jeremy because I earn handsome forex. Indigo and I hope to continue our relationship. I want to make the most of the next ten days with Indigo here, so it you don't mind, I'll not be particularly hands-on for the remainder of her holiday. Are okay with that?"

"Yes, of course. Make the most of the time you have together. She's a lovely girl."

"Thanks Dad. When will we be placing Garth's ashes beneath the Lemonwood tree?"

"In a few days. Mum can't do it yet."

That night, when the house was quiet and all the lights were off, Brad snuck into Indigo's room without making a sound. Indigo had been asleep since they got back from their ride. He expected to see her in bed, but she was in the shower and had left the door ajar.

He let her know he was there and lay on the bed. He could see her. Her head was back, her long blonde hair hung wet down her back. While she soaped herself, he thought how graceful she was performing such a simple task. She should be a top international model, he thought, though he knew she didn't want that fame. Like him, her sole reason for modelling was to help achieve her dream of buying her own farm.

He heard the water stop and waited with anticipation. She stepped out of the shower, leant forward and grabbed a towel, covering herself. Then, patting her breasts dry, she walked toward the bed.

"Was that good?" he asked, taken by the perfection of her body. He couldn't help but whisper.

"Divine." Brad could see she felt a little self-conscious with him lying on his side watching her towel herself dry. "Take that grin off your face," she teased. "I still have body lotion to smear all over me."

"How about I do that for you?" Brad suggested. The thought, and the sight of her made his groin tingle.

Indigo handed Brad the body lotion and sat on the edge of the bed with her back to him. He squeezed the sweet-smelling lotion onto the palm of his hand and rubbed it into her back, caressing the top of her shoulders and over the top of her firm buttocks. She turned and faced him, pert nipples erect and aroused. Brad squeezed more cream into the palm of his hands, rubbed them together, then placed them over her perfect breasts, but the pressure in his groin grew too painful to finish. "I think you'd better do the rest," he said and slipped self-consciously beneath the sheets. A few minutes later Indigo lay beside naked beside him.

"You are truly exquisite, babe," Brad took her hand and placed it over him. She held him and whispered, "I'm also a virgin, babe. I'm not too sure what you want me to do," she kissed his cheek shyly. "I started taking the pill a month ago, in anticipation of coming here, so you don't need to worry."

Naked and pressed together, Brad uttered, "Good. I don't want to repeat what Garth did, but I can't tell you how honoured I feel that a beauty like you has kept herself as a virgin for so long. That is unique and rare nowadays. So what if we're a little clumsy together this first time, we can have fun perfecting it."

"Sounds like a good idea." She rolled onto her back and stretched her arms above her head, changing the shape of her breasts and smiled tantalisingly. Brad moved on top of her.

"Ooooh, babe, you feel amazing. We've waited so long for this moment." Indigo looked into his beautiful green eyes. With him just lying on top of her, feeling his manhood she admitted to herself she was falling in love with this man, and she wanted urgently now.

"We certainly have," Brad groaned with desire and felt for her opening. She reached up in search of his lips and moved her legs a little wider as he eased himself inside her. The sensation so exquisite he had to stop moving or he'd let go.

"Can we just lie still for a moment, or I'll orgasm too quickly. I want you to enjoy this first time too." Indigo nodded. Her eyes filled with tears of ecstasy. He could feel her nipples harden against his chest. The urgency of release was too power-ful, and Indigo began to rotate her hips and gasped as they came together to loud applause, then Indigo burst out laughing. "Oh honey, that was heaven,"

"I love you, Indigo," Brad whispered, expressing his feelings for the first time.

"I love you too, Bradley Whitaker." She squealed.

Brad held himself up and gazed at her beautiful face. "It happened so fast. I'm sorry. We'll take our time from now on." He rolled off her.

"I don't think either of us could have held on. It wasn't just you, babe." She slipped the towel out from underneath her and popped to the bathroom to wash away the evidence of her lost virginity, then took a quick shower and came back to bed.

They lay together talking in each other's arms and soon a contented sleep took them happily into LaLa land.

Brad had set the alarm on his phone for five a.m.

It beeped and woke them.

They bounced out of bed, dressed quickly and hurried down to the track, arriving in time to see the first group of young horses warming up.

Standing against the snow-white rails on the edge of the turf track, the wind was cold, and the horses felt it. "Look at the steam rising beneath the quarter sheets" Indigo said as she lifted the hoodie over her head. "I've always loved watching horses blow puffs of steam from their noses on a cold morning. I used to imitate them when I was a little girl," she giggled, "and this morning I feel like one." She bounced around Brad playfully to keep warm and blew steam rings from her mouth.

Brad watched, smitten.

The early morning sun had just begun to filter through the trees, but the rays brought no warmth yet and Indigo snuggled into him. "I don't think I've ever seen, or noticed, such a beautiful soft light, and it's shining in your amazing green eyes, babe.

I think we should go back to bed." She giggled wickedly and cupped his face with her frozen hands.

Brad bounced backwards a little and grabbed her hands. "Geez, your hands are freezing. Your suggestion sounds awfully tempting, but Mum and Dad will be up by now."

Chapter Twenty-Seven

THE TIME HAD COME to decide what to do with their world champion horses who were still in Dubai with Chase. Moving them home would take them out of the running for the Qatar Prix de L'Arc de Triomphe in Longchamp, Paris. Chase wanted them to run in this grand race, but Brad wanted to get to America. Hesitant because of the loss of his brother, he kept his plans under wraps, but he thought he'd share them now.

Indigo had flown back to America, but she called in the middle of the night and woke Brad.

"Hi babe, what's up?" He asked sleepily.

My Dad suggested you send the two horses to us. He is a registered trainer and has some of the top jockeys riding for him. Your two horses will draw huge attention here in Kentucky. Isn't your mum's dream to have her horses race in America?"

"Yeah. What a brilliant idea. I'll put it to them. Thank you, my sweet treasure, for thinking of us. God, I'm missing you and you've only been gone four days."

"I'm missing you too, that's why I called. I want you here., but I'd better let you sleep. Mwah. Call me when you've chatted to your folks."

Despite not wanting to upset his parents, he felt relieved by Indigo's suggestion. He wanted to get out of South Africa and leave the Solomon tension behind.

That evening, sitting in the lounge after dinner, he put Indigo's idea to his parents after worrying all day about putting it to them. He knew his mother would be devastated by him leaving.

"I couldn't sleep last night wondering where the bullet with my name on it might come from. A call from Indigo changed things. She suggested we send the horses directly from Dubai to America. Her father, a registered trainer will train and race them for us there. I'll go over and stay there for a few months. Mum, her father thought you should come with me and stay for a few weeks. This way, it will prevent the horse having to come back here and go into quarantine again. What do you think?"

"Sounds like a pretty good idea to me, "Gary said and looked at Mel for confirmation. Brad had a feeling her reaction would be such. The pain of his words wrenched, and Gary's thoughts were on Steve's earlier call.

The mood in the room was fraught with emotion while Mel sat quietly. It was this that Brad had dreaded.

"Mum, I won't be gone that long, but I need to get away and I think Indigo's idea ties it all together nicely. It is your dream to have our horses race in Kentucky, isn't it?"

A flicker of a smile rose on her face, and she looked at Brad. "Sweetheart, I'm just trying to process an empty house, but it's a great idea and I will come with you, if Dad doesn't mind being left behind."

Brad's shoulders seemed to fold inward from relief.

"Time is like a blur for Mum and me nowadays. I understand you wanting a break away and I think the idea is great. Darling, you need to get away too." Pain was etched into the grooves of Gary's brow like the deep furrows in a ploughed field. Brad had always admired his father's inner strength, but Garth's death was really showing now.

"Dad, I think you need a break from all this too. Why don't we all go. Tinus can manage everything for two weeks."

"That would be brilliant, Darling. Time over there will give Brad and Indigo a chance to see where their relationship might go and our horses will take Kentucky by storm, as they say." Mel's smile widened for the first time in weeks.

"I also thought of going to the UK afterwards. Work in Newmarket for a month or two with your friends the Beresfords, but I'll come home first." Brad said enthusiastically.

"Yeah, I'd like to meet Blair and Francis and see their operation. It would be fun to go together, sweetheart. It will do us all good." Gary smiled lovingly at Mel. As hard as it seemed, it was time to move on with their lives now.

Chapter Twenty-Eight

Sitting in her office gazing out at the ocean, Tanya sipped the hot coffee she'd just made. Tanya favoured this hour of quiet time alone, working out her day before the staff arrived at eight.

Just as the staff began to filter in to start their day, her phone rang. "Hello grandfather," she answered her mobile, his name showed on her screen. She removed herself from her office and wandered down the stairs, across the hallway, and stepped outside into the communal gardens.

"I'll be arriving in Durban tomorrow." He began using his charming tone. It didn't take long for the rude, commanding tone to be back though. "Pick me up at the airport. Two forty-three. I'll stay with you as usual."

"That's fine, grandfather." Tanya raised her eyebrows. She wasn't looking forward to having him.

"Arrange the hire of a black Mercedes. Make sure the windows are darkened, and I want a driver." He put the phone down.

Irritated, Tanya wandered around the gardens for a few

minutes to walk off her mood. The sky was a rich blue today. Not a cloud lingered. She began to wonder why she helped him. She wanted her life back, like the clear blue skies above her. He clouded her life and now he ordered a young life to be taken. NO! She had to stop him. On the way back to her office she wondered how, but it was too late, her secretary had brought in the morning paper and she read of the suspected murder of Garth Whitaker. She went cold.

She knew the consequences of letting him down. She'd end up like Garth Whitaker. Dead.

'Get out,' the voice in her head kept urging and by the time she sat at her desk she'd made up her mind. She'd take the risk. He could deal with his stupid vendetta on his own. She'd notify Nkizwi not to contact her. She read the article about Garth Whitaker and the rest of her day was consumed by research on the family. She discovered an exemplary track record and a disconnect between the image she'd formed of the Whitakers, particularly Melonie from what her grandfather had told her, and what she'd researched, didn't link together.

She thought about the 'three fugitives', as her grandfather called them. Jackson had called her from the police station on her private cell number. He said he'd been brutally interrogated. There'd been little fed back since, though some filtered through from Nkizwi. After a few days in holding cells, the police let the 'fugitives' go. A few days later Jackson had called to tell her he wanted nothing more to do with her grandfather. He'd lost his job because of him. She never heard what happened to the other two.

Shortly after that incidence, she remembered with considerable dis-ease the tone in her grandfather's voice when he said Melonie Whitaker deserved to die. She wanted to meet Melonie. Julie had said she liked her. A pang of regret tightened her stomach when she remembered Julie saying she'd hated doing what she did, but Solomon had threatened her with her life if she disobeyed him.

Tanya discovered the Whitaker's had a great reputation with the unions. So much so their staff had refused got involved with the Trade Union strikes of 2006. That spoke volumes as far as she was concerned. Soon she'd be moving to Nelspruit to live with the man of her dreams. She'd not let anything disrupt her new life, least of all her embittered grandfather.

She dialled her boss's internal number. "Hi Mr. Carsen, may I have the day off tomorrow, please. I have some family matters to deal with?"

Being his key worker, he never had an issue giving Tanya a day off. He'd not write it up as leave, she always went the extra mile, and put in, goodness knows how many extra hours for the company. "Of course, Tanya. Hope it's nothing serious."

"No, not at all, anything but, in fact. Thank you, Mr. Carsen." She then arranged the car hire for her evil grandfather.

Sitting at her dressing table, Mel leaned in closer to the mirror. "God, Gary, I'm looking pale and wan and bloody awful, but I really like Brad's suggestion. I've always wanted to race our horses in America, but darling, are you sure you want to be left alone here?"

"Sweetheart, I'm not the target, as Steve's man said. I might join you, but just for a week." Oh, how he admired his wonderful wife. Despite herself, she was always quick to think of everyone else's welfare and happiness before her own. His thoughts went again to Steve's call. He hated keeping anything from her, but under the circumstances, Steve's intel was best left unsaid for now. Especially the report that Solomon felt he'd hurt her more by disposing of her two sons first, then he'd deal with her.

Gary felt the burden of what he silently carried. He knew the strain showed like the light beaming from a lighthouse across the ocean of his handsome face, but for now, he had to deal with it alone.

"I'll see you in the office just before breakfast, sweetheart." He leant over her shoulder and pecked her on the cheek. "I love you. The break will do you good."

Mel smiled, "I love you too, even more." She went on brushing her hair, feeling the love of him stir in her insides.

"CHANTING CLOVER STUD, GOOD MORNING," Anette answered the internal phone on her desk.

"He's in Durban. Staying with Tanya." Nkizwi said and cut the call.

Taken aback, she raced through to Mel's office. How did Nkizwi know where she worked? Gary and Brad were sitting with Mel, they'd just joined her having finished at the track.

"What on earth is the matter?" Gary asked as she barged in.

Shaking, she closed the office door and uttered, "I've just had a weird call from Nkizwi. Solomon's in Durban, staying with his granddaughter, Tanya." She leant against the door, her legs too shaky to support her. "But" she put her index finger over her mouth, "I heard Iris speaking to Nkizwi in Shona, and he called on the office landline, asking for me."

"He could've got the number out of the telephone directory." Gary said logically.

"Yes, but he wouldn't have phoned me using that number unless Iris told him, plus, she's from Zim. She speaks Shona like it's her mother tongue. There's a sinister message for me in this call. I've never trusted that woman. During the funeral arrangements, Indigo said she got a bad vibe from her too."

"This is exactly what scares me and the reason I need to get the hell out of Africa." Brad fidgeted nervously in his chair then stood up and paced about rubbing his hands together. "What's up with our internal security? If Iris is on the Colonel's pay roll, and she's from Zim, they're not doing what we pay them for." Brad said, the anger in his voice clear.

Anette looked at Brad. "The colonel pays no-one for his dirty deeds." She reminded them, 'so Iris is a volunteer."

"Anette, get Willem on the phone. Ask Iris to call from the switchboard." Anette frowned, but she did as Gary instructed. He had his reasons, no doubt, she thought as she walked to reception, her legs still felt like jelly, but she gave nothing away.

Gary quickly called Willem from his cell phone. "Willem record the incoming call from our switchboard. I think we are onto someone." He ended the call.

"It's scary not knowing what's on that son-of-a-bitch's agenda, and why he's in Durban." Mel felt a rear deep fear now.

"I've only shared half the contents of the intel from Steve's call the other day. For the moment, I cannot share the rest, but I can say thank God you two are getting out of the country."

"What a blessing Anette is. I'm worried about her safety though. We need to get her out of the offices while security corner Iris."

Gary glanced at Mel. This was the second time, in a matter of hours, she thought of the safety of someone else before considering herself. He shook his head in awe.

Ten minutes later Willem called. "Under cover Zulus on their way." He said to Gary and cut the call.

"How are we going to get rid of Iris?" Brad asked, having not heard what Willem had just said to his father.

"That's for security to deal with, my boy. If Solomon comes near this farm, he'll be taken out."

"Bring it on," Brad said happily. "He's mine." But noticed a happy expression on his dad's face too. "Why do you look so happy suddenly?" Brad was curious to know.

"I'll let you know just now, but for the next two weeks all Chanting Clover owned horses will remain on the farm. No racing. We'll have to race the outside horses, and Steve's Harare contact says Solomon can't be out of the country for more than two weeks. He's also a target, apparently. A wanted man in Zimbabwe. A brutal bastard whose actions will catch him one day and let's hope his enemies in Zim do it for us."

"That would solve our problems, but I'd love to end the mother fucker's life, and I'd do it very, very slowly."

"BRAD!" Mel felt his anger burn as deeply as her own. Her anger was entwined with guilt, though, but she'd just witnessed another side to her gentle, kind, youngest son and she couldn't believe the hatred she'd seen on his face. No wonder he wanted to leave.

Mel walked through to Anette's office after lunch. "Has Iris been removed?"

"YES! By two large Zulu men." Anette beaming happily, rubbing her hands together. "And good riddance."

"While I'm here, a thought struck me at lunch. I feel so selfish not asking how your children and mother are doing. I've been so self-absorbed. I'm sorry my dear."

Anette looked at Mel with wonder in her eyes. "I would never have expected you to remember them after what you've been through. My goodness, Mel! Moses and Shinzi are fine, and my mother's well too. At least Moses has a little income, but the money doesn't go far and there's often precious little in the shops. Shinzi asked if she can come here and live with me and now that Iris is no longer here, could I train her as the receptionist?"

"Perfect timing. Will she manage receptionist duties?"

"She'd need training but she's very good with people. She has her 'O' level and she's nearly nineteen. She's bright and learns quickly. I think she'd be an asset."

"Get her here as soon as possible. Why don't you bring all three of them here?

"I'd never thought of that. I'll ask, but what will they do?"

"Moses can help anywhere on the farm and your mum can relieve you of your household chores. How does that sound?"

"Amazing. But........"

Mel cocked her head to one side, "But what?"

"I can't afford their passage here." Anette cried. "I'd love nothing more than to have my family here at Chanting Clover."

"Get Prime to arrange their security. We'll pay for their flights. A security detail can collect them at the airport, not you."

"I....I...."

"No arguments, if they're all happy to come, go ahead and arrange it. You've looked after us, now it's our turn to say thank you."

Chapter Twenty-Nine

BRAD AND MEL arrived at Louisville International airport on the 19th of August, exhausted. Indigo saw them pushing their trolleys and shrieked 'hello' at the top of her voice. Her long blonde hair hung down her back and she was wearing denim dungaree's, with a white T shirt under the top and white trainers. She looked every bit the beautiful pin-up all-American farm gal, Mel thought.

She ran into Brad's arms, kissed, and hugged him, then turned to Mel and gave her a hug. "It's so wonderful to have you both here." Indigo whipped the luggage trolley away from Mel. "It's time for me to spoil you."

"Feels surreal to be near the home of the famous Kentucky Derby," Mel sounded as tired as she felt sitting on the back seat of Indigo's deep red Chevy Suburban SUV. She gazed out the window while Indigo and Brad chatted madly. It wasn't long before Mel fell asleep — a combination of jet lag, emotional exhaustion, and relief. Thousands of miles from home she was no longer being held hostage to the perils of the vendetta.

Brooks End farm was a forty-five-minute drive from Louisville. Tsotsi and Warriors Rival were already there. They'd been transported by Emirates SkyCargo in a Boeing 777 and had been collected by professional horse carriers that Indigo had arranged.

The entrance to the farm and the farmhouse was exactly as Mel imagined. The road leading up to the farmhouse was like back home; lined with lovely old trees, only their road wasn't gravel, it was tarmac and beyond the line of trees she could see white post and rail fences demarcating the paddocks. Passing through the tree line avenue she saw snatches of some fine young Thoroughbreds.

The farmhouse, a huge rambling cream-coloured brick bungalow with a green roof and painted green window frames was like how she'd pictured it. A terraced garden banked one side of the driveway and parking area and filled with blue and white agapanthus that reminded Mel of home.

Indigo pulled up outside the front door. A white gabled entrance porch covered the front door. A black, cast-iron racehorse was mounted against the white board at the face of the porch. There was no doubt that racehorse owners lived here, she smiled and opened the car door.

Blair and Francis welcomed them into their home.

Mel loved the open plan, simplistic, ultra-modern design. Francis wasn't one for endless ornaments but what she did have were hundreds of photos of their horses on every wall, plus some magnificent bronze sculptures of horses. The one that caught Mel's eye was a beautifully sculptured bronze mare and foal. She guessed it was about a foot in height and about the same length and sat in the middle of the long, twelve-seater wooden dining room table.

Francis liked large glass vases of flowers. Arum lilies with an assortment of other white flowers and greenery filled many spaces and though Mel loved it, it felt more like a show house than a home.

The following morning, after catching up on some much-needed sleep, Mel and Brad were shown to the stable complex. Blair had said the vet who'd travelled with the Whitaker horses reported the two champions had been a pleasure to handle. Quiet, obedient, confident horses. They'd been the last drop-off and Mel could only imagine her poor babies were exhausted, but she couldn't wait to see them.

They met Indigo at the stables. "I doubled their bedding and wrapped their legs, so hopefully they rested well." She told Mel and gave Brad a kiss and led them to the horses. Tsotsi nickered when she saw them and Warrior Rival, who was busy pulling at his hay, spun around and reached his head over the door. Mel gave them each her customary greeting, a kiss on the nose and big bear hug.

"My darling babies are looking so well considering. Thank you, Indigo."

"My pleasure," And for some reason Mel thought her accent sounded broader than when she was at Chanting Clover, but probably not!

Mel and Francis hit it off, but Brad could see she didn't like Blair. He'd ask her when they had a moment alone. Likely she understood why Indigo's brother would be given everything when he passed away. If he could speak for her, he'd guess she would have summed him up as a classic chauvinist with the old-fashioned belief that women weren't designed to run a business, any business and he knew that would raise his mother's hackles.

When Mel joined Brad and Indigo after a guided tour with

Francis and Blair, she found a moment to whisper to Brad. "How are you getting on with Benjamin?"

Brad grimaced. "It's going to be a challenge. The rough edges of youthful arrogance haven't been chipped away by life yet, and I guess he's spoilt rotten. A classic brat in my opinion." Mel covered her mouth, she wanted to laugh. She agreed. If anything got in the way of this endeavour, it would be the two B's, she thought.

Indigo had inherited her flashing good looks and broad smile from her father. Thank the Lord she didn't have his personality, Mel reflected as she followed to view young Thoroughbreds in another barn. She led the way down to the end of the barn. A pretty young yearling reached for Mel as she passed. Mel flet her energetic pull and turned back. The filly snuggled her nose into Mel and nickered gently. Blair had turned to watch.

"You're not a bloody bunny hugger, are you?"

"No, not at all. But I do love horses and most of them love me." She said sharply, making her stance abundantly clear as he stood with a sarcastic expression on his all-American, tooth perfect smile, strong jaw lined face. There was no doubt he was a good-looking man, as was Benjamin, but their loud, arrogant and egotistical ways removed any natural charisma. Indigo had inherited charisma from Francis, Mel thought as she turned away from Blairs penetrating glare.

Blair looked at Francis, shrugged his shoulders and they moved outside the barn and wandered back to the house. Brad and Indigo joined them for breakfast a little later.

In Harare, Solomon sat at his desk in Army Headquarters, seething. His mole had been caught. He wondered how Brad and Mel had escaped to America before he'd finalised the slaying of that last Whitaker boy. The pain of Tanya's desertion still stung and weighed heavily on his mind. He had to find out the real reason for her leaving before he decided what to do about it. But first, he had to find out why his instructions had, yet again, been foiled.

He shifted his enormous frame in his chair and poured a robust treble tot of Johnny Walker Blue Label whiskey into a glass, then gulped the amber liquid back. It burned down the back of his throat. The same feeling he had when Tanya told him to do his own dirty work.

He began to wonder if the new mole had been influenced by her. He'd have to get rid of her. He couldn't live with Tanya's words screaming inside his head, burning him up, like the whiskey was doing to his throat right now.

He repeated her words aloud. "That's what your stupid vengeance does to your brain, grandfather. It fucks it up. It's why all your plans go astray. You only plan when you've had half a bottle of fucking Johnny Walker first." She'd yelled at him.

He lifted the empty glass, looked at it, and sloshed in another treble tot. More of her words flooded in. 'You're too old for all this crap. You've had three wives, all of whom have left you, and hate you, and now, Grandfather, I want nothing more to do with you — ever. It embarrasses and shames me to think I'm related to you.'

Those words hurt deeply, though the whiskey helped dull the pain.

It pained him just a fraction more to think his henchmen would now have to get rid of his granddaughter too. More words. 'Your stupid plans have jeopardised my life and my job. I want you out of my life forever. I've booked you into the Maharani hotel. I don't want you near me, or my flat. I'll pay the rent from now on. You make the plans for the return of the hired car.' Her words rattled in his brain. He felt his heart thump with anger.

She'd shoved him out of her flat. He remembered her high-pitched yell. 'Now leave. GET OUT.' The angry pitch gave him a headache. He remembered trying to calm her, but she'd slammed the door in his face. Another big mistake.

The confrontation rankled. He took another gulp of his dearly beloved liquor and felt the warmth sooth him this time. He wondered if she'd really meant what she'd said.

After his third glass of whiskey, he put his thoughts to the test and called her number. It no longer existed. He smashed his whiskey tumbler on his desk.

"HI HONEY," Mel responded to her beloved husband's voice. He'd called earlier than expected, she wasn't out of bed yet. Perhaps he'd miscalculated the time difference? "Is there a problem?"

"No, sweetheart, on the contrary. Good news. We've been honoured with the South African Breeders Championship title. Can you believe it?"

"Oh wow, that is good news."

"Well, it is, but it's caused a bit of an issue for me. They suggested that Brad may like to receive the award, after one of us has given a speech. The TBA are dedicating the evening in memory of Garth." Emotion wobbled his speech. "Do.... you think .... Brad will be up to it?"

"I'll ask him, darling. I'm sure he'd be delighted," she said bravely. "When is the function?"

"In three weeks. It means both of you will have to fly back

at the end of next week, which is only a week earlier for you, but I guess, a bit of a pain for Brad. Missing you stacks too, and how are the horses?"

"I'll be ready to come home. I miss you too. The horses seem to be doing well. They've settled in. Blair handles it all very differently, though. He's made it clear he wants no input from me, calls me a bunny hugger and accused me of being far too emotional. Their farm is stunning and the whole operation is well organised, I'll give them that, but...." Mel stopped. "I'll explain it when I get home. It's a pity I'll miss their first race booked at Keenland racecourse. I'm hoping they qualify to race at the famous Churchill Downs. I'm going there with them this coming Saturday. Very exciting. I'm not sure Brad and I'll come home together, but I'll ask and let you know later."

"Shall I call you back, or will you call me?"

"I'll call you, sweetheart. The time differences are difficult." Mel put the phone down and suddenly yearned to be home beside her husband. The break, as short as it would be now, will have done her good.

Mel spent half an hour during the next two evenings sitting with her two champions, talking to them both and thinking about being home, the excitement of attending the famous Kentucky Derby, where the brilliant horse Secretariat became internationally recognised as one of the world's finest racehorses and her husband.

To her surprise, Brad and Indigo said they'd fly home with her, but first it was the Kentucky races.

Mel, Brad and Indigo travelled in Indigo's car. Blair, Francis and Benjamin travelled in the family's Mercedes saloon. Their destination, the Churchill Downs racecourse.

Mel had spoken to Gary earlier. He was most envious of their opportunity.

They parked in the VIP parking. A very grand set of stadiums made Mel hold her breath as they made their way to the VIP box. "Gosh, this is spectacular." Mel looked about her as they took their seats, and she gazed across the lawned infield.

"I love the brick paved parade ring and the fancy winner's area, Mel said to Francis when they arrived. "This is such a treat. I've always dreamt of having my homebred horses race here."

"The grassed infield is the only place where cheap tickets can be had," Francis explained, noticing it was still almost empty. It'll fill up soon and you won't see a blade of green grass. Did you enjoy the partying folk outside the main gates and up the avenues?"

"Yes, I did, very entertaining, brings on a jovial atmosphere, doesn't it? Nothing like that happens in South Africa. It's like a carnival."

Spectators and punters began to gather for the first races and the grandstands were filling quickly. From where Mel sat, she could see the twenty starting stalls on the sand track, but the track was nothing like the one in Dubai.

She leant close to Brad, "Wonderful, isn't it? And to think the main race is only run this evening at seven. As a breeder and trainer, it always makes me wonder why we do it. The total race time lasts just on or over two minutes, yet it takes years and vast expense to get a horse ready for a race, or even breed one that has the potential to qualify to run in a feature race." Mel pondered and Brad laughed.

"I'd never thought about it like that before. But you're right. Let's hope Blair gets our two to run on this track."

Blair overheard her. "We'll have to turn them into proper horses, not cuddly bunnies if they stand a chance of qualifying."

Mel looked away and scowled. Brad seethed inside. Blair was trying hard to ruin their day.

Mel turned back to face him. She wasn't going to let such an arrogant pig get away with that nasty statement. "My two horses won the world's richest races in Dubai. From what I gather none of your home bred horses have run there, not have you won the feature race here. We're paying you good money to get them to the top here, so I'd like to see it being done, and done with care. Any brutality and we'll ship them home."

Blair shrugged his shoulders. "I suppose you sat in their stables in Dubai and spoke sweet nothings into their ears, and miraculously they won for you."

This time Mel didn't bother to answer. She got up and wandered around below the grandstands watching costume parties begin below the grandstands.

Brad came after her. "Indigo is so embarrassed and apologises. I don't think Francis dares say a thing. Indigo and I are going to watch from the general grandstands if you want to join us, Mum."

"I'd like that. I'll wait for the two of you down here." She needed to be alone for a few minutes to make her decision.

Chapter Thirty

In 1979, Iris Paige had won the coveted title of The South African Breeders Champion. And now, thirty years later, Gary and Mel were to wrench it back. She hoped 2009 marked the turn of better things for the family.

A most prestigious title, one of the highest honours in the horse racing world, and even this didn't impress Blair. Mel knew he'd be happy to see the back of her, just she would be him. She found him to be the rudest, most despicable human being she'd ever met, bar one, of course.

Mel, Brad and Indigo were on the same flight home. She didn't want to miss the celebration, especially as Brad was to give a speech to honour national breeders and his late brother, Garth.

Douglas Wakefield, the then Director of the TBA, had thought it fitting that Brad receive the coveted award after Gary had made his speech, then he'd present his as normal.

Indigo helped Brad prepare his speech before they flew, and he'd recited it a few times.

. . .

DOUGLAS HAD CHANGED the traditional protocols of the evening for the Whitaker family's input into South African horse racing was admirable on many levels and had been consistent with Iris Paige's legacy.

They'd not only bred numerous champions and many of the finest horses ever bred in the country to date, but they'd imported four fine stallions to improve the national gene pool, they'd rehabilitated the famous international jockey, John MacIntosh.

Gary collected them at the airport in Johannesburg. They spent the night at the City Lodge Hotel that night and the following evening the awards ceremony was held in the Sandton Southern Sun, where Gary had booked them into.

They arrived early and had a drink in the rooftop bar where John met them.

What the Whitaker's didn't know was Douglas had prepared an in depth look at the amazing lives of Gary and Melonie. Not only had they rehabilitated John, who'd been told by numerous doctors he'd never walk again, let alone ride, plus they'd opened their home and cottages to young jockeys desperate for that one important all-important break. No other South African racing family had been inflicted with the number of tragedies the Whitaker's had endured.

Of course, the family knew none of these plans. After a few drinks with John, they went to change. The dress code was formal. Gary looked dashing in his black suit and bow ties and Brad looked outstanding, dressed in a navy Ralph Lauren three piece tailored Polo suit. Mel wore a forest green three-quarter sleeve velvet dress and Indigo wore a structured ivory two-piece trouser suit. They took their allocated seats close to the stage where Douglas met them.

By seven the tables were full and starters were served.

Douglas stood up, gave his welcome speech and explained that the evening would begin with the first two course, then the awards and then a tribute to the Whitaker family and the late Garth Whitaker.

The evening was a great success. Gary received the award for Chanting Clover stud, then Brad gave his speech. He kept it amusing with anecdotes taken from the last nineteen years of Chanting Clovers history and touched very briefly on Garth. He'd been advised that John was reading the eulogy at the end of the evening.

Indigo felt deeply honoured to be a part of the evening awards ceremony. She loved the funny little bits he'd added and faltered only when he touched on bits about Garth.

"I hasten to add, Garth Whitaker, my beloved late brother, is still with us all." He said boldly, holding his emotions together for the last part of his speech. "He's here in this room with us, and he'll be with us at every race meeting across the world." Brad held the trophy his father had passed to him and held it up proudly. "Till we meet again, boet."

The audience were on their feet and clapping. Someone shouted from the back, 'Here, here, Bradley.'

Dessert was then served, and platters of cheese and biscuits were put on each table.

Douglas gave everyone half an hour to finish, then he stood up and tapped his beer tankard with his spoon. There were over a hundred guests in the room.

"I'm not getting up on the stage again. I've eaten far too much." Everyone laughed and most of the audience agreed.

"Tonight is not only about the prestigious awards we've given out, but I'd like to end this evening with a tribute to the late Garth Whitaker who was tragically killed."

Douglas gave a heartfelt eulogy having done his research

well. He ended by wishing the Whitakers all the best, and success with the two horses in America. When he finished there was not a dry eye in the room.

It had been an exceptionally difficult evening for Gary, Mel and Brad. They thanked everyone for their support and retired to their rooms feeling the loss of their beloved Garth in an even more profound way. The wounds had been exposed once more even though Douglas's intentions were honourable and sympathetic.

Brad drove them home the following day. Gary felt too drained to drive safely. He and Mel sat on the back seat and slept. Indigo sat in front with Brad, and they chatted quietly about how they were going to deal with her father and brother when they got back to the US.

An armed security detailed followed closely.

As soon as they got back to Chanting Clover Brad called to confirm his and Indigo's return tickets to America. He didn't want to hang around knowing his safety wasn't guaranteed. His concern for Indigo's safety was a top priority too.

"Let's start your day with some good news." Steve said. Gary stretched back in his office chair, "I need it. I'd like to start every day with good news."

"Tanya has moved to Nelspruit with her fiancé. She booted the evil grandfather out of her flat. George, our Zim contact says he's floundering, and this has impacted his already bad health. Too much whiskey. Too bloody fat. And another little bit of information — Iris flew to Zim a few days ago."

"Brilliant. I hope the bitch is in his firing line. Mel will be overjoyed to hear this. Perhaps soon we can settle into a normal life at last. Will be weird not looking over our shoulders the whole time and worrying about little moles hiding in our offices, home, or elsewhere on the farm."

"Yes, you won't know yourselves. I hate to add a bit of bad news though. Nkizwi is still working with him, so we're not in the clear yet. But our plans are coming together nicely. Any news on how Tsotsi is doing?"

"Well, apparently. Brad and Indigo fly back tomorrow."

"How was the Awards evening?"

"Oh God, heartrending and painful. We both feel a bit raw. Sorry you weren't there with us."

BRAD SAID a difficult goodbye to his parents. Gary and Mel hugged Indigo, and they set off for the airport. Tinus was driving, he had a batch of vaccinations to pick up Durban after he'd dropped them off.

"How are you doing, babe? That evening was hard for you." Indigo squeezed his arm affectionately.

"Yeah, it was tough, but I'm proud of the family and our achievements. My focus now is getting out of here."

"I can see you're very edgy."

"All sorts of different thoughts keep popping into my mind. I just need to put my head back, close my eyes and be quiet for ten minutes. I'm exhausted."

"Me too, now you mention it."

Before Brad put his head back, he checked security were close behind. Satisfied, he closed his eyes.

Tinus asked Indigo about the American racing scene, and she answered candidly, then noticed Brad's fists were balled and his jaw clenched. She was worried about him, but she knew once they were on the plane, he'd relax.

Brad opened his eyes. "How ya doing, Tinus." He asked.

"Yeah good."

But something didn't feel right. Sometimes Brad cursed his sixth sense.

"What's the matter, Brad?" Indigo felt his leg begin to shake.

"I don't know what it is, but it's making me nervous. I'm going to call Dad. Tinus, would you mind pulling over, please."

"Sure," Tinus slowed, then glanced in the rear-view mirror. Unfortunately, he saw it too late.

"MR. WHITAKER, MR. WHITAKER," Brad heard his name being called. The voices sounded distant, like they were coming from inside a tunnel and echoed in his head. He tried to move, but he couldn't. He tried to answer, but he couldn't. Blinking rapidly, he slowly opened his eyes.

"Where am I?" He looked into the eyes of the nurse leaning over him.

"You're in hospital, Mr. Whitaker." Brad suddenly sat up, but his head spun so violently he lay back. Crystal-like patterns danced across his vision. "Where's Indigo? Where's she? What happened?" Brad asked, panic-stricken.

"You were in a car accident, Mr. Whitaker. Your friend is in the ward next door. She has been asking for you."

"Oh, thank God. Can I see her, please?" Brad moved as if to get out of bed, but the nurse stopped him.

"Mr. Whitaker, you cannot move from this bed. Doctors' orders."

"Is she injured?"

"Not badly. She can walk. I'll go and call her and tell her you've woken."

A few moments later, Indigo appeared at the door to Brad's

private room in a white hospital gown and limped toward his bed.

"Thank God you're alive and awake now." Indigo cried and kissed him.

"You're hurt, babe." Brad gently touched her swollen left eye, bruised black and blue and yellow.

Indigo held his hand. "Apart from smashing my eye, stitches in my arm, bruises all over me and a very sore hip, I'm okay. They X-rayed my hip, nothing's broken." She showed Brad the stitches in her arm. "What the hell happened?"

"I guess we're supposed to be dead. Solomon's plan for us it would seem." Brad's eyes burned with rage, his voice laced with venom as he thought about the evil colonel. Indigo felt his anger, but when he looked at her again, his eyes were gentle and loving. "Thank God your wounds are superficial. Do your parents know?"

"Yes, they do. Your mum called. I've spoken to her. They should be here shortly."

"How's Tinus?" Indigo dreaded him asking that question.

"I'm so sorry, babe. He died in the ambulance. It was horrible. I travelled with him. You were taken in another ambulance. You were unconscious. The medics thought you'd broken your back. I watched the medics work on Tinus, but as hard as they tried, they couldn't save him. His family have been notified."

"Jesus, no! NO. NO. That fucking bastard," Brad swore, and two nurses came running. His lips were quivering, and tears overflowed.

"Is everything okay?" One of the nurses asked Indigo.

"Yes, thank you." She held Brad and he cried. "This is getting out of hand now."

Indigo felt her heart would break for him. He was

devastated.

Gary and Mel burst into Brad's private room, panic-stricken, but relieved to see Indigo standing next to Brad, groggy, tearful, but awake and alive.

Mel hugged him and sobbed with relief, then Gary rubbed Brad's arm. "Thank God you are alive."

Brad had taken a hard knock to the head. He'd been unconscious for a few hours which had worried everyone and long enough for the Doctor to insist on x-rays of the skull when he woke.

"Will you excuse us. Doctor's orders are to get Mr. Whitaker to the Xray department." The nurse said politely and helped Brad into the waiting wheelchair.

"The cops said the Landcruiser is a right off. You were hit by a speeding BMW." Gary said.

"Really, is that what hit us?" Indigo shook her head. She was interested to know more. "Gary, do you know whether the car that hot us belonged to that man?"

"We are waiting to hear who the driver was. He's dead too."

"I remember the vehicle rolling and Tinus screaming. His injuries were too severe to save him."

"Well, he took the brunt of the speeding BMW. You were all pulled from the wreckage by the jaws of life. It's a miracle you two are alive. Do you remember that?"

"No, not really. It's all quite a blur."

"Sit, Indigo. I'm so sorry this has happened to you." Indigo was close to tears now.

"After I'd been seen to and the wounds stitched and I'd showered, I sat next to Brad for an hour praying he'd wake up, but the tranquilisers they'd given me made me so sleepy I went back to bed. Just before the car hit us Brad said he had a gut feel something wasn't right. He asked Tinus to pull over so he could call you, Gary. It was as we were slowing down that we were hit."

The screeching of rubber wheels on the vinyl tiled flooring meant Brad was back from the X-rays.

"Two fractures to my skull." He rubbed his head carefully. Gary and the nurse helped him get into bed.

"Dad, do you know if the driver of the BMW lived or who he was?"

"He died at the scene and once he's been identified we'll know." Gary watched Brad's eyelids flicker. "Go to sleep, my boy?" Within seconds Brad had drifted off.

Gary and Mel left the hospital with Indigo. Mel couldn't bear the thought of her sleeping on the pull-out chair with her painful hip. Besides, Brad would be asleep all night. They'd be back in the morning.

"Hello, sleepyhead," Indigo kissed him. Gary and Mel were there too. They'd been escorted into the hospital by armed security guards.

"Morning." Brad said, still groggy.

"Are you allowed home today?" Mel asked.

"Yes, I am. I saw the doc earlier. Indigo and I need to get the fuck out of the country as soon as possible. I'm sad, I'm angry, frustrated, enraged, and feel fucking vulnerable. I'm sure you understand, Mum." He sat up. "I woke twice last night from nightmares about killing Solomon."

"Dad and I fell all those emotions too. Unfortunately, you're not cleared to fly yet. You must wait a week for the swelling in your brain to subside."

"Really?" That news didn't impress Brad.

"Indigo booked your new flights for Monday week."

She'd also brought a change of clothes for him and stuffed the filthy, blood-stained ones in a bag.

Just as they were about to leave, Doctor Sneddon arrived. "Bradley, you're one lucky man." He pulled a little flashlight from his top pocket. "Let me check those pupils once more." Blinding Brad with the penetrating light, he said, "take it easy, Brad. Here's a prescription. You should feel much stronger in a day or two. The headaches will subside as the swelling of the brain goes down. Get as much sleep as you can, and don't go racing around. You know you can't fly for a week?"

Brad managed a faint smile. "Can't race around like this. Thanks Doc."

Outside the hospital the two-armed security men waited. Brad shook their hands in the traditional African way. "We're happy to see you," one of them said in Zulu and they followed the Whitakers back to the farm.

THE FOLLOWING Monday Brad and Indigo boarded a Boeing for America. Happy to be flying to safety, but sad they would miss Tinus's funeral.

Indigo held Brad's hand as the Boeing gathered speed down the runway then lifted into the sky.

"I can't stop thinking about Tinus. I'm really sad to miss the funeral. He was such a brilliant trainer and friend. He'll be sorely missed and now Dad has no help, other than Mum." That worried Brad.

It took a full two days before Indigo and Brad finally arrived back at Brooks End Farm. Brad called his parents the moment they drove onto the property. He knew they'd be waiting for the call.

"Hi Ma, we're here, tired, but safe."

"Good. Glad you had a good flight, tiring though. How are the headaches?"

"Not too bad, thanks."

"The driver of the car has been identified. It was Nkizwi. When I told Anette, she rejoiced, threw her arms up and said, "Praise be to God. He's the last link in the chain now that Iris is no longer in our midst."

"That is good news, but how did the bastard know Indigo and I were in that car?"

Mel went silent for a moment. "Good point. From Nkizwi, I guess. But yeah, how did he know. Willem's team have missed something again."

"Was it ever confirmed that Iris flew to Zim? I'm amazed Nkizwi took his life. Like a fucking suicide bomber. That shows you the effect Solomon had on him. The man is evil beyond evil, if that's possible." Brad took a deep breath. "Mum, you're not safe until that bloody man is in a box, buried very deep underground. Put the proverbial bomb under Willem."

"We will, today. Dad wants a word."

"Hi Dad."

"Encouraging news from Steve. Solomon's circle is getting smaller, and his health is a concern." Gary said.

"I hope his fucking heart stops beating. Anyway, Dad, we're safe. I'll miss you both like crazy, but we'll chat regularly."

"Of course. Now look after yourself, son."

"I will. Bye for now."

It took Brad and Indigo another fortnight to fully recover from their wounds, bruises and swellings. They missed Tsotsi and Warriors first race.

Tsotsi ran below her usual standard, coming in third. Warriors Rival ran a bit better and placed second.

Hugely disappointed, Brad said so. Though Blair was furious, he suggested they'd not fully recovered from the long flight.

Brad had no option but to agree, but the horses had been in America for six weeks.

"Come on babe, you should know six weeks is not a long recovery time." Indigo said, but Brad could hear she was annoyed with him.

"Yes, I guess you're right, but I'd like to introduce some Chanting Clover tips during their training sessions and improve their nutrition."

Indigo mentioned it to Blair and Benjamin. Both turned crimson with anger and refused to take Brad's valuable advice.

Brad had an inkling that things would not work out as planned for their horses in America. He'd keep quiet for now, but if nothing radically improved, he'd step in. They were his horses. It worried Brad that Indigo was so wary of her father. He mentioned it but Indigo was very reactive. He'd touched a part of her she wasn't ready to deal with. It was their first real disagreement.

Just before the qualifying race for the Kentucky Derby, an associate of Blair's offered an exorbitant price for Warriors Rival.

Brad called his parents. "Mum it's for the best. Blairs training methods are not suitable." Saddened by the news, Gary and Mel mulled over the options and decided in the interests of the horse's welfare Warriors Rival could go to stud and they let Brad know.

Blair was turning out to be a very disappointing trainer, and Mel was concerned.

Gary called Blair and expressed his concerns about Tsotsi. Blair's temper flared. His oversized ego was being questioned.

"Brad is also not happy with the way things are going."

"I suppose you're going to send your wife over to give the horses a hug and a talking to." Blair's smarmy, sarcasm didn't go down well with Gary.

"Fuck you, Blair. You've not proved yourself and my son is taking the brunt of it. If Tsotsi doesn't perform in the qualifying race next week, she's coming home." Gary slammed the phone down, fuming with indignation.

Mel was in tears. She'd not ever seen Gary so angry. "Honey, Blair is ruining our precious Tsotsi and he's charging us the earth to do it. Bring her home."

Early in the evening, two days after the battle with Blair, Gary found Mel sitting with Master Vision. The stallion had a dreamy look in his eyes while he stood beside her, and he wished Blair could see her and the response she was getting from the powerful Thoroughbred stallion. But in reality, Gary knew he wouldn't give a shit, anyway.

He entered the stable, leant down and whispered in her ear. "I'm also pining for Garth, my darling. I liken the sensation to losing a leg — the feelings are still there, but the limb is missing." Mel burst into tears and when she finally stopped crying, she stood up and rested against Gary's chest. "I relate to that. Let's get Tsotsi home, then maybe Brad will come with her."

Chapter Thirty-One

"Hi, Julie. It's me, Tanya. How are you?"

"Great, thanks. Wow, it's so nice to hear from you. How's life in Nelspruit?" Julie missed Tanya, but life with a baby took up most of her time and though she didn't forget about her friends, by the time evening arrived, she was too exhausted to chat for half an hour.

"Just awesome. I love it. Super friendly place, weather's awesome and being I love tops it all. How's your little bundle of joy?"

"She's good. Thabo's brilliant with her, even though he's away such a lot. He's flying to Australia next month. I'm so proud of him. Envious too, of course. But nothing compares to being a mother. Hey! When are you getting married?"

"Next month, on Valentine's Day, which luckily falls on a Saturday. Can you come? Will Thabo be in Aus by then? Simon would love to meet him."

Julie shrieked happily. "Of course we can come. Thabo

leaves on the 22nd of February. Yippee, then you'll see our beautiful, Zinzi."

"I can't wait. I hate to change the subject, but..." she paused, "back to the evil grandfather. Did you hear Nkizwi wiped himself out in the car accident my bloody grandfather set up? Another almighty fuckup. He doesn't learn. Someone must deal with him, talk some sense into his thick head. He didn't listen to me, the stupid old fool. The whiskey consumes his brain and fuels the ridiculous vendetta. It blows my mind how someone can hate so rabidly."

"Sorry to say, but he's the most vicious, evil man I've ever encountered. I'm so glad I've had nothing to do with him for years. I follow what happens to the Whitakers, though. It saddens me, to be honest. It saddens Thabo too. He knows them well. Everyone likes them so much. I have nasty nightmares about what I did. They don't deserve what your grandfather is doing to them, and though I don't hold anything against you for getting me involved, I'll never forgive myself for what I did. Fear kept me there, but you know the story, hey?"

"Unfortunately, I do, and believe me Julie, I will always hate myself for getting you involved. What I love so much about you is, we are still such devoted friends. I'll treasure that for life. Obviously, he never received an invite to the wedding, he can keep his personal vendetta and thirst for violence all to himself now he's knocked off Nkizwi. I pray he has no idea I live in Nelspruit. I don't doubt he'll eventually find us, though. There must still be a mole at that stud."

"Surely there are none of your family left who'd want anything to do with him? And Prime security constantly check the stud for moles, but they can slip through, I guess., but who in their right mind would want to help a man who's festered such hatred inside him for years, twisting his thoughts."

"One can never be too sure. You know what he's like. Anyway, we're going to Zim for our honeymoon. I know it's a dodgy decision, but Simon has never been to Zim, nor has he met family of his that live in Bulawayo and won't make it to our wedding. Things are dire there. Simon sends them money every month, or I'm sure they'd die of starvation. It's too awful. We're spending four days in Victoria Falls, stopping in Bulawayo for two nights first, and one night in Harare. Pity we can't be away longer."

"Sounds great." Julie sighed. "I can't believe we were such idiots. Your grandfather has ruined our lives. We're criminals, Tanya. Shit, if it were all exposed, we'd be had for murder."

"I know. I pray I can cross the border without any shit. Thankfully Simon has connections in his debt collecting business, but you never know, by then grandfather may have got someone else on my tail. When I slammed the phone down on him and told him never to contact me again, I changed my mobile number. But when he finds me, he'll throw the book at me, as they say."

"That was quick thinking. Well done, but surely, he wouldn't kill you. His own granddaughter."

"He wouldn't think twice."

THE SITUATION at Brooks End farm had turned into a disaster. Tsotsi was miserable, she'd lost weight and wasn't performing which broke Brad's heart. It was time to leave, but he didn't know how to tell Indigo. If he didn't leave soon, he'd punch her arrogant brother.

Two days before Christmas, when everyone was asleep, he snuck outside and called his parents. He wished them a happy Christmas before telling them of the situation.

"Goodness, what time is it there?" Gary asked.

"Late. I need to come home, with Tsotsi." Gary could hear the frustration in Brad's voice, he'd thought they should've come home a month ago.

"We'd love you here. Good timing, son. We've just hired a new trainer, so things have eased up a bit for mum and I. You'll like Shane, but I sense something else is worrying you."

"It's bad here, Dad. Tsotsi looks like a fucking greyhound, in fact she's the reason for my call. They've fucked her up. Just yesterday I had another argument with Blair over her feed. He's completely irrational. He's a bloody narcissist, I'm sure of it, and Indigo and I are going nowhere. She's too terrified to say anything to her father, or her brother for that matter. I checked her feed, it's not too bad, but nowhere near enough of it and I'm sure she has stomach ulcers from stress."

"Hang in there, son. I'll get Mum to book the flights, and I'll call Blair."

"That would be great. Tell Mum I'll fly in the hold with Tsotsi. I'll tell Indigo in the morning."

"Okay. Mum will call you with the flight details tomorrow. I'm sorry it hasn't worked out."

Brad crept back into the house and slid into bed next to Indigo, making sure he didn't wake her. He'd be sad to leave her in many ways, but it was time to get home.

The following morning early, Brad knocked on Blair's office door.

"Can I have a word with you?"

"Have a seat." He drew on his pipe and pointed at the empty chair.

"Dad's flying Tsotsi home and I'll be leaving here simultaneously. He'll call you to arrange the necessary details today."

Blair blew the smoke from his mouth. Brad watched the

swirls circle up toward the roof. "That's fine, Bradley. Have you told my daughter?"

"Not yet. I only got the call from my father late last night." He lied to keep a semblance of peace.

"Very well. I'll cancel Tsotsi's race. She's no good, anyway. I told you that from the start." That comment set Brad off. The stress and tension over the last few weeks he could no longer contain.

"Because you don't fucking feed her, she looks like a greyhound, that's why she's no good here, and combined with your fucking useless training. You know they sports coaches when they don't perform and bring the best out in their team. Well Dad's just fired you because you are fucking useless, so is that arrogant son of yours. I hope you reimburse my father for fucking up an international champion." Brad stormed out and ran to the stables to find Indigo. Never in his life had he been so outspoken in anger. Anger and rudeness were not part of his character. He didn't know how to cope with it. By the time he'd located Indigo his gentle nature was almost under control.

"Hi," he leant over the stable door, "can we chat?" He was panting from exertion.

"Yeah, of course."

"Open your beautiful eyes, my girl." He said breathlessly. "Look at Tsotsi, she's dying of fucking starvation. Can't you see what your father and brother have done to her. It fucking breaks my heart." Brad went inside the stable, "I'm sorry, babe, but we are both going home as soon as Mum can get us a flight. I'll travel in the hold with Tsotsi."

"Oh!" She stood the rake against the wall and looked into Brad's eyes. Though she agreed, she didn't dare admit it. "Your decision has come at the perfect time. I've just landed a modelling contract in Milan. I'll be leaving soon. I guess the universe had a hand in this. She stepped forward and hugged Brad. "I'll miss you and I hope we remain friends."

"Of course. Our relationship has been memorable, and I'll treasure our time together." Their lives were set on two different paths, but he had thought Indigo might have shown a bit more emotion.

From the 24th of December to the 7th of January passed in a turmoil of emotions for Brad. He spent most of his time either in Tsotsi's stable, grooming her and feeding her carrots and apples and extra hay, especially on Christmas day. He couldn't face this family on such a day. When he an Tsotsi weren't together in her stable, she and Brad went walking. Though Brad carried a lead, Tsotsi followed like a happy dog, unrestricted. Some days he'd take her out on a walking hack, but he didn't want to stress her with carrying weight. The rest of the time he'd wander through the fields where the other horses grazed, or take a taxi into the nearby village and chat to the locals in the pub.

THERE WERE no goodbyes from Indigo's family. She gave Brad a hug and a kiss before he led Tsotsi into the horse transporter. There was certainly no sadness, more relief. Brad left knowing he'd never promote Brooks End as a racehorse training venue.

Brad and Tsotsi arrived back in Johannesburg early in the morning on the 9th of January 2010.

Shane Roberts, the stud's new trainer was there to meet them. His wife Elly was with him. Shane shook Brad's hand, introduced Elly and said, shaking his head like a puppet on wobbly string.

"Oh my God, she does look like an S.P.C.A. rescue case. So

sorry, Brad. Your folks should arrive any minute. They are going to be shattered."

"Now you know why I insisted she come home, but God," Brad looked around, "despite being so tired, it's good to take in a breath of African air." Brad pulled the dry, warm air into his lungs with a few deep breaths and heard the toot, toot, from his parents' car as they parked close.

Shane held Tsotsi while Brad rushed over to greet them. Mel's hand was already over her mouth as she stepped out the car. "Thank God, you brought her home. What have they done to our beautiful girl?" Mel wheezed.

Shane and Elly hadn't been with the Whitaker's long, but what they witnessed today would stay in their memory forever.

Airport personal guided them to the overnight confinement area.

Tsotsi ambled tiredly into the stable and lay down, exhausted. Gary had brought a bale of wheat straw from the farm. Bedding was supplied, but it was often precious little. What hurt Elly watched the greeting. Mel knelt beside the broken mare and spoke to her, she nickered, and Mel wrapped her arms around her neck and kissed her. "We'll collect you in the morning, sweetheart," she looked up at Brad and Gary and noticed Elly sobbing.

"I've never... witnessed anything more.... Poignant... in my life." She uttered. Mel stood up and hugged Elly, then she turned to Gary, "Thank God you arranged with the Department of Agriculture that she doesn't have to travel all the way down to the Western Cape for endless quarantine. That would've killed her."

Shane hung up the tightly packed hay net, then dumped a generous mound beside her so she could eat lying down. The five of them watched Tsotsi for a while. She stood up, took in a few litres of water, shook herself and started pulling at the hay net but she soon lay down again.

"Does jetlag affect them too?" Elly asked.

"You bet it does," Shane answered and moved the mound of sweet, homegrown teff close to her.

The following morning Shane and Elly collected a well-rested Tsotsi and headed for home. As usual, armed undercover security tailed them. Gary followed the security vehicle.

"This bloody traffic is hell. I hate Joburg." Gary grumbled, but soon the city was behind them.

"Two security vehicles?" Brad said.

"Yes, unfortunately, but they've been marvellous. One looking out for us and one scrutinising the horse box. We don't want to lose another horse or trainer."

Brad put a hand on his mother's shoulder. "You're still in shock over Tsotsi's condition, aren't you Mum?"

"I'm afraid so. Sorry, my darling child, I've not said how happy we are you're home and that you made the decision to bring our beautiful Tsotsi back to us. It'll take her six months or more before she can race again. I wasn't expecting her to be quite so emaciated." She covered Brad's hand with hers. "Sorry about you and Indigo."

"Oh, don't be, it was great while it lasted. We'll be friends on Facebook now, "he chuckled. "How's everything else going, and all the horses?"

"Horses are doing well. We plug along. Mum and I find daily life hard to cope with now. It's been a horrid, traumatic ten months, hasn't it?"

"Sure has. I don't even want to think back. I'll try hard to fill the void. I think about Garth so much. Being home will make me miss him even more. Did Willem trace the mole?"

"Not yet. It's a massive concern, but they're working on it.

Storm in a Teacup, the little fiery colt who Garth fell for before he died has just started a little in hand training. He's as bright as the brightest star in the sky. He gives me hope. You'll love working with him." Mel smiled, thinking about the young exuberant colt.

"I'm so glad you are working with the babies. You're so good with them."

"They are what gets me out of bed in the morning, but sometimes I feel I'm just operating on autopilot. It's awful. Dad and I have to chivvy each other along, don't we darling?"

Gary answered with what sounded like a grunt as he concentrated on the road ahead, but the journey went surprisingly quickly and soon they were pulling into the parking bay at the stables.

It took Brad two full days to recover and on the third morning he decided not to switch off his alarm clock, roll over and go back to sleep. He met Shane at the main stable block.

"Bad news. Tsotsi must go into quarantine. I'm taking her down tomorrow."

"At least she's had some rest poor girl. How's she this morning?"

"Looking perkier. Christ it must've been a shocker watching your horse's gradual demise."

"It was. If I'd stayed another day, I'd have punched the arseholes and got myself into a lot of trouble."

"I wish you had punched the arseholes." Gary came up behind them and put his arm around Brad's shoulders. "Such a shame she's got to go into quarantine, but I've spoken to Barbara, they'll nurture her back to good health."

"What time are you leaving tomorrow, Shane?" Brad asked.

"Early. I want to be loaded and on the road by three o'clock."

Brad whistled. "Is Elly going with you?"

"Yes, and armed security. Not taking chances."

"Good man," Brad patted Shane's back. "Drive safely, mate and call me if you need anything along the way and hey, take your time."

"Thanks. We'll make sure she arrives safely. Elly has a bag of apples, Tsotsi's favourite, I'm told."

Nothing kept Brad in bed the next morning, except he wasn't up when Shane and Elly left. A time when owls are still hunting, he still slept.

Brad made his way to the track and arrived as the first eight horses were coming down from the ready-to-run barn.

The crisp morning air, azure, blue skies unblotched by cloud, and the calls of a multitude of birds, over-shadowed by the screech of the Hadadas Ibis, confirmed he was very much back in Africa. Dressed in a pair of jeans and a T shirt, the air was warm and comforting.

"Morning, Mr. Brad. We're glad you're back." Siyanda greeted, then Johnny came over.

"Morning, morning. It's very good to be back. Tell me, Siyanda, who's that horse?" Brad pointed to a dark bay two-year-old who bounced this way and that with his back up.

Siyanda smiled. "Another Master Vision, Brad. Another one for over the seas."

Brad cringed. "Not to America, though."

"No, no, no Sir. Dubai, Mauritius, Mr Chase. YES!"

When the horses had warmed up, the dark bay colt left the circle and galloped down to the start of the gallop.

"My goodness me, look at that action. That baby can cover ground. WOW! So, what's his name, Siyanda. They all change so much once they start full training."

"It's Big Vision, Mr Brad."

Brad shook his head. NO! He's magnificent."

Siyanda chuckled. "The old men, they still giving us fine young stock. Even old men can do it." Siyanda roared with laughter at his joke.

Brad patted him on the back, "you're not old Siyanda, but you're not making children anymore."

"Hau, Mr. Brad." Siyanda flicked his fingers playfully. But Brad had to agree, the old stallions were still producing top quality foals.

Suddenly Siyanda looked serious. "Mr. Brad, can I talk to you?"

"Yes of course. What's up?"

Siyanda cupped one hand over his mouth. "Johnny tells me there's a bad man here. A groom who used to work with Jackson."

Brad nodded, whistled loudly and pointed to the horses on the track. "Thanks for telling me Siyanda, it's got to look like we are chatting about the horses, not private stuff in case that someone is watching."

Siyanda got it. He burst out laughing and patted Brad's back.

Shane wasn't standing far away and wondered what the two men were laughing about. He walked across to join them.

"I'M POPPING BACK to the house quickly. I'll be back shortly." Brad said and left Shane and Siyanda chatting.

"Morning Mum, Morning Dad." His parents were sitting in the lounge with their morning tea.

"Good to see Siyanda at the track, but he pulled me to one side and said the mole here is a friend of Jackson's. He's a groom at the ready-to-run barn."

Gary put his cup down. It wobbled in the saucer. "That's good of Siyanda. He's not normally at the track, but I guess he was there to greet you and share this information."

"He's still pretty spritely for his age and joked about the old stallions still producing top quality progeny. That Big Vision is spectacular."

"He told me if he stops, he'll die. I guess he probably would. He's been an absolute godsend for years." Mel finished her tea and stood up. "Honey, I guess you need to let Willem know as soon as possible."

Chapter Thirty-Two

THABO ARRIVED BACK from Australia to a particularly stressed wife. As he walked into the house Julie threw her arms around him, almost bowling him over.

"Jeepers! What on earth's the matter?" Though weary from the long-haul flight, alarm echoed in his voice. Thabo pushed her gently away and closed the front door.

"Sorry," she kissed him quickly, "It's Solomon, of course." She shrieked, panic-stricken.

Thabo went cold. He'd always dreaded those words. That name. "Let me put my suitcase down, sweet pea, then you can tell me what happened."

Julie followed him to their room. He dumped his case and loosened his tie enough to pull it over his head and tossed it on the bed. "I hate wearing those things." He rolled the sleeves of his shirt up. "What happened. Tell me." He took Julie's hand and sat on the bed.

"I got a nasty, threatening phone call last night, and of course, I couldn't contact you. I'm scared, really scared."

"Come, my love," he said, and pulled her into his arms.

"He's going to kill me, Thabo. We always knew I'd be the first on his hit list after the Whitakers."

"Sweetheart, take a breath. Relax. Let's sit in the lounge and calmly go through what the caller said."

They tiptoed through to the sitting room. Zinzi was still asleep. Thabo was longing to see his little girl, but pacifying Julie took priority while Zinzi slept.

"Whoever spoke, said in a low, threatening tone, 'You let him down. You failed him. Be warned.' Then the phone went dead. Sorry, my love, I haven't even said hello properly, and you must be exhausted." Feeling more secure with Thabo home she realised how panicked she was and had forgotten about everything else. "You'll see how little Zinzi has grown."

Too tired to think straight and make rational decisions, Thabo suggested they do nothing until they'd both had a good night's sleep, but his mind raced. If Julie was exposed, the police would lock her up for good. She'd already escaped them once. He found it amazing there was no record of that escape. Someone paid somebody handsomely, no doubt.

"I'm going to take a shower before Zinzi wakes." Julie followed him to their room, unpacked his suitcase and threw his dirty clothes in the wash, then she heard Zinzi cry.

"Daddy's home." She picked her up. In moments she was gurgling and chuckling after a good sleep.

Thabo had heard his daughter and stepped in her room and her little face lit up. She reached out to him. Thabo took her and kissed her little button nose which made her gurgle with delight, blew bubbles with her lips and bounced on his hip as he carried her through to the lounge.

While Thabo sat drinking coffee and playing with Zinzi a thought came to him. A rather off-the-charts thought, he had to admit. What if he linked up with Gary Whitaker. He didn't share his thoughts with Julie for now.

Zinzi was a great distraction. They'd have a restful night and then he could think clearly, but at one-forty-five another call came through. Thabo answered.

"Stop harassing us. We know who you are. One more call and you're a dead man," He slammed the phone down, but struggled to go back to sleep. He got up and paced around the lounge considering his approach to Gary.

Julie, reassured her beloved Thabo would find a solution, fell asleep again. An hour of pacing and thinking, Thabo climbed back into bed and succumbed to exhaustion.

Aware the reception wouldn't be courteous once Gary learned who he'd married, but Thabo had to try. The thought of Julie being murdered gave him the courage to pursue his plan. If Gary saw the logic in them joining forces, not only would their security company trace the mysterious caller, but in exchange he and Julie would provide vital information about Solomon Tlale.

Though Julie had had no contact with Solomon for years, she knew all about his plans from Tanya. Thabo felt sure he could offer this as a win/win for both parties. This vital information, which included the names of who was still working with the colonel in South Africa, may help clinch a deal.

Thabo had a meeting with a new trainer at nine-thirty at the Summerveld racehorse training centre near Shongweni. He'd call Gary after the meeting.

He secured rides for two new trainers, and, feeling rather upbeat, he dialled Gary's number.

"Whitaker," Gary answered.

"Good morning, Mr. Whitaker. It is Thabo Biyela here."

"Good morning, Thabo. Looking for a ride?"

"I'd always be happy to ride for you, Mr. Whitaker, but that's not why I'm calling. I have something rather pressing to discuss and would prefer not to do it on the telephone."

"Oh? Sounds ominous."

"I'm sure it does, but it isn't. I'm at Summerveld and wondered if I could drive up to you this afternoon."

"Well, yes, but give me an idea what you want to discuss. Our security is very tight. I'll have to inform them of your reason for visiting the stud." Gary advised.

Thabo hesitated a moment, not feeling as confident as he had earlier. "Let me try to explain briefly. Please don't put the phone down on me."

"Go ahead," Gary said, intrigued by Thabo's nervous approach.

"It's about the Colonel in Zimbabwe. I'd like to discuss the formation of an alliance with you to stop the man."

"What has he done to you? And what is your connection to that murdering son-of-a-bitch?" Gary asked.

"He's done nothing to me. I've never been connected to the man, but my wife was, a long time ago. Suddenly, out of the blue, she got a death threat. Solomon is after her. The nameless caller has called twice in the last four days. The first call came when I was away."

"I see. Not pleasant at all, Thabo. Who's your wife?"

"Julie." There was an extended, uncomfortable silence. "It's for this reason I would rather sit in front of you to explain. Then you can see I genuinely want to help. I'm sure you understand I don't want my wife killed, and I want you to know Julie deeply regrets what she did to your horses. She was young and scared and misguided. Afraid he'd kill her if she didn't carry out the Colonel's instructions. She finally found the courage to make the break."

Gary's thoughts were racing, though he admired Thabo's bravery.

"Thabo, I tell you what. I'm not particularly happy that you come to the stud, but I can hear in your voice you're deeply troubled, so I'll agree. When you get to Reception, ask for me. Can you make it here by two?"

"Thank you, Mr. Whitaker I'll be there at two." He clicked off the call.

Gary immediately alerted security to trace the call and advised Willem the jockey would be at the stud at two o'clock.

Half an hour later, Willem called to confirm the caller was indeed Thabo Biyela and the cell phone number was registered in his name. They confirmed he's a professional jockey, and gave his registration ID number, confirmed his residential address and his marital status, and told Gary he'd just returned from racing in Australia and was apparently going back at the end of February.

Security would be waiting for his arrival at the main gates at two o'clock.

With Brad at the ready-to-run barn with Shane, and Mel sorting out the yearling sales list at the house, Gary felt comfortable neither of them would bump into Thabo.

Security waited for Thabo's arrival. Thabo's visit would appear normal. Jockeys, owners, and trainers visited regularly.

Cleared by security, Thabo pulled into the demarcated parking outside the main office. He switched off the engine and prayed the conversation would go in his favour. Glancing around before ascending the steps into the reception, the manicured gardens impressed him. First impressions always count, he thought.

Anette and Shinzi greeted him warmly. Shinzi was still in training.

"Hi, I have a two o'clock appointment with Gary Whitaker."

"He's waiting. This way, please." Anette beckoned.

Thabo followed her through to the small boardroom. Gary and Mel's offices were on either side of it. Gary stood up. He towered over Thabo and shook his hand. "Have a seat. I believe you've just returned from Australia."

"Yes, I have. I got back the day before yesterday. Great experience."

"Anything to drink? Tea, coffee, water?" Anette asked before leaving.

"Coffee would be lovely." Thabo said.

"Make that two, Anette. Thanks."

Gary and Thabo chatted about racing in Australia and only got down to business after Shinzi had brought the coffee.

"So, Thabo. Before we tackle what you have to offer, anybody remotely connected to Solomon not only creates instant suspicion, but a feeling of dread for us. You obviously understand that. The man and his collaborators have taken so much from us, and unfortunately, that includes your wife. If we could, without breaking the law, we would find a way to send him to hell tomorrow, for that's where he deserves to be. However, after much deliberation, I don't think they'd want him down there either." Thabo smiled. "I want you to know our conversation is being recorded. So, without wasting time, what alliance are we talking about? It's not lost on me that you are also taking a risk, and in everyone's interest, total transparency is vital if this is going to help us both."

"I understand and agree. I can only offer transparency in my proposal," Thabo said sincerely.

"This isn't easy for me. I can assure you. Your wife did considerable damage here. It was a long time ago, and I know she told Solomon to go to hell, but it doesn't detract from what she cost us emotionally. After she escaped from police custody, our security was the first to establish her whereabouts. We reasoned that keeping our eyes on her meant we would be better informed of Tlale's next moves. Accordingly, we dropped charges so we could monitor her movements. We had her followed for a long time before our security company realised that the line of communication to Tlale no longer existed, probably before the two of you married."

Thabo listened intently, surprised by what Gary revealed, then he outlined his thoughts on a proposed alliance. "The plan is a bit loose, but it only occurred to me forty-eight hours ago."

At the end of the conversation, Gary suggested they meet at Prime Security offices in Durban. Gary wanted Willem, Steve, Julie, and Thabo present. Though Gary wasn't particularly keen on seeing Julie. He'd put those emotions aside for the sake of his wife and son.

"Gary, I have a daughter who is fourteen months old. I need her and Julie protected. Can we meet tomorrow?"

Gary looked at Thabo. He picked up the phone and called Willem.

"Howzit Willem. Are you in your offices at ten tomorrow?"

"Yes, I think so. Let me check." Gary heard him turn the page of his diary. "Perfect. I have another meeting at eleven-thirty, so plenty of time."

"I'll be bringing Thabo Biyela, his wife and one other person with me." Gary didn't want to mention Steve's name with Thabo present. Caution had long been imbedded in his subconscious.

"No problem. See you in the morning." Willem ended the call.

Gary turned his attention back to Thabo. "So, apart from

this issue with your wife, and her connection to my wife's adversary, I must congratulate you on your successes over the past two years. I'd often wondered why you'd never contacted us for a ride, but it all adds up now."

"Thank you, Gary." Thabo stood up and shook Gary's hand. "I'll see you in Durban tomorrow."

Deep in thought, Gary sat at his desk for a long time. He felt positive about Thabo's proposal. The man seemed genuine. Security check proved to be somewhat juxtaposed. Good that Julie was no longer associated with Solomon. Bad that it gave them less to work on keeping tabs on Tlale's current movements.

Remarkable, Gary thought, what a curved ball. Who would ever have thought that Julie's husband would voluntarily help them in their fight against Solomon? Yes, sure, there was a good reason, Thabo wanted protection for his wife and daughter, but somehow the link seemed outrageous. Gary's immediate concerns were how to share the information with Mel.

He left the office and called out to Anette. "Going to the stables to meet Brad."

"Okay," she shouted back.

Gary strode down to the stables. Brad saw him coming. "Hi Dad, Mum and I will be at the track early with Shane. Will you join her?"

"Probably, but not for long. I have a meeting with Willem at ten."

"Oh, Mum will be disappointed. She's feeling
enthusiastic again, and you know how she values you being with her."

"There's still time, come to think about it. I only need to leave for Durban at seven."

"She'll love that, Dad."

Gary rarely kept anything from Mel, but for the moment, telling her now would simply complicate things. He didn't feel good about it, particularly as it involved Julie, whom they both loathed in equal measure.

'Climbing into bed with the enemy,' he thought to himself and prayed he wasn't making a fatal error of judgement. He also felt sure Thabo had withheld a certain amount of information, but Willem had a knack of gleaning information from people.

GARY WATCHED Mel dress and noticed the way she hauled on her clothes, excited to be out with horses at this time of the morning. Not to disappoint her, he dressed quickly and together they joined Brad at the gallops.

It was five thirty a.m., and a light breeze rustled the leaves in the trees. Brad's return had been a godsend. It was just a pity Tsotsi wasn't with them, but Gary knew Barbara would have her back in good health as soon as possible. According to the Department of Agriculture ruling, she'd be there for at least a month.

Gary watched Big Vision run his training race, then he left for Durban and joined the rush hour traffic. He arrived at Prime Security offices five minutes before the start of the scheduled meeting. He parked next to a red BMW Z4.

'Could only belong to Thabo,' he thought with a smile, running his fingers over the bonnet. Many of the top professional jockey's Gary knew drove BMWs of a sort. Jockeys and fast cars seemed to go hand in hand. Steve's Mercedes wasn't in the car park yet, he noticed.

Willem's office was on the first floor. Instead of taking the elevator Gary ran up the stairs like a man in twenties. Thabo, Julie, and Willem were standing on the landing chatting and sipping coffee. Gary greeted the two men and curtly nodded in Julie's direction without making eye contact. Julie visibly wilted at seeing Gary again and the sight of her sickened Gary.

He'd expected to feel that way.

Willem ushered them into the boardroom. As they were finishing coffee, Steve arrived.

"Apologies for being late." He glanced at Thabo and Julie and pulled out a chair next to Gary.

By the end of the meeting, Steve felt assured that Thabo was friend, not foe. A great relief for Gary, for he liked Thabo.

As it turned out, Julie would be pivotal in stopping Solomon doing any more damage to the Whitakers, their horses, or their staff. Privy to information they'd never have known without Julie's input, it also provided vital information for Steve's Harare connection.

The net was closing in on the soulless Colonel Tlale and for the first time Gary felt a flicker of excitement.

Once Julie had provided them with everything, she could give them, Thabo stood. "I'd like to thank you all for offering respect and kindness to my wife. We know she did horrendous things for Solomon in the past. Your co-operation proves what wonderful people you are."

The way it had turned out intensified Julie's feelings of regret. Nevertheless, it was comforting for Thabo to know that his family would be under formal protection within twenty-four hours.

Chapter Thirty-Three

"Hi, Tanya. I've been meaning to call you. Thanks for all the beautiful wedding photos. Did you have a good time in Zim?"

"I wondered when you'd call. Is Thabo back from Aus?"

"Yes, he is, thank goodness. It was only a two-week stint away this time, but I've got something to share with you. After your evil grandfather had someone call me in the middle of the night with death threats, my precious Thabo has managed the absolute extraordinary."

"Oh my God." Tanya shivered, if grandfather was onto Julie already, she'd be next. "Fuck! So, what has Thabo done that's so extraordinary?"

"This is really going to shock you. Yesterday we had a meeting with Gary Whitaker, the head of their security, Willem, and a bloke called Steve." She heard Tanya gasp. "Remember when I escaped police custody, well the Whitakers dropped all charges against me so their security company could use me to lead them to your grandfather. As you know, I haven't had any contact for years. It was for that reason that Mr. Whitaker agreed to the initial meeting with Thabo. How it's going to work. We feed them all the information we have, old and new. The moment the caller calls again Prime Security will be monitoring the call, and we're under their full protection, but I still can't discount the fact that I live in absolute fear of what your grandfather could still do to me, given what he's done to them. He's so evil, revenge for him has become an art. If he can, he'll find a way around all this, and because I'm not related, he'll take me out first. I know you've said you're on his hit list, but I still can't imagine he'd go after you." Julie felt the burn of fear rise in the back of her throat, and her mouth filled with the metallic taste of dread.

"My God, Julie. That is incredible. If I get nasty calls in the middle of the night, that would be enough to set the wheels of Simon's wrath into motion. He's been waiting for such an eventuality. He has business there, debt collecting. People seem to think if they gap it across borders, they are untouchable. Well, I tell you, Julie, nothing escapes Simon. He uses some brutal debt collectors for his business. Men that are so big they can snap a man's arm like a dry twig and feel nothing. My grandfather had better watch out. I'm going to talk this over with Simon tonight. We've both been waiting for this, haven't we?"

"Yeah. I told Mr. Whitaker how much I regret killing his horses and I still cannot believe I did it. I fucking love horses, but I was so scared, and I believed, like you did, that Melonie Whitaker was the evil one. I hope I don't die because of it. I am so scared."

"I'm sure you are, my friend. I'm sickened by the fact I got you involved."

"It was my choice. We both had choices, we both believed the fucker. It's history and we're still friends. Stop blaming yourself."

"You're so special. Thank you for always being you. As absurd as it sounds, try not to overthink things. Fear will only remove any rational thinking. God, how I wish I'd never believed my grandfather."

"HEY, Mum! Did you watch the race on the telly?" Brad called from the Greyville racecourse.

"I certainly did. Would not have missed it for the world. Lord Vision is an exciting horse. Kgabu must be delighted with his win today."

"Yeah, he is. Jabulile also ran a fabulous race. I'm telling you, Mum, if he hadn't got snarled up at the beginning, he would have beaten Lord Vision."

"Perhaps." She teased with a smile on her face.

"Aaah, come on, Mum. It's because you're looking through those Master Vision tinted glasses of yours." Mel laughed, enjoying the banter with her son again.

"We'll see. It's only their third race."

"Third for Jabulile, fourth for Lord Vision."

"He's a fabulous horse, I agree, but wait till we see what Big Vision does. He gives me goosebumps. When are you coming home?"

"We're leaving the course in about ten minutes. See you later." Mel stared out the window feeling warm and gooey inside.

WHEN THE GROUP got back to the farm, Mel was sitting with her feet up, reading a newsletter from the TBA. Thoroughbred Breeders Association. Gary was at the stallion barn. Golden

Chancellor had hurt himself and the physiotherapist was working on him.

Golden Chancellor — new to Chanting Clover. A beautiful, Irish bred horse, multiple Group One winner, eleven years old and the first brilliant chestnut with a flaxen mane they'd ever owned, but it wasn't his glorious colouring that caught Mel's attention, on the contrary, his pedigree went all the way back to the famous chaser, Red Rum. The great British horse who won the Grand National an unprecedented three times, among other first-class National Hunt races. Golden Chancellor's grandfather had won the English Derby three times and his dam, a runaway success at Ascot. They were truly blessed to have this horse standing at Chanting Clover, all thanks in part to Warriors Rival US dollar input, Tsotsi and Warriors wins in Dubai and Steve and Synthia's investment.

"Hey Mum, where's Dad?" Brad asked.

"With Golden Chancellor. He'll be back in a mo."

"When did you last see Tsotsi in work?" Barbara had done a fabulous job of getting Tsotsi back in condition. She'd been back at the stud for a week and was starting to look like the old Tsotsi.

"Yesterday. She's looking fabulous, isn't she? But a long way to go before she's on the circuit."

"I'm riding her tomorrow. Taking her out on a hack. How about coming with me?"

Shane and Elly joined Brad and Mel on the veranda.

"You've settled in well, Elly. You're clearly soaking up the wonderful African sun, looking at that wonderful tan."

"Oh, I love it here, Mrs. Whitaker. It's lush. So nice and warm. No sloshing around in mud with no sunshine for months at a time. And thank you for being so hospitable." Elly sank into one of the comfortable loungers on the veranda.

The afternoon extended into the evening. Lots of beer and wine was consumed and there were many more moments of laughter than there were unhappy thoughts. When they finally got to bed around eleven, Gary cuddled Mel. "You're looking happier, my lovely."

"I am. I love the enthusiasm and youthful energy that Brad, Shane, and Elly bring to our lives. Being at the track almost every morning gives me a sense of purpose again." Mel yawned. They fell fallen asleep in each other's arms and when they woke in the morning, their bedside lamps were still on.

GARY'S MIND had been so distracted by trying to calculate the right moment to tell Mel about Thabo and Julie. His gut burned from the stress. The sooner he told her, the better. He and Mel had never hidden anything from each other.

"Sweetheart, I have something to tell you." He sat up in bed and rested his back against the headboard and explained. He knew she'd be furious. Her cheeks were flushed crimson. She jumped out of bed and stormed across their room and stood at the bay window. Gary watched her without saying a word, wondering how he was going to finish telling her the whole story.

Eventually she turned to face him. "I'm sorry, but I couldn't face that girl without wanting to tear her eyes out. She killed some of our best horses. This is far too much to ask of me, and I still can't believe you met with her." She didn't know whether to spit or cry.

"I understand you're mad at me, my love. Believe it or not I'm also struggling with it. I pacify myself knowing she was driven by a fear only you would understand. She turned on us for no reason that we gave her. Her head was filled with who knows what lies about you. She's hurting too, and bitterly regrets what she did."

"That's all very well, but that still doesn't mean I have to meet her or forgive her, and I do not want to see her, and certainly not here in my house."

Gary's eyes pleaded. "I know this is hard. It took me days to digest. They thought we were the villains, or you were, for killing Funani. She didn't have a clue about the circumstances or what had happened to you in the past. When I thought about it from her perspective and saw it through different eyes, I decided not to carry the toxins of her awful acts in my heart any longer, especially as this is an opportunity to begin closure and get rid of Solomon. They want him dead as much as we do."

Gary's words touched a chord. She sat on the edge of the bed. "There's a lot of truth in what you say, my love, but surely that's not enough to kill two horses in the worst way possible." Honey, their golden Labrador had wandered into their room. Mel played with her velvety ears.

"Perhaps forgiveness was the way forward, but I still cannot imagine sitting in Willem's office with Julie in the room. I wouldn't be able to hold my tongue. It'd be like a hot knife cutting words into Julie's heart." Behaving uncharacteristically wasn't her style. It made Mel extremely uncomfortable. What Julie had done still pained her deeply.

"Let me think on it a little more, Gary. Let's not overlook the fact that Solomon has been eroding my inner strength for the last thirty-odd years. We all know what he's capable of and how brutal he is. He hauled me across kilometres of harsh terrain and subjected me to all kinds of violence when I was only seventeen." Mel fidgeted and felt close to tears now. "So, though I understand what you're saying about Julie and her fears, I need to piece together what you've said, and it's not going to happen in any kind of hurry, nor will I be pushed into it." Mel sniffed and held back the tears. "What has Willem and Steve said about this strange turn of events?"

"There're happy about it. Comparable to the beast entering the cage on its own. The mysterious caller has not threatened Julie again. We know they're playing a tactical game with her, based on fear and it's nasty, as we all know." Gary noticed Mel's body wither like a rose going over. The drama of opening old wounds, hurt.

"Thabo loathes Solomon too, perhaps not as much as we do. He understands the dangers. Tanya is all for Thabo and Julie working with us, which is interesting. She has even suggested a trade-off. Her information for protection and she knows a lot more than Julie does. One thing is for sure, Solomon is finally running out of people he can trust. Thabo mentioned that Simon, Tanya's husband, uses some of the most violent men in the business to get people to pay old debts. He has his own debt collecting company and is well connected in the legal world, which will be to our advantage. Apparently, if anyone threatens Tanya, he'll not hesitate to mobilise his team of brutal Zulu's. No questions asked."

Mel focussed on Honey's soft ears. There was a comfort feeling the velvety hair in her fingers. Gary knew she was thinking, then she looked up at him. "How vile. What a dreadful world it is sometimes. I'm still not sure I'm comfortable about all this, perhaps because it's so off the wall."

"I know, my love. I agree. We'll deal with it in your time. I'll let Thabo know."

Chapter Thirty-Four

TSOTSI WAS ready to race again. Mel was delighted for the excitement eased her constant thoughts about Thabo and Julie.

Her beloved mare was entered into the Tsogo Sun 1200 metre sprint, run on the last Saturday in May at the Scottsville racetrack. As she'd made a significant recovery in four months, Mel felt she was ready.

An argument ensued over who would riding her. Gary tossed a coin. James was heads, Kgabu tails. James won the toss. Kgabu would ride Lord Vision in the second race, which he wasn't at all displeased about. He loved riding Lord Vision, but he wanted to ride Big Vision. Shane put one of the new apprentices on Lord Vision. Two, magnificent half-brothers racing each other was going to be fun to watch.

Richard Wilkinson, a young Academy jockey had caught Shane and Gary's attention at the morning gallops at the Summerveld training academy. They'd been to look for a talented, second-year apprentice and chatted to him in the club house at breakfast. He would ride Lord Vision.

Shane offloaded the three horses at the course stables then wandered up to the Members lounge where he found Brad and Gary.

An hour later, Tsotsi and seven other mares pranced around the parade paddock. Johnny legged James into the saddle and gave Tsotsi a comforting rub down her shoulder and they filtered out of the parade ring and cantered slowly down to the start. Tsotsi was the favourite. It was a small field of eight mares.

Brad watched Tsotsi gallop down to the start, relaxed and attentive, just as she used to be. How he wished Blair, Ben and Indigo could see her now.

The gates flew open. James placed Tsotsi centre field early on, giving her time to drift across to the rails where she liked to run. Tsotsi's galloping hooves ate up the ground. She finished to loud applause. The punters darling was back in fine form. She won the race by two lengths in effortless style which secured her a place in the Durban July.

"That's my girl," Brad yelled, grabbed Mel's hand and they ran downstairs to meet them coming in off the track. James shouted when he saw them. "I told you she'd win."

"Well ridden, my man." Brad praised James.

"I was a happy passenger," James laughed. "She did it all."

After the sash had been placed around Tsotsi's neck, Brad snapped a photo of her in the winner's box and sent it to Indigo. Tsotsi in the winner's box. Her first race since arriving home. He never heard back.

Big Vision and Lord Vision both ran a brilliant race. Big Vision beat his half-brother by a length, running second and third respectively. Young Richard had proved himself.

. . .

THOUGH THE WHITAKERS and their staff had seen many Durban July's come and go, this one had a different feel. It was also Shane's first and he couldn't wait to get to the course.

Tsotsi had crawled back into the heart of punters country wide, and the staff voted unanimously that it was a lady's year. Tsotsi's work ethic had always been unquestionable — she was a world champion after all.

Brad had a meeting with Jeremy. A new and very lucrative modelling contract he was keen to learn more about so organising he left in Shane's capable hands. He got back to Greyville in time for the first race.

The jovial, colourful vibe at the Durban July could not be compared to what he and Mel had enjoyed at the Kentucky Derby, even though Blair had ruined it for Mel.

The first race, a maiden race for fillies, was about to start. Mistress Mel and Gatsha were running their first race. Mistress Mel, a classy, flashy red bay, named by the staff when she was born because the colour of her coat matched Mel's hair colour. Gatsha, almost black in colour, sired by Bold Warrior, was of equal looks and ability as her stablemate and they ran well together. James was riding Mistress Mel.

Running parallel, galloping at the same speed but Mistress Mel gave a sudden burst of energy and beat her stable mate by a head. James was delighted. Mel was overjoyed too.

"How did your meeting go with Jeremy?"

"Excellent. I'll tell you all about it after we've seen Mistress Mel in."

In between the first and third races, Brad explained to his parents all about the contract Jeremy had offered him, then they dashed downstairs just as the first horse entered the parade ring for the third race.

Brad's favourite, Jabulile was racing against Big Vision, and though he knew his favourite boy didn't really stand a chance against the big colt, he didn't care.

"How are you feeling, son?" He and Gary stood side by side waiting for Big Vision to come off the track.

"I'm not disappointed. All three horses ran superbly."

"They certainly did. Jabulile will have his chance to win. Nothing wrong with a close second. You and Shane are doing a splendid job. Mum and I are enjoying doing the watching."

Richard shouted, "Big Vision is the best horse I've ever ridden. Hell, I enjoyed that ride." Brad praised the young jockey. As he turned, he saw a triumphant Julie running to meet Thabo with Zinzi on her hip.

His stomach cramped. That was the drawback of having Thabo ride for them. Julie no longer needed to hide. Thabo had ridden Jabulile.

"Seeing Julie makes me angry, but I know it's all for the best in the end."

"Celebrate the good stuff, my boy. Don't let it eat you. It's been on my mind too. I've gone over the forgiveness thing a million times. Poor Dad has been wonderful listening to me throw my wild thoughts around on the matter. He's dealing with it with such calm and logic. It's so admirable. I didn't think forgiveness was possible, but it is time to forgive her. We won't ever forget what she did, but our anger and resentment only make us sadder. As Dad says, keeping it inside is toxic. We all have to face her in a meeting next week."

"I guess you're right, Mum. I'll do the right thing, I promise."

Mel put her arm around him. "All we can do is pray it all works out."

"I'm going down to meet Jeremy. He's got models doing

the Rising Star fashion parade and it's starting in," he glanced at his watch, "ten minutes."

Brad found Jeremy in his curtained cubicle back of the stage knocking back imported French champagne.

"Do you want a flute full?" Jeremy asked.

"Yeah, why not. It's not every day I drink real French champagne. It'll either settle me for the feature race or make me vomit."

"Oh dear," Jeremy chortled. "I see Tsotsi is second favourite today. My money's on her. I've won a nice little nest egg so far today." Jeremy poured the champagne and handed the flute to Brad. "Cheers, quality like this won't make you vomit, Bradley. It's over a thousand bucks a bottle — that makes me want to vomit."

Brad smiled and took a sip. "Ooh, that's good. I seldom drink champagne, and I would never buy a bottle of hooch for that price."

"Hooch? Oh, deary me, Bradley, this doesn't fall into such a classless category." Jeremy said, his little finger theatrically held away from the stem of the crystal glass.

Brad stayed hidden behind the curtains sipping the champagne while Jeremy fussed about with his models. When the show was over, he wandered back to join his parents. James and Kgabu were there too, discussing their nerves.

"No matter how many feature races I ride, I can't control the nerves. I get these stupid churning sensations in my gut, and my feet tingle. Do you get that?" James asked Kgabu

"Yeah, except mine is with every race, not just feature races," Kgabu responded. "And the smell of sweat, deodorant and carbolic soap makes me bilious." Brad sat listening to the two jockeys' share their nerve sensations prior to a race. They'd have to report to the jockey's rooms in five minutes to prepare for the feature race.

"Wouldn't it be amazing to win on Tsotsi."

"Fuck, I wish I was riding her." Kgabu admitted. "James, we must go."

"Yeah, go and concentrate on your tactics for the race. I'm told nerves are a good thing before a race. Stops one from becoming complacent." Brad teased.

Forty-five minutes later the two jockeys walked into the collecting ring and were lifted onto their mounts.

"Mum, Dad, I'm heading back upstairs." Brad left the ring. He wanted to watch Tsotsi canter down to the start.

"Despite Tsotsi looking amazing, she's up against some good horses and this is quite a distance for her." Mel said seriously, but Gary was in a playful mood.

"Nah, Silver Flame, my dressage horse will win." He teased and she tickled him which made him squirm.

"Brad won't be disappointed if she doesn't win. The betting public don't know what she went through, all they see is a world champion back home."

It had been an unusually hot day in Durban. A glorious, brilliant blue sky, the wind was gentle off the ocean, and the late afternoon temperature hovered around 25°C.

The track looked immaculate. The turf, a deep forest green waited for the galloping hooves of the nation's top Thoroughbreds once more. Tsotsi preferred running on turf.

Gary, Mel, Brad, Shane and Elly, stood in a line along the windows of the member's lounge. "Pity Steve and Synthia aren't with us this year." Mel said, without removing the binoculars from her eyes.

Brad remained silent as he watched the field load. Then the gates flew open. The announcers voice echoed from the loudspeakers, calling Tsotsi's name more often than the other horses, and the crowds were shouting for her. The electric energy rippled through the stadiums giving power to the punters voices as the stood and screamed for their favourite.

At the thousand-meter mark, Brad said in a low voice to Mel, "I think she's holding her own. God she's a wonderful mare."

Mel didn't answer, too choked with emotion.

Tsotsi galloped on, gaining steadily on the leaders. The roar from the crowd became deafening as Tsotsi won the 2010 Durban July.

James stood up in the saddle and punched the air as she slowed to a trot, and he turned her around to come down the walkway to the winner's enclosure.

Silver Flame had run fourth. "Not so bad for a dressage horse." Gary poked a finger into Mel's side. She spun around and into his arms and they hugged. Gary held her for a little longer, happy to see her so excited.

Brad ran downstairs before even Shane had had a chance to move.

At the winner's enclosure the sun lit up Mel's face and her smile shone as brightly. Brad answered all the questions from the interviewer.

"Her poor show in America. Why was that?" The man asked.

Brad felt sorely tempted to say why, but he didn't.

"She did very well in Dubai." He began. "Us humans take it for granted when we fly around the world, but flying really takes it out on horses. They have no idea what to expect. It's frightening and stressful and the sounds are so foreign to them. Adapting to different altitudes, climatic conditions and different training methods is equally tough. She's a sensitive mare and perhaps the trainer asked a little too much too soon. But she's home and in fine form now, as you can see." Brad patted Tsotsi. She knew she'd won. She recognised the sounds from the crowds. She almost looked like she was smiling while trying to get her breath back. The race hadn't been easy for her.

The interviewer moved the microphone to James.

"A lovely race for you, James. Talk us through it."

"Yeah, I felt her tire in the last fifty meters. I got a bit worried, but she responded to me and ran on. She's an incredible mare, not once did I touch her with my whip, she's a voice responder." James laughed. "That last burst of speed choked me up."

"I'll bet it did. It was close call, but she did it. An astonishing ride. Well done." The interviewer then moved away and spoke for the television cameraman.

Thabo came across to congratulate James and Brad. He left Julie and Zinzi sitting in the restaurant.

Brad got back to the farm late that night after celebrating two wins. The most lucrative modelling contract to date, and Tsotsi's win. Before he switched his light off, he sent a picture of Tsotsi in the winner's box to Indigo. The caption read, 'Tsotsi won South Africa's prestigious feature race.'

She never responded.

Chapter Thirty-Five

"BRADLEY, you are flying SAA to Paris. I've emailed you the itinerary. The first show is called, 'Where style meets energy.' The launch of the wonderful Hugo Boss's new range. He's one of my fave's, darling. Oh gosh, so exciting and so clever, the range still respects the signature colours of grey's, white and black, but now there's a splash of colour. Such fun Bradley, such fun."

"Sounds good, Jeremy. Confirm the number of days for that show."

"Three-days. Yes, I know daaarling, you hate all the make-up and fussing. Never mind, it's all part of the fun. Oh, and some more exciting news. At the show, there will be scouts looking for the new face of Hugo Boss men's clothing range for 2011. Get that, Bradley darling and you'll buy yourself a mansion, not just another one-bedroom flat in Durban."

"Sounds cool. I'm looking forward to being in Paris, but not the titivating crap. Has your travel agent booked me an onward flight to Heathrow?"

"Yes, Bradley, all taken care of. You'll see everything you need to know in the itinerary, and your airline ticket is attached."

"Awesome. Thanks, Jeremy."

The email came through as promised. Brad's flight to Paris on the 8th of August he put in his diary and while he read through the itinerary, his thoughts drifted to Garth. They could have been doing this assignment together. A little over a year had gone by since he lost his brother. His sombre thoughts were gradually replaced when he calculated the income. He'd fulfil his property dream. That thought made him smile. Garth had left a legacy, and he'd inherited it. A love of money. Only Brad invested his differently. He liked the security it gave him, not the status. But this would be his final assignment. His loyalty lay with his parents and the horses.

Brad learned that the Hugo Boss company were also in search of a suitable male, Hollywood actor to launch their new male fragrance. After the selections were made and the contracts signed with the winners, a combined launch would take place in February 2011. If Brad put February 2011 out of his mind — he didn't stand a chance.

From Paris, a hop across the ocean to Newmarket. Alex and Emily Beresford at South End Stud wanted Brad to help with their horses. He looked forward to that far more than Paris.

BRAD AND JEREMY landed at Charles de Gaulle and took a taxi to the hotel. Jeremy had booked the Hôtel Duquesne Eiffel. The tower stood, in all its engineering glory, only a kilometre away and the view of it from Brad's bedroom window was perfect. He could see the whole tower, and the hotel was a short taxi ride to the Hugo Boss showroom in the Avenues des

Champs-Elysée's where the initial introductions would take place.

Brad and Jeremy had one day to rest and relax. They met for breakfast in the cosy dining room, its walls painted in a warm cream. The hidden, soft glow lighting gave an even cosier ambiance.

Brad chose to spend the day on his own and wondered across to the Eiffel Tower, bought an ice cream and a ticket and climbed six hundred and seventy-four steps to the second floor, then he bought a few little trinket souvenirs and walked slowly back to the hotel and slept in the afternoon.

They had a very early start. Brad and Jeremy joined the other models at 5.50 a.m. at the Hugo Boss showroom. In a large auditorium at the back of the building the introductions, general rules and protocols of the shoot were read out, then the models hung around waiting for their make-up and hair to be done.

Then the 3D artists arrived with teams of IT specialists, photographers, system engineers, fashion directors, agents, and other helpers.

Backstage, where Brad and a sea of male models lounged around, Brad watched the crew set up. Most of the other models took no interest and plugged themselves into their earphones or had cell phones or iPads to capture their interests. Conversation wasn't top of their agenda. Brad didn't mind, they had nothing in common.

Brad and Jeremy left the studio at nine that night. Both tired and moody.

"Fuck, this is exhausting, Jeremy. Once this assignment is done, so am I."

"Now, now, Bradley. Don't let me down by thinking like that. You're going to be the next international male super-model. I'm sure you'll win this competition. I watched the judges today. Didn't you notice that tall Italian man standing next to you while you were having your hair done? Well, darling, he's one of the main judges. He has a big say in the final selection of the next Hugo Boss male model for 2011."

"Come on, Jeremy, I don't stand a chance."

"Bradley Whitaker. You do. You're in line, I can promise."

Bradley gave a weary smile. All he wanted to do was get to bed. "See you in the morning, Jeremy. Good night."

THE FAMOUS LOUVRE was the first shoot. Underneath the looming lass pyramid, the open courtyard was transformed into a makeshift fashion set. The sharp, geometric line of the Louvre's architecture contrasted beautifully with the clean-cut elegance of the new summer range.

Brad enjoyed wearing the clothing range. Quality of the garments let good on one's body and he understood why people went for the top name brands. The poses were casual, but there was an air of silent competition. Subtle glances exchanged, smirks barely hidden. Male models with impeccable chiselled features. The atmosphere buzzed with tension, but Brad never craved for the attention. He knew he'd not win after seeing some top international models stunning faces and equally perfect bodies.

The photographer, a seasoned pro with a sharp eye, gave brisk, no-nonsense directions from behind the camera.

Brad found the assignment, stressful and boring, but he had a chuckle. André muttered, 'Where's my light? after Pierre was told to lose the pout. He rolled his eyes slightly.' The lighting crew were used to divas like these. But Pierre got a response.

"Right here, darling, relax." one of the engineers call back sarcastically, eliciting a low chuckle from the crew.

"Marc, can we get a little more intensity? Less moody, more Boss. I want confidence, like Bradley has just shown us."

Marc shot Brad a look of mild irritation, but he adjusted his stance as requested.

The session wrapped up and the tension dissolved into the early evening air.

The fourth and final day, held in the grounds at the Palace of Versailles turned into a breathtaking display of grandeur. Although Brad was fascinated by the symmetrical pathways lined with perfectly trimmed trees, he preferred the haphazard layout at home. The Grand Canal, a massive cross-shaped body of water was a perfect setting for the first photo shot. The sky was a perfect blue and reflected I the water with the palace in the background. It could not have been a more perfect location for the theme — where style meets energy.

Brad appreciated the blend of artistic expression and natural beauty and wished his mother could have been with him to see it.

Clearly designed to impress and showcase the power and taste of the French monarchy and a masterpiece of the Baroque style. It was a most enjoyable day and finished at lunch. After lunch the models were given a guided tour of inside the Châteaux.

Marc, whom Brad disliked intensely kept interrupting the tour guide with silly remarks to capture her attention. Not wanting the man to ruin his Palace of Versailles excursion, he warned Marc to keep his mouth shut, the others were interested in what the guide had to say. He did shut up eventually when the tour guide took no notice of him.

On their way back to the hotel, Jeremy let Brad in a little secret. Jeremy wasn't good at keeping secrets. "The model was chosen at the palace shoot. I'll be advised in the next few days."

"It won't be me. There were far better-looking models with the chiselled high cheek bone, square jaw look. Have a good flight and I'll see you in December, I guess." Brad couldn't wait to get to the Beresford's and the smell of horse. He was sick of the intoxicating smell of aftershave lotions and hairspray.

That night Brad chatted to Alex Beresford on the phone.

"Once I get to Heathrow, I'll let you know what time my train will get into Newmarket. I'm certainly looking forward to a few months with you." Brad loved the sound of Alex's Etonian British accent. So posh.

"Wonderful. Emily and I look forward to seeing you again. You were a boy of twelve, I think, when we last saw you."

"Yes, that's right. You visited us at Chanting Clover."

"We certainly did, and what an awfully good job your wonderful parents do with the horses. Chanting Clover is about four times the size of our small farm, but it's perfectly adequate for what we do. My dear Dad fell in love with this farm because of its wildness, the trees and the brook that marks one of the boundaries. It was once an apple producing farm in 1947. It's six hundred and four acres."

"That's quite a fair-sized piece of ground for England, isn't it?

"Yes, it is. Especially its location being so close to Newmarket."

"I'm looking forward to seeing it and working with some of your horses, Alex." Brad was tired and he felt sure his excitement hadn't come across in the way he'd hoped, but he'd be rested by the time they met.

"We'll have lots to talk about, I'm sure. Have a safe trip. We'll see you tomorrow."

Brad fell into a deep and peaceful sleep and when he woke, he felt truly alive for the first time in years.

Chapter Thirty-Six

London had been blessed warmer weather. Standing outside the bus terminal at Heathrow he could scarcely believe he was in England. The sky was blue but filled with criss-crossing contrails. He seldom saw them overhead at Chanting Clover. On a cloudless day back home, the skies were always a glorious uninterrupted desert of blue.

He grabbed a ham, cheese and lettuce sandwich and a cup of coffee and sat in the corner café and called home called home. He had forty-five minutes to spare.

"Hi Mum, I'm at Heathrow waiting at the bus terminal for my bus to Newmarket. How's everything at home?" Brad loved the way she sounded so cheerful, and he had her in hysterics telling her about the photo shoots, then she passed the phone to Gary. They chatted briefly, he still had to call Alex. The call for passengers to Newmarket was leaving in ten minutes.

As pre-arranged, Alex collected Brad. The bus rolled into the bus stop in Newmarket at exactly four thirty-eight.

"How nice to meet you again, Bradley," Alex shook Brad's

hand. "I'm so sorry about the tragic death of your brother. What a terrible shock for you all."

"Thank you. It was indeed," Brad responded sadly. The mention of Garth's name would always make his chest contract with sadness.

"Welcome to England. Did you have a good flight?"

"Yes, thank you, I did. It's a quick hop, skip, and a jump across the channel, isn't it? And the bus services here are fabulous. All on time."

"Yes. Yes, of course. The system is awfully punctual, which is rather nice." Alex walked toward his parked car. Brad followed. "A week's modelling for Hugo Boss is awfully impressive, young man. A bit different from training horses, what." Alex smiled broadly.

"Yeah, for sure. Done purely for the money, I assure you. But no more for me. But it has put me on the property ladder at nineteen."

"Goodness, no wonder you did it." Alex opened the driver's door to his pale blue Jaguar SUV. "Jump in, let's get back. Emily has tea waiting for us."

Alex did a little detour or two and pointed out the Whitaker family flat, the one Mel had inherited from Hector Willis.

Brad made a mental note of the landmarks close to the flat so he wouldn't get lost when he came into the village.

They passed the beautiful bronze statues near the entrance to the famous Rowley Mile racecourse and a few miles further on, Alex turned off the A1304, the London Road, down a long avenue of ancient Beechwood trees that led to the house.

"I love these trees. We have the London Plane lining the driveway to the house and Grandmama also planted vast quantities of Sycamore trees. I guess you remember."

"I certainly do. Chanting Clover is a very beautiful estate."

"It is, isn't it? I hope I'll be of value to you." Brad said as they pulled up in front of the Beresford's grand home.

Emily came rushing out to greet them. Brad didn't remember her clearly but seeing her now, he thought she couldn't have been a more perfect example of an aristocratic English lady. She wore a fashionable tweed skirt, camel-coloured jersey and matching bolero and expensive leather shoes. She gave Brad a hug, then stepped back, "It's wonderful to have you here with us, Bradley. My goodness me, you are a handsome lad."

Brad felt his face flush.

"Your mother tells us how well you've done with the horses. I wonder what on earth we can teach you." Emily ushered Brad into their grand home.

As grand as his mum had said. Filled with a lifetime collection of beautiful antiques, pictures, silver, and precious ornaments made in any number of mediums. Tasteful, but not cluttered, Emily had mingled the old and the new with style. Brad instantly understood why his mum loved staying with Emily and Alex.

"Come along upstairs. Let me show you to your room." Emily led the way up the sweeping stairs to a spare bedroom that overlooked the stables.

"This is perfect. I love the view. Thank you, Mrs. Beresford."

Emily stopped in the doorway. "Bradley, do call me Emily, won't you."

"Oh, okay. Yes, certainly." Brad stammered with uncertainty.

"Now, make yourself comfortable. I'm sure you want to

unpack and have a bit of a wash. When you're ready, come down for tea, then we'll stroll down to the stables."

"Is that teatime like we have in Africa or tea as a meal like you have here in England."

Emily burst out laughing. "Just like you have in Africa, with a few tasty biscuits and some cake. Alex and I like to have a cuppa at five-thirty, and we may or may not have anything with it. Then we take a stroll. These glorious late summer evenings are perfect to be outside. It stays light until around 8:30 p.m. We go down to the stables again after supper. Once we've done our rounds this evening, I'll cook a light supper which we eat on our laps, watch telly for half an hour and catch up on the world news. Beastly information nowadays. Hardly worth watching. I find it awfully depressing, but Alex likes to keep informed. Anyway, come down when you're ready, Bradley."

Brad felt instantly at home. He unpacked, splashed water on his face, washed his hands and went down to join Alex and Emily.

After tea and a slice of the most delicious walnut cake, they set off. Charging ahead were the Beresford's two gregarious cocker spaniels, Ginger and Biscuit. Ginger, a red cocker, and Biscuit a tricolour, had their noses to the ground sniffing for interesting smells that were likely new since the morning walk.

They chatted as they strolled down the lane to the stable complex.

"Do not mention to my stable lads that you are a volunteer. I never take in volunteers, it's just too risky nowadays. I employ, pay good money and hope they remain loyal, and so far, it's working." Alex said as they rounded the bend and the stable block, built of stone with a slate roof appeared.

"Nothing as fancy as Chanting Clover, I'm afraid." Alex said apologetically as if it mattered.

"Looks wonderful to me. How many stables do you have?"

"Twenty-two in this block and six in another block you can't see from here. That block houses Emily's passion. She'll tell you all about that later."

They were met by three hard-working stable lads' poop-scooping and doing the late afternoon chores.

"Guess I'll be doing that too." Brad laughed.

Emily turned to Brad, "not entirely. You'll be turning a few of our lazier racehorses into champions."

"Oh goodness. No pressure," Brad said with a touch of playful sarcasm and popped his head over a stable door to have a look at the bay horse within.

"Oh, hello." A stable lass was bent over cleaning out a hoof. She looked up and smiled at Brad, looked back at the hoof she was cleaning, then spun her head up again to take another look.

"Hey, mister good-looking. Be rather lush having you around for a few months. I guess you are Bradley." She grinned and picked up the other hoof. Brad blushed and moved on. Emily had missed none of it. She smiled at Brad, raised her eyebrows and said in a low voice, "take no notice of Gina, she fools around and jokes with everyone. She's great fun. You'll love her. Everyone does. She is full of nonsense, but a very hard worker and the horses adore her, plus she's a darn good rider. As fit as a fiddle and always cheerful. She lives with her parents not far from where your parents flat is situated. Catches the early bus out here every day."

Brad nodded. "So, how many people are employed here?"

"Four, plus Alex and me. Our staff have been with us for a long time, except Gina, who's been here a little over a year. It's a busy, physically hard day that ends at 7:30 in the summer."

"Wow, that is a long day. We're spoilt in Africa, but I'm not scared to get down and dirty, muck out stables and groom, so shove me in where you want me. I'm here to learn how you lot do it in England."

"Well, before you get stuck into, the-get-down-and-dirty, I want you with me at our training track, Bradley." Alex chipped in.

"Of course. I'm looking forward to that. So, who will I be working with?" Brad asked as they wandered back to the beginning of the stable block and stopped outside the stable where Gina was working.

"This boy. He's more like a Labrador than a racehorse. The bugger is 'bred in the pink', as they say. He has outstanding bloodlines and can go like the wind, but only when it suits him. If you can't get anything out of him, I'll flog him. He would make a lady rider a lovely quiet, sensible hack."

"What's his name?"

"Fantasy Flight. I'd hoped he'd win at Ascot last year. He has that sort of potential, but as the ladies say, that day he had a bad hair day." Alex looked disappointed.

Bradley whistled, "he's lovely. I look forward to taking him out."

"He's been a favourite often enough. But he's one of those horses that's difficult to read. If the mood doesn't take him or he gets stressed by the crowds and the noise, he'll almost break into a trot at the back of the field. The jockey is held to ransom. He will not gallop faster than he wants to. But, for all his character, he's a wonderful horse with a great temperament. I'd like you to ride him on the track tomorrow and see what you think."

"So, he's my first project, is he?"

"Yes. And you'll take over grooming, feeding and mucking out of his stable. In fact, everything to do with him."

"Sounds good to me. Training in the morning, hacking in the afternoon? Something like that?"

"Exactly. You'll use the horse walks around here. There are horses on them all day, every day. They lead to a variety of marvellous gallops, but we will show you all that in due course. Crack on with him in the morning and see how you get on."

BRAD WALKED DOWN to the stable at seven. Another cracker of a day. Bright and sunny and surprisingly warm. Brad headed straight to Fantasy's stable, where he bumped into Gina. "Hiya. I've placed his grooming box at his stable. It has his name on it. Grooming kits are not shared here." Gina had put the training saddle and bridle on the rack nearby and on the floor was a pair of neoprene brushing boots. Gina had already slipped on the overreach boots.

"Fantasy must always wear overreach boots. I've put them on for you today, but me laddie, that's your job from now on. When this chap gets going, he overreaches badly." She laughed, "well, that's if you can get Mr Plod going. Do what you do best, bring him back, cool the boy off, groom him again, clean out his feet and put him out." She pointed to a small paddock to the left of where they stood. "Check the water trough in his paddock every day. Mr Beresford insists on sparkling clean water. In the feed room, what he eats, and when, plus the quantity is written up on the board. Nothing more, nothing less, he's a pig is this boy. I'll show you when you get back."

Gina spun around suddenly, dropped the bucket she was carrying and ran down to the sixth stable. She shouted, "sounds like a horse down."

"What the fuck," Gina yelled and reached for a halter. "Someone call Alex, horse down with colic."

"I'll go." Brad ran back toward the house and met Alex on his way down to the stables.

"Alex, you have a horse down with colic. Stable number six"

"Oh, blimey." Alex did an about turn and hurried back to the house. "I'll get the pain killer and call the vet."

Brad jogged back help Gina. She'd got the horse up and was gently walking him around.

"Must've just started. He was fine when I got here at six. He's known for rushing his food. Another bloody pig is this one. He should go to the knacker's yard. He colic's too often and he's never won a race. He ain't going to give 'em any kinda return." Gina said.

'Go to the knacker's yard,' Brad thought. Pretty harsh. He wondered if it happened a lot here. He didn't say anything, but it did prompt memories of what James had told.

Alex arrived with the medicine and administered the intravenous injection. It didn't take long for the horse to respond and look more comfortable. "Seems like a mild spasmodic colic." Brad said observing the horse's reaction time.

"You know about colic's, do ya?" Gina smiled.

"Yeah, I've dealt with a few. Luckily, we don't have it occur often." Brad went back to Fantasy's stable and gave the horse a good grooming. He could hear the steps from the sick horse become almost normal by the time the vet arrived.

Brad saddled up and rode Fantasy down to the home track. It was a small oval track, from start to finish, less than a mile, but perfectly adequate. The going was good, bordering on hard, unlike England at this time of year, but Alex had said there'd been no rain for a week and the ground dries out fast.

'Quick,' Brad had heard Alex describe the going.

To feel a new horse, Brad liked to do it at walk first. From what he'd been told he presumed Fantasy Flight had soured. On the track, with a change of pace and a new rider, Fantasy's attitude became fidgety and questioning. Normally when a horse and rider had warmed up and entered the track, it meant gallop.

"Not today, sonny." Brad ran a hand down Fantasy's shoulder. Fantasy settled into a good, bridle slapping walk around the track. Brad made him shorten his stride and lengthen to leg aids. The aim of the exercise to get a sour horse to concentrate again.

Brad chatted to Fantasy and watched what his ears were doing. When they began the second circuit, Fantasy was listening to Brad's aids, all of them. Fantasy's ears flicked this way and that, he'd settled and appeared to be enjoying this new schooling.

For Brad, this exercise told him a lot about the horse and what sort of mouth he had and how responsive he was to the bridle, and the requests through the rein aids as well as his leg aids.

By the time they'd completed the second circuit, Brad asked for some lateral bending. Fantasy's back muscles were nice and soft and elastic even though the exercise was new to Fantasy, but he learned quickly.

The third circuit he trotted it, and played with Fantasy, introducing some basic dressage moves. After an hour and a half, Fantasy was sneezing, his jaw had relaxed, and his shoulder movement was more fluid and open. By the time he walked back to the stables, Fantasy had a lovely, dreamy look in his eye. He hadn't raised much of a sweat when Brad untacked him. When Brad gently removed the bridle, Fantasy mouthed, then yawned appreciatively.

"How was he on the track?" Alex asked, coming out of the tack room.

"Very good." Brad was washing the saliva from his bit.

"How did you manage that?" Alex was curious.

Brad explained what he'd done. Teaching the horse obedience to rider commands and aids and introduced some basic dressage. Alex looked horrified.

Exasperated, he said, "Good God, son, this is a racing yard."

There was a glint in Brad's eye. "I know. Every horse needs to have the basic groundwork done before they race. Lateral work, which is part of basic dressage, is vital for good musculoskeletal health along the horse's top line. It's the foundation upon which a good horse can develop a strong, supple back. Before our horses go to the ready-to-run barn, they've undergone six months basic dressage moves taught from the ground, then it's reinforced under saddle. The backing process is a simple, pleasant experience for the young horse after that. No trauma because they already understand what is being asked. The exercises and routines are varied so the horse doesn't get 'nappy' and bored and go sour like Fantasy, plus it makes for a safer ride and a thinking horse. It teaches good self-carriage and hock action." Brad noted he had Alex's attention.

"That's fascinating, young man. I'd like to ride out with you this afternoon."

"I'd like that." Brad felt confident that in a few days Fantasy would be willing to do anything with an enthusiastic attitude.

That afternoon Alex noticed Fantasy Flights dramatic change in attitude. "I can't believe what a change in attitude after just one morning session. Well done."

"I learned from the best. My mother. She always swears that by forcing a horse to learn things too quickly is like building a wonky house foundation. When the cracks appear, there's problems."

"What a simply marvellous analogy." Alex stood examining

Fantasy more closely as he walked. "He appears bigger some-how, or am I just imagining things?"

"No, you're not imagining anything." Brad demonstrated that Fantasy understood the leg yield command. "This move-ment is good for their back. Fantasy is a quick learner. Intelli-gent horses often go sour quickly if not stimulated. By tomorrow, he'll give me six correct strides in leg yield instead of the three he's just shown. But I'm happy with that."

"Aren't you going to give him a good gallop?" Alex asked, trying to settle his horse who cavorted around, expecting to gallop down the track.

"No. These early lessons are all about teaching the horse to think, listen and enjoy the work. The slower the gait, the better. I like to teach them to listen to my aids at walk. I don't want the horse to anticipate my next command. Besides, I've asked enough of Fantasy for one day."

Alex was in awe and immediately saw the value of what Brad had done with Fantasy Flight. "I'd like to come out with you on my idiot, Rising Dawn. Nothing settles him, even a good fast gallop. I want to know is how the hell you got Fantasy so chilled and listening to every command. Normally he's either galloping flat out or refusing to do anything."

"Aaah, that's where so many people go wrong. The Thor-oughbred knows how to gallop. No teaching required, it's in their DNA. It's our responsibility to teach them to think while carrying a load. Teaching at the walk is the best place to start. Believe it or not, at home we teach our horses to walk correctly from a few weeks old. A balanced walk is the foun-dation on which they will learn to perform in balanced motion throughout the gaits. You see, moving off from a balanced walk will ensure this. Keeping a horse structurally aligned and balanced helps prevent the early breakdown of limb and back. This in turn, prevents enormous cost to the horse's health and one's bank balance." Alex could relate to that. "The moves are dead simple. I look forward to showing you. Resistance that shows in the walk, will get worse in trot, canter and gallop. The horse will naturally adjust to cater for any discomfort."

"Sounds fair logic. I'll get Emily to join us too. I'd like her to understand all this."

When they got back to the stables, Alex and Brad were still engaged in conversation about these early training principles Alex had known nothing about, but he was keen to learn.

"Teach me too," Gina asked suggestively, leaning over the top of the stable door with a naughty glint in her eye.

"Brad will teach you once he's taught Emily and me first." Gina went back to her work, whistling happily.

Brad untacked, then rubbed Fantasy's back. The horse moaned with satisfaction as he rubbed in circular motions.

"Hey, mister handsome, tell me what did you do with this lazy horse today? Tell me, tell me." She quipped like a child.

"We walked," Brad responded playfully, testing her reaction.

"Huh? What kind of training is that?"

"The right training." The two dimples on either cheek appeared with his smile.

Gina stood staring, mesmerised by this handsome hunk that stood in front of her when Alex interrupted.

"I've never seen racehorse training done like it either, but Fantasy's attitude toward his basic dressage is starkly different."

"Dressage? What the f......" She stopped herself, but the first letter left her lips. Alex and Emily strongly disapproved of that word. Gina often wondered why. It being the most expressive word in the English Dictionary. When Alex was out of earshot,

Gina grabbed Brad's sleeve, "Hey, do you mind me using the 'F' word?"

"No Gina, I don't mind. I use it myself, but not often."

THE FOLLOWING morning Alex was at the stables early with Brad. Gina saddled up Rising Dawn for Alex, and Brad got Fantasy tacked up.

"Ready for this?" Brad asked.

"You bet," Alex put his foot in the stirrup and mounted his favourite horse. In moments Rising Dawn anticipated a gallop. Fantasy Flight showed no anticipation, instead he waited for Brad's command and walked along side Rising Dawn to the gallops. Rising Dawn had only had four days of lessons with Brad, and he hadn't galloped for a week. He settled into the walk without bouncing sideways. When they started to trot, a flamboyant cadence of a horse ready to dance in all gaits began to show.

Alex couldn't stop talking about the change. Fantasy was now the most enthusiastic of the two. Rising Dawn no longer used up all his energy prancing around pointlessly. His jaw had softened, his shoulders were loose and free, and he listened to Alex's every command without a fight.

Emily watched from the edge of the home track. She couldn't believe her eyes. "A joy to watch." She shouted to Alex and Brad when they'd completed one circuit in trot.

"I'd like Gina to bring a horse out to race against me on Fantasy later this morning. If that's okay with you?" Brad asked Alex while they ambled back to the stables, with Emily walking beside a very relaxed Fantasy.

A gentle, soft light fell over the mile track and dew still twinkled like diamonds in the grass. "A good early morning gallop now will stretch Fantasy's top line nicely." Brad said to Gina.

Alex was out of range to hear her swear. "Fuck, I can't believe what you've done with two horses in a bloody week."

Gina was riding Tango, who Brad hadn't seen gallop yet.

Gina had already warmed-up Tango, and Fantasy had done his exercise with Rising Dawn twenty minutes earlier.

"You ready," Brad asked as they approached the start.

"Fucking right I'm ready, mate. I'd be ready for anything with you." Brad ignored the comment and Fantasy burst into a gallop stretching himself to his fullest extent. He'd got his mojo back!

When they pulled up, Brad looked back. Gina and Tango were a few lengths behind. Brad's turn to tease Gina. "I thought you said Fantasy would never outrun Tango!"

They brought the horses back to a walk and noticed Alex and Emily standing under the trees nearby, clapping.

Gina yanked her helmet off. "Aaaw, fuck off." Gina's face was flushed, and she hadn't seen Alex and Emily standing nearby. "Oops, sorry," she shouted when she them.

The training of the Beresford's horses continued to progress over the following week. Brad's training regime was welcomed with enthusiasm.

"So where did you learn all these tricks, Brad." Gina wanted to know. No-one had ever done it this way where she'd worked before.

"From the master herself. My mother." And, at the end of the week, early that Friday evening, Mel called.

"Hi ma, how super to hear from you."

"How has the second week been? I'm curious to know."

"Amazing. Fantasy loves his work. He'll be ready for Alex to enter him into a race in another two weeks. Not sure which course he'll run on, but I'll let you know."

"That's great news. I also have some good news."

"I'm always open to good news."

"Well, you, Mister Bradley Whitaker, have won the vote. You're the fashion model selected for the 2011 Hugo Boss men's range."

"WHAT! You're kidding." Brad shouted. "Really? I mean, really and truly?" He couldn't believe it. Mel was laughing happily. "You're pulling my leg, aren't you?"

"No, I'm not. Jeremy has just called. He's over the moon, and so are we. You're famous."

"That's the last thing I want. But WOW! I'm in shock. Who did they nominate for the men's cologne range?"

"Oh, I'm not sure. Does Jamie Dornan ring a bell?"

"Ma. You obviously don't watch movies. Jamie Dornan. Wow, that's great."

"Jeremy mentioned another name. I think it may have been Orlando Bloom, whoever he is, to launch a fragrance called Orange for Men."

"Now I know you definitely don't watch movies. Orlando Bloom? Mum! This is going to take ages to sink in. I can't believe it." He half laughed; half choked. "Did Jeremy mention when the launch is?"

"He did, but I'm so excited I can't remember. He'll call you. I told him I wanted to tell you first. He did mention something about February, which I think you know. We're so proud of you. Dad will call you later but sends congratulations."

"My God, Ma, this is mind-blowing. I'm in shock."

"I'm sure you are. Dad also wants to know what condition the flat is in. He's with Steve right now. Send our love to Alex and Emily. Must dash. I'm joining the meeting."

"Okay, love to Dad. Bye Mum."

To compose himself Brad took a walk around the garden a few times taking in snatches of breath as he chortled with delight at the thought of his income. When he felt poised enough to tell the Beresford's without grinning like a schoolgirl, he joined them in the conservatory.

"Hello, Brad, cuppa for you?" Emily asked.

"Yes please. Mums just called. She sends her love to you both and shared some amazing news. I've been selected as the model to launch the Hugo Boss range. Can you believe it?"

Emily stopped pouring the tea and looked up at Brad. "Oh yes, I can believe it. A well-deserved win. Darling, I think we should take Bradley out tonight and celebrate, don't you?" She continued pouring the tea.

"And we can celebrate how well Fantasy is going at the same time. Brad reckons he'll be ready to race in two weeks. For me, that's far more exciting news." Alex jested, then added. "Congratulations, young man."

They popped into the village and dined at the local pub and while they were there Jeremy called to gave Brad the contract details and to congratulate him.

It didn't take long for the news to circulate on social media. Either forgetting, or ignoring the time difference, friends from across South Africa began calling. Eventually Brad had to switch his phone off.

When he got to the stables the next morning, Gina was waiting for him.

"I never thought I'd be working with someone so famous." Gina had seen the news posted all over Facebook.

"How the hell did you know?" Brad asked.

"Social media. You're famous. You should have been a film star."

"I never wanted fame. Horses are my life, besides it's the last contract I'll ever do." He said humbly and walked down to Fantasy's stable, grabbed the grooming kit and got to work. Once he'd done Fantasy's stable, he moved down to Emily's barn to groom and muck out her four mares' stables.

Emily had bred two foals this year, both now weanlings. There were six stables to clean. When her foals reached eighteen months old, she handed them on to Alex for training. Tango was one of the horses she'd bred. Emily had been breeding for the last fifteen years and had produced some quality horses for Alex.

Once he'd finished up with Emily's six, Brad went back to the house for breakfast and listened to Alex's gripes to Emily. "A sight for sore eyes those bloody solar fields. Carving up the British countryside everywhere now, and the idiot next door tells me he's putting in another hundred acres and the field that butts onto our land."

Alex moaned about the changing landscape every morning. In a few weeks Alex's south boundary would be an expanse of solar panels scaring the countryside.

The proximity of South End farm to two good equine hospitals and the numerous gallops supplied by The Jockey Club on all corners of the town benefitted Alex's set up though. "I suppose I shouldn't grumble, we are perfectly positioned here with an assortment of surfaces to train on at our finger tips. Turf, synthetic, flat and jumps, and the racecourse, and we use the Pete Moss track too.

Alex trained mainly for flat racing, but he four excellent chasers in his stables that held Brad's interest. He'd never done it before, and where better to start than Newmarket where The National Hunt Schooling facility at the Links was based. There they had steeplechase fences and hurdles on turf. Brad could see himself trying that soon.

By the end of the fourth week Brad's training of Fantasy was to be tested on the Rowley One mile track at Newmarket and he cracked it, winning his race by a whopping two lengths. Brad's first win on British soil.

"Here's to you, Bradley Whitaker," Alex clinked his beer tumbler against Brad's.

"Thanks Alex. A horse with loads of talent"

"Oh Mr. Humble, what utter rubbish," Gina slurred, "you're gifted with being able to bring out the best in horses, isn't he?" She directed the question at her employers.

"I am rather inclined to agree with you, Gina, and Fantasy happened to be one of those fortunate horses." Alex said. Emily whole-heartedly agreed.

"Lazy Fantasy Flight proved himself. Cheers to Brad." Emily lifted her glass of wine.

Arthur, one of the lads from the yard had taken Fantasy back to the farm, and joined the Beresford's and crew at the pub.

Arthur had been after Gina for some months, but now he felt intimidated by Brad's presence and only stayed for one drink because Gina eyes were for Brad, and he knew he couldn't compete. Alex and Emily watched with amusement. They knew all about Gina's nymphomaniac ways.

Apart from work riding together and stable work, Brad hadn't paid much attention to Gina over the past four weeks. She had a great sense of humour, but looking at her now, he had to admit she cleaned up rather well. Her mass of thick strawberry blonde hair hung loosely tonight and framed her round, freckled face. He'd not seen her with make-up on before, but getting involved hadn't been written up on his to-do-list.

Feeling euphoric from both windfalls, two Foster's down the hatch, and staying in the folks flat again, he might be persuaded.

Brad downed the last of his beer and said goodnight. It was a brisk five-minute walk to the flat from the pub, or a ten-minute stagger. Alex and Emily were tired and left the pub at the same time.

Brad switched on the heating as soon as he got in. In just a week there was a hint of a musty, unlived-in smell in the flat. He'd just filled the kettle and switched it on when his phone vibrated on the kitchen counter.

"Hi, Gina, what's up?"

"Nothing yet," she giggled. "Hey! Can I come to your flat?" Brad hesitated a moment, then agreed. "Yeah, okay. Do you know where it is?"

"Yes, you told me during the first week you were here. I'll see you in a mo."

Could be interesting, he thought and pulled two coffee mugs from the cupboard, deciding not to encourage Gina by offering her alcohol. Besides, he'd not let Alex down by being late the next day. Besides, she'd probably had enough alcohol already.

The knock on the door startled him. She must've sprinted from the pub. He opened the door, and a breathless Gina stood in front of him.

"What a lush little flat you have here. Real cosy."

"Yes, it's lovely, isn't it? Has lots of family history. We love it. Mum has furnished it so well, hasn't she?"

"Yeah, it's very classy." Brad heard the slur in her voice.

"I popped the kettle on when I got in. Tea, coffee or hot chocolate?" Brad asked as she leant over the couch to look more closely at a photograph of a horse winning at some racecourse she'd not heard of.

"Nothing a little stronger?" Her hand slipped off the bridge of the sofa as she turned, and she slumped into the seat in an undignified heap.

"Afraid not, Gina. I don't keep it here," he lied. "Sounds like you've had a few anyway."

"Pity, coffee then. Thanks. Who's the 'orse?" She asked making a poor show of sitting upright and proper.

"Tropical Sun. Of all the horses my mother has ever owned, he was her number one equine soul mate. And what a horse."

"Good-looking chap. Big too." Gina struggled to stay upright.

"Do you have milk and sugar?" Brad asked.

"Yes, please. Half a spoon of sugar. Thanks."

Brad put the coffee mug on a coaster beside her and sat next to her on the couch. The flat, open plan in design, made the living area seem more significant in size than it was. Hung on the walls were a set of old-fashioned racing prints and photographs of some of the past Chanting Clover champions.

"What a win today, hey Brad?" She held her coffee mug with both hands.

"Yeah, I'm chuffed. Fantasy enjoyed his seven-furlong gallop, didn't he?"

"You're an amazing fucking horseman, and so fucking good looking" Gina fluttered her eyelids.

"Thank you. Pretty girls like you shouldn't swear so much," he gently chastised. "My skills are all learned from my amazing mother. She's a brilliant horsewoman. Though my dad is first class too, but even he listens to Mum."

"Are you looking forward to going home?"

"Not yet," Brad said honestly without going into why. "What I'm excited about is getting those four chasers of Alex's ready. I've never raced over jumps before. It's only flat racing in Southern Africa. Reckon it must be pretty good fun."

"Shoot, Brad, it's fucking scary. I'll never do it again. I went flying over a jump once and broke my collar bone." She pulled her lower leg up and tucked it under her. "Nope, that's not for me, but I love going to watch and knocking about with friends."

"Knocking about?" Brad asked, a little taken aback.

"Yes! What's so wrong with that?"

"Nothing at all, I guess. It's just the expression. Back home it would mean you'd be looking for a roll in the hay, so to speak."

Gina burst out laughing. "Nothing wrong with that either, Brad."

Brad didn't comment.

"Season opens soon, ya know. There's a great meet at Cottenham near Cambridge in November. Wanna go? I mean to go and watch. I don't think Alex's horses will be ready to chase until January." The coffee was starting to help sober her.

"Yeah, I'd love to. I'm going to chat to Alex about it on Monday morning. I'll be back in South Africa in January." She edged a little closer to Brad, reached over him and put her coffee mug down on the table deliberately rubbing her breasts across his legs.

Brad inched away enough for Gina to notice. "Not up for a bit of fun then, Bradley Whitaker? A romp in the hay, or a little knocking about?" She'd just confirmed the reason why she'd been so keen to get to his flat.

"Hadn't given it a thought, to be honest." He wasn't being honest. He had thought about it, but...............

"Where's your toilet? I've had too many gins."

"Through there. First on the left." Brad pointed. A couple

of minutes later her heard the toilet flush and Gina entered the room, stark naked.

"Gina!" Brad exclaimed. "What are you......?" She didn't let him finish.

"Come on, Bradley, you want it as much as I do. Nothing wrong with a good romp between work mates now, is there?" She rubbed herself against him.

"Well, um, no. I guess there isn't." He choked on his words but appreciated her petit, firm body and well-rounded breasts that were almost in his face giving away her desire. He felt his groin tingle as she pushed her bosom into his face. Brad held her waist and gently pushed her back, but one erect nipple was tantalisingly close. He placed his lips over it and flicked his tongue around it playfully while Gina giggled and began undressing him as quickly as she could.

"Phew, Gina." She had him naked and lying on the fur pile carpet beside the couch before he knew it. There was no point in resisting.

"My goodness, you're a randy little wench."

"Oh, I notice you're not saying no." She said sarcastically, her breasts bouncing around as she turned away from him, then sunk herself down and had him in her mouth before he could answer.

Brad felt his body mould with the carpet as if invisible threads had tied him down. He couldn't move. He held onto her strawberry blonde hair as she worked him for a moment longer, then he gently pulled her off him and rolled her onto her back and mounted her. Their sexual interlude ended all too quickly.

"Sorry, I couldn't hold on." Brad apologised, but Gina's smile stretched across her face triumphantly.

"I think I can safely say I've just been fucked by the best-looking man in Europe" She rejoiced. "Can I stay the night?"

"Not a shit, Gina. I'll not be able to walk in the morning if you do. Time to get dressed and get home, young lady." And he meant it. Gina whinged, but she pulled on her jeans and slipped her jumper over her head.

She knew she'd get her way again.

Chapter Thirty-Seven

STEVE'S ZIMBABWE connection's latest report suggested the colonel may be ramping up his plans to murder Bradley on his return from the UK, and slay the famous Tsotsi, before going for Melonie Whitaker's jugular. Willem decided not to let the Whitaker's know, as discussed with Steve.

In their Kloof home, Steve read George's report to Kgabu and Synthia.

"Oh my God, Dad, you've got to stop the bastard. We can't lose Tsotsi, Brad and Mel. I damned well hope I'm not a target too. Would your connection in Zim know if I was on the hit list? Or any of the other jockeys?"

"They certainly would. No jockeys are on the list this time, but this calls for extreme vigilance. Prime Security are working in full co-operation with my connection in Zim now. The Whitakers could not wish to have better protection, but that bastard is cunning."

"Do the Whitakers know about this?" Synthia's face had

paled. She sat in her armchair with her legs crossed underneath her looking very distressed.

"No, they don't, for obvious reasons. Poor Gary carries enough of the burden." Steve said with admiration. "But I may have to warn him. I'll do it sensitively and find the right moment, but for now it's between us."

"Dad, I think Gary should know. He'll handle it. Just don't tell Mel. Since Garth was murdered, she's not been the same, and though I don't blame her, I wish Brad hadn't gone to Newmarket. She needs him now and I must admit, I worry about riding for them now."

"I understand. You, my boy, are the primary reason mum and I got involved. Apart from being horrified by what the swine has put the Whitakers through already, we have a huge investment in Tsotsi. Mum and I are taking no chances with your life, and you were born to ride, so never think of giving it up or letting the Whitakers down. The harsh and sordid reality is, Mel is the ultimate target. The very thought makes us go cold." Steve shuddered involuntarily.

"God, it must be awful living like that. I feel so sorry for them." Kgabu got up and stood at the sitting room bay window and looked out over the lush, manicured tropical garden to his little hide-away at the bottom of the lawn.

"Dad, didn't you say the colonel is reportedly getting scared now that Tanya is no longer working with him? He's killed off Nkizwi and now it seems Julie and Tanya may be next."

"For sure. Everything depends on who he has conned into working with him. We're getting feedback every day from Harare which keeps us one step ahead of the swine."

"You hope," Kgabu said, still standing at the window. "Iris slipped through the net." He turned and faced his father.

"What about the groom that worked under Jackson. Where is he?"

"Arrested, taken into custody and interrogated. He quickly spilled the secrets. Pissed on the floor of the cell and was released. The colonel took care of him, two days later he was dead. Killed in a car accident."

"That man isn't human, he's a beast." Kgabu spat in disgust.

"Solomon will be stopped soon, and you'll be fine. I won't let anything happen to you, Mel, Brad or Tsotsi."

"Gee, I hope so. I miss Brad. He has his mother's Midas touch with horses, and he's such fun."

"Well, he'll be home in a month. Yes, I agree, the Whitakers outclass so many owners, breeders and trainers. We've seen that and value them enormously, as you know."

Kgabu left the bay window and walked across to his mother and hugged her. He sat in the chair beside her and held her hand. "Ma you look like you've seen a ghost."

"It feels that way too. I can't bear the thought of any more tragedy. Lucky Brad and Indigo weren't killed in that awful car accident that killed poor Tinus." Kgabu flet her hand shaking. "Any talk of horses going to Dubai or Mauritius? I could do with another holiday."

"Yes, there is, but at this stage, it's talk. They want to take a stab at Paris this time." Steve turned to Synthia. "Relax sweetheart, we'll conquer the evil."

A week later George called Steve from Harare and the moment he placed the receiver of his private line, Steve called Gary.

"Gary, morning. I have mixed news. George says things are

almost in place." Steve's tone immediately alerted Gary who'd not long been out of bed. He'd had a nasty flu bug for three days.

"Elaborate, Steve. What's the meaning of, almost? I thought everything would take place last week. I've been rather anxiously waiting to hear. Lying in bed, feeling vile, I've been over thinking."

"The delay, you'll be interested to know, is because Jackson made attempt to take Solomon out, but he messed up and got himself killed. Dam shame Jackson didn't take the bastard out. However, the wheels are in motion despite the minor setback."

"Have you spoken to Willem?" Gary asked.

"Not yet. I'll get hold of him when we've finished this call. The circle is tightening, my friend. We'll get that son-of-a-bitch, and my God, he deserves the worst. When's the next meeting with Thabo and crew?"

"Next week, Thursday. I'll see you there. Hopefully I'm over this blasted flu."

"Knowing the plans are settling into place should make you feel better. Cheers for now." Steve knew more but he was loath to talk about it on the phone. They'd discuss it in the meeting on Thursday.

The Thursday meeting Mel dreaded was starting in fifteen minutes. She looked at her watch, fidgeted with her hair and checked her minimal make-up in front of the mirror in the Prime Security offices ladies' room, then took a tissue from her bag and wiped her sweaty brow. When she came out Gary held her. "Take a nice deep breath, honey. You know this meeting is for the safety of all of us, including our horses." Gary's gentle, soothing tone calmed her stretched, fragile nerves.

Thabo and Julie were expected to arrive in the next five minutes.

Tanya and Simon had driven from Nelspruit for this important meeting. A large city in the north of the country, and roughly a nine-hour drive to Durban. They were being escorted from Durban central by one of Willems security vans.

Gary led Mel through to the boardroom and they took a set at the large oval table.

"Some water, sweetheart?" Mel nodded and placed her handbag on the floor beside her. Gary poured her a glass of lemon infused water and she sipped on it, likely tasting nothing, silently dreading the confrontation with Julie, Tanya and their husbands.

Mel understood, on a very deep level, just how difficult the moment would be when she laid eyes on Julie again and met Tanya for the first time. These two women were instrumental in killing Garth, their trainer, Tinus and two of their prize horses. Apart from injuring Brad, James and Indigo. The days of disquiet leading to this meeting gave Mel terrible stomach cramps and sleepless nights.

Tanya and Simon were joining this meeting to offer a trade-off. Their lives for security and protection from the legal system. Tanya and Julie knew they would be jailed for what they'd done should everything be exposed, not just on the Whitaker level. Tanya would be had for murder and attempted murder, with Julie as her accomplice.

Mel's two enemies arrived and were ushered into the boardroom with their husbands. Mel didn't move, nor did she greet them. The blood seemed to drain from her face. The atmosphere was strained like a bow string and the point of Mel's arrow held fixed as her stare.

Gary opened the meeting.

"I cannot express how hard this is for my wife and me to be seated here with the two people directly responsible for the murder of our son, the death of two of our top horses, and injuries to one of our jockeys, our youngest son and his American girlfriend in the car crash that killed Tinus, our trainer." Gary paused and focussed his attention on Tanya and Julie's expressions. The silence in the room spoke volumes.

Gary pointed his first question at Tanya. "Are you willing to turn state witness as a trade-off for your protection from Solomon and prosecution for the murder of our son, Garth and the death our trainer?" Emotion caught in Gary's throat as he asked. His mouth had dried. He felt his body internally tremble. He took a sip of water and glanced at Mel, whose head was now bowed.

Simon glanced at Tanya. He too felt the enormity of what his wife and Julie had done in collaboration with Solomon as Gary spelt it out.

"Yes, I am," Tanya answered and glanced at Julie. "I hate my grandfather more than I've ever hated anyone. I will tell you everything I know."

Willem switched on the voice recorder and Tanya began. Occasionally Julie interrupted and added things she'd forgotten to say in the first meeting when Tanya wasn't present. What Tanya revealed left them all aghast, and it became clearer just how vulnerable Mel's life was.

Willem had already conferred with Steve after their first meeting, and through George in Zimbabwe, it had been agreed they'd work with an external undercover agent from South Africa. His brief was to extract Solomon from Zimbabwe.

The room was hot and clammy. The air conditioning wasn't working efficiently as the sun reached its zenith and baked the top of the building. Mel couldn't wait to get out of the building. She uttered a few words of thanks, then she and Gary left.

Chapter Thirty-Eight

Opening the Herald newspaper, Jules, Mel's old school friend, read aloud to her husband Allan while they were seated on the veranda of their Harare home.

"There's a photo of Solomon, as fat as a toad, sweat dripping of his brow. God he's evil."

"Go on. Who's he's brutally murdered this time?" Allan asked stretching back in his deck chair.

"Someone tried to kill him. Pity they didn't. He's not seriously injured, is in a stable condition and will be released from hospital today. Well," Jules laughed, "perhaps stable in body, but not in mind, though looking at him I can't see how he'd be stable in body either." She read on. "Investigating officers seem to think the attack came from a woman." She moved the newspaper away from her face. "As always, the article is clouded with dramatic bullshit."

"Damn shame he wasn't killed, but I think you should let Mel know. Send her a scan of the article." Allan suggested.

"Oh God he's a disgusting, enormous fat toad no doubt

living off fraudulent earnings, as most of them are. Ugh, the photograph of him gives me the shivers. Here's the newspaper, I can't read more." She handed it to Allan.

Jules called Mel. "Hey, how awesome to hear from you. I hope this is a friendship call and not more scary info about my bloody nemesis?"

"I always want to find out how you are, but this time your ghastly tormenter was attacked by a woman, but unfortunately she didn't kill him."

"What a shame. What is the name of the woman who attacked him? An ex-wife?"

"It doesn't say. The search is on to find her, apparently. I'll scan the article in today's paper and send it to you."

"Wonderful. Our informants tell us he's out of favour with many of his henchmen here in South Africa, which is good news, but you never know. I hope he's been taken out by the time Brad gets back from the UK. I haven't shared with you yet an extraordinary turn of events. Gary and I met with Solomon's granddaughter, Tanya and that bitch, Julie, the one who killed our horses."

"Good God. Why on earth did you do that for?"

"I had the same reaction when Gary told me they'd contacted him. I was utterly devastated. Poor Gary bore the brunt of my anger, but as it's turned out there were many good reasons to meet. I'm not going to lie, the meeting took it out of me, I was an emotional wreck, and I couldn't look at either of them throughout the meeting. Julie's nice jockey husband, Thabo, instigated the whole thing. After 'Jockey Julie' killed our horse in Cape Town, the police found her and arrested her, as you may remember. It took the police a day to lose her again which didn't shock any of us. She escaped. More accurately, we think Solomon bribed for blind eyes. She disappeared off the radar, but our security soon found her. Instead of turning her over to the police, we dropped the charges so our security company could tail her." Mel breathed in deeply before going on. Jules stayed silent. Mel thought the phone had gone dead. "Jules, are you still there?"

"Yeah, I'm listening. I'm enthralled. Incredible lengths you and Gary must go to ensure you stay alive. God, it must be awful living under that constant threat."

"It's stressful, for sure. Anyway, as it turned out, Julie got word back to Solomon that she wanted nothing further to do with him. She changed her address and telephone phone number, and we tracked her for months after that to satisfy ourselves she had indeed left the bastard. However, Solomon's men recently found her and threatened to kill her. Thabo was in an absolute state about it and contacted Gary, which by any accounts was a bold thing to do."

"And brave."

"Yeah, and brave. Anyway, Gary, being darling Gary, agreed to meet Thabo. At that point, I had no idea of the arrangement. You can imagine how I felt when he told me, but common sense prevailed. All I can do now is pray the plan works in our favour. Gary is currently negotiating the next move."

"Gosh, I admire your courage. You're one brave lady. I must go. Have a dentist appointment. I'll call if I hear who put him in hospital, except you'll probably know before me."

"Thanks, my friend. Chat soon. Love to Allan."

"Yes, of course and all our love to Brad and Gary." Typical of two lady friends chatting on the phone, Jules went on. Mel smiled. "Oh, and hearty congrats to young Brad. Gosh, what a contract. You must be so proud of him, but he is rather drop-dead gorgeous, isn't he? That's danger for him with a capital D.

Guard him carefully, Mel. You'll be inundated with women when he's home."

Mel sighed, thinking of Garth. "We are proud, but prouder of the way he's remained humble and genuine throughout all this ghastly modelling. Testament to his lovely character, but he's stopping the modelling now, thank God."

"Why? He must milk it and make himself a fortune." Mel loved Jules's attitude.

"This latest contract will make him a fortune. Anyway, chat soon or you'll be late for your appointment."

"Yes. I really must go this time."

Mel hung up and sat thinking about Solomon, wishing he was leaving hospital in a box. Those and other thoughts flitted through her mind when Gary walked into the sitting room.

"Jules has just called. She tells me Solomon has been hospitalised from another attempt on his life, but he's being discharged today, sadly."

"I've just this moment heard. Steve called and I came to tell you. News travels fast, doesn't it? Did she tell you who tried to knock him off?"

"No. Apparently, it was a woman."

Gary smiled. "Yes, it was, and guess who?"

"I give up."

"Our ex-receptionist, Iris." Mel shook her head, not in disbelief, but she did wonder what Solomon may have done to her for her to turn on him like Jackson did.

"Really? Have you told Anette?"

"Not yet."

"Let's go together. I want to see her face when you tell her."

. . .

Solomon's bodyguard collected him from hospital. He sat at home brooding in his over-sized, custom-made armchair and doused his anger by sharing his thoughts with his best friend: Johnny Walker Blue label whiskey.

Solomon's home in Borrowdale was palatial and surrounded by an eight-foot wall. The sitting room, furnished like the room you'd find in a home belonging to royalty, his chair was positioned so he could not only see himself in the giant-sized, Mahogony engraved mirror, but anyone else entering the room.

"Cheers," he said to himself and raised the glass to his reflection. The smooth, expensive liquid helped relieve the pain from the stab wounds, but didn't help with the waves of depression. He'd felt visceral fear before and it felt similar now. Why had Cousin Iris wanted to kill him?

Fear. Would he ever forget the day the Rhodesian air force flew over the burning camp in Mozambique. The one that bitch Melonie had escaped from. After finding refuge in a huge cluster of banana trees, he'd watched the remainder of the camp being pummelled by bombs from the Rhodesian Hunter jets. He could still hear those terrifying sounds. Somehow, he'd got away unharmed, but his life was in danger once more.

Questions raged through his mind. The most pressing one. Why had his family turned on him? Tanya? His granddaughter. The one who knew of all his activities. She'd have to be silenced. Once his man in South Africa had dealt with Julie, he'd get rid of Tanya. Cousin Iris would meet her end soon, but in Harare.

Suddenly, like an explosion from the burning camp, he erupted. In loud bellows he shouted for the resident nurse who scurried through to the sitting room. There was little she could do to help.

"Do you need painkillers, Sir?" She asked, wanting to tell

the Colonel the antibiotics wouldn't work with half a bottle of neat whiskey in his system, but she didn't dare. She gave him painkillers and a sleeping tablet. He swallowed the tablets with one gulp of neat whiskey.

"Do you want to stay in your chair, or should I help you to your room?"

"I'll stay here," he slurred. She hung around close by. He'd be asleep in a few minutes. She felt sad for him in a weird way, though she was unaware of all his nefarious activities from the past.

Chapter Thirty-Nine

OBLIVIOUS TO WHAT his parents were enduring, Brad was having the best time in England, but he was paying for it this morning. He felt vile as he blundered through the hedge, cursing himself for allowing Gina to lead him astray. He'd taken in far too much alcohol and needed to bring up. He heaved emptily, rested, and dozed, rocking on his haunches, then heaved again. Little but saliva. He squatted for several minutes, waiting for nausea to either manifest or subside. Soon his stomach started to ease, and his breathing became less urgent, then he heard a voice approaching along the path on the other side of the hedge.

"I want Penzance to lose." Brad overheard the voice say. He remained crouched, hoping no-one would discover him at his most undignified.

From what he could hear, the man who'd spoken appeared to be middle-aged and local. Brad surmised, a local trainer and accent his suggested a public-school education. The voice. There was something familiar about it.

In his blurred reasoning, Brad realised that the man's sentiment was not for public consumption. He peered through the hedge branches to get a better view of the man, but all he could see was brown corduroys and green gumboots, but the man had a limp. He couldn't see anyone else on the pathway and realised the man was talking on his mobile phone.

The mist lay heavily over the Heath, so before he froze, he staggered back to the warmth of his flat. On the way back, the fate of Penzance's next race kept playing over in his foggy mind. And that voice. Did he recognise it?

After cooking himself breakfast fit for a king, he felt better. 'I want Penzance to lose', the words still reverberating through his thoughts. Although he could do with more sleep, he'd have to catch up later. He called Gina.

"Hiya," She answered.

"What the fuck did you give me to drink last night?" He asked. She roared with laughter.

"Ya feeling it, mate?" She chuckled.

"Bloody hell, I feel like death. I'll be down at the yard in half an hour. Hey, are Alex and Emily there?"

"Yes, they are, but they always have a quiet Sunday. Why?"

"I don't want to bump into them looking and feeling like I do. Not again, Madam Gina, not again. However, I've something pressing I need to ask you when I get there."

"Righty ho. Need another romp around the carpet?" she squealed with mirth and hung up.

Brad hired himself a BMW after being in Newmarket for two weeks. It was small and nifty for parking in Newmarket is a nightmare. As he was spending more nights in the flat than at the Beresford's, he'd needed his own transport to avoid standing in the freezing cold waiting for the bus. Besides, he reckoned he'd well-earned the luxury of a hire car.

He pulled into the yard and parked, hauled himself out of the car, still feeling a bit queasy. He didn't want to let go of his breakfast. He needed it to absorb the alcohol. Settled, he made his way to Fantasy's stable and hung over the door like a dirty mop. Gina cackled like a hyena.

"Don't laugh," Brad held his head.

"Hey, I'm mighty curious about this pressing thing you need to ask me."

"Do you know the horse, Penzance?"

"Yes, you should too. He was in the same race when Fantasy won last Saturday."

"It's been niggling at me, but my minds too blurred by excess alcohol thanks to you. Somewhere in the darkest depths of my alcohol distorted mind, dulled further by a strawberry blonde nymph, I thought I recognised the name." Brad teased and when he smiled shyly Gina groaned.

"Ooooh, you tease," she punched his arm, "but fuck, you're even sexier hung over."

Brad ignored the comment. "Can you ask your friend Laura, the one who works at the Club's Rooms in the Jockey Club Estates, who owns him? I presume it's a, him, not a, her."

"Yeah, sure. Why?"

Brad gave Gina the details of what he'd heard while hidden behind the hedge. He explained that he'd gone for a walk earlier to ease the hangover. "A greasy fried egg breakfast worked better than a brisk early morning walk, though. Are they into doping in this country?" He asked casually, though he knew it was done. He wanted to hear it from Gina, who he knew would offer the truth.

"Oh yeah, blimey mate, it happens all the time. The drugs get harder and harder to detect, which is an ongoing headache for the authorities."

"Well, from what I heard of the phone conversation while squatting in the hedge, it sounds to me like Penzance will be doped with something nasty for his upcoming race. How does one report this, or what would be the next step in preventing it?"

"Jeez, Brad, best to let Alex know. You know, if ever there is doubt in the racing industry, it has a permanent parking bay outside the betting shops. Doping is bad news for the bookmakers and betting agencies, and they are always fighting it."

"Okay, I'll talk to Alex, but only once Laura gives us the owner's and trainer's names."

"I'll call her when I finish mucking out."

Brad grabbed a poop-scoop and a wheelbarrow and worked in the stable next door. The voice. It still bugged him. He couldn't place it, and why should he? He'd only been in the UK four weeks. He went on mucking out, then moved to the first of the three chasers. There'd be no work riding today. He'd head home in an hour.

Just before he'd finished the chaser's stables, Gina appeared at the door of the last stable. "Laura says she can't get the info today. She'll look in the Horses in Training book tomorrow morning and call me."

"Great, thank you, Gina. What's the Horses in Training book?"

"A record of every single horse registered to race in the UK. It tells the gender, age, colour, and names of its mum and dad. Plus, of course, who the owner is and who's training the horse. Penzance is a racer. He'll be listed. So, what are you doing this afternoon, mister good-looking?"

"Sleeping, Gina. Don't get any ideas."

"Spoil sport." She muttered. "You owe me one."

Brad smiled, finished up and gapped it as fast as he could.

. . .

Early Monday morning saw Brad rested and re-booted after ten hours of uninterrupted sleep and arrived at the yard before anyone else.

New Destiny, a horse with a big heart and as bold as 'brass', Brad was training today, and when he got back, he told Gina he'd almost followed her history on the first jump. "I nearly went flying," he laughed.

Though Brad had done well in show jumping and eventing as a junior, jumping a fence made of birch, four foot in height at full gallop in a racing saddle was quite different as he'd found out.

It took three days to pluck up the courage to try again. He also knew it was a big ask of the horse. He was no lightweight, though he rode with such grace and balance, he still weighed considerably more than the jockeys, but the three chaser geldings seemed to manage.

"These are three super horses. So solid, super temperament and they try so hard for me. I believe they were bred in Ireland?"

"Yip, ya guessed right, mate," Gina grinned. "No falls today?"

"Tease." Brad enjoyed the banter with Gina, she was both fun at the stables and great in bed. "New Destiny, Classy Lad and Next Exhibition are all doing me proud. An no falls."

To everyone's amazement, Alex handed his favourite horse, Rising Dawn, to Brad to train too. His days were brim full now and the fittest he'd been in years. But a momentary lapse in concentration resulted in him nearly falling at the first fence this morning. He hung on and wasn't going to tell Gina.

When he got back from the hurdles he asked, "What time do you expect Laura to call you, Gina?"

"This Penzance horse has got to you, hasn't he?"

"You bet. I detest this sort of dishonesty. It's always the poor horse who pays the price."

Gine nodded. "She gets to work at ten, Brad. Not everyone starts work at five-thirty in the morning. Did you wet the bed?"

"No, but the same could be asked of you. I had ten hours of uninterrupted sleep, and if I hadn't woken when I did, I probably would've wet it. What I need to find out is when he next runs."

"Oh, that you'll find in the Racing Post, or Laura can have a quick peep in the Flat Form Book or the Flat Programme Books. Remember, the line-up for any race is not confirmed until a few days before the race."

"Yeah. It'll probably result in us finding out nothing before the horse runs again, but if we can stop it, let's give it a bash."

Gina agreed, thought the likelihood was slim.

That evening, he ruminated once more about the elusive voice. Where the hell had he heard it? Was it perhaps on TV during a screening of a race and subsequent interviews?

Still, at a loss, he called his parents. He needed to convey that the handyman would be in the following day to begin with the minor roof repairs and the fitting of a new boiler. He'd get a break from Gina too, for he'd have to stay with the Beresford's until Friday.

Brad moved back to the flat on Friday afternoon and for some unknown reason he decided to have a bit of a lie in on Saturday morning. Lying in bed thinking about home, the new modelling contract, and other events, he heard horses passing on the street below. They'd be on their way to the Heath for their morning exercise. He heard the voice.

He lay there for a moment thinking back to the first trip to the Beresford's in his hired car. He was not used to driving in England and recalled an unpleasant exchange he'd had travelling towards the T-junction of Parsonage and New Base Road. The road is narrow and as he approached the T-junction, two horses turned into Parsonage and came towards him. Logically they should have adopted a single file. Instead, one of them was guided by its rider onto Brad's side of the road and walked boldly towards him. Brad had to stop. He rolled down the window and leaned out to ask if there was a problem. Very purposefully, the rider, middle-aged and somewhat overweight, rode right up to the car. He pompously bellowed something about the special bylaw in Newmarket that states motorists are to give way to horses. Brad apologised, though he'd done nothing wrong. It was one of those occasions where one would be left feeling thoroughly offended and growing in wisdom about what he should have said in reply.

Newmarket is littered with hidden stable yards, and behind most of the housing, the real secret of Newmarket is revealed. Stables, lots of them. Lots of horses, exercise rings, you name it. They are there, tucked away down alleyways and back streets which Brad was learning.

A WEEK LATER, it happened again. This time Brad had been crawling behind another car. Eight horses came out of the stables onto Parsonage Road. This time, the direction of travel was reversed. He was heading south. The riders shimmied into single file, and the cars inched forward carefully. Then suddenly, from near the back of the file, Brad noticed the dreaded toff strike again. He had immediately blocked off the line of oncoming traffic, which was now four deep. They all stopped.

How unnecessary, Brad thought, but held his tongue. Under his breath, he practised what he wanted to say. Staring straight ahead as the riders walked past, he muttered to himself, 'Chalk it up, just chalk it up.' Brad was mindful of the wisdom his father often repeated — a quote by James Bond's author, Ian Fleming. 'Once is happenstance. Twice is a coincidence. Three times is enemy action.'

Reflecting on these recent events, he thought about the voice he'd heard through the hedge. Convinced it was that same little-big-man toff. It seemed he enjoyed lording it over motorists from the lofty height of a 16hand Thoroughbred. What was he doing work riding a racehorse anyway? His age and physical condition didn't come anywhere close to fitting the bill. And that accent?

Later that day, Gina got a call from Laura. Penzance exists. A four-year-old. Good form; 1302. This meant that in his last four races, he came 1st, 3rd, not placed, and 2nd. She passed this information onto Brad.

"Brad, Penzance is running again next weekend at Lingfield Park. Oh! And the trainer is local, I know of him, his name is Des Smart, and he's not a popular fella."

"Where are his stables?" Brad asked.

"Somewhere in town. Off Old Station Road. It's very near the Heath." Gina explained.

"I have a hunch, but it's only a hunch, so I'm going to let Alex and Emily know I'll be staying at the folks' flat again tonight. If everything turns out the way I hope it will, I'll gloat in the morning! He's up to no good if he is who I'm sure he is."

The following morning, Brad was earlier than usual at the newsagent. It was a long shot, but he fancied his chances of catching the jerk pulling his typical traffic control stunt. Brad just needed to be positioned strategically to see the riders moving out. If he got snookered, he still had their return to try again.

Taking a circuitous route, he turned into Parsonage. He wanted to be facing the entrance to the stables. This meant he needed to be parked where all the overnight cars parked, the only problem was finding a space. Brad drove slowly. An early commuter was just leaving. He took her place. Parked, he could see the stables entrance. He waited. As if scripted, about ten minutes later, out came a string of six horses. Brad felt certain number five was the toff, sitting deep in the saddle. God, he rides badly, Bradly observed, started his engine and checked his rear-view mirror. All clear, he pulled out onto the road.

Right on cue, Bullyboy broke rank and moved over to the opposite side of the road. The car in front gave him the finger but managed to get past. Aah, shot, thought Brad, he was now positioned perfectly.

Bullyboy shook his fist at Car No. 1, then focused on Brad. He aimed his mount directly at Brad, arm raised. Brad stopped, put the handbrake on and switched the engine off. Bullyboy faltered. The other horses were passing by. Brad got out of the car and walked straight up to the horse and slipped his hand into the bit-ring. The horse had to stop. Bullyboy was mute for a moment, and then he started to protest loudly. "Let my horse go. Wot, do you think you are doing, young man? You have no right to touch my horse. HEY! I say, let me GO."

Brad hadn't said a word. The clip-clop of the other horses had changed to a cacophony of clattering hooves as the horses stopped and the riders turned around to watch.

Brad noticed they were in no hurry to intervene.

Facing Bullyboy squarely, he said, "Good morning, sir. I would appreciate the opportunity to discuss your traffic controlling antics. This is the third time you have inconvenienced me on this stretch of the road. The first time you read me the riot act about cars giving way to horses. It was a bit thick because I was barely moving. Question for you, sir. Does the bylaw say, 'Give way' or does it say, 'Stop?'"

"You were driving too fast. It's very dangerous for us riders..." He blustered, avoiding the question. "You are not from these parts, are you lad?"

Ignoring his question. "Actually," Brad pulled his Blackberry out of his pocket, "I have filmed this morning's episode. I have my dashboard on-screen, and it shows you approaching the car that has just squeezed past. I continued filming until I stopped. Would you like me to show you how fast I was going?"

Bullyboy was speechless, but his face spoke volumes through the colour red. He tried to yank the horses head out of Brad's grasp. The horse jumped backwards, slipping on the tarmac. Brad quickly pocketed his phone and, using that hand, grabbed the bit-ring on the other side of the horse's mouth and calmed it down. Bullyboy was huffing and puffing, going nowhere.

As calmly as ever, Brad looked back up at the man and said, "Sir, can we agree that you will never stem the flow of traffic again. I promise you that I, and I'm sure I speak for 99.9% of all the other drivers in Newmarket, will continue to watch out for these beautiful animals by GIVING WAY. Don't ever ask us to stop again. It's not your job. If you want our courtesy? Earn it. You and your fellow riders can return the favour by riding in single file as a courtesy to us. How's that for a fair deal?" Brad stated.

Bullyboy was flustered.

"Now, sir," Brad continued, "one more thing." He stepped to the side but remained in firm control of Bullyboy's horse's head. He needed to have a clear vision of Bullyboy's face. In measured syllables, Brad hit him with the question, "Does the name Penzance mean anything to you?"

Bullyboy's reaction was electric. His eyes shot open. He didn't know what to say. It was all the proof Brad needed. Two of the more curious riders had walked back to where Brad held court.

"What happened to your leg? I noticed you walk with a limp. Not wearing your brown corduroys today, I see."

This was too much for Bullyboy. "Who are you? And who do you think you are? You never answered my question, you not from these parts, are you?"

"Someone you unwittingly encountered. But never mind that. We're holding up the traffic. Penzance is running on Saturday at Lingfield Park. I want you to know that unless there is a placing; 1st, 2nd or 3rd, we shall be requesting the Steward to get an official blood test done." Raising his voice like a schoolteacher, Brad shot him another question, "What's your name?"

Bullyboy blurted it out before he could catch himself, "Smithers, Reg."

"OK, Smithers-Reg. Thank you. So, you work for Des Smart, is that right? I think you know we have your number. Stop your shit on the roads and, for the sake of what appears to be a good, honest horse on the rise, no luminal sodium or whatever the hell dope you use nowadays. Do that, and this encounter will fade into the mists of time. Have a good day."

Brad felt proud of outwitting the smug toff. When he got to the farm, he briefed Alex and Gina on what had taken place. Brad had nothing to lose; he'd be gone in a few weeks. Smithers-Reg was someone they might want to keep an eye on.

Brad had torpedoed a big lay bet and was likely to motivate a reaction by goons in the underworld. He hoped it wouldn't include a modification to Smithers-Reg's good leg. In Brad's estimation of street justice, it would be sufficient if, instead of a financial gain, he would suffer, at the very least, a jolly good loss.

Alex agreed, he loathed this sort of skullduggery and together they strategized. If Penzance failed, all they had to do was follow through with the blood test.

"He's one of the most unpopular assistant trainers in Newmarket. Man am I happy with what you did, Brad. Might stop his nonsense now he knows he's being watched."

THE FOLLOWING Saturday satisfied them all. Smithers-Reg had done the wise thing. Penzance ran a comfortable second place.

Brad would still encounter the 'Smithers-Reg' riders making their way to or from the Gallops when staying in town. They rode in single file. Courtesy had been restored, and friendly waves became the customary greeting, except from the toff.

Chapter Forty

"Morning Gary, are you able to meet me at Prime's offices later today?" Steve asked.

"Yes, certainly. Good news? Bad news?"

"Good news. Solomon's been kidnapped. George will provide the exact details a bit later. I thought it justified to meet."

"That's music to my ears, Steve. What time?" Relief surged through Gary, he felt it in every pore of his body. How many years had this bastard been trying to kill his wife? He'd held her ransom since she was seventeen years old.

"Eleven, suit you?"

"Absolutely."

Gary crossed the passage and told Mel. She sat at her desk, speechless. Finally, she said, "I'm anxious but excited, if that makes any sense at all?"

"Yes, it does. Let's get going. We're meeting Steve at eleven in Durban." They were keen to learn the details of Solomon's capture.

"Let's pray it's nearly all over and we can live a free life. I wonder where they've taken him. Who's got him, and how they got that enormous mound of blubber out of his house."

"Well, we'll find out soon enough. I'm curious to know if they used those Zulu bone-breakers of Simon's. A couple of those 125 pounders with muscles like an ox would have made the fat toad compliant, I expect. God, how I wish I could've been a fly on the wall, but I won't rest until he's incarcerated."

"Yeah, me neither. George or whoever George got to do it would've had to have planned this well to have executed it without alerting security."

They arrived at the Prime Security offices with minutes to spare. Steve was already upstairs with Willem sitting in the boardroom.

"Hi Steve, this is remarkable. Is it really true?" Mel hugged Steve and greeted Willem. Gary shook hands with the two men.

"Tea? Coffee? Something cold?" Willem asked.

"Iced water for me," Mel said.

They made their way through to the board room. Willem closed the door and handed the meeting over to Steve.

"The details I have to hand are that Thale is in the hands of his captor's. Who they are I've not yet heard, but what amused me, his security guards were fast asleep at the time."

"Figures," Willem said with tilt to his mouth.

"Were Simon's heavyweights a part of this?" Mel asked.

"I'm not sure yet, but I've a good feeling they were. The most important thing is that the son-of-a-bitch is held captive in a safe house on a smallholding near Ruwa. You know where Ruwa is, Mel. I'm not familiar with Harare and its satellite towns?"

Mel nodded; she knew precisely where Ruwa was.

"The plan is to move him by car to somewhere near Beitbridge under cover of darkness and as soon as things are tied up with the border control authorities, he'll be walked across the Limpopo at a given point and formally arrested."

Gary burst out laughing. "Walk? Have you seen the size of him? How the hell is he going to move clandestinely in the dark through thick Mopani scrub, spikey stubs of old trees even the goats can't gnaw through and stick out the ground like the left-over spears of Lobengula's warriors. Impossible."

"They believe their plan is watertight. They won't be gentle with him, and he won't be in great condition when he arrives on South African soil, if he hasn't died of a heart attack before they reach the pre-arranged rendezvous. Given that a formal court case will be fraught with politics and a consequential cost to the South African taxpayer, they'll have to escort him careful-ly." Steve explained.

"It won't work, Steve." Gary was shaking his head. "The plan is fraught with impossibilities."

"I have my doubts too, but George is reliable, and if he's got the full support of Simon's team who has the latitude to apply unconventional methods for a cheaper and cleaner way to make the problem go away, there's no point in us getting involved. The only drawback is, if Mugabe's men get wind of Solomon's arrest, he could insist the Colonel be returned to Zimbabwe without trial. If he makes it to South African soil, that is."

Mel listened intently. Gary noticed there was hope in her eyes even though the logistics seemed impossible. Visions of Solomon being forced to walk great distances over difficult terrain by bullies like himself flashed in her mind. In between those visions, memories of Solomon dragging her over harsh terrain at high speeds, numbed by fear and dehydration came to mind.

She broke her silence. "One reassuring thought is Simon and Tanya have been true to their word."

"They certainly have. Simons deployed all his resources. He's been in constant contact and has been a pleasure to work alongside." Willem announced. "And there's no love lost between Tanya and her grandfather. She holds considerable remorse for what she was involved with and is eternally grateful to you two for being open to this plan. The torture that lies ahead for the Colonel is something he has to look forward to." Willem left the statement hanging.

Mel shifted in her chair. Wishing the worst on any human being went against her gentle nature and beliefs, but the sensation wasn't matched where Solomon was concerned. "May the torture be slow and painful as the deaths he inflicted on our beloved son and our horses." The tone in her voice caused an uncomfortable silence in the room.

Steve glanced at Gary and stood up. "Please excuse me, I've got to get back to the office." He bent down and gave Mel a kiss on the cheek. "It'll be over soon."

Chapter Forty-One

THE ROOM smelt musty and cold. Solomon landed with a thud on the cement floor. Blindfolded and bound. Climbing down the ladder had been an ordeal, and once he was down, he was thrown to the floor. No sooner had he got his breath back, he cried out as a boot landed in his kidneys. He pulled his legs toward his gargantuan gut, growling from the pain and babbling that no-one should be doing this to him, he was far too important.

To make him understand he was no longer of any importance one of his captors grabbed his right hand and broke the index finger, then the small finger, snapping them like twigs. The pain was excruciating.

"Leave me, you foul beast," he sobbed with terror, but the captor hadn't finished and repeated the process on Solomon's left hand. The torture drew on. Solomon had never known pain like this. Trapped, unable to see, the heat in what he assumed was a concrete dungeon was stifling, like being trapped in a bread oven, barely able to breathe, and his thirst became another terrible torment.

He knew he'd not been taken far from Harare, but he had no idea in which direction they had left the city. His senses reeled and he was hauled from the floor to a sitting position. His legs and feet burned as the horrors of his predicament hit full force and he groaned.

Solomon had once learned attack was the finest form of defence, but he was no match for the two brutes who'd roughed him up at the house and now there was no hope of attack. He'd have to use his mouth and talk his way out of this predicament. But judging by the brutal nature of the two men, he had a hunch there'd be no mercy. They'd drive him beyond the bounds of sanity. This he knew.

He seethed. "Who are you?"

There was silence.

He heard the ladder being drawn up and the trapdoor above his head close.

"I need water." He yelled. The sound of his voice was muffled by the walls. His request lost on deaf ears. Thirst clogged his swollen tongue, and his broken fingers throbbed. He cried like a child for the first time since that day when he found the commanders charred remains. Charred by Melonie Whitaker. His hatred brewed to an all-time high.

Simon hid, waiting for his two heavyweights to appear. He heard the ladder being drawn up and the trap door close. "Psst," he called to Zulu One who moved over to where Simon stood. "Not to be too vicious. We have days." Theirs was to subdue Solomon, then torture him.

It was three a.m. "Good that we changed plan, this safe house is in the perfect position."

"Where are we exactly, Sir," Zulu Two asked.

Near Ruwa. It's a tiny village about twenty kilometres east of Harare. What's the underground shelter like?"

"Hot, dusty. Perfect for this fucker to burn in hell." Zulu One said with a snarl.

The farmhouse, a ransacked, derelict place failed War Vets had long since abandoned. With Solomon gagged, bound and blindfold, they'd turned off the main road, crossed over the Marondera/Harare railway line and three kilometres down the gravel road they drew up alongside a roofless, windowless shell of what had once been a respectable farmhouse.

Blindfolded and lying on the floor in the back of the truck, Solomon could not figure out where they were and with his mouth severely taped, only muffled sounds could be heard when he tried to shout.

Simon had purchased an aged Land Cruiser with a full canopy that covered the cargo bed. The dented and rusted doors bore the logo and name of Mabvuku Boreholes and Pump Services.

Arguably, a bit early for engineers to be setting up for a hydrological and geological survey, Simon thought, but such is the drive of small business.

George, working in the headlights of the stationary Land Cruiser, created a perfect distraction as he busied himself, setting up something that might pass as a seismographic survey. Then, using a theodolite, he marked off and planted red and white poles all over the place. A ruse to mislead local commuters heading to Ruwa to catch the early taxis into the city.

Meanwhile, Simon's heavyweights had dragged Solomon down the overgrown track, away from the vehicle lights. They passed the old house and came to another dilapidated build-ing. It had no roof, but the walls stood. A trapdoor swung freely. Using a make-do ladder they'd found stashed behind the building, the two men laboriously guided the blindfolded Solomon down into a dungeon-like room beneath the surface of the old floor and did it with only the light of a quarter moon to show them down. The descent took longer than anticipated. They closed the trapdoor above them and lit a paraffin lamp, pushed Solomon to the floor and the torture began.

They left Solomon lying on the floor, moaning and growling like a rabid dog but before they climbed up the ladder, Zulu Two delivered a thunderous kick to Solomon's side and heard him vomit as he hauled the ladder up and closed the trap door. "Good we removed the tape from his mouth. Bad that we did, he would have drowned in his vomit." Zulu Two stood up and smiled. Zulu One walked across to Simon.

Commuters living in the vicinity started passing by. Taxis would be queued up along the main Harare/ Marondera road waiting for these passengers.

To appear authentic, Zulu One, Zulu Two and Simon joined George and continued with their phoney survey work, leaving the area after eight-thirty.

"The room where Solomon is stowed had been used as a bunker during the Rhodesian bush war by the farmer who'd once occupied this smallholding." George told the men. The sound-deadening tarpaulin-cum-blanket they'd used to cover Solomon in the cargo-bed of the Land Cruiser they used to cover the trap door.

"We did not respond to the Colonel's plea for water. We climbed out, pulled up the ladder and locked the trapdoor, then threw down the cover and arranged dried branches and leaves all over it to replicate the derelict appearance and hid the ladder in the thick bush behind that building," Zulu Two pointed out, knowing that even the Colonel's screams wouldn't be heard.

As the dawn broke, George got a call from Steve. "How's it going?"

"Well. We'll warn the son-of-bitch that police are waiting across the border. He'll be arrested on two counts of murder, three attempted murders and the poisoning of valuable racehorses, plus read out a list of all his other misdemeanours that we know of. Scare the shit out of him. It's important to stress upon Solomon that this outcome is to be his reality. His prospect. His future. An illegal extradition. He is to understand that there will be no room for diplomatic interference from Mugabe."

The bush along the border is crisscrossed with paths leading thousands of desperate and starving Zimbabweans into South Africa. A new corridor had been scouted in case they reverted to this original plan. A corridor Mugabe's security forces knew nothing of.

"Things are being tied up with the South African border control authorities in case. This will ensure Solomon is plausibly arrested trying to gain illegal entry into a sovereign state."

They'd meet their guide in Masvingo. A town halfway to the border. Details were to follow.

"I'm pretty sure it won't resort to this." George said.

The men understood the gravity of this instruction. If they were caught, their lives would be on the line. Zulu One and Zulu Two were aware of the havoc Solomon had caused in KwaZulu-Natal. Zulu One, said to Simon he wondered why he was risking his life for this despot.

Simon laughed. "No risk to your life, I'll make sure of that." He was not going to be seen to be in defiance of his paymaster. The question. How were they to meet both objectives?

• • •

THE MOMENTS PASSED in thought and intermittent conversation between the two Zulu men. Then Zulu One spawned another plan. "Solomon is going to commit suicide!" He said, happy with his idea.

The suggestion immediately struck a chord with the others. It seemed to be the neatest, cleanest way to tick both boxes.

They had three days, or he'd be moved.

Solomon represented the worst of African politics. Having fought to break the shackles of colonialism, he proceeded to rake off as much as possible for selfish gain, with no thought or care whatsoever for future generations. All three of Solomon's captors were motivated to see this man suffer.

The next problem. Where to dispose of the body?

No problem. George worked with a person who'd served in the Rhodesian African Rifles during the war. After the peace accord in 1980, Julius opted to serve in the combined forces comprising members of the Rhodesian forces, ZIPRA, trained by Russians and ZANLA, trained by the Chinese. However, as time progressed, he found it increasingly difficult to serve shoulder to shoulder with the terrorists who'd murdered his entire family in Mudzi during the war. So, he resigned, and a chance meeting brought him together with George. They both had an unhealthy hatred for the Mugabe dictatorship.

During Julius's brief service in the new Zimbabwe army, about a year after independence, he joined a troop who'd acted on intelligence that ZIPRA had used an old mine to stash Russian weapons. This plan had been in preparation for the aborted final push on the Capital, Salisbury as it was then, during the war. This mineshaft, on a farm north of the city, still housed the cache of weapons, but they were never used. Peace came before the weaponry was deployed. The weapons had started to rust, and the ammunition, unstable so the whole lot had been blown up right next to the mineshaft, and all vestiges were shovelled back down the mineshaft. The mine was in rugged countryside and access to it, difficult. Even cattle found little to sustain them amongst the boulders and stunted Msasa trees. Knowing something about the rabbit-warren of shafts and underground passages in this old mine, Julius felt sure that Solomon's body would be easily hidden in perpetuity.

Solomon manoeuvred his enormous frame from side to side. His buttocks had gone numb. Cold, hungry, thirsty, in pain and frightened. Still bound and blindfolded, he had but to think and reflect. Being alone, in darkness in the musty chamber, was torture alone.

Where had his guards been when these brutes had entered his Borrowdale, high-security home? He wondered helplessly. Who would ever know he'd gone missing until it was too late? Being semi-retired did not require him to be in his office at Army Headquarters at specific times every day. It would be two or three days before anyone would realise there could be a problem.

His telephone would ring at home unanswered. His family had turned against him. There was no one to help. He slid down the wall and screamed for mercy. He screamed out his fears. Because two of the captors spoke Zulu, it was clear to Solomon that this had something to do with Melonie Whitaker. He had other enemies, but this was not them.

In his mind, he relived her abduction. He'd carried her like a rag doll from the Johns' comfortable farmhouse in the Eastern Highlands of his beloved Zimbabwe. He had hauled her over unforgiving territory to the terrorist camp deep inside Mozambique. He remembered the commander, Antonio, being very proud of him, especially as Joe, the leader of the group assigned to abduct Melonie lay dead outside the farmhouse, slain by Ivan

Johns, the late owner of Blue Winds and Solomon had taken command. Antonio had promoted him for his bravery. Perhaps, he mused, Antonio's magnanimity was somewhat influenced by his nocturnal activities with this young, white prize. His thoughts moved on. Fearsome images replaced the erotic ones. Images of the camp going up in smoke after he and Jacob had bolted from their underground bunker. Most of his comrades had perished in the fire and others in the bombing raid by Rhodesian aircraft later that morning. How had she done it? How had she escaped the commander? He'd never know.

But there lay the seed of his unquenching thirst for revenge. Even now, it raged on. Unfortunately, his present reality was still weaker than his bloodlust.

She had fled into the unknown Mozambiquan wilderness. Then she'd got away from him in the Monomatapa hotel years later. Though his hands pained him, he could feel the soft flesh of her throat now. It had got that close to killing her, yet, once again, she'd cheated death.

She deserved to die. She had to die. He sat in the darkness gloating on the trauma and loss he'd caused her. She'd never forget Colonel Solomon Tlale, but he would be saved. He'd become a national hero. Mugabe would send out the army to search for him, if he hadn't done so already. They had intel. He had to get away from here before these thugs lugged him across the border into South Africa. He'd heard their plan. His number one priority was to stay alive a few more days.

That evening the two Zulu heavyweights returned. They'd brought bread but no drinking water. Only dirty muddy water from the nearby marshland. The same muddy puddle the locals' cattle drank from and defecated in. Torture was their trade — suffocating water treatment and nasty body blows delivered. Solomon was beginning to realise what his cruelty felt like.

When the men were finished, Zulu One and Zulu Two climbed back up the ladder, drew it up, locked it up and covered it.

Solomon had a lot more to think about. His eyes dripped from the dust and the pain. His concentration wavered and he slipped into unconsciousness.

THE PAIN of a violent kick woke him the following morning and torture resumed. But he wasn't giving in. Somehow, he'd get away from these thugs. He wasn't sure how yet, but Solomon was a clever man, he'd work it out. They gave him the same filthy water and bits of dry bred one would feed a pet pigeon. Solomon was hungry. What he'd do for a tumbler of Johnny Walker Blue. The thought brought saliva to his dry mouth, and he swirled it over his parched, cracked, bulbous lips. It stung.

That afternoon the Zulus were back. Solomon's growing fear of them began to erode his arrogance. He felt his resolve weaken. Something he'd promised himself not to allow. He'd not eaten for sixteen hours. His mouth wouldn't allow the dry bits of bread to fit between the spaces left by his swollen tongue. He'd not drunk clean water for thirty-six hours.

That night they returned. His swollen tongue filled his mouth, even sipping the muddy water became impossible. The torture became more vicious than before. One of them crashed a fist into his nose. He heard it break. His resolve wavered. But he still didn't give in. Frankly, there was nothing to give in to for they asked no further questions. The silence became an ugly form of torture.

Solomon slept in fits and starts for the remainder of the night. Ravenous and dehydrating to dangerous levels. He'd none of his diabetes meds. He'd soon slip into a coma. Nightmares of horrifying intensity woke him from short moments of sleep. The long, long lonely night had him weeping and crying out for forgiveness. His pleas drifted into the room, unheard by anyone but himself.

The following morning the thugs upped the ante. Solomon broke. He pleaded. He wept. He urinated and the final humiliation, he defecated in his pyjama trousers to loud, raucous laughter from the Zulus.

Zulu One spoke. "You're a fucking coward. You whimper like a child, and you dirty yourself like a baby. Let's see if we can end this. We have an offer for you. Want it?" Solomon, almost relieved to hear a voice, nodded, then he began begging for water. Fresh, clean water.

Zulu One lit the paraffin lamp for the first time and placed it on one side of the room. Solomon was to see his torturers for the first time. Next to the lamp Zulu One placed a glass of clear water.

"Give it to me. Give me water, give me that water," Solomon pleaded.

Zulu One spoke again and pointed to the water. "There is water. But there's a catch. You will find that it is mixed with an old friend of yours. The exact same poison used to kill Melonie Whitaker's son and one of their horses."

Solomon snarled. He'd been right about the origin of his abduction.

"Never let it be said that your captors didn't give you water." Zulu Two added.

"We will return tomorrow, and again tomorrow night. And again, and again until you do what you must do."

As Zulu One spoke, Zulu Two untied Solomon's swollen hands. The blood surged and delivered a shock of pain to his fingertips that clawed its way up his arms. He screamed in agony, like fire had engulfed him.

Zulu One spoke when Solomon quietened. "Take the glass when you're ready. If you are not willing to suffer as Garth Whitaker did, you might consider tipping over the paraffin lamp or throwing it against a wall. There is enough room to warm the place up a bit if you get my meaning. You will remember how your commander Antonio was burnt to death. Is it not shameful to you? A soft seventeen-year-old schoolgirl, who you abducted, fought for her life. She was taken from her home at night by you, separated from her mother and father, terrified. Your commander ruthlessly raped her in that bush camp. Your old friend, Antonio, burnt to death, overcome by the pure animal determination of a frightened schoolgirl with a will to live?" Zulu One's voice had raised in anger and a dribble of saliva ran down one side of his chin. Solomon revolted him. "Real men, real soldiers, don't behave with such savagery."

Then Zulu Two spoke. "ZANLA has little to commend itself. You guys were pathetic! We watched from South Africa. We were not impressed. You shot off a few rounds then ran away." He kicked one of Solomon's swollen hands. Solomon screamed, half expecting his hand to burst open. "Stop whimpering. Be a man and take what's coming to you like a man, not a snivelling brat."

Zulu One spoke again. "We're black. We supported the liberation movement. But you snivelling bastard forgot that the objective was to obtain your country's independence and consolidate it. Not go after a young girl on some personal and unreasonable vendetta that, so far, has taken some thirty years to achieve nothing but fear, unhappiness and inexplicable misery. The directive delivered from your office while you sat smugly, unseeing, unfeeling, and dished out instruction for destruction. Fucking coward. What earthly use is that to the Zimbabwean people? Huh?" Zulu One delivered another blow to the other hand. "You liberators had the responsibility to continue living in the economic freedom set up by your predecessors and you royally fucked it up. How many lives have you fucked up because of the greed and madness?" This time he sunk a boot into Solomon's side.

"Well, no more. Mrs. Whitaker is a proud citizen of South Africa. A good person who has endured your vicious attacks on her, her family, and her horses. She's done everything we would want the Whites to do. To integrate, to coexist, to help indigenous people grow, to make our country richer, to bring peace out of the burning ashes of our transition. How can we support idiots like you? You have achieved nothing but division and hatred. Fuck you." Zulu One's anger and disdain allowed his him to deliver an almighty blow to Solomon's kidneys. Urine seeped across the floor.

"We will leave now. We will not be back tonight. We will see you tomorrow. If you delay the water, remember that the paraffin will run out. When feeling your way around, be careful not to knock the water over. Then there will be only one option left to you. To die of thirst."

The Zulus were not receptive to any protestations. They'd been tempted to kill him with their bare hands, but resisted. They exited the underground cell to the sounds of wailing and pleading. Solomon heard the bolts being slid into place, and the padlocks snapped shut. Once again, he was subjected to his own miserable company. His ribs hurt. His kidneys burned red-hot after emptying his bladder from the blow to his kidneys. He looked at the cup of water in the flickering light from the paraffin lamp. He was hungry and filthy.

It felt to him like an eternity, but at about eleven o'clock that night, he capitulated. It was time.

He crawled to the cup and took it up between his middle finger and thumb. The light from the lamp played through the white wall of the plastic cup and made eerie patterns. His hand shook. Tears ran from his eyes, making seeing more difficult. He stared at the cup for several minutes, undecided, hesitating, hoping for a miracle. Where were his army? The men he'd trained. He desperately wanted to taste water in his mouth, but he knew what it would cost.

He placed the cup back on the floor and sat staring at it — his back to the wall, knees at chin level, his painful arms tried hugging his legs, but they were too weak to hold them. Hope was lost. The intensity of the pain overwhelmed him. All alone. Abandoned to his regrets. He wished he could write to his family and say sorry. He dropped his head and wept. Then it came to him. He would like to write a message to his family. He drew a line in the floor with his uninjured middle finger, the nail scratching through the dirt. It made a mark.

To my dear family. I've realised how bad I am. I have caused suffering to myself and to you. I have caused grief to many other people. I am sor.......

Solomon stopped writing. This was bullshit. Steadying himself, he grasped the cup again and very deliberately slugged back the entire contents. It tasted like nectar. Still savouring the moment, he squeezed the empty cup and tossed it across the room. He then moved as far from his letter as he could, and sitting with his back to the wall, legs flat and spread apart, he sat and waited for the inevitable.

· · ·

By morning, Solomon felt dizzy and disorientated. His skin itched and his breathing laboured. Then the vomiting began. When he'd prescribed this poison for Garth Whitaker, he'd not bothered to read the small print. Had he done so, he would have known to keep his head below the level of his lungs. But he didn't know that. The fumes and ingress of his contaminated vomit raced into his lungs. Soon he was gasping for air. His organs went into revolt. He writhed and convulsed, rolling around in agony then he lost control of his bowels and soiled himself. By now, he was scarcely aware. The pain and discomfort excruciating. "Air. I need air." He gasped in a whisper.

Natural light shone from above, but he was no longer able to identify it or appreciate it by then.

Zulu One lowered the ladder and descended into the foul-smelling cavern. He quickly surveyed the scene and called up to his partner. "He's done it, but he's still alive."

Zulu Two came down. They stood staring at the pitiful apparition in the shadows, slumped sideways on the floor.

They agreed that it was a matter of time. They had to wait it out. But not down in the cell. It stank.

As they were about to climb out, Zulu Two reached to extinguish the paraffin lamp and noticed the message in the dusty floor. "Hey, come and look at this." He shouted to Zulu One.

Zulu One came alongside. They read what Solomon had written. "This is important. Take a photo of this." Zulu One said.

He reached into his pocket and drew out his cell phone. Zulu Two caught on as quickly and took the photos. One picture of the scribbled note, and the other of Solomon. He wasn't quite dead, but he'd leave for the afterlife within in minutes now. This evidence was going to make life a whole lot easier for them.

Having checked that the photos were good, they pocketed their phones. Trained as they were, they wiped the lamp and the cup, then carefully offered them up to Solomon's clammy hand and rubbed his fingers over them — all to the non-rhythmic laboured breathing of the dying man.

Zulu One bent down and relit the paraffin lamp. It needed to be found to have run out of fuel. They then scoured the room for any other evidence of their presence. There was the tiny glass bottle that had contained the poison concentrate and the plastic Coke bottle that had been used to bring water into the underground room. They wiped these clean of their fingerprints and again took Solomon's hand and rubbed his fingers over the coke bottle. Satisfied that there was nothing left, they retreated towards the ladder, brushing away their footprints. They removed their shirts to cover their hands, so their fingerprints were no longer evident on the ladder and trapdoor. Once out, they left the ladder in place with the trapdoor open, then folded up the canvas cover and carried it to the Landcruiser, where they met George. He had been busy doing his 'borehole work' whilst standing guard.

"We won't be needing the mineshaft after all," said Zulu One. "Let's go."

Want More?

Tangled Reins of Fate
The final book in the Whitaker trilogy

BRADLEY WHITAKER returns from England, as 2010 ends. With his mother's nemesis, Colonel Solomon Tlale dead, Brad believes peace will reign for the family, and he can get on and build his dream eco-home on the farm and train racehorses without a having security guard his every move.

Only days after his return from England the vendetta raises its ugly head again, proving that even in death, the Colonel is still dangerous.

After signing with a suitable architect in Durban, Brad drives home, excited. But as he pulls up in the parking outside the admin offices at the stud, he sees Thabo standing on the veranda sobbing. Julie, his wife has been murdered and Zinzi their toddler, kidnapped.

The colonel once warned those who betrayed him would

not live a happy life, long life. Julie was the first on the unknown executioner's list.

A frenzied police search for the murderer and the missing toddler gets underway. But after a few months the case goes cold, all leads have been exhausted and the child is still missing.

Guided by the famous clairvoyant, Lerato leads police to a shallow grave in the middle of a cornfield and they uncover a gruesome find in the hills surrounding Shongweni.

The vendetta reaches new levels, and Bradley finds himself caught in the middle, while the Colonel's granddaughter becomes the next target on the assassin's list, thus relieving the pressure from the ultimate target, Melonie Whitaker.

But the blood feud takes another unexpected turn.

Also by Diana K Robinson

Fiction

Winds of Change

Don't Blame Me

Non-Fiction Reference

Connect–An Equus Soul Technique

Available on Amazon and in bookstores.

Visit the author website to see what is coming soon.

www.dianakrobinson.com

Diana K Publications